The Light over the Solway

THE LIGHT OVER THE SOLWAY

John Little

Illustrations by Claire Ball

© 2018 John Little

Illustrations © 2018 Claire Ball

All rights reserved.

No part of this publication may be reproduced, stored in a retrieval system, stored in a database and / or published in any form or by any means, electronic, mechanical, photocopying, recording or otherwise, without the prior written permission of the publisher.

ISBN-13: 978-1986411042

ISBN-10: 1986411044

Contents

VII	Preface
1	Chapter 1 — The Nurse
14	Chapter 2 — Human Fragments
24	Chapter 3 — The Sands of Normality
40	Chapter 4 — Family
47	Chapter 5 — Disaster
62	Chapter 6 — A Friend
70	Chapter 7 — War Comes to Margaret
91	Chapter 8 — The Dentist
104	Chapter 9 — Recruiting
118	Chapter 10 — The Munitionette
130	Chapter 11 — The Devil's Porridge
145	Chapter 12 — Barwise on War
161	Chapter 13 — The Big Push
176	Chapter 14 — The Red Cross
196	Chapter 15 — Paddy to the Rescue
206	Chapter 16 — A Bit of a Kick About
216	Chapter 17 — Of Football and of Danger
230	Chapter 18 — The Royal Wink
246	Chapter 19 — Saving Lives

262	Chapter 20 — The Soldier
285	Chapter 21 — A Time out of War
306	Chapter 22 — Special Service
327	Chapter 23 — Ripon North Camp
348	Chapter 24 — Defence in Depth
371	Chapter 25 — At the Front
395	Chapter 26 — Retreat
415	Chapter 27 — A Family Gathering
435	Chapter 28 — Battle
458	Chapter 29 — Explosion
479	Chapter 30 — Fit for Heroes
503	Epilogue
505	Glossary
507	Family Tree

Preface

I have a photograph taken in 1918 and in it are a soldier and a nurse. Obviously they did something in the First World War, but I know next to nothing about their actual experiences. There is also a young woman of age to have done something, but I knew nothing about her contribution either. It seemed to me that there was a novel here, because I could not write it as history; the things that would happen to them could not be things that they actually experienced. There was however a story to be told if I made them representative of their generation and gave them lives in fiction. The soldier was in the Border Regiment and of an age to serve in 1918, which he did. Using the regimental history and researching sources it would be possible to put him through experiences that would not be too far removed from what a recruit to that unit would have gone through at that time. Weaving the sketchy details that I knew in with the research could show something often ignored in stories; what the ordinary working class lad went through on his way to war.

The nurse, I knew nothing about, but strangely, she was easier. There is so much material available from nurses who did write down what they went through that synthesizing a story that would be a reasonable facsimile of one woman's experiences was not hard. Weaving this fiction with actual events, real people and medical features of the day enabled me to put together a story that may seem extraordinary for one young woman to go through. That thought I suppress, because compared to the actual experiences of some real nurses, my heroine comes off rather lightly in many respects. I think she is not a caricature and that her experiences, if not historical, are at least plausible.

I decided to make my third character Nancy a munitionette to represent her generation of young women, hundreds of thousands of whom spent their war making ammunition, often under dangerous conditions. This seemed a reasonable thing to do as in her hometown was a National Shell Factory and it was therefore probable. On reflection though I decided to place her forty miles north of Workington and have her manufacturing explosives at Gretna Green, because it was the largest ammunition factory in the world at that time. It would be easier for me as a writer because of the material available, though I confess I did feel as if it was ducking out of writing about life in the National Shell factory.

After I had written the first Gretna chapter I was rather taken aback by the receipt of a message from Nancy's granddaughter telling me of an old letter she had referring to Nancy's time at Gretna. This was followed the next day by a phone call and news of the discovery of a photograph of Nancy in munitionette uniform, and on the back of it was written 'Gretna 1917.' My fiction was actually fact. The reader must make up their own mind what they make of that, because frankly I have no idea what to think of such coincidences.

Each of my characters served their country in their own way, but they had a family back home. The war affected them too and their experience would be of their time and of their place. In a steel town with everyone working flat out and earning wartime wages they might not have had things as bad as many in the country. Nonetheless, they had to go through food shortages, the attentions of the enemy, doing their bit to feed the demands of the war, and also to get on with their own lives. Normal activity is not suspended in wartime though it may be disrupted; they still needed entertainment, time off, days out and for some of the time the war was not very relevant to what they were doing; this was especially true in the first few months, even years, after the declaration. In 1914 this generation of Britons found themselves faced with a war on a global scale and challenges that nobody had ever faced in the whole of British history. They rose to it in an extraordinary way, sent their sons to war and their daughters to provide care, and ammunition along with a whole range of things not permitted before. They gritted their teeth, saw it through and defeated their enemy. In the process they revolutionized the lives of women, made stupendous technological advances and elevated their hopes into a dream of a better world. The home fit for heroes that they were promised may not have materialized but their wish for wider democracy; that their children could have and could expect something better, still inspires today.

This book then, is not a history. It is a novel; a vision of how one working class family might have been; what they might have gone through, and within the bounds of plausibility, what they might have seen for themselves. Some of the characters are real; some are not. I hope that the reader enjoys the experiences in a tale, which if not pure fact, is at least within the bounds of possibility.

I wish to thank my wife Ruth and David Banks of Nova Scotia for their eagle eyed editing and proofing of this book, a great boon to me. I am also grateful to Margaret May, Judith Harris and Penny Durham for use of their relatives' names and for their help with research. I also wish to thank David Lister for the use of his stunning photograph of a Solway sunset on my back cover and Andrew Sutton for his artistry in cover design and typesetting. To Claire Ball I owe a great debt for the wonderful illustrations she has provided throughout the book, evoking various actions and scenes so well. Because of the nature of the research needed for this book I have chosen a list of beta readers who have expertise in particular fields so that my discrepancies may be laid bare before publication, and I am very grateful indeed to all these people for their time and help. David Gilhepsy of the Her Citi Café, Maryport (Military), Belinda Linden (Medical), Sarah Harper of the Devil's Porridge Museum (HM Gretna), Betty Telford (Local knowledge and critical), Irene Martin (Critical). I am fortunate in their acquaintance.

I must also record a debt of gratitude to the authors whose works I read which provided me with information and anecdote to flesh out my narrative. These include several excellent books on Workington by Richard Byers, Keith Wallace and other works by Derek Woodruff. The latter is particular in providing me with the 'Yis lad, arl ave yan' tale from the cemetery; all I had to do was provide a reverse protagonist. The excellent works on the First World War and various towns in Cumberland by Ruth Mansergh made for fascinating reading and were also very useful. The British Newspaper archive was invaluable and a host of online sources too numerous to mention. All have enabled me to concoct a narrative that I hope the reader may find of some enjoyment; the proof of any pudding is in the eating.

For some guidance, a glossary and a family tree may be found at the back of the book.

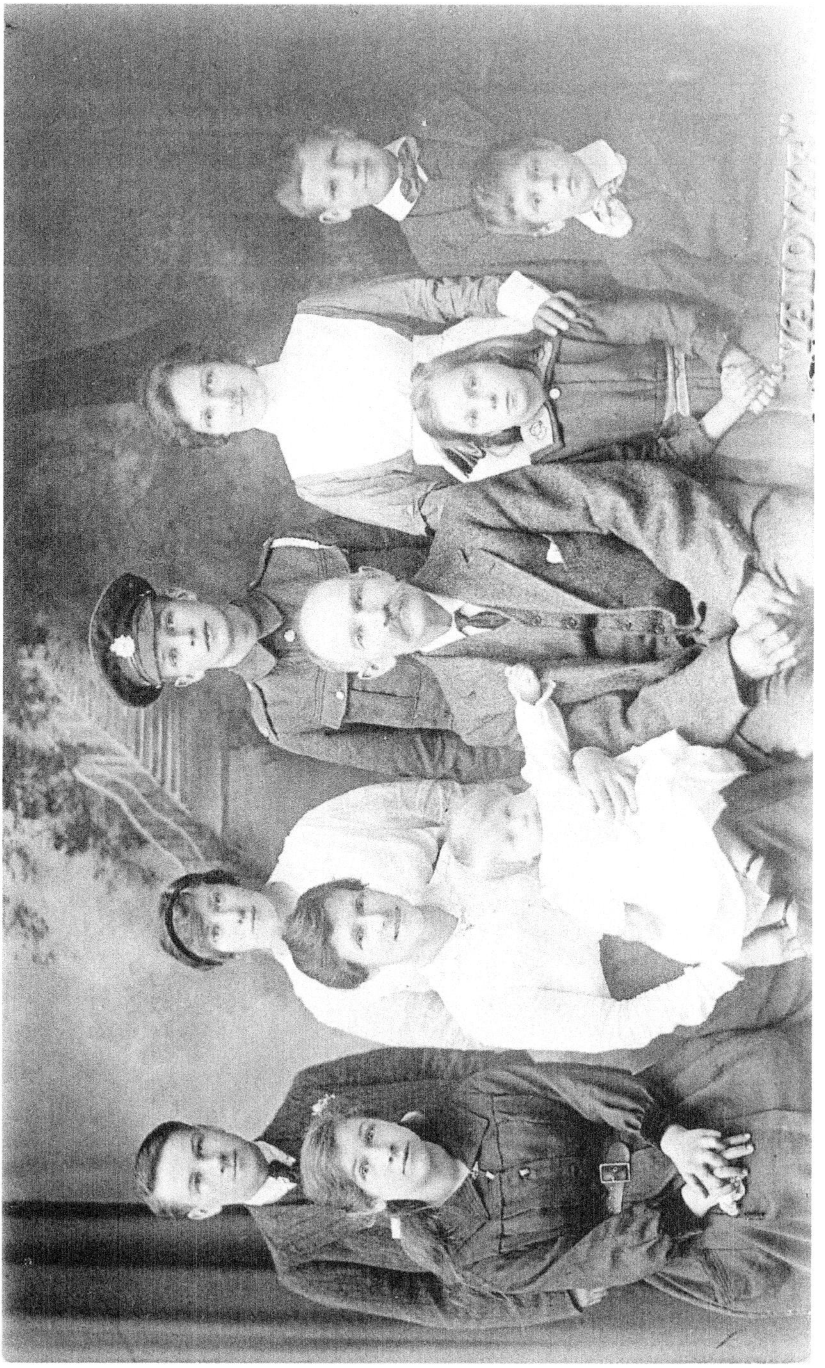

Chapter 1

The Nurse

In West Cumberland the sun rises over the mountains of the Lake District that lie to the east, and beyond the miracle of a new day, most people would not notice it, especially in the streets of the coastal towns. It is true that people further inland may look out of their windows and see the dawn come up over the high fells, especially if there is snow on the tops, and marvel at the beauty of it, yet the growing of the light has a rival that in this area is unbeatable. At the end of the day the sun goes down in a spectacular blaze of glory to the western horizon of the sea, the light over the Solway slowly fading in red gold splendour that makes the sunsets famous the world over, and Cumbrians far from home to miss them. Between the sun's rising and setting the engines of industry and commerce once drove this area into a hubbub of frenetic energy that made it of great importance to the whole British nation and to the empire it had acquired. Living and working, loving and breeding, walking and breathing in this region, were thousands of artisan people, miners, steelworkers, servants and labourers, mothers and children, each with their own story, each with their own drama. Amongst them, in a terraced house in Workington, were Margaret, *nee* Adams, her husband Thomas Little (Tom) and their eight children. It is to them and mainly three of their children that this tale relates.

The working day started early at number 55 Devonshire Street, Workington; at five o'clock in the morning to be precise;

and Monday 10 May 1915 was no exception. There had been some disturbances in town over the weekend that Tom and Margaret Little had forbidden their children to take part in, however understandable they were. The news of the sinking of the Lusitania three days earlier had caused a wave of indignation across the country and riots had taken place in several cities, whilst anyone suspected of being of German descent was in danger of being attacked and beaten up or worse. Tom and Margaret observed this, but they also considered themselves to be good people and would not permit themselves or any in their house to tar all Germans with the same brush, or to engage in law breaking. Some of their neighbours might speak of 'Germ-huns' and smash windows of suspect shops in town, but the Little household was having none of it. Tom's views on the matter were both trenchant, and stern.

'I expect my children to show some self-restraint. If I thought that any of them could not show sufficient control of their own minds and brains to stop judging people for what they are rather than who they are, then I would be offended by the thought that I had been a bad parent. We abide by the law or we are no better than the Germans.'

Tom was adamant that he would not be over-ridden in this, and his boys knew well that none of them was big enough to avoid being told to fetch the strap hanging on the grandfather clock if they did not do their father's bidding. The punishment for the girls was the same, but the infliction of it was much rarer.

'If any of you are taken up by the police and birched for doing something you should not have been doing, then you will get no sympathy from me; indeed for each stroke they give you, I will give the same when you get home. Be in no doubt.'

For all that he was a stern father, he was also a kind one, as his children knew. In the house his word was law, as was

Margaret's because that was how they had set it to be. With so many people in such a small house there had to be order; therefore there was. Tom was the sort of man that people did not like to argue with for all his diminutive size. At five feet and one inch tall he was well below the five feet five inch average for a man, but that did not detract from the air of him. On top he was bald with a fringe of iron-grey hair, usually surmounted by a flat cap that was uniform in this time and this town. His eyes, however, told a different tale, for they were iron grey, direct, and seemed to penetrate a person they were directed at, as if to see clear through to the other side. The whole was set off by a ferocious 'Kitchener' style moustache; if he had been set in the Wild West with a Stetson on his head he would have been the model of a gunslinger. The overall effect spoke of a man not to be trifled with, and generally people did not.

At number 55 on this particular morning the mood was much as that of any other working day. The sun was coming up at 5.15am and the older members of the Little family were tucking into bowls of pobbies soaked with hot milk and sprinkled with a little sugar, though this last was getting to be rather expensive and difficult to find. They took little notice of their mother's exortation to use less of it.

'Be canny wid the sugar; I had enough trouble finding it.' Of the milk she was less cautious in its use, but did not allow them to flood their plate with it. 'That's 'ot cream! Leave some for your sisters!'

By 5.30am Tom was sitting in the corner by the black range with his first roll-up cigarette of the day clasped in a wire loop made from a paperclip, and the fragrant smell of Golden Virginia filled the room while he sipped occasionally from a white mug of strong tea made up with condensed milk. He made his smokes thin these days as tobacco was also becoming scarce, and consequently more expensive. Ten minutes later it was time to go. Tom's bait box and flask of cold tea were tucked into his haversack and he was marching his way through the back lonnings on his way to Moss Bay Steelworks where he did a job that he liked, working with horses. He was lucky in this because most men probably did not like their work; it was a way to make a living, but Tom had once been a farmer and he had found a way to support his family and be with animals. This is not to say that the men in the local community did not take a pride in their work, or that they did not cherish the sense of professionalism and purpose which they got from doing a good job, but most of them did hard and heavy physical jobs which exhausted them, so 'liking' what they did was a hard ask.

John, whom the family called Jack, was with his father, as he always was every working day since leaving school two years previously. At fifteen he was, as writers of old novels might have it, 'a stripling youth'. Yet some inches smaller than his father, he resembled him in a few features, but though his mouth and nose were even, and the eyes grey, he took after his mother in the respect that one eyebrow was slightly higher than the other which tended, with the lop-sided smile he had, to give him a cynical air, though his nature was anything but. He was quiet, determined when he had set upon a path to follow, and did not speak much unless he had something worth saying. In this he appeared more of an interested observer of life rather than an active participant, and there was much of truth in this in his overall character. His job at the steelworks was rather different to his father's. Although young and small his work was quite important; the furnace floors of the steelworks were apt to become covered in small splashes of molten metal, bits of slag and other debris which could turn men's feet or trip them up. His job was to sweep and scrape this 'skull' off the floor and it had to be done well. If he missed any he was apt to get a clip round his ear or sworn at for not grafting properly. A rough furnace floor could, and did sometimes cost men their lives. He did not mind the blows so much, considering it part of the job, and besides which, he was ambitious and he knew that new lads took a lot of stick and pummelling. The job that he really had his eye on for when he was older was engineman working the rolling mills and he had already made this clear, so it was in his interest to keep his head down and serve his time until he reached that goal.

Barwise, the oldest boy, also took hold of his bait box and did not hang round at home, setting off as quickly as possible to the Marshside on the other side of the lower station where he was employed at Workington Bridge and Boiler Company. His position was lowly, although it was grandiosely titled 'apprentice hammerer'. This was the position he hoped to attain one day for it paid well, but he also had to run the gauntlet of curses and sore ears if he was not quick enough in keeping his team supplied with fresh rivets. For the moment it was work, paid him eight shillings a week, and helped him earn his keep. His appearance was singular in that a first glance at him gave the impression of a rather innocent young man with even features and blue eyes and a rather wistful expression, yet he was no ingénue. Within a few minutes everyone who met him was aware of an aura of 'dash' and this was no misleading thing. Barwise liked to take risks and to play practical jokes, which were sometimes beyond normal limits. If there was a tree, he liked to climb it; a river in summer, then he had to jump in it; of all Tom and Margaret's children he had the hottest of tempers and his fists were always ready to avenge perceived insults or injustice.

Up in the girls' room Annie Eleanor, known to the family as Nellie, and her seventeen year old sister Nancy had to dress quickly and very neatly. Nellie's uniform had to be spotless and especially so as she was, at nineteen, becoming quite senior in her profession with five years experience under her belt. When she was fourteen Nellie had been about to leave school, perhaps to go into service, when Margaret had introduced her to a stern looking lady, Miss Winter, whom she knew through Church. The boys all served their turns as choirboys at St John's, just up the road from their old school and were listened to with much appreciation by this formidable woman who was the Matron of the Workington Hospital. As a result of this connection Nellie had commenced sweeping under beds and mopping floors as a trainee nurse at the hospital. She had come on quite a lot since then.

Nancy's uniform was rather different, for hers was that of a maid at the Central Hotel, a large and rather prestigious establishment just outside the Central Station. Neither girl needed a bait box for they would take their lunch where they worked in their respective canteens. Alpha Omega, or 'Ommie' at age twelve was still asleep because her school day at Guard Street Girl's School would not begin until nine o'clock. Also asleep was Esther (Ettie) aged six, and in the boy's room William and Joe aged eight and five respectively, would also slumber on until 7.30am. Joe, though small, would get up because his parents did not wish him to cultivate the habit of lying abed in the morning.

Nellie liked her job, though at first she had not been so sure. Initially she had found it rather boring in that what she did every day was pretty much what a scullery maid did. Sweeping, cleaning beds, scouring and sluicing out bedpans, washing dishes and mopping floors did not hold out much allure. She was also very much at the beck and call of all the other young women training to be nurses because she was the junior and answered to the call of 'Little!' Sometimes it made her feel as if she was a dog being told to fetch things. It was possibly the first realisation that a qualified nurse could earn £40 a year that concentrated her mind, for that was very good money to her and opened up worlds of possibility. She also found that she had, by association, garnered a great deal of enhanced status in the neighbourhood, simply by virtue of working at the hospital. More accurately it was known as the Workington Infirmary and was a source of great civic pride to the town. It had seemed absurd to the dignitaries who ran the town, the mines and the great steelworks back in 1886 that such a burgeoning and prosperous place did not have its own hospital. Without any messing about they had subscribed to, built, and opened one. Not only that, but it was financed by a scheme where workers in the community paid into an insurance pot, and in return, if ill, they received medical care without further charge; this was universally acknowledged to be an excellent and pioneering idea. Originally it had three wards with twelve male and four female beds, but it had expanded since and was continuing to do so. Nellie found that after a while she was proud to work there and felt she was doing something worthwhile. During the last five years she had learned to clean and dress cuts, burns as long as there was a nurse present; the sight of blood, wounds and pus, that once made her feel squeamish now had no effect on her. She could bathe people in bed, assist at births, change dressings, make proper hospital beds and had learned how to keep awake when watching through the night shifts among many other things. What she was not allowed to do was to administer medicine for that was strictly within the province of doctors, and they guarded their procedures jealously. Eventually, at the age of seventeen she had been told that she could take her nursing examination and had to sit with other candidates for two hours answering questions on such matters as how to proceed with bad cases of *pediculi capitis* or how to prepare a room for an operation for strangulated hernia. She knew the ways in which typhoid could be carried, why the common fly was dangerous and how to treat cases of whiteleg in an artisan's dwelling; she also knew how to cope with a breech birth, having seen several. Rather to her surprise the answering of a volume of questions on such matters did not make her head spin, and a week later she was very pleased to have been told that she had passed.

Her new qualification led to an elevation in status when she was told to draw a uniform from the stores: from then on she was no longer 'Little', but 'Nurse Little'. She could carry out her duties without supervision. If she kept her nose clean and her luck held then eventually she would become 'Sister Little' by recommendation from Matron and any attempt by family or friends to call her that was stopped immediately. The hierarchy of nursing was a rigid system of caste; the public might think that all nurses were 'Sister', but they were not and a great deal of anger could be caused if seniors assumed you were taking a title which was not yours to take. 'Sister' was a dizzying height to attain and pay was consequently much higher than for a mere nurse.

A final check in the downstairs hallway mirror was necessary; blue uniform dress ironed and free of creases all the way down to the bottom of her skirt with a two-inch hem. At the end of each sleeve, loose at the top, tighter round the forearms, was a spotless white and detachable cuff. Over the front of this was a starched white apron secured round the waist with a two inch wide white belt, buttoned to one side, the ensemble being topped with a high white collar buttoned at the neck. Her dark hair was swept back and up, pinned tightly at the back of her head and secured on top was a pure white 'Sister Dora' cap. If she had been told that she was a pretty girl she would have tutted at the remark, but the lustrous hair, arched and prominent eyebrows, the grey eyes of her mother, straight nose and even mouth made her more than presentable. Every time she inspected herself she reflected how lucky she was that Workington Infirmary supplied uniform, when she knew that many nurses across the country had to pay for their own. Satisfied that she would pass Miss Winter's gimlet eye, she pulled on her dark coat and was soon on her way down John Street, to Harrington Road and into Infirmary Road, a mere ten minute stroll but less if she hurried.

Shortly after ten o'clock in the morning one of the junior trainees came into the men's ward where Nellie had just finished changing the dressing on a nasty gash in the arm of a man from the Derwent Steelworks.

'Please Nurse Little, Matron wants to see you in her room straight away please.'

'Did she say what it was about Burdon?'

'No Nurse Little. Just that you should come as soon as you could.'

'Well go and tell her that I will be there directly as soon as I've washed my hands.'

Nellie knew very well that Miss Winter would not be happy if she did not wash her hands after wound dressing, but it was by now second nature to her. Soon she stood in Matron's Office and Miss Winter told her to take a seat.

'Now then Nurse Little, I expect you're wondering why I've

called you in here, so I'll come straight to the point. As you know, our army in France has been involved in a number of big battles in the last few months, that business at Neuve Chapelle being particularly nasty.'

Nellie nodded her assent.

'Well there have been too many casualties for the hospitals right across the south of England to cope with and there's more arriving every day. It's been decided that the serious cases will be dealt with in the south because they are closer to the action, but many of the less critical ones and many of the moribund ones will be brought up here by train and taken care of in hospitals across the north. You're looking puzzled. What is it?'

'We've only got sixteen beds Matron; how will we manage more?'

'I think we may have to squeeze some more beds in considering the scale of what is happening, but the point is we will need nurses used to dealing with wounds when the doctors are overwhelmed with serious cases. That's why I want to send you up to Carlisle for a month's course helping in one of the military hospitals. You'll see some bad cases up there and gain a lot of experience.'

'Me Matron? But why? Do you not think I'm too young? You've always said that we have to grow into our responsibilities. I'm not sure I could cope with really badly wounded men.'

'Oh believe me Nellie, I spoke to your mam after church last night and she thinks you could cope with anything.'

'You've spoken to her? She didn't mention it.'

'No, because I asked her not to. I wanted to tell you myself. I've had my eye on you for a while and I think you've got the makings of a fine nurse. I chose you because it's an opportunity for advancement and I think you can cope.'

'I'm to go to Carlisle Hospital?'

'Not exactly. An auxiliary hospital opened there two

months ago at Murrell Hill House. Because Carlisle's on the mainline from London they've been shipping some critical cases up there by express train for treatment. You're to have four weeks intensive training in dealing with wounds, infected and gangrenous. Ordinarily it would be a lot longer, but this is wartime and there's a shortage of nurses. I hope you feel a little honoured because I would not let myself down by sending someone I did not think was up to it.'

'Oh I am Matron, believe me, I am; just a little taken aback, but I'd like to do more for the war.'

'Well this will help you do that I think, though you will be seeing some very serious wounds and injuries and it will not be pleasant. There will be a certificate at the end of the course, so it's another step on the way for you. There's a bed for you in the nurses' hostel up there. Your last shift here is Friday, so that you'll have the Saturday and some of Sunday to get ready. They will be expecting you Sunday evening. When you finish come and see me and I'll sign you a rail warrant for the journey because this is government business.'

To say that Nellie's brain was set awhirl by this development would be an understatement. She had never been away from home before, yet here she was going to Carlisle, which to her seemed a far off metropolis, for four weeks and to tend real wounded soldiers instead of the contusions and broken limbs that she assisted with in Workington. There was also a certain apprehension about what she might see, but she knew that young women of her age were helping the war effort in this way all over the country and that her training made her better placed to carry out the task than many. Her mother certainly thought so.

'You've been training four years Nellie. If it's not somebody like you helping with those poor men, then who? Some neat and tidy little society lady who'll pass out at the sight of blood or cry if she gets a mark on her pinny. No, Miss Winter's given you a plum opportunity and I'm beholden to her, because I think she's done her best for you. I knew that she would.'

Margaret, at 38 was as grounded and as sensible as ever. She had given birth to eight children since her twentieth birthday and as far as she was concerned, you coped with whatever life sent you. If anything 'you cope' was something of a motto with her, though the message sometimes varied to 'you manage'. Still vital, far from worn out by her children, she sustained herself by an unfussy attachment to her church, which, although it meant a lot to her, she was unostentatious about. Two years previously she had felt so deeply, that she was confirmed into the Church of England at the lovely old St Michael's Church by the Bishop of Carlisle. When Nellie was in her last year at school Margaret had given her a prayer book of her own for Christmas, which was one of the first things into her case for the journey and what she wrote in it was indicative of her own faith:

'Do not steal this book for fear of shame
For here is the owner's name (N Little)
For when you die the Lord will say,
Where is that book you stole that day?
And if you say you do not know,
The Lord will cast you down below.'

During that week great events were happening in London and the government shook. Final negotiations were going on to bring Italy into the war on the Allied side, but Nellie knew nothing of this; her head was full of Carlisle.

Chapter 2

Human Fragments

At four o'clock in the afternoon of Sunday 16 May Nellie said goodbye to her family, took her case and walked to Oxford Street, which ran into Station Road, at the far end of which was the Low Station. Workington had three stations and Central Station was not far from her home; indeed the end of her street abutted onto the railway and the trains passing were loud and often made her mother annoyed at sooty smuts on the washing if the wind blew their way. Despite its grandiose name it was never on the main passenger line for the town and was used mostly for the transport of ore and coal. Worse, there was no Sunday service, so Nellie had to trek the three quarters of a mile down to where was the proper station for the town. Here, even on Sunday there was much activity inside the great locomotive repair sheds and the large marshalling yards that serviced Cumberland's extensive railway network. Passing into the elegant honey-brick building she was soon waiting on the northbound platform, her travel warrant stamped, and on the way to Carlisle. It was only when she was part way up the line towards Maryport that she gave a slight laugh as she recollected that she actually had no directions to where she was going. It did not matter for she was not a shy person and asked a porter, who looked a nice old chap, for help at Carlisle station.

'It's out on the Dalston Road, lass. It's a big spot about where Shaddongate turns to Dalston Road, but ask the conductor and she'll set you right. That bus right there – yes the 62.'

She! Female bus conductors had not reached Workington yet, but Carlisle was leading the way; Nellie approved. The bus drove slowly out of Carlisle along a road lined with neat red brick terraced houses and shops that all looked rather clean. Workington always had a pall of smoke hanging over it and many of the buildings were black with soot, but that was not the case here. It was not long before the bus came to a halt and the conductor pointed out a large and handsome mansion set back in its own grounds off the road as Murrell Hill House; Nellie reported herself at a desk and the woman sitting there sent an orderly to find the Matron, Mrs Bennett-Brown who was also the Commandant. Like Miss Winter she was a solid and determined looking woman with an air of authority to her and Nellie wondered momentarily if they were related; it might be the height of absurdity to think that there was a factory somewhere where they turned out Matrons of this type.

'Nurse Little! Well thank goodness you've arrived in time.'

'In time Matron?'

'Yes, in time. Now you, orderly, take the nurse up to room three on the top floor and show her which bed is hers. Then, Nurse, I want you back down here right away before the first ambulance arrives.'

'Are there many ambulances coming Matron?'

'I should think five and we will have enough to do when they get here. At this moment you and I and two others are the only nurses in this place and we've got to deal with whatever happens.'

Nellie looked around at figures in white with nurse's pinafores on their fronts.

'They're Voluntary Aid Detachment nurses (VAD). Most of them have good hearts and are willing to learn and in time a lot of them will be of use, but not quite yet; now just listen.'

Over the next few minutes Mrs Bennett-Brown briefed Nellie on the situation facing them. There was a battle going on in France at a place called Festubert near Ypres, and there were thousands of casualties. The wounded men had been tended to in base hospitals, but then the problems began. They had to be shipped back to Britain and the resources in the south were overwhelmed by the sheer numbers of men arriving. Many of the wounded were being sent to Scotland, but there were plans to turn Carlisle into a hospital city and Murrell Hill House was merely one of the first new hospitals.

'The normal procedure for new arrivals is to show you photographs of men with very bad wounds, partly to see if you can cope with it, and partly to harden you up, but we have no time for that now. It's in at the deep end for you I'm afraid. Do you think you can handle it?'

Nellie replied that she thought she could.

'Very well. We are empty right now, but when they arrive, every bed will be full; we are an officer's hospital. Our work is simple enough. Every man will not have been tended to properly since leaving the base hospitals in France. So each of them will need their dressings changed, their wounds cleaned and many of them will need operations. Some will be very dirty because they have not had any sort of bath for days, and some will still be verminous. We have to do all that. The doctors will be standing by, because there will be operations to carry out, so it's going to be very busy; get yourself a cup of tea from the canteen over there. It's likely to be your last for a long time.'

Nellie's thought, though she did not articulate it was, 'Talk about being thrown in the deep end!'

Soon the ambulances were arriving and orderlies carried in the first of the wounded men. Nellie's world changed forever as fragments of suffering humanity entered her life. Each man had to be set on a bed with a waterproof sheet so that he could be tended to. Many of them still wore the uniforms they had been wearing when wounded, and although they had been tended at the hospitals in France, for some that was three days previously. As the evening went on Nellie was to discover that at least half of them had eaten and drunk nothing for at least two days. The base hospitals were overwhelmed by the numbers of casualties and many of the wounded were marked for England straight away and sent over the Channel as quickly as the ferries could carry them. Limbs and parts of men's bodies were swathed in bandages that in some cases were caked hard and blackened through being soaked in blood during their train journey. Although precautions had been taken in France, some of the men were still lousy. Every man was tired out, hanging on, and in need of care. Some were in great pain, yet there was very little moaning as they were moved from the hallway to the beds allocated to them. The VADs set about washing each man and giving them water, while Nellie, Matron and the other two nurses began changing dressings. In many cases the soldiers' uniforms were so caked with mud and filth that they had to be cut off them. It was quite encouraging to see how many of the volunteers, a number of them lately from genteel homes, lost all trace of fastidiousness and got on with what needed to be done. They were not all sheltered young ladies of course; many were local women who volunteered in their spare time. For example, there was a local schoolmistress who could not come before five o'clock in the afternoon, then stayed every night until nine. The VAD would accept any and all help. Others were local girls who came in for three hours a day, every day, but every third week. They did all sorts of jobs, sweeping, scrubbing, helping in the kitchens, but now they began to give men water, to wash dirt from them, and in some cases, to remove soiled bandages. As they did so the surgeons appeared to assess who needed most urgent attention. Over the whole scene hung a strange, sweet smell that one of the orderlies identified to Nellie upon inquiry as chlorate of lime, used to sanitise things in the trenches.

Nellie's first patient was a man who had no left leg below the knee; the surgeons in France had made a good job of the amputation, but the dressing had not been changed since. One of the VADs brought a bowl of Eusol and Nellie began taking the bandages off with scissors. It took some time, because of the congealed and blackened blood stiffening the outside, but as she began to unwind it the whole thing came away as an evil smell filled the air and pus dripped onto the waterproof sheet. The whole area of the wound was suppurating though the stump itself seemed to have been properly closed. The VAD turned a funny colour and swayed; Nellie caught her by an arm and steered her to a chair.

'Put your head between your knees; you'll feel better soon.'

'She feels worse than I do Sister,' remarked her patient whose grey face betrayed his exhaustion and pain.

'I doubt that somehow, now just grit your teeth because I'm going to have a look at this.'

Nellie fought back the rising gorge in her own throat and looked at the stump. It was odd how revulsion spread from one human to another, but there was a job to be done here and the feeling soon passed. She had been told never to show bad feelings to a patient in face of a wound, no matter how nauseated she felt, and she smiled her professional smile and told her soldier that she'd soon have him sorted out.

'Doctor,' she called, and a doctor came over, looked at the stump and at the patient, then said, 'Clean it up; it's gas gangrene. Plenty of Eusol. Then Eusol and lint all round it and dress. Two aspirin tablets when done. You'll be fine, Lieutenant; I've seen far worse.'

The doctor went away to examine a comatose man who apparently had a bullet lodged next to his spine and Nellie went to work as the now recovered VAD held the bowl. The patient was very stoic as she gently but firmly elevated the stump and washed it down thoroughly with Eusol. When that was done she told the VAD to bring fresh, and when it arrived she soaked a large piece of lint in it, which she wrapped all around the stump. Around the whole she wrapped Jackinette, a waterproof type of bandage and was done.

'That's you done until tomorrow. If there's anything you want tell the VAD and they'll do what they can.'

'Thanks Sister; I could use some food and a cup of tea with those aspirin. Do I have to go through that again tomorrow?'

'I'm afraid you have to. You've got an infection and it has to be done every day. And I'm not a Sister; I'm a nurse.'

'Yes Sister.'

Nellie gave up.

This was her introduction to large battle wounds and over the next few hours she cleaned, dressed and disinfected until she was almost dropping. When she had finished her last patient it was after two o'clock in the morning and she had been awake for twenty hours. There were four beds in her room and by the time she crept into hers, the other nurses were already asleep.

Her official duty was supposed to begin at the start of morning shift, at 6.00am, but to her horror she did not wake until eight o'clock. She scrambled out of bed, then noticed that the other nurses were also just waking up. Well if she was going to be in trouble then so were they. As she made her way towards the washroom the Matron came along the corridor.

'Ah Nurse Little, I'm glad to see you are up.'

'I'm sorry to be up so late Matron; it won't happen again.'

'Oh, it will never you fear, I let you sleep on because I need you alert. You were tending wounded until the early hours and needed to sleep. I know that; I have learned in this war that we sleep when we can. It'll get worse. There are nurses in France twenty-four hours and more on their feet and we must take it as it comes. There are plenty of VADs for the routine stuff. Now as you are first up it'll have to be you in theatre.'

'Theatre? I have no experience in theatre.'

'That's what you're here for. All you have to do is what the surgeon says, and pass him things. Now get on down to the theatre because they are operating in half an hour. There's no trained theatre nurse available and only the surgeon and an anaesthetist in there; we are stretched very thinly with all these casualties. Any idea of larger surgical teams has been abandoned for now. There's a poor lad with a bullet close to his spine and the surgeon in France put a note in his pocket that he dared not attempt it. He's very ill and it's got to come out, so get a move on.'

The patient had been brought in the previous night in a very bad condition and had been carried on a chair. The reason he had not been taken care of in a southern hospital was because he had been classified as 'moribund'; that is to say he was likely to die, and hospital beds were given to the men they knew they could save. Second Lieutenant Reeves however, clung on to life and had, seemingly against the odds, reached Carlisle. Now he lay face down and anaesthetised on the operating table. Mr Plugg, the elderly surgeon told Nellie to wash him well with Lysol around the wound area, which was in the middle of his back between the shoulder blades. Poor Reeves lay grey, barely breathing and looking already a corpse, waiting for his attentions. The only people present were Nellie, Plugg, and Mr Murphy the anaesthetist.

'Now then, Nurse, pull that dressing off and let's see what we've got.'

Nellie pulled off a patch of sticky dressing to disclose a small red-black hole where a bullet had entered, then she cleaned the area and dried it with lint.

'So we have a small entrance wound and no exit so let us see. Hand me those forceps Nurse – yes the thin ones with teeth.'

Mr Plugg inserted the forceps very gently into the wound and began to feel around.

'Trainee aren't you? First time in theatre? Well watch and learn. What am I doing?'

'Probing for a bullet Sir.'

'Well, it's a good guess, but not quite. Not yet. Do you see where this bullet has gone in? Yes? So what am I looking for?'

'Bone fragments Sir.'

'Very good Nurse. Very good. Yes, and since a superannuated old fool like me has been doing this for nearly forty years, how do you think I find them?'

'By touch Sir?'

'Well done Nurse. Yes indeed. If I feel my way very carefully I can feel a gentle grate vibrating up the metal where it touches bone. And if it touches bone where there should be no bone?'

'Then it's a fragment Sir.'

'Exactly! Now just wipe the sweat of my face will you or it'll steam my glasses up. Aha.'

With an air of triumph the doctor pulled out a chunk of bone, smashed off a vertebrae. Over the next few minutes he pulled out three more pieces of bone and probed even deeper.

'I can see why my colleague over in France did not wish to attempt this even in a base hospital. Yes indeed I can. Now Nurse I have, as Murphy there can tell you, a kind of mental picture in my head of where exactly the tip of these forceps are and I can tell you now that I am very close to the spinal cord, which makes me a tad nervous because this chap is not paralysed and I have no wish to damage it. In fact I'm pulling out.'

Mr Plugg removed the forceps and asked instead for a long probe which he inserted very gently into the wound, advancing it delicately, almost imperceptibly, and to Nellie's astonishment he closed his eyes. After a minute or two he let out a breath.

'Ah! Got it. It's actually embedded in the spine Murph. It's pressing on the cord, but I believe that I can take it out the way it went in. Nurse, there's a slightly thicker set of forceps over there; yes those. Thank you.'

Mr Plugg inserted the new forceps and felt around, then he gripped them very hard, rotated slightly and pulled. With the forceps came a flattened chunk of lead. To Nellie's astonishment the effect on the unconscious patient was immediate. Within two minutes his breathing became deeper and more natural. Colour slowly returned and he no longer looked grey.

'I know Nurse. I'm a cast iron number one genius, no need to tell me; I'm well aware of it. Now clean that thoroughly and I'll apply a few stitches; then you apply a dressing. The patient is to be put to bed between two firm pillows and in a semi-upright position; please see that he is watched for the next two days around the clock and kept in that position. After that he should be fine.'

Over the next few days Nellie got to know the other nurses in her room, became friendly, but not too friendly, with some of the VADs, and assisted in theatre again dealing with the removal of deep shrapnel and in one case the removal of an arm which was too gangrenous to leave attached. It was hard work and long hours, and because she lived in, she was liable to be called at any time. It was with some relief that she heard Matron tell her that she had done well and that she could have the coming Saturday afternoon off. On 22 May Nellie started her morning shift at 6.00am. Mr Asquith was putting together his new Cabinet, and the second battle of Ypres was raging over the Channel, but Nellie was looking forward to going to see a film in Carlisle with one of the other nurses who also had that afternoon off; cinemas were considered quite respectable places to go these days. Her world had shifted into a place and shape where she was doing things that she had not imagined that she would ever be called upon to do just a week before. Nellie's war had begun in earnest and she wondered what they would say back home if they could see what she was engaged in. For them industrial Workington was, as yet a peaceful haven, but the war was to change and mark them all before it was done, though some in more ways than others.

Chapter 3

The Sands of Normality

For the Little family life in Workington continued much as it always had since they had moved to the town from Dearham. Tom had long wished to leave coal mining, an occupation he had held for several years, where he had oversight of the pit ponies down the Crosshow pit. However, he had been born and raised a farmer and the contrast between the wide-open spaces of the Solway Plain and the dark close tunnels of the mine had been particularly large to him. As the years went by he fretted more and more each day as he disappeared into the bowels of the earth, away from the sun and the wind and the flowers of earth, and he yearned for something different. When the mine had closed he was lucky enough to land a job working with horses at the Moss Bay Steelworks in Workington which paid him enough to support Margaret and a growing family without too much of a pinch. It is true that their lives would have had more quality if they had not chosen to have eight children, but that was how things turned out and somehow they managed to get by and never go hungry. The only really difficult time they had gone through since arriving in the town was during the great coal strike of 1912, which caused great hardship because people had to heat and do their cooking with coal and there was none to be bought. Like most other people in Workington the family had to recourse to gathering coals on the beach or going to an outcrop such as was found on open ground in St Michael's road where the measures rose to the surface. This was not a thing they would normally have considered because like most families they liked to give the impression that they were coping well, but since perhaps 80% of the population were eking out their fuel supplies in the same way, somehow the stigma melted.

It was during this time also that the family discovered that Workington had a rather strong community spirit of its own because people really did go out of their way to help each other. This was not perhaps so surprising as many of them were people who had once lived in rural areas where co-operative activities were ingrained by centuries in small communities, but the impulse to do it was particularly strong in Cumberland. During the coal strike the women had used their set pots in the back yards, not for laundry but for cooking. It seemed wasteful and foolish to have each household cooking its own meal so whole streets took to communal cooking, lighting fires to heat vast pots of broth into which every household would contribute something of what they had, or nothing if they had nought, and would take a pan out of when it was cooked. In this way a nourishing meal, padded out with bread, could be had for a large number of people. It is true that this had ceased once the strike was over, but the life of the community now took place in back lonnings when special occasions made an excuse for it. The lonnings were kept clean and neat, and on party days, tables and chairs were placed outside each yard. Whole streets and neighbourhoods knew each other, worked with each other, played with each other and lived the life of a full and vibrant commune. Margaret liked living here, which was strange because, coming from a small mining village, she had never thought to live in a large town or that she would like it, crowded though it was. The collier's daughter was content with her lot, and although she had an idea that it would be nice to have a larger house, she had no intentions of moving from number

55 Devonshire Street, her neighbours, friends, congregation at St John's Church and the huge variety of shops and things to do; why should she? She and Tom slept downstairs in the front room, which was comfortable and quiet, whilst upstairs four well behaved boys and four smart girls slept soundly.

Barwise was dreaming adventurous things; this was by no means unusual, but he occasionally mumbled in his sleep which Jack found disturbing, quite literally because it kept him awake. He did not dare to awaken his elder brother because Barwise was evidently enjoying his dream in which he was a local hero. This year on 6 April he had taken part in his first Uppies and Downies match which he had enjoyed very much, though he had been very much on the fringes of the players, being far too small to compete with some of the larger men chasing the ball. This event took place every year at Easter and its origins were lost in the mists of antiquity; as well they might be for to all intents and purposes it was tribal warfare loosely described as a game of football, not that you would want to kick it. Anyone who did kick it would regret it because the heavy ball was made of thick hand-stitched leather and well stuffed with sawdust. The 'teams' were known as Uppies and Downies though these days it was often referred to as ironworkers versus sailors, but even that gives the loosest idea of who was on what side. There were, apart from this broad description, no teams and no limits to how many were on each side. The 'goals' were three quarters of a mile apart, the Uppies' being the gates of Curwen Hall, and the Downies' placed at the capstan at Workington Harbour. To win, a team had to get the ball into their own goal where it was 'hailed'. Having so captured it, the victory was theirs. And there were no rules.

In his dream Barwise was at the centre of a mob down by the Brewery beck on the Cloffocks, a wide meadow sort of area that ran beside the town in the river valley. The whole mass of men were struggling to gain possession of the ball, and no holds were barred. Barwise got hold of the ball and headed off upstream only to find his way blocked by a group of determined Downies.

Whole families were there and although they did not wish to kill the man with the ball, they were not too fussy about where they grabbed him. Shouting pushing and struggling men by the hundred grappled with each other, the only restraint being that this was a small town and people knew each other. If you were too nasty then grudges would be borne. Barwise lost the ball as someone ran into the river and headed downstream splashing through the shallows, then as the water grew deeper, began to swim downstream with it. The Downies were up to this trick and had rowing boats stationed in the river so a melee of swimming men and boats went for the ball and the Uppies lost possession of it. Over the next three hours the cries of 'Up wid her' and 'Down wid her' echoed across the meadow. At one point the baying mob moved up Dolly's Brow, but a strong body of police were not having that. The game had spilled into the town before where windows were broken, premises damaged, and bystanders hurt.

After six hours of play the ball was the subject of a huge fist fight in the shallow part of the River Derwent, and the hero of the day Barwise Little grabbed the ball and headed for Curwen Hall. It was very odd that try as they might, no-one could lay a hand on him. All they could do was yell and try to stop him as he hurtled up the Black Pad, but he was so fast that no-one could stop him. Finally, with a mighty yell he reached the gates of Curwen Hall and leapt to ring the bell that hung there, throwing the ball into the air, 'hailing' it. As people shouted his name and pounded his back, the hero felt someone shaking him and opened his eyes to see his mother holding a candle near him.

'Barwise, what on earth were you dreaming about? That's quite a nightmare you've been having. You've woken the whole house and maybe the neighbours too.'

'I'm sorry Mother; it was just a dream.'

'Well then, go back to sleep. From the sound of it, it was a rather violent dream and you were punching people.'

'Only because they were punching me!'

'Hmmm – don't do it in the real world or your father will want to say something about it. Now go back to sleep.'

Margaret looked round the room, 'And that goes for the rest of you, except Joe. Goodnight.'

With that she was gone and Barwise looked at little Joe who, at five years of age evidently placed sleep as a priority, even in his unconscious mind, for he had slept through the whole thing.

'It wasn't you anyway,' said Jack.

'Wasn't me what?'

'Who hailed the ball this year.'

'How did you know what I was dreaming?'
'Couldn't avoid it; you were loud enough. Local hero.'
'Shut up Jack.'
'It was that wrestler from Grasmere who did it. Clark.'
'I know. Shut up.'
'One of those girls taking part could have done it before you…'

Barwise hit him with a pillow, which could have been the start of trouble but a male voice from below shouted, 'Go to sleep, now!'

Jack added, 'And even if he hadn't Curly Hill would have taken you apart if you'd got near the ball…'

Although this was undoubtedly true of the local and muscular legend, Barwise did not press the point. Wise men did not argue with Father; they went to sleep. Getting back at Jack could wait until the time was ripe, for Barwise tried never to let such things go unavenged. This was especially true at work where he had undergone the usual initiations when he started at the boiler work with a reasonable humour. Being sent to the stores for some elbow grease or the long end of a short plank was fairly mild stuff, but if it gained acceptance among his workmates then he did not mind because he knew that everyone had been through it. Even the ceremony of having his trousers dragged down and his buttocks liberally painted with grease had passed him by because he knew it was a tradition, if a rather stupid one. The problem was Matthew Roach who was the chief hammerer or 'basher' of his team, because he appeared to be a bully and for almost a year after Barwise had started work, the bullying had been fairly relentless. If Roach had known the boy better he might have realised that he was never going to let it continue indefinitely.

Barwise was a 'catcher' in a four-man team skilled in the hot riveting of boilers for steam engines. The shaped steel sheets of a boiler would come down to them from the machine sheds into the assembly area with holes already drilled, spaced, and burrs removed by the precision craftsmen whose speciality this was. The heavy pieces would be lifted by block and tackle by the shed labourers and pinned into place and then the riveters would move in. 'Cook' would set up his coke brazier near the work site, ply his bellows and get a good hot flame going in which he heated the steel rivets until red / white glowing. When he was satisfied that they were ready he would lift a rivet out of the brazier with tongs and throw it into a leather lined bucket with ash at the bottom held by Barwise. It was then Barwise's job to take it quickly to the hole it was destined for and the basher would insert it. Then the basher tapped it home with his hammer and his mate, the 'holder on' would push a shaped metal dolly against the rounded end to hold the rivet in place while the other end was bashed flat. Barwise had been so fascinated by this the first time he saw it that he lingered too long looking at the skill displayed by the basher and was recalled by an angry shout from the cook that he was a lazy little bugger and better get his arse in gear. That was the first time that Roach had smacked the side of his head and told him he'd better learn to get a ripple on or he'd get a pasting he wouldn't forget.

After that he got slapped for everything; not getting the water for tea ready quickly enough in the corrugated iron hut where they took their bait, taking too long at the toilet, or even for looking at Roach in a 'cheeky way'. Barwise, it seemed, could do no right. One morning he was even called a 'jam-eater' because of what he had in his sandwiches that day instead of meat, but Barwise preferred jam, having a sweet tooth. Nonetheless, he even swallowed this, the ultimate local insult, which implied that he came from Whitehaven along the coast, because he hoped that eventually it would stop. Of

Chapter 3 — The Sands of Normality

course anyone having a degree in the university of life could have told him that bullies do not stop of their own volition. You have to stop them; the two elderly men who were the cook and the holder on began to feel sorry for Barwise, but they did not say anything against the younger and more muscular Roach because he was the team leader. The truth was that Roach was not a natural bully, but was one of those men inclined to not restrain themselves if he saw weakness. It's a fine distinction, but the true bully actively enjoys the victimisation of another. With Roach it was different. He did not enjoy bullying Barwise; he never gave it a second thought, just doing it because he could, almost unconsciously. If he could be brought to think about it, then he would probably stop, but as yet, he had not thought about it. The matter came to a head one night at knocking off time when he told Barwise to carry his hammer and toolbag to the hut, which the boy did. In the hut he swung the bag under the bench where Roach usually sat, where they would sit until the next day, but on this occasion there came the sound of breaking glass. Beer was not allowed in the yard, but Roach had brought a bottle of beer into the hut for when he finished his work, and now it spilled all over the floor. In the Marsh and Harbour area were many pubs because the men employed in the area did hard and sweaty work. At clocking off time they would swarm by the hundred into these pubs where the landlords would have dozens of already drawn pints ready to slake their thirst, but Roach had wanted to steal a march on this process; now he could not.

Bellowing in rage he grabbed Barwise who struggled hard but to no avail and he put him over his knee. He then thrashed him with a batten of wood that leaned in the corner of the hut and he made the boy cry. When he was done, Barwise left and went home where he said nothing about what had happened; it was an affair that he was fully determined to see to himself, though Roach was a grown man and far stronger than he. It took two days for Nemesis to fall. It being November, knocking off time was after dark, and Roach always went home on his old bicycle without lights that was kept during the working day in a corner of the yard. Barwise was watching from the hut as the basher got onto his bike and cycled away only to come to a sudden and unexpected halt as the bike, held from behind, stopped dead and he sailed over the handlebars onto the hard ground where he sustained several cuts and bruises, and in particular a gash on his head where it came in to contact with the cobbles.

Staggering to his feet he saw a rope, unobserved in the darkness, attached to his bike, with the other end tied to an iron fence post. Several men around were laughing, thinking it a great practical joke and the funniest thing they'd ever seen, but Roach failed to see the humour. The showdown came the very next morning in the hut.

'It was you you little bastard wasn't it? You fixed my bike so I'd come off.'

'It was me alright and next time I'll think of summat better so it kills thew proper.'

Roach may have reflected on looking at his smaller workmate that there was a certain wonder in being the cause of such hatred, but this thought did not come immediately.

'Kill me? I'll give you a thrashing you won't forget you little swine.'

'Aye you might you bullying sod, but you won't forget doing it though you put me in the hospital.'

With that, Barwise did not wait for commencement of hostilities because he knew that if he was grabbed, he would be helpless. He jumped off the opposite bench, punched Roach straight on the nose and dashed out the door to the open air. Once there he did not run, but turned and waited in a posture of defence, his fists up and absolute defiance in his eyes. To his great surprise Roach burst out laughing.

'Well you're a game little bugger, I'll give you that.' He came out of the hut dabbing at his nose, which was more than a little tender. 'Aye, I've been riding you hard haven't I?'

'You have and I'll not stand for it.'

'You won't have to. I like pluck in a lad and you'll get no more trouble from me. I shouldn't have thrashed you like that the other night and I knew it as soon as I cooled down a bit. I'm sorry I did it. Now give me your hand on it 'cos we're going to be marras.'

Bemused at this turn of events, Barwise stood a moment, his brain working like a fast clock, then decided not to look a gift horse in the mouth. He stepped forward holding out his hand, half expecting Roach to grab him and give him a hammering. Instead the man spat on his hand and shook hands with him as a few spectators around grinned. The trouble was over, and since that day Barwise had been happy at work.

Now, in May 1915 he was quite content for the moment to sit against the wall where Devonshire Street ended against the railway embankment and soak up the Saturday afternoon sun. A lot, even most of the local men were away watching the football at Lonsdale Stadium, but he and Jack thought it nice and warm to just relax, for they had both been at work until one o'clock. Down the pavement they watched Nancy, who also had the afternoon off with Joe and Ettie, teaching them to play hopscotch on the markings newly re-chalked on the road. To their left and just a little way down, their mother Margaret was chatting on the pavement to Mrs Beeby, their next door neighbour and Mrs Smith from across the road.

'Shall we walk along and see what's happening at the fair?'
'Yes Jack, but not just now. I'm feeling lazy so just sit a bit eh?'
'Fair enough. I like sitting here when it's sunny.' Jack paused

a few seconds. 'Do you remember sitting here when the comet came?'

'Well it'd be hard not to. I've never seen anything like that in my life. It was like a great golden sword in the sky.'

'Aye, but then you told me that if it touched that chimney pot up there we'd all be blown to kingdom come. I was scared out of my wits for days until it left.'

Barwise grinned at his brother, 'You'd believe anything then, though it's a bit harder to fool you now. You were wet behind the ears then.

'I've grown up a bit since then.'

'Just a bit maybe. Just a bit.'

'Aieee aiee aiee tush tush tush!'

'What are you kids doing now?'

Barwise's question to William was followed by a blank look from the smaller boy as he rushed away down the street followed by Ettie, then Joe all shouting the same thing, joined by various infants from the Smith and Beeby households.

'Why are they shouting that Nancy?'

The girl called over, 'They don't know. They just think it sounds good.'

Down the street came the paper lad from Smith's newsagents down on Finkle Street, pushing papers through doors. Later in the day he would be out with a sack selling the *Star* on various street corners.

'Now look Jack, here's Tommy Wilson. Hey Tommy, have you been out after dark lately?'

The paper-boy looked abashed, shook his head and went on his way.

'You shouldn't tease him Barwise. He saw a boggle last year I heard and he won't sell papers in the evening any more. Why rag him like that?'

'Because he asked for it. Look Jack, do you remember him

a year or so back at school when he used to slap your ears and pull Ommie's hair?'

'Yes, but that was school and he's turned over a new leaf since then. He won't say boo to a goose now and he's completely different.'

Barwise grinned broadly. 'Yes he is isn't he?'

Jack looked at him and realised all of a sudden that his information was incomplete.

'You know something about this don't you?'

Barwise continued to grin.

'You might as well tell me as not now.'

'Alright, but not a word to anyone?' Jack having agreed to this, Barwise told his tale.

'You'll remember that he used to sell papers down the Harrington Road? Well it was just after the last time he pulled Ommie's hair that I decided to get him back for it. Anyway he's the son of a Dronnie so that's nearly enough on its own. Last November I was at St Paul's and I just came out and saw him coming down towards me with his bag, yelling 'Evening Star' like he did, and I saw my chance. I knew he liked to sell some to men coming out of the pubs down there and it was a good wide place to stand.'

'You mean Pisshaven?'

'Call it what you like but that's where I was.'

Barwise was referring to a cast iron urinal of the French pissoir style that stood on a triangle of pavement across the road from the gates of Harrington Road cemetery which had several whimsical names; St Paul's, for its domed roof, Peacehaven to some or Pisshaven to those who appreciated the real relief it afforded to the drinker on his way home. Dronnies were the steelworkers who had migrated up to Workington in 1883 when Cammel's had closed their works at Dronfield in Derbyshire and shipped hundreds of people up to Workington and their new plant. The town was divided in hostility between locals and Dronnies.

'To continue; I nipped into the cemetery gate in the dark and hid behind the wall. Sure enough, he came along and stood outside the gate and carried on yelling and he sold a couple, and that's when I had my idea. Originally I was going to just jump up and scare him but I decided to do something else better.'

'What did you do?'

'Well I rolled my jacket sleeve up and covered my arm and hand in mud and dirt and waited till he came to lean against the wall for a rest. Then I held a penny out through the railings over his shoulder and said as deep and hoarse as I could manage, "Yis lad – Arl 'ave yan"'

'What did he do?'

'What did he do? Well first I thought his eyes were going to come out of his head. Then he let out a scream that I thought would waken every man jack out of his grave in the cemetery and then he took off like a rocket up the road towards Harrington. I've never seen anyone move so fast in my life.'

'And since then he doesn't sell papers at night.'

'That's right Jack. Exactly so. And he's nicer too. Glad to have friendly folk round him and not boggles.'

'Well I suppose it did him good then.'

'I think it did. I'm not sorry about it, but it gave him far more of a fright than I thought. Never mind, it paid him off and that makes me happy.'

'Were you not afraid to go in the cemetery in the dark?'

'No. Why should I be. If there was 'owt to worry about they'd lock the gates.'

'Well, I wouldn't go in there again.'

'Why not? I don't believe in boggles.'

'Maybe but there's a lad over in Brayton Street tells different.'

'Go on.'

'His uncle had a few pints last August and was on his way home after eleven. It was a warm night and he felt sleepy so as he was passing the cemetery he decided to pop through the gates, lie on the grass and have a little doze. He closed his eyes and was just about to nod off when a voice whispered to him; "There's only thew and me in here." Anyway he sat up and there's no one there so he thought he'd imagined it and lay back down again. A couple of minutes later the voice said "There's only thew and me in here." So he got up and looked round behind a couple of gravestones to see who was playing tricks, but there was no one there. As he stood thinking about it a voice said right in his ear "There's only thew and me in here." "Aye" he says, "and in ten seconds there'll only be thew." He was out of there pretty quick.'

Barwise thought about this for a moment then he shivered.
'You pulling my leg?'
'Aye. I am.'
'Well, I ain't going into that cemetery after dark again, I can tell you that!'
'But I just made it up.'
'That's as maybe, but it's creepy enough to keep me the right side of them gates after dark. Come on; let's go up the Buttermarket and see the hirings.'
'Alright. Well I might as well tell you; I didn't make it up…'

Margaret, their mother, watched them go with a sense of pride in her two eldest boys and was, yet again glad that they were not old enough to go off to war. There were terrible tales circulating of battles in France with thousands of casualties and it was a good thing that the war would be over before either of them had to go and fight. Taking 'Thou shalt not kill' as a literal commandment, it was not just fear for their lives that set her mind against them joining up. Nellie was going to nurse wounded soldiers and that was a good thing, but she could not see her children shooting other men. Tom of course was too old, but he would not have wished to fight in a war; a more unmilitary man she never met despite his fierce look. No, what was important was to work hard and bring their children up well and that was what they were doing. This was their purpose and the point of their living and she accepted her place in life with relish, for it gave her meaning. For the moment at least, life was normal though the sands of time were running out on normality and much would change before long.

Chapter 4

Family

Across the street Nancy's mind was full of thoughts about, of all things, Mr Lloyd George. The Chancellor had signed an agreement with the unions in March, and Nancy knew girls who were working in factories where they had not been allowed to previously. Women were doing all sorts of jobs they had not done before, because so many men had gone off to war. Nancy had heard that some of them were earning nearly £3 a week and that made her wages seem very paltry indeed. She had been a maid at the Central Hotel for three years now, at first as a junior, but £7 for a half year was tiny in comparison to the riches that were on offer. She had recently been 'promoted' to waitress at £18 a year, but it was still not much. There was also a nagging doubt in her mind that this was what she really wished to be doing. Of all Margaret's children it was Nancy who most closely fitted the description of 'little mother' and she always had displayed a nurturing personality, which was why it was she who kept an eye on the small ones whilst Margaret worked in and around the house. Handsome rather than pretty, Nancy had inherited her mother's determination and strength of will, a matriarch in the making if she should have her own family; for now she supervised and mentored her own siblings. She would not be doing it for much longer on this particular day, because she had an evening shift at work starting at 6.00pm, but at least it meant that she would be around when the family went to church the following morning. At first she had enjoyed the idea that she was bringing home a wage and contributing her bit to the house, but three years of long shifts, hard work and low pay had left her wondering if this was all there was to be in life before marriage. The new pathway that had opened up for girls in war work was of great interest to her and it was no longer just the germ of an idea. It was early days yet, but the rumour mill was saying that huge numbers of young women would be needed in factories in the coming months where they would receive full training and be paid well. Nancy had a firm and determined nature and her mind was quite set that when opportunity knocked, she would answer the call.

Church was a binding glue to Margaret's family and they knew it well; the ceremony of it was as important as sitting down together to family dinner. The church they went to was rather special because it was a Waterloo church, St John's, built with government money in 1823 as a thanks to God for victory against Napoleon. It was a little gloomy inside and not beautiful at all; even the layout was odd because the congregation faced towards the main door and the altar was just inside it. Nonetheless, it was spectacular in its size and had a very dedicated and enthusiastic congregation of which Margaret was a member. Her religion took the form of high church and she would have wished to do her worship, which was very important to her, in a place that was more handsome, but for the moment she was happy with it. A choir of men and boys complete with surplices was introduced in 1904 and all her boys took their parts in it, and, from what she heard, had carved their initials in the wood of the choir stalls. She had always had faith, but as with many people, it manifested itself more solidly as she grew older; her confirmation into the Church of England was taken as a mature decision in 1913, although she was quite pleased that the ceremony had taken place in St Michael's Church and not her own. The solemnly beautiful Victorian gothic setting had seemed very fitting to her for such an important event in her life, and she had loved all the pomp of the Bishop of Carlisle with his robes and mitre, with similarly attired attendants, because they lent splendour to what she had decided. A new vicar, Reverend Croft, had arrived in 1914 and he had great plans for the beautification of St John's, which Margaret wholly supported, but of course it would have to wait until after the war. Some of the congregation were involved in raising funds for their church and how they wished it to be and the better off ones could be very generous with gifts of money. For those with less to spare like Margaret, there was a host of activities she helped with, like the celebrated St John's sales of work or fetes, coffee mornings, afternoon teas and a never ending list of tasks that could be undertaken. Somehow she managed to fit this in with all that was needed in running a household and raising eight children; the girls did help of course. Age and motherhood had not served to make her plump nor slatternly as it did with some in the locality; rather it had fined her down and her still dark and lustrous hair worn tidily behind her head was abundant. There were thin lines on her face, at her eyes and round her mouth, but they were nice lines that spoke of a woman who smiled, who laughed, and was happy.

Margaret's younger children did not over complicate her life, because they were simply not old enough to think difficult things. Like young birds, they needed food, a warm nest and sufficient nurture; all these they received in plenty. Ommie still had two years to run at school before she would have to leave or go to Guard Street Grammar for girls. It would have been nice to have one of the boys stay on and go to the technical school, but this was not in reach of their purse and none of them had so far shown aspirations to do so. Ommie, her hair in bunches, a flower to the side of her hair on Sundays, her best dress a severe and scratchy coverall with a thick leather belt, also her school uniform, did not appear to have her head replete of serious thoughts. In fact, she was rather the reverse, full of fun and activity, a twinkle in her eye and never able to sit still long. She always had a little foible to her at different stages of growing up and at one time her nose was too big, then it was her ears that were too big; her current obsession was her handkerchief for she had to have a clean one about her person at all times, and usually it was clutched in her right hand. If Margaret had known the term 'security blanket' then she would have applied it to Ommie's hanky.

It was possible that Billy and Joe might show more academic ambitions as they grew up, but it was doubtful. The impulse among male children as they grew up round here was to get out and earn a wage because that was what men did. As it was, these younger brothers were a boisterous pair and their mother hardly ever saw them during the day; they were out at school, but then played in the streets and lonnings at all sorts of games with other children in the neighbourhood. It may not be said that she let them run wild, for they had jobs to do, young as they were. They were not to be allowed to grow up feeling that they were there to be waited on. Billy was a well set up type of lad, big for his age and even at his early years, developing a sense of self reliance that made Margaret think of him as her little man. He looked out for Joe, who was of a more delicate constitution, though healthy enough. Finally, there was Esther and quite simply, she was Margaret's pet. At six, her hair was light and long with a ribbon tied in the right hand side, and she looked the picture of Margaret at her age; she had her mother's grey eyes and that air of self-possession that told an observer she was sure of herself, grounded and with a gentle direct gaze that suggested much intelligence. Of the girls, this one was most like her mother in appearance and temperament, and a glance at her was enough to make Margaret's heart ache.

Tom at 51 was, like his wife, of a happy disposition. Perhaps he should not have been, for in some senses he had come down in the world. Once he had lived as the prosperous son of a prosperous farmer, but his own ventures in that business had led to his losing all that he had save a couple of hundred pounds. For several years he had supported his family by working down a coalmine in Dearham as the ostler, looking after the pit ponies and the draught horses on the surface. When the mine had closed because the economics of it no longer worked, he had been lucky enough to get a job at Moss Bay Steelworks on the plate-laying gang, but with an added responsibility. Plate-laying was, for him, not a full time job; he was only required when rails needed to be replaced on the steelworks' extensive network of sidings, and this was not constant. The work did not bother him over-much because he was as strong as an ox, and used to working outdoors on the farm in all weathers. The rest of the time he worked with a large Clydesdale called Skiddaw. When asked why he had given the horse this name he would reply, 'Because it's a big lump and so is this one.'

Even with the horse, the work was varied. Although steam engines did much of the haulage work round the steelworks, there were wagons to be pulled from one place to another, and there was even shunting when it was not worth summoning an engine. The size of the railway freight wagons was enormous and when he first attached his horse to one of them Tom doubted if he would be able to shift it, but to his surprise the big horse leaned into his collar and the huge mass just smoothed along the track with little apparent effort. He knew nothing of friction coefficients, but steel wheels on steel rails meant that Skiddaw could move several wagons at a time. Once the mass was moving, it was a different matter so the horse never pulled the wagons straight on, but from a chain attached to the side

Chapter 4 — Family

of one wheel bogey. That was so he could not become trapped and crushed between wagons and buffers when they arrived at their destination.

Tom was fond of his horse and his duty was to make sure that he was fed, groomed, watered and his general welfare attended to, whether he was at work or not. Even on Sundays Tom had to trail down to the steelworks for an hour or so to see to Skiddaw, but he did not mind at all. In some senses the big Clydesdale reminded him of his former life as a farmer, and of his own little attempt to set up on his own, breeding Clydesdales. They had all died in 1903, and it was only years later that Tom, speaking to old farming acquaintances, had found out the probable cause of their deaths.

In 1907 the first cases of a newly recognised condition had been reported and termed 'grass fever'; it had apparently been around for some time previously. There was apparently no cure for this, and dozens of Clydesdales had fallen victim to it. Tom found this somehow a comfort because it made him understand that he had done all he could to save his farm and horses, but that ultimately he was powerless against it. What he did not like to dwell on was the aftermath where he had taken to drink and hit his wife, causing her to leave him. Although they had been reconciled Tom had sworn off drink and kept his pledge, because in the end his love for wife and family mattered more to him than did the spirits he had been so enamoured of. His sworn pledge was on the wall of their own bedroom; he and Margaret and the children took part in Temperance parades and saw them as a cause for festivity and celebration. Their work, their church, their sober and respectable habits all gave them a good name in their neighbourhood and in the town and generally speaking their move to Workington had brought them nothing but good.

Like many families in Britain at this time, the Littles had

not felt the full effects of the war that they, like most people, had thought would be over by Christmas 1914. No doubt there was an effect on their community, because many men had volunteered and gone away to train and fight, but directly, the family remained untouched. It was true that new open hearth furnaces were being installed at Moss Bay and that production was switching from railway lines to armour plate and steel for ships, but that did not affect Tom's work in what he actually did. Some foodstuffs were getting hard to find and prices had gone up a bit, but so far Nellie was the only family member who had any direct contact with the war or its effects. Normality had continued in their lives, though a little changed in colour, but the sands of time, and what passed for normal, were running out. War, that unwanted intruder, was to mark three of their lives to a significant degree, and in the marking, was also to impact upon the others before it was ended.

Chapter 5

Disaster

Murrell Hill House was full so they could not, for the moment, accept any more casualties. Nellie was expecting to be sent to another of the city hospitals for her wound treatment course to continue, because much of the work being done was simple changes of dressings and straightforward nursing. The VADs were able to manage a lot of this work, and there were so many of them that occasionally she felt almost surplus to requirements. After some of the injuries she had to attend to when she first arrived, a routine had set in which would not vary until the next casualties came in, but that would not be until some of the current patients had been moved out to convalescent centres.

She did not hear the telephone ring down in the office, and was aware of no change in her routine until Matron Bennett-Brown came almost running up the stairs and into the ward.

'Nurse I want you downstairs now and ready to go and the other three nurses too. Now you girls gather round me and listen.'

The VADs gathered round in a gaggle and listened attentively, for Matron was in no mood for argument.

'There has been an accident on the railway and word is going round that every trained nurse that can be spared is wanted. That means that myself and the nurses from here are going now, and you will have to cope with this hospital. Ainslie; you are in charge until I get back.'

This word to the oldest of the VADs was enough, and she strode off to meet the four nurses in the hospital foyer. There she bundled them into a waiting Crossley ambulance, and as they drove she handed each of them a bag that had been stuffed hastily with bandages, plasters and bottles of Eusol, together with scissors, pins, short splints and other items for medical emergency.

'What's happening Matron please?'

'I don't know anything other than what I've told you. There has been some sort of accident on the railway line and they want every nurse that can be spared.'

At Carlisle Citadel station order was being wrought out of chaos; the place was packed with steam locomotives as every train north had been stopped and many were being diverted onto other lines. The concourse was a mass of nurses' uniforms, doctors, soldiers, railway officials, and a special train was being assembled with haste from the carriages that were available. As each carriage arrived it was filled with blankets, stretchers and all sorts of supplies as men argued loudly as to the haste with which they should leave. In charge was a senior military officer who was quite firm that the train would not leave until it was ready to do its job.

'I have been in touch with people near the wreck site and am assured that there are many helpers on the site and many wounded. They do not need willing hands and well meaning people; they need trained personnel and medical supplies and that is what I shall send them.'

The first medical train was sent at 7.43am, but Nellie did not notice the exact moment of departure. Afterwards she remembered that it was 8.10am when they arrived at Quintinshill just outside Gretna Green, because she had just looked at her fob watch and thought that her family back home would be in the Sunday morning service. Not until a soldier helped her climb out of the carriage did she realise what she had arrived at, because the scene of devastation in front of her was almost incomprehensible, the horror of what she saw being compounded by the fact that the wreckage was on fire and screams were coming from it. She could barely see how many carriages were involved, but thought she could see at least three smashed locomotives; for the moment there was work enough for her away from the wreck, but she found herself wishing not to go near it, unable to bear the thought of what she might see. Behind her was a peaceful green field studded with buttercups and daisies but in front of her for a huge area was nothing but twisted metal, wreckage of all sizes and a vast fire from which came sounds she wished she could not hear. Desperate figures of rescuers swarmed round it, hacking at carriages, smashing windows and tunnelling into the pile of chaos to try to reach people trapped inside who were calling for help. Many of the men were in uniform and had obviously been on the train; it was a troop train, and at least one civilian train she realised with horror. They attacked the wreckage as if attacking an enemy and fighting a battle, a task in which they were assisted by numerous local people, but their efforts were hampered by lack of equipment.

In the middle where the train gas tanks had exploded and set alight to the wooden carriages there were people unable to get out and who could not be rescued because there were no tools to tackle the twisted metal and spars. Some of the train crew had obtained a hand pump from a nearby farm and were desperately trying to quench the fire with water from their tenders, but it was of no use. Indelibly printed on her mind was one officer up on a carriage, flames licking up around him, whom people were calling desperately to in order to get down and save himself. With a face drawn in combined horror and determination, he drew his pistol, deliberately took aim at something in the fire and shot. Then, and only then did he jump down and stagger away from the pyre; she noticed that he was shaking uncontrollably.

Nellie, wide-eyed said aloud, without realising it, 'Did he just shoot a man?'

A grim faced Scot passing by caught her by the arm. 'Aye Nurse; he did. And you know what? If I'd have been the poor devil trapped where that one was, I'd want him to shoot me too. Better a clean bullet than burn to death. That officer's a man; they drew lots for who would shoot the poor devils and it was him that got the job. I advise you that you did not see that. That's not the only poor lad that's been spared agony this morning by a mercy and a blessing; some that could manage it did away with themselves before the flames took them. One officer took his own arm off with a sword that he begged his friend to pass to him.'

Nellie could do nothing but to nod, speechlessly.

The soldier softened to her. 'You've enough work to do without worrying about that lassie. There's men that need you.'

She looked round and nodded.

'Yes. You're right. They do.'

The field around her was covered in dozens of prone figures, some covered with their greatcoats, and some not; she took her bag and commenced to walk towards them, but another soldier stopped her and said;

'No Sister. You can't help them and some of them it's best you don't see.'

'I've seen the dead before Sergeant. Are they all dead?'

'Yes Miss. Every man woman and child. The wounded are on the other side in the meadow.'

'Children?' asked Nellie, aghast.

'Aye,' was all he replied.

Walking round the front of the train Nellie found her mission set plain for her as men in various stages of injury lay, many moaning in distress. Among the other nurses spreading out,

Nellie headed into the melee and picked the first man she saw being unattended. He lay, unprotesting, his lower body covered by a blanket, but his face grey and obviously in some distress.

'Are you in pain Private?'

'No Nurse. The doctor gave me some morphine a wee while back, but I was in pain; a lot of it.'

'Where are you hurt?'

'It's my foot Nurse. It's off.'

Nellie gently removed the blanket from his foot, using it to keep the upper part of his body warm. It was the most beautiful sunny day, getting warmer by the minute with the sky a clear blue, but patients who lost a lot of blood could feel the cold badly. When she looked at where his foot should have been, she caught her breath.

'How did this happen?'

'A local man cut it off with a woodsaw.'

Nellie blenched inwardly but retained her outward composure.

'Why did he do that?'

'Because, Nurse, I was trapped in there, near the top and it caught fire. A man smashed his way in through a whole carriage on top of me and then down into my compartment where I was caught by my foot. There was another man with tools nearby and he shouted to get a saw; the flames were licking round us and he cut my foot off there and then he and his pal and got me out of that Hell. I'll bless him till the day I die for doing it because there were others they could not get to.'

'That's his belt round your leg?'

'I think that's what's keeping me alive.'

'You are right. Have you been seen by a doctor since being given morphine?'

'No Miss. I don't like to fuss. There's others worse than me.'

'Well you are not wrong, but you need a surgeon, not me

and I'm not going to cover that wound. Orderly!'

She saw her patient into an ambulance where two orderlies attended each vehicle and handed him over with the information that he had a tourniquet and needed immediate surgery. Since there were already five other injured men racked on stretchers in the ambulance, she had the satisfaction of seeing it speed off down the road back towards Carlisle. From then on she was engaged in tending men with a range of injuries, but the astonishing thing was that there were very few intermediate injuries in this disaster. They were either mortal or an immediate threat to life, or light. The men who were badly burned, she could do little for except make as comfortable as they could be and get them onto the train. The four doctors in attendance on the first train were men of miracles, stitching and repairing men where they could, despatching them to hospital at Carlisle or Longtown and administering morphine where necessary.

The main pile of the wreck was by now an inferno yet still men attempted to get at it with twelve fire extinguishers from the medical train, and fire buckets. Along the road at about 9.30am a bell signalled the arrival of a pump engine from Carlisle Fire Brigade, but there was no water supply. The engine was parked half a mile away and three hoses led to the river Sark and from the pump to the wreck site. This had all taken time and by ten o'clock they were pumping tons of water onto the flames, but they had taken too firm a hold. Nellie, glancing up from wrapping a tight dressing round the arm of a man who had gashed it open jumping for his life out of a carriage window, saw with disbelief the jets of water having no perceptible effect on the roaring flames. Mercifully the noises from the epicentre of the flames had ceased; although she did not know it yet, they were to trouble her dreams on occasions for the rest of her life. Around the edges where the fire had not

Chapter 5 — Disaster

yet caught, the struggle for life and death went on.

At 10.42am Nellie looked up at a train whistle and saw that a fully equipped hospital train had arrived and a flock of nurses and doctors descended on the field. At that she could restrain herself no longer and dashed towards the wreck to do what she could, though what she did not know. As she ran she almost marvelled at herself overcoming her fears, amazed that the desire to help had removed all her nausea and dread of what might reveal itself.

'Nurse! Over here and give me a hand. Hold this fellow's head up.'

While two men struggled to hold a man horizontal, the doctor was attempting to amputate his legs while flames were three feet away.

'I've had to put him out with ether but I can't get him out of here. If his legs don't come off he's done for. His head's flopping backwards and I need him to breathe properly.'

The heat was intense and Nellie winced as a large flame probed out in their direction, but gamely stood doing as she was directed. Within five minutes the surgeon had done what he had to do with a speed that beggared belief and they carried the patient clear. Shortly after they did so flames gouted out of where he had been.

'My grandfather was a surgeon too Nurse and he used to say that he could have a leg off in twenty seconds. I took one leg off another fellow half an hour ago and he died in minutes from the shock I think. This one's alive so look lively you men and get him onto the ambulance; he needs to be in theatre as soon as possible.'

Surrounded by scenes of utter destruction the rescuers, the doctors and the nurses worked on with almost superhuman will. Two men nearby had tunnelled under the wreck, hacking their way with axes and crowbars and dragged out four men. The heat in their tunnel was appalling as the fire had caught above them so they backed out to drink some water and steady their nerves with a cigarette, but as they left the hole they had worked at so hard, it collapsed in on itself and the way was closed.

It was now that Nellie became even more aware that there were civilians in the crash as well as soldiers, for the bodies of a woman and a child were carried away past her and the sight overwhelmed her and for a few seconds she stood staring in horror, tears starting at her eyes, but an elder nurse grasped her by the arm.

'Steady my girl. I've watched you and you've done well. But you have to hold on because you are still needed. There's time enough for that later.'

Nellie looked at her, steeled her nerves and managed a small smile of thanks.

'I'm alright. I know and there's work to do.'

Far to her right she heard cries for help and ran to find that she could be of no assistance at all. There was a man lying trapped under the tender of one of the crashed engines while fire burned above him. On top of the heap a young soldier hacked away at a carriage seemingly heedless of the flames round him, desperately trying to save the people inside. Several men were standing by the toppled locomotive and one of them, a corporal, dropped to his belly and began to wriggle under the tender.

'Maloney come back! Ye cannae save him and you'll get yersel killed'

'Awa; I'm no standing here listening tae a man die that I can save.'

The plates of the tender were a dull red as the corporal wriggled out backwards a few minutes later, but with him he dragged a man with a broken leg, a broken arm and extensive burns. The clothes of both men were smouldering and the small pump hose was turned on them to stop them bursting into flame.

'Ach now look what you've done! I'm all soaked.'

Nellie was now busy and retrieved her bag that she had dropped nearby. A doctor came, gave morphine and put the broken bones back into place as best he could. Then with Nellie's help he splinted the broken limbs and moved on to another patient, leaving Nellie to tend to the burns. As she had been taught, she cleaned the burns of the unconscious patient with Eusol and left them uncovered. The lessons she had been given had included the strict dictum that burns healed best if they were left open to the air. What was needful was to keep them clean and free of infection if possible. These burns were not too deep and hopefully the man would recover though he would always bear the marks of them. Soon he was on the ambulance train and no longer in her care.

'Here lass. I've brought you some tea and a bit of bread and butter. You look exhausted. I wish I had more to give, but I had nowt in t'cupboard but this.'

A local woman who was one of many doing similar kindnesses offered her the first food she had eaten since breakfast, and she realised that she was hungry so accepted it gratefully along with a mug of tea from a bucket which was proffered. It was when they saw she was available that some of the rescuers began to come to her and she realised that many of them, in the frenzied efforts to free the trapped passengers had hurt themselves and some rather badly. Their wounds ranged from minor cuts to great gashes from broken glass which needed stitching, but Nellie was not qualified or allowed to do that part; thankfully there were now quite a large number of doctors round the field. It seemed to her that a never-ending stream of abrasions, scrapes, cuts and minor burns came her way and that no sooner had she finished with one than another came along. Finally, about three o'clock she heard a whistle down the track towards Carlisle and realised that a larger hospital train had inched as close to the scene of devastation as it could, and at that point things moved very rapidly. Dozens of men swarmed over the field where the wounded lay and within a very short time they had transported all of them into the train. She had noticed that there were body parts lying round the wreckage, so great had been the impact of the collision in the front carriages, but her fascinated horror made her eyes keep coming back to a bucket in which someone had placed a foot and lower leg, still with its sock and boot on, presumably to get it off the floor in an attempt to tidy things up.

Matron Bennett-Brown appeared, blood on her apron, her face dirty and her hands, like Nellie's, grimy with blood and ash. With her were the other nurses from Murrell Hill House.

'We are finished here Nurse Little and must head back to our own place. We've been ordered back as there are enough people here to finish what has to be done. All of you back onto the hospital train now; it's leaving for the Citadel in three minutes.'

'A moment please Matron.' Mr Edwards, the surgeon whom Nellie had helped with the amputation came up. 'Before you go I'd like to say thank you to this nurse. I know you have all done great service here today, but I can only speak from my own experience. If this young woman is an example of what you are training then all I can say is that she is a credit to you. She's done marvellously and I thank you too.'

Mrs Bennett-Brown visibly radiated professional pride and positively beamed as the doctor shook her hand before they headed back to Carlisle. The large cobbled courtyard of the station was thronged with ambulances taking wounded to various hospitals where beds could be found, but many were being taken across the road to the Central Hotel where a local headmistress called Miss Lucy Reynolds, had organised a team of volunteers and nurses to care for them. From there they

Chapter 5 — Disaster

would be transported to various hospitals all over the north of England and southern Scotland. The problem with Carlisle was that so many hospitals were full with the wounded from Ypres and this included Murrell Hill House. When Nellie and her comrades got back to Murrell Hill they found that the VADs had held the fort admirably and so Matron Bennett-Brown dismissed them to have a meal, to find clean clothes, and in most cases, to go to bed. It was less than an hour after she had returned, just when she was beginning to feel human again, that Nellie received a call from Mr Plugg.

'We've got one of those poor fellows from Gretna downstairs Nurse and he needs seeing to now. We have an operating theatre so they've sent him to us. I need a theatre nurse again. I know you've had a day of it, but will you help?'

She could not refuse of course and wondered why he had chosen her, but it was not long until he enlightened her. The patient was a man who had a large jagged piece of metal embedded in his upper leg and it would have to be removed.

'Now Nurse, this fellow is lucky in a way because I believe that this nasty piece has missed the artery. If it had not then I think he would be dead. It's got to come out, but it might have crossed your mind to wonder why I sent for you and not one of the others? After all it's Buggin's turn.'

Seeing that Nellie's eyes confirmed the query, he continued.

'It's partly because the other day you were not squeamish, but mainly because I received a phone call earlier this evening from a colleague of mine, a Mister Edwards.'

Nellie's face furrowed in puzzlement.

'Ah. You did not think to ask the name of the surgeon you assisted with the amputation this afternoon?'

'No Sir. I did, but I can't think why he should call you.'

'Can you not? Oh there's no need to be puzzled on that I assure you. He was actually impressed by you Nurse! He also watched you tending to many other injuries to such a degree that he wished to commend you and have it noted on your record. That really is quite a compliment I think. So I've decided to give you this opportunity.'

'Opportunity Sir?'

'Oh yes. Do not doubt it. There are so many wounds in the battles these days that nurses are having to remove debris and treat quite serious hurts by themselves for there are not enough doctors. This being a serious wound but straightforward enough by reason of the fact that it's sticking out, I want you to remove it.'

'Me Sir?' Nellie's face was a picture of dismay.

'Yes. You Miss! Or are you not able to cope…?'

Waving a red rag at a bull is never a good idea, but implying that Nellie could not cope was probably just that. She moved forward to examine her task.

'Good Nurse. Now I suggest you grasp the end with these. Now give it a slight pull. No? Very well, try angling it to the left and pull ever so slightly. Why Nurse you are quite sweating!'

'I've never done something like this before. I don't want to hurt him.'

'I know that but you can't. He's flat out in the land of Nod. Ah now, there you have it.'

Nellie was holding a jagged piece of metal in her forceps.

'Now what do we do?'

'Clean the wound Sir.'

'Yes indeed, though it might be well to swab some of that blood out of the way. Now do you know what this is?'

'It's a retractor Sir.'

'Very good. Now watch.'

Nellie watched as Mr Plugg inserted the L shaped steel instrument into the wound to hold it open.

'Now swab that clear. Why am I doing this?'

Chapter 5 — Disaster

'To see if there's any more?'

'Correct. That includes anything that should not be in there, dirt, paint flakes, cloth, more metal, but I cannot see any and that's as far as I can see. It's quite deep and it's got to be cleaned out. How do I do that?'

'I don't know Sir.'

'And that is why you are here my girl! Now I want you to watch me very carefully because I am going to irrigate this wound. There are dozens of young nurses out in France doing this now, so you must learn.'

Nellie watched intently as the surgeon inserted a rubber tube into the wound, pushing it as far as it could go, then attached a small metal funnel to the end.

'Now then, I want you to take this solution and pour it into this funnel if you please.'

Nellie obeyed and for a few minutes slowly poured the liquid into the tube, and it poured out of the wound, presumably having flushed out any dirt and germs on the way though it made quite a mess on the floor.

'What is it Sir?

'Well they call it Dakin's solution, but it's really sodium hypochloride and it's a very useful antiseptic. This is called the Dakin-Carrell technique; you can force the solution into the wound with a rubber bulb, but the point is to irrigate it so that it is thoroughly clean. In this case, I think it is. What now?'

'Dry it and stitch it up, then dress it Sir?'

'Exactly. If this were a battlefield wound with sepsis present then you would have to use a lot of this solution and maybe more than one tube, but when objects are removed and the irrigation is done thoroughly, the rest is in the hands of the almighty. We still lose an awful lot of patients through sepsis, but we will have done all that we can.'

Nellie carefully dried the area round the seeping wound

then placed a pad over it as the surgeon prepared to close. She watched as he held the edges together and began to carefully stitch it closed. He started at the centre of the wound.

'Do you sew Nurse?'

'I've made quite a lot of my own clothes Sir.'

'Aye well it's not so different. Here you are – finished this off.'

He offered her the curved needle and thread.

'Me Sir?'

'Well yes of course you. There's no-one else here. Just stitch it up girl. It's not embroidery. Take the forceps and put the needle through at exactly the same distance as I have. Insert it at a ninety degree angle to the skin and it should come out the other side of the wound that distance, if you are doing it properly.'

Reluctantly Nellie took the forceps holding the needle and placed her left hand to hold the wound closed.'

'Come on Nurse; stick it through there and stop pussy footing around, for I want a cup of tea.'

Nellie thought to herself 'Right! I'll show you,' and finding that the needle passed through the flesh quite easily, and she pulled the thread through after it.

'Good. That's the first one. Now let me show you a surgeon's knot.'

Nellie watched intently as Mr Plugg showed her how to tie a square knot and then proceeded to place four more sutures and tie them off on her own.

'Well done Nurse Little. A bit slower than me of course, but that's to be expected. A little more practice and you'll do just fine. Now just dress the wound will you and I'll be away.'

To Nellie's astonishment he then left, leaving her with Mr Murphy the anaethetist.

'Oh don't look so puzzled Nurse. He likes you and he knows you'll do the dressing just fine. Just patch him up and I'll stand by. When you're done he can go back to his bed and wake up in a wee while.'

It did not take Nellie long to place a Lysol impregnated dry pad over the wound and apply a sticky dressing over the top of it. Then she wrapped a bandage round the leg to keep all in place, and was done; orderlies took the sleeping patient away. Finally she was free and exhausted; then she had one of the great moments of her life, for as she crossed the foyer over towards the stairs and her bed, Matron Bennett-Brown looked at her and said simply, 'Well done.'

Chapter 6

A Friend

Over the weeks of training remaining to her Nellie assisted at other operations and stitched, dressed, and redressed many great wounds in men's bodies. Patients were removed from Murrell Hill and taken away to convalescent homes and all the while new casualties were brought in from the battles raging round Ypres. Plans were afoot to create great new hospitals in Carlisle and she knew that, but they were not yet put into practice; she thought that ultimately she would not mind being posted to one of them. The work was having a curious effect on her in that she felt useful. She was contributing, playing her part; doing her bit. It was a strange validation and it would not be fair to say that she enjoyed her work, for she did not. However, if feeling valued and part of something bigger than herself was any measure of worth, then she felt worth more in herself. She hated war when she saw what it did, but although association with it tainted her thoughts and made her feel part of a species of brute beast, the healing of men brought a sense of mission. If the thought crossed her mind occasionally that civilisation itself was being destroyed in the battle of good and evil then her faith in it and in humanity was somewhat restored by the sacrifice, the effort and the care she saw around her. Brought up in a religious household her faith told her that the struggle between nations was of greatest importance between a world where people would have to obey masters and one where they at least had the right to aspire towards some form of freedom. If not that, then all that was being done was for nothing. This was going to be a long struggle and she had taken a side, not because of country or flag but because of a cause she believed in. Nellie knew, after her month in Carlisle, some of the meaning of war; the first of her family to do so. It did not occur to her that all these things she was doing and all the horrors she was seeing should have a lasting impact on her. There was simply no time to think about it, so anything she might have felt was simply battened down in the face of the expediency of having to get on with things. There was, as there were all over the country, a huge parade in Carlisle on Monday 24 May as everyone celebrated Empire Day. Every street was decked with flags and patriotic fervour washed over the land, as it does when a nation is at war. Some of the VAD nurses had been given time off to head into the centre of the city for the national holiday, some so happy and so young that they sang as they went, the song they had learned in school:

> 'Brightly, brightly, sun of spring upon this happy day
> Shine upon us as we sing this 24th of May.
> Shine upon our brothers too,
> Far across the ocean blue,
> As we raise our song of praise,
> On this our glorious Empire Day.'

Nellie heard the drums thumping and the distant sound of brass and cheering, but was on duty in her ward and thankful for it. She was not there to deal with the pomp of war but its results and felt rather removed from the great and glittering show that encouraged men to sign their lives up to death and misery. She focused on dealing with the wounded who came in a steady stream, varied by the influx of some injured sailors from a great battle that had taken place out in the North Sea at a place called Jutland Bank.

On Saturday 12 June Nellie's time at Murrell Hill was done. It was only a small hospital with one theatre but it had taught her a lot in a very short time. In her bag was a certificate stating that she had undergone a course of dealing with severe wounds and had passed, a letter from Mr Edwards commending her help at Gretna, and another letter from Matron Bennett-Brown recommending that Miss Winter make her up to Sister as soon as possible. Her four weeks had been a high-octane experience and she had been worked almost off her feet, short of sleep and bereft of recreation and she was tired. She thought that it would be good to rest, but a strange thing began to happen as the train clattered south; an overpowering urge to go back came upon her. At first she could not identify it, but staring moodily out to sea as they left Flimby, she realised that there was a new world back there that needed her. At least that is how she felt at the time, and the thought came upon her that part of her was still back in Carlisle. A feeling of regret, then of guilt, then of loss came over her. As she thought on these lines images of what she had seen and done came back to her and for the first time she began to think of them instead of just dealing with them. 227 men had died in the train wreck and 246 had been injured; and she had been there! Then she had spent the aftermath dealing with men broken by explosions, shrapnel and bullets. Most people could go through their entire lives and not see what she had seen. Remembrances rushed in on her and a great tidal wave of emotion welled up like a balloon of gas in her head which she thought would burst. Eventually she stood on Workington Low Station down platform as the train left, and she picked up her bag, crossed the road by the Station Hotel, and began to walk up Station Road. It was all the same; the neat little shops all the way up towards Oxford Street, the sunshades pulled down to shelter the pavement from the sun and rain, the smells, the salty sulphur tang in the air, and all round her the sounds of industry. Everything was peaceful and normal and as far removed from where she had been as the moon. She got as far as Hagg Hill and looked across the road to where the market bustled and the women, dressed neatly to keep up appearances shopped among the stalls, and she put her bag down on the ground. Nellie took in the complete and utter normality of it, and felt disconnected, as though she was somehow no longer part of it because the people around her were completely oblivious to the alien world she had been in and she was no longer part of their existence, but outside it. Quite suddenly all her experiences caught up with her and washed her social mask away. Her face crumpled and she began to cry standing on the pavement, in silent misery. If she had sobbed or cried out then this being Workington, she would have quickly been surrounded by solicitous people, many of whom she would have known, but she turned her face away from the crowds over the road, took out her handkerchief and surreptitiously dabbed at her face. Despite her wish to avoid making a fuss however, she was not unobserved.

'Nellie; is that you Nellie? Whatever is wrong?'

The question was delivered in a deep male voice with a strong accent that people thought of as 'American' though he assured them that it was from Chicago South Side. Nellie turned to see Joe Johnson, a friend of her father's and as exotic a person as Workington could offer because Joe was an African American known to the whole town for he was the only person of colour living there, and so they called him 'Darky Joe'. A man of great height, being six feet four inches tall, his reaction to this was an easy chuckle because having such a nickname in the local community was something he took as an indication of a certain respect, for it was used with affection. As he had told Tom Little he certainly was dark and his name was Joe, and he had seen and heard many more things than this in his life that he could get offended at. Joe had been a stoker on a steamship and had seen much of the world and of life since his birth in 1852 to a former slave family, who had escaped north before the American Civil War. Just before the turn of the century his ship had docked in Workington and Joe had been taken to the hospital after scalding his feet. After his treatment, his ship had sailed without him, and although he could have found another berth he decided that he liked the town and the people and was going to stay. At first he made a living doing labouring jobs, but eventually gained a job as a porter at Low Station; that is where he met Tom Little with his horse, shunting wagons, for Joe was fascinated by the Clydesdale and Tom was fascinated by Joe, never having conversed with a black man before, though he had seen him in church and knew of his nickname. He quickly saw Joe for what he was; just like him, a working man, earning to support himself and decent with it; in the Little household he was never 'Darky Joe', but 'Mr Johnson'. Nellie could not answer him at first.

'Come along Nellie. I think you need to be home and I'm taking you there.'

'But Mr Johnson, are you not on the way to work?'

'Yes I was, but that can wait. There are things more important in the world, and this is one of them.'

Joe Johnson picked up Nellie's bag, took her elbow and gently steered her up Oxford Street, and, glad of his solicitude, she obeyed and went with him.

'Have you been doing war work Nellie?'

The question was a perspicacious one, but Joe had a reason for it.

'Only I think I know the look on your face, because I've seen it before.'

'Oh. Where Mr Johnson?'

'On the faces of men at war.'

'You've been to war?'

'Yes Nellie; I was in Cuba back in '98 and saw what happens. It was not a pretty sight, and the men engaged in it wore the look that you have now. What I saw there put the look on my own face and I saw it in the mirror. Want to talk about it?'

Joe Johnson, at 62 years old, was an imposing figure, especially in a town where the average male height was around five feet four inches. If he had been an aggressive man then his life might have been rather different, but his stature, combined with an easy cool manner and a temper that was quiet and mild, made him many friends. As he and Nellie walked up Oxford Street he listened to her, nodding his understanding and fending off with a smile the numerous people who tried to greet him to pass the time of day. She found that she could talk to him, for his professions had shown her that he had seen something of what she had seen. Passing Central Station he knew that she could not finish before he had seen her home and would not be able to talk there, so suggested that they divert a little into St John's Church, which they did. For nearly an hour she talked, getting the mighty load off her chest, while he listened, occasionally interjecting with a gentle question. Eventually, she had unburdened of all she could think of and brought out a tearful smile.

'Goodness, Mr Johnson; whatever must you think of me? I've been talking thirteen to the dozen and you're supposed to be at work.'

'That's no matter Nellie; I will go there shortly, but before I do I want to say something. It was not anything that you did that caused the death and injury, the war and the wounds. What you do is different. You put people back together and try to heal them after they are broken. Isn't that the case?'

'I suppose it is, yes.'

'Well then, I have no instant cures or any snake oil to heal the hurts you have in your head. All I know is that sometimes it is necessary to talk about them. But remember this Nellie. You are on the side of light in this because you try to heal people and to help them. I'm quite a religious man and to me that's God's work. I know you are of a similar mind, because I've seen you in church and so you must know that your faith can help you at times like this. You might try praying for help, for I have often found it to be a comfort to me, but what I think in this case is that we are in a struggle of good versus evil and you are most definitely on the side of good, an angel of mercy. Just remember that if you forget anything else, and remember that I can listen. If you need to talk then come and find me and just talk.'

'I will Mr Johnson and thank you. I may well take up your offer, because I don't think my parents would really understand what has happened to me this last few weeks.'

'I suspect that there are few in this little town that would; a few ex-military types perhaps, or some older nurses, but although I like and respect your father I think that this is beyond his experience. Stay strong Nellie. There are people who are going to need you before this war is over and you have it in you to heal and save life. Do it and all that you have seen in the last few weeks will not have been for nothing. Now, my watch tells me I really must get to work. There's a train due in fifteen minutes and there will be baggage to tote. Find me if you need to talk.'

'I will Mr Johnson; and thank you.'

'Nellie took his hand gratefully and then stayed in the pew as he left. Sitting in the quiet of the church for the next ten minutes, she blanked her mind; then she prayed a prayer that was between her and the God she believed in. When it was done, she felt better, picked up her bag and left, on her way home. Though what she had seen was still there, the horrors of it were back in their box and she could move on. By the time she arrived home she had regained her poise and reserve, was able to muster up her smile and when asked what she had been doing in Carlisle she replied;

'Oh just this and that, mostly boring medical stuff; you know, bandages and plasters.'

'Did you see anything about that awful train crash?'

'Yes we all helped deal with the wounded; there were a lot of them, but it's all under control now.

As with soldiers from the wars returning, she did not wish to talk of what she had seen, dwell on what she had seen, and pushed it to the back of her mind. That was what people did, for post-traumatic stress disorder was an unknown thing, and people who dwelt on what they had seen or done in war were likely to get a label slapped on them of LMF, and of low moral fibre she certainly was not. She had learned much in a very short time and she hoped that she would be able to be of real use and help to wounded men in future because of it; failing that, she prayed that the war would end, because she had seen what it did to men and had learned to hate it.

Chapter 7

War Comes to Margaret

'This is very precise Margaret,' said Tom waving a piece of paper at her. 'I've always hated forms and always will.'

'That makes no difference one way or another. You've still got to fill it in.'

'Yes I know, but it's daft having you to fill in another with the same information on it.'

'Now that I do agree with, but since grumbling about it will get us exactly nowhere, I suggest that we get on with it. Now let me dip my pen again and stop hogging the inkwell.'

The form that Tom was irritated by was the National Registration form which every man and woman in the UK had to fill in as the government determined, to find out exactly what they had in the way of labour. So many men had joined the forces that the balance of production was disturbed and they had to find out who could be spared to join the forces, and who would be needed at home doing vital war work and had skills which could not easily be replaced.

'Well just look at it.'

'Oh Dad; it's got to be done. Just fill it in and have done.'

'And that's another thing Barwise. Why do you have to fill one in? And Nancy; and Nellie; and Jack of all people.'

'I'm fifteen Dad,' came the answer from Jack, 'and Barwise is sixteen. It's the law and we have to obey the law, or at least so you've always told us.'

'Yes, but I am also head of this household, and in my

opinion it should be like the national census. There should be one form per household and I should fill it in on behalf of my wife and children.'

Barwise laughed. 'I think you'll find Dad that the government disagrees with you. If we don't do this we'll be fined or sent to jail.'

'Aye and I know whose idea that was. Mr Walter Long! He's a damned Tory. What's he doing in office anyway? They have won no election.'

'Yes Dad, but Mr Asquith did and he's entitled to ask whoever he likes to be in the government so he's asked the Tories to join him. It's about national unity in time of war. How can we beat the Germans if we're divided among ourselves.'

'That may be. That may very well be, but to me my lad, you are still boys. And Nancy is a maid. Why do they want to know all about you eh? This war will be well over by the time either of you are of an age to fight, so why do they want all this?'

'Perhaps they think that the war is going to go on for a long time and they'll need to call on us all to fight.'

'I don't see how they can do that unless they compel people Barwise. Our armed forces are all volunteers.'

'I know that Dad, but if there's not enough men coming forward then they might have to force them. We can't lose because of lack of men!'

'I think that the unions would have something to say about that. It's nothing more than our rulers trying to regiment working men into uniform and get them to do as they're told.'

'I don't agree Dad. That's Ramsay McDonald speaking for some of the Labour Party, but I think we are in a fight for the right here.'

'What do you mean Barwise?' asked Margaret. 'The Bible says that we are not to kill. That's what's right, and it seems a clear enough thing to me.'

'Yes Mam, but I also know that if you lie down and let people walk over you, then evil wins. I'm thinking of Belgium; the Germans had no right to go marching in there like they did, let alone shooting priests and women and children.'

'Mam,' interjected Jack, 'I agree with Barwise. If we allow big countries to attack little countries and get away with it, then what sort of world is that? That's not how the meek shall inherit the earth. That's how the Kaiser inherits the earth and that's not the sort of world I want for me or my children, when I have them. Frankly he needs to be stopped and if I get my chance I'll try and help stop him. And don't forget he's attacked us too.'

'You mean the Zeppelins? Well yes, it is wrong to bomb civilians, especially women and children in that manner, but he'll be punished for it in the end.'

'I'd rather he was punished here on earth and sooner Dad. Look at what he did last back end sending his ships to bombard the East coast; they killed loads of folk in Hartlepool including babies. There's no cause for that; it's no wonder Mr Bottomley calls them Germ-huns. For two pins I'd go down to Edkin Street and sign up.'

Barwise was referring to the local Drill Hall, where the recruiting office was located for the district.

'You need not think that I will stand by and let you two join up,' said their father. 'You are both underage, and if there's any funny business about faking ages and joining up then I shall inform the authorities and have you sent back right away, so don't go wasting your time. As for Bottomley, I detest the man. He's a low sort of jingo and you my lad should not be taken in by what you might see in *John Bull*. I advise you to ignore it.'

'And I will not let my sons go and get shot by some German they have never met, or worse!' vowed Margaret.

'In fact,' growled Tom, 'Fetch the Bible Jack.'

Five minutes later he had extracted a promise from each of

his sons that they would not volunteer to join the Army.

'And I hold you to that as I am your father and you are my sons. Now your mother and I can rest easy knowing that you will not do anything foolish. Until you are twenty-one you are minors and bound to do my bidding. Now let's have an end to that discussion. There are more important things to worry about.'

'What's more important than the war Dad?'

'Cooking my dinner is what I am thinking of. We are running out of coal and because it's in short supply, it's a bit expensive, so we'll need to do what we did during the coal strike. That range goes out and there'll be no more hot meals.'

'Dig our own?'

'We could do that, but it's very popular up there at the moment and sometimes difficult to get close enough. Your mother had a notion that you could all get up a bit earlier tomorrow morning and go down to Salterbeck shore. There's a high tide tonight and it's been choppy lately; you might get a good load of smush.'

'All of us?'

'No Jack. The little ones stay in bed; they are too young and would need watching. I won't be there because I have to see to the horse and I'm shunting at six though I should be able to get a bag of cinder from the tracks.'

'Well Barwise and I have to be at work at six as well!'

'True enough, but if you get up early enough you'll have time for a trip to the shore with your mother and still get to work on time. I'll not hear arguments on this; you like your dinner hot as well as any of us. Up at four, out as soon as you can and on your way. The sun's up at ten to five so you'll be among the first on the beach for the pickings. Leave it any later and you'll like as not get nothing. It has to be done.'

'We could get the gas laid in and get rid of the old range instead.'

'Yes Barwise, and we could pay for it too. I know it's convenient, but it's a lot more expensive.'

'And I like the range anyway,' butted in Margaret. 'It's what I'm used to and I'm not minded to change. And you,' here she looked at Jack, 'Go canny wid that sugar!'

'And as far as I am concerned,' said Tom 'Your mother's word in the kitchen is law, so find me some smush; and stop using so much sugar.'

Tom's word was final, so whatever might have been felt about it was firmly bottled up and unsaid. Ommie was to go too as it was the summer holidays from school. So it was that the alarm went early next morning and shortly before 4.30 am Margaret led her task force out along the Harrington Road heading for Salterbeck where the shore could be accessed. They were not alone by any means for the whole town knew that coal could be gathered where they were bound; however, the numbers were quite low, the hour being so early. Barwise dragged the children's cartie along by a rope with Ommie sitting in it. Tom had knocked this together out of an orange box, some old planks and the wheels off a rusting old perambulator after the children had begged him to. The occasion of this had been a trip to the picture palace at Hagg Hill the previous year where a film called 'The Pest' had shown children racing these 'cars' in America. The star of the film was a man called Charlie Chaplin and he was becoming very popular as he was so funny; however it was the carts that had caught the imagination of the youngsters. The craze for these had spread across the UK too, but they were very useful for carting loads of coal as well.

Workington is a town literally built on coal and in some places it comes to the surface and in times of fuel shortage townsfolk could just dig what they wanted from where the outcrops showed as they had done in the national coal strike of 1912. However, sometimes these areas got rather crowded and this was where smush came in useful. The coal seams ran out to sea and lumps of sea coal were washed up on the Salterbeck shore where the backward swash of the waves let it be caught in crannies, nooks in the rocks and in the depressions of the wave cut platform stretching out from the bottom of the low cliffs. The rounded and clean lumps varied in size from that of a marble up to fist sized lumps and it burned very well and brightly. Smush, as they called it, was better, so people said, than dug coal. No wonder that even now, just at dawn, the shore was dotted with a few dozen people, each holding a sack in which to place their black gleanings which had been thrown up on the overnight tide.

Alongside Margaret, absorbed in the same task were four of her eight children, each doing their bit to help the family coal stocks before starting work; Nellie, Nancy, Barwise and Jack. Ommie was up on the cliffs about 20 feet above the shore guarding the family cart which was really the children's precious 'cartie'; she wore her oldest pinafore to protect her dress from the coal and Margaret would clean it later as it was washday. Tom was back home with William, Joe and Esther; he was due at the steelworks at six o'clock and needed the extra sleep as the main breadwinner of the house; William at eight years old was deemed old enough to keep an eye on the younger ones until Margaret returned. The sea coal was very important to the Little household because the price of coal for cooking and heating had gone up considerably since the start of the war. Miners generally had turned out to be a patriotic set of men and since August 1914 over a third of the entire UK mining force had joined the Army. This had sent production nose-diving but the need for domestic coal was no less. Although they should not do it the older boys had taken to scaling the wall at the end of Devonshire Street where they lived and picking along the sidings of Workington Central Station with sacks to find stray lumps of coal and cinder dumped from the fireboxes of passing locomotives. These days Tom would eke out their supplies with bags of cinder gathered from the sidings at the steelworks. Once they might have looked down on such activity as scavenging, but more than half the town were doing it too; the more coal could be garnered for nothing, the more money was left to spend on other things. They could see well enough and began to look in the grey light of first morning, but at 4.49 am the sun began to climb out from the western horizon.

Margaret did not see the U-boat surface behind her, and there was really no reason that she should because her attention was not on the sea but the beach at her feet. Ommie was jumping up and down on top of the cliff squealing something and pointing, but none of the family could make out what she was saying at distance. Margaret was just about to send John back up the narrow gulley which provided the only way down to the shore to ask what she was upset about when a loud explosion out to sea made explanation unnecessary. Another brief noise followed, like a large paper bag being torn and then further along the coast, round the looming mass of Lowca pit, which sloped almost into the sea, there came a 'whump' as of a distant explosion. Now Margaret saw the U-boat, as did everyone else, and the consternation was instant as people ran to get away from the shore. The Little family scrambled up the gully onto the flat terrace formed by the slag dumped over many years from the steelworks and down into the dip between the slagheap and the railway line. There they lay down and looked wide-eyed out to sea where the German submarine lay off Parton Bay sending a shell every minute or so at the industrial buildings on the coast to the other side of Lowca. They could not see round Lowca to Parton village or Whitehaven, but the U-Boat looked to be very close into shore.

Chapter 7 — War Comes to Margaret

Kapitanleutnant Rudolph Schneider's task was not an easy one in some respects. His orders were clear enough; he had to take U-24 around Britain to the coast of Cumberland and bombard the Harrington Coke-Works that were attached to Lowca pit. The installations there had been put in place before the war by Koppers, a German chemical company and thus they knew that synthetic toluene was produced there; a component in the making of explosives and vital to the British war effort. It was a legitimate target and Schneider had done well to reach it. The English Channel was closed by dense minefields and guarded by the formidable destroyer force known as the Dover Patrol. U-24 had managed the difficult passage through the mines of the North Sea, then gone far north around the Orkney islands to avoid destroyer sweeps near the Scapa Flow naval base. Swinging out into the Atlantic she had come down through the North Channel between Ireland and Scotland, arriving during the hours of darkness off Parton Bay. It was a considerable and very intrepid feat of navigation; now she surfaced at precisely 4.55am, six minutes after sunrise, and Schneider began the bombardment to destroy the toluene plant. The first shells ripped into the buildings at Lowca and a new one arrived each minute. The local population fled inland, hid in cellars and prayed, for there were no shore batteries and no British warships for miles. U-24 could do as she wished.

Lying flat beside her mother Nancy looked at the flashes out to sea and asked rather anxiously, 'Are they Germans?'

'Well of course they're Germans! What else do you think they might be? Men from the Moon?'

'Now Barwise don't be nasty to your sister; she's only asking a question.'

'I know Mam, but it's a daft question.'

'No question is daft if it looks for information. She's very worried is all.'

Ommie began to cry, 'If they see us will they shoot us too?'

'They can't see us if we keep our heads down.' This was from Jack, who normally said very little unless it was worth saying, but on this occasion it was. All of them kept their heads down, as indeed did the many other people crouched beside them along the bank.

'I don't think we are in any danger,' said Margaret. 'They would gain nothing from shooting at us; and look behind us – there are no buildings to shoot at, so it would be a waste of their time. Just stay down for now and sooner or later they'll have finished.'

'Well they've shown they don't mind shelling women and children already,' spat Barwise. 'They might fire at us if they see us.'

That only made Ommie cry more, so Margaret told her eldest son to be quiet and say nothing more.

The watchers on the shore could not see Schneider any more than he could see them, but his binoculars were trained at the toluene plant with a concentration appropriate to the import of his orders. Back at the Wilhelmshaven base he had been told that his mission was of great importance, and that the Lowca plant must be destroyed at all costs. He and his First Officer were counting the number of hits registered on the installation and he was pleased that his gun crew were making such good work of it. In thirty-five minutes they counted thirty hits on the buildings. With no defenders anywhere near, he intended to continue his work until he was satisfied his mission was complete; his duty then would be to remove his crew and his ship from the area in safety so that they could continue to be of use to the Fatherland.

It was perhaps a lucky thing that Schneider did not realise that he was actually engaged in a game of wits, because if he had known, the outcome of this incident might have been very different. As far as he was concerned he was simply bombarding a coastal target, and that was the end of the matter. To the men who operated the toluene plant, however, it was rather different and their minds were more subtle. They knew full well that their facility was important to the war effort; they also knew that there was no defence force nearby and that there were no coastal guns. Realising months before that the only real threats they faced were either from Zeppelins or from submarines off the coast, they had set in place plans to deal with both. For the Zeppelins they simply enforced a blackout after dark. For the submarines, since they had no way of hitting back, they resorted to subterfuge.

As the shells began to land round the chemical installations, the workforce left very quickly, fleeing inland. The damage looked spectacular as a fifty-gallon drum of naptha was set alight and flames shot up into the sky. In the still gloomy dawn the inferno from this looked enormous, causing the German gun crew to cheer at their hitting a target; this was quickly stilled by Schneider who told them to get on with their duty without the noise. Two huge 11,000 gallon Naptha tanks had punctures to them, but did not take fire whilst a shell passed through the chimney of the generator house without exploding. The duty engineer Oscar Ohlson was in no doubts as to what to do as the attack began and quickly went to the steam whistle that normally sounded the beginning and end of shifts. He pulled the lanyard sending six prolonged blasts into the surrounding area, which alerted all workers and the villagers in Parton to run for their lives. Then with remarkable calmness he went to meet the valve man Daniel Thompson at a pre-arranged place.

'Hello Dan. I'm glad to see you in one piece with all this going on around!'

'Likewise Ozzie; I take it we've got to put the plan into operation.'

Both men winced and crouched down for instinctive shelter as yet another shell flew overhead to explode on the brow above them.

'Well yes. No point in waiting; let's do it.'

Oscar walked quietly a few yards away and opened a valve in a large steam pipe, which vented an enormous cloud of steam into the atmosphere. Daniel stayed where he was and opened another valve which was rather more serious because huge gouts of black smoke, evil smelling and shot through with tongues of flame belched like a volcano out into the morning air. Soon the whole area was enveloped in a vast cloud of vapour that billowed and glowed in a most gratifying manner. A few more shells whistled in from the sea, but it was plain to Ohlson and Thompson that the fog of war they had created meant that as a target they were now invisible.

Kapitanleutnant Schneider, on the conning tower of U-24 was satisfied. He had been on the surface for fifty-five minutes and had fired fifty-five shells. It was quite evident to him that the target had been, if not destroyed, then at least greatly damaged. He could take his men home. He had discretion to continue the bombardment if he saw fit to attack the shipping in Whitehaven harbour, and having sailed across Parton bay he now turned his attention and his binoculars in that direction.

'My God! Do you see that?'

'I do Karl, and most peculiar it is too,' replied Schneider to his First Officer.

'What on earth do they think they are doing?'

'They appear to be...waving; and listen.'

Across the water came the distant sound of cheering.

'I imagine that we are the first submarine that they have ever seen.'

'But look at them. There must be hundreds of them.'

'I agree; and a lot of them are women and children.'

'Do we open fire Captain?'

Schneider looked at his number one and said with a somewhat pained expression; 'Karl, the German submarine service is not composed of barbarians. Fire on women and children? What are you thinking of?'

With the gun crew looking up at him expectantly the First Officer asked, 'Well what shall we do?'

'Do? Why wave back of course!

The gun crew grinned broadly, drew handkerchiefs or hanks of waste from various pockets and waved back at the spectators on the shore. After a minute or so of this Schneider decided enough was enough and gave the order to prepare to dive. In the most efficient manner possible his men housed their gun, went below, secured the hatches and submerged. The

Lowca toluene plant lost a few hours production as repairs were quickly made, and the only casualty was a black dog named Lion who received a shell splinter from which he later died.

On Salterbeck shore Ommie asked, 'Has it sunk?'

'It's a submarine Ommie,' replied her mother. 'They don't sink, they submerge.'

'So they haven't all drowned then?'

'No. They come up again later.'

'I hate them. If I had a gun I'd shoot the lot of them.'

'That's very bloodthirsty talk Barwise. They're just men though they are the enemy. They are doing their job.'

'They're cowards, Mother. They attack sneakily from under the sea at people who can't fight back. Remember the Lusitania!'

'It's true that the Lusitania was a nasty thing to do, but they are still men Barwise and I do not like to hear you saying you'd like to kill people. It might be war, but we are a Christian country and the Bible says "Thou shalt not kill."'

'Christians or not Mother I think they are a bunch of cowards and if I get a chance I'll kill a few of them.'

'Well I do not think that likely to happen. You are only sixteen and with any luck the war will be over by the time you are old enough to join up.'

'I could fake my age and join up anyway.'

His mother looked at him with her level grey stare and said, 'Yes. You could; if you broke your promise to your father, which would make you a liar.' Here Barwise flushed, for Margaret knew him well and he hated that anyone should hold him to be a liar.

'But then again I doubt they'd take you. You're not tall enough yet and anyway if you did your father would be down the depot like a dose of salts telling them you're under age. So you might as well forget it Barwise. I do not want a son of mine to go and get his head shot off. There's far better things to do with your life than that! Now the Germans have gone and we came to get smush. Jump to it and let's get what we can or there'll be no hot dinners for you.'

The enemy having departed, Margaret's pragmatism kicked into gear and the family spent another thirty minutes gathering coal before finally wheeling their cart with a fair haul, down the narrow path which led to the low tunnel under the railway and along the track known as Shore Road. They were soon back at 55 Devonshire Street and the real bustle of the day began; the boys simply peeled off and went straight to work. For Margaret, as ever, Monday was washday, but she considered herself lucky. Her house had been occupied previously by a blacksmith who liked to be clean. In the back scullery was a work surface that folded back to reveal a full length bath which was plumbed into a hot water boiler behind the range in the living room. It made her washing day far easier than for many of her neighbours who still had to contend with the set-pot or copper in a back outhouse. 55 Devonshire Street did have such a copper, but she hardly used it. She could heat water whilst cooking meals; though it was true that reliance on a range cooker did make the living room very hot in summer. This being the day after the compulsory filling in of the National Registration forms, it was a more interesting wash-day than most. In Workington, as in every other town and village throughout the land, a large army of volunteers swarmed out onto the streets on this day and subsequent days in order to collect the registration forms. It was not quite as simple as that, because many people, despite all the advice in the newspapers, were still not sure of what to say, or even unaware that there were severe penalties in law for not filling the forms in. Such people would need help to fill in forms, or if they had lost them, get another from the volunteer. Margaret had the household forms waiting when the knock came at about three o'clock, but she also had a question to ask.

It was a woman who came to the door and as it turned out she was a teacher from the Technical School and quite able to supply the information Margaret wanted. As she handed over the completed forms she asked;

'I'm not quite clear what the government wants these for, but there you are. Have you any idea what they are about?'

'Well it's been in all the papers Mrs Little…'

'We do not take a daily paper in this house I'm afraid, just an occasional one, and most in our street don't either.'

Margaret did not need to say that money was tight and they could not afford to buy papers, for the matter was plain enough.

'Very well then. It's my understanding that the government intends to have these papers sorted into those whose work is needed at home so that they may supply what we need to win the war, and those who can go to fight. There are a lot of young idle men who could go to do their duty, but who are lingering at home and not doing what every man should be doing.'

'Are they going to force men to join up?'

'Oh I shouldn't think so. There are enough men around. No, I think the problem is that there are too many idlers and shirkers about and we have to find out who they are, then persuade them to do what is right.'

'So no forcing.'

'That's the way I am seeing it. I gather that men who are needed at home will have a star placed at the top of their forms and that men whose work is not essential will be unstarred. The ones who are unstarred will be the ones to persuade.'

'I see. And who will be starred?'

'I imagine that a lot of men in this town will be starred. If they are steelworkers then we need steel for ships and guns and all sorts of things. To send skilled steel workers off to war would not be a very good idea, for who would then supply the Army? I doubt that any men who work with metal will be required to join the Army. I would think that a lot of other men will not be allowed to go because they will be in reserved occupations; people like miners, railwaymen, engineers and so on. They won't like it but they'll serve their country far better by staying at home.'

'That makes me easier in my mind; thank you.'

A wave of relief flooded Margaret's thoughts. Even if the war lasted another year or two, there was no prospect of her sons being forced into the Army because they both worked in metal. The idea of either of them marching away to foreign shores to be shot at or blown to pieces was a growing terror to her that haunted her dreams. Although the household did not take a daily newspaper she was quite aware, as was everyone, of the stories coming from the Western Front. Every so often, when the children were at school, Margaret would continue a practice she had begun as a serving maid at Edderside years before. On Finkle Street was the Carnegie Library where the family borrowed their books, but it had a reading room of a fair size in which there were seats and angled stands into which the latest newspapers were clipped. It was a nice place to pop into when shopping on her own and when Joe and Ettie had been left with Mrs Beeby. The scale of the casualties appalled her and she had early in the war made up her mind that she never wanted to see either of her older boys' pictures in the paper in those little postage stamp sized photographs that spoke of their 'gallant conduct'. She hated the phrases they used like 'fallen with honour'; it meant that they were dead and buried in some foreign country and their mothers would never see them again. As yet Margaret knew no-one who had lost sons, but she dreaded it happening, and even more to her own. Every night she prayed with increasing fervour, that the war would end, but every day it went on.

It must not be thought that she was not supportive of her country at war, but her mind was conflicted. She thought the Kaiser an evil man, and what the Germans had done in Belgium to be the work of devils, but fear for her boys, and obedience of the sixth commandment made her hate the war itself, though she wanted Britain to win. She had been in the crowd back in April when Private James Smith had arrived home to Workington. He and another man, Abraham Acton from Whitehaven, had been in a trench near Armentieres in France when they could stand no longer to hear the cries of a wounded man out in no-man's land. The poor lad had been out there almost at the enemy's trench, for seventy-five hours and no-one had made a move to help him. The two Cumbrians had gone out under fire and dragged him back to receive aid, with bullets slapping into the ground all around them. After that they had gone out again and spent an hour dragging other wounded men to cover. When Smith was wounded in March 1915 he had been shipped home and received his VC and then been granted home leave in April. When he arrived at Workington it was late at night, but the news of his arrival had been sent round the streets and they were full. He was hoisted shoulder high and carried home through cheering crowds. Barwise and Jack had been there too, cheering themselves fit to burst, but she wanted to tell them that she knew that war was not all like that. It was not all heroes and glory; but this was from her reading. She was a woman and had never been to war; any words from her about dirt and squalor would fall on stony ground and would be dismissed as the natural worry of a mother. The fate of the Whitehaven VC was the one that filled her with dread, for in May 1915 just three months ago, Acton had been killed aged twenty-two and his body never found. That they were brave, and that they were heroes, she did not doubt for a second, but ultimately she wanted live sons rather than dead heroes. Just let the war end!

Her faith was under strain too, because she could not bring herself to believe that God was taking sides in a war among men. Miss Beatrix Potter had written many books for children and Margaret had found some old copies of Peter Rabbit which had helped to stimulate her own infants into learning to read more quickly. Miss Potter, or more correctly, Mrs Heelis, lived about forty miles away from Workington and sometimes featured in the local newspapers. She had a large degree of fame and this in turn had brought public attention onto some members of her immediate circle of friends. One of these was Canon Hardwicke Rawnsley and when he heard about the West Cumbrian VCs, he had written a poem about them that Margaret found disturbing when she read it:

*'When at Red Banks, companions tried and true,
You ventured to save a brother man,
When with your precious burdens, back you ran
And showed what gallant Borderers dare and do,
More than your soldier mates took note of you,
The very angels who with your longing scan
This earthly stage were glad; your saviour plan
Thrilled heaven's great armies watching from the blue.
Wherefore today all Cumbrian hearts rejoice
To think the Viking warrior in your blood
Has learned of Christ the noblest knightliest thing;
To know you fearless made it the hero's choice,
And for your country's honour and your king,
Have proved the deathless might of brotherhood.'*

It was very hard for Margaret to reconcile the glorifying of heroism in war with the approval of Christ for she did not think the Jesus she prayed to would approve of people killing each other. All around her she saw Bishops and Canons and all kinds of other religious people exhorting men to join up and she often found herself wondering if some woman like her over in Germany felt the same dread of sending her boys to war. It was the one thing that she really envied her sister Omega in. Omega had repeated her unfortunate pattern of 1897 in 1906 when she had again become pregnant by a man who intended to marry her. Unfortunately, he had been killed at work before this could happen and Omega had to stop work when her condition became apparent. Her son, John Adams, named for her father, was far too young at nine years to be remotely considered for military service in this war. Omega had married Stephen Martin, a steelworker in 1910, a true love match, and their son Thomas was born that same year. They all lived over in Brayton Street at number 35, snug as bugs in rugs and three times as happy. Thinking of this drew her mind to her other family members; Father and Mother were still living down the Dib at Dearham. Thomas was a miner and now a solid family man aged 32, married to Harriet and with three children. If what the lady from the National Register had said was true then probably mining would be a reserved occupation and he would not have to go; the country needed coal. Johnny was also married to Isabelle, with two children and another on the way; he was an engineer on steam engines and though 28, that surely had to be a vital war job.

Lastly, but not least was her younger sister Alpha Nancy, of whom the family were inordinately proud and quite rightly so. Margaret certainly admired her little sister who had turned into a serene young woman of twenty-four who seemed to be absolutely imperturbable. She had grown up loving children and had determined to become a nurse midwife so had set upon a course of training to do exactly that. In 1914 the Central Midwives' Board in London had granted her a certificate stating that she had passed their examinations and was entitled to practice as a midwife in accordance with the provisions of their rules and regulations. Shortly after that she had been appointed to be West Cumberland's first District Nurse and now went all over the area delivering babies in their own homes and inspecting them for a time after they were born. There would be no danger of her going off to war because she had said so. Her business was not to help people out of the world, but to bring new life into it; that process went on regardless of whether there was a war or not and there were hundreds and eventually thousands of women who would need her help. Of all the family she was the one who, so far, had distinguished herself most in any field of qualification.

Tom's brothers were all too old to serve in the Army; Joe at fifty-five was still farming at Edderside, whilst William was a Clerk of Works living out at Bothel. Joe's two sons were only little and his daughter was a lovely little thing. Annie Eleanor was married to her Mr Metcalfe and had two little girls, still living out near Allonby though she had stuck to her determination not to play the farmer's wife, but ran a busy clothes shop for women in Maryport.

The U-boat had shaken Margaret, though it had not been without its comic moments. The grapevine in West Cumberland worked very quickly and the gossip on the streets from about lunchtime was about how all them daft jam-eaters had come out and waved at the Germans and how they had waved back. There was also a story about a woman in Parton, a Mrs Holliday, who was very lucky because she had been in her house and a shell had come in through the front wall, made a neat hole and passed right by her, then out through the back wall where it buried itself in the brow without exploding. Some men had come and dug it out to take away, but she was apparently charging folk a penny each to come into her house and look at the holes! It might, Margaret thought, almost be worth having a shell come through her house at that rate; heaven knew they could use the extra money. Apparently, although the works looked as if it had been heavily damaged, they had not been and would be back in full production in a day or so. It was an incident that had made her feel very vulnerable and all her feelings were thrown up in the air as if hit by an enemy shell herself. It was all very well reading about such things in the papers and welcoming home local heroes, but this was her country that had been attacked. Her neighbours just along the coast had been shot at and that made her feel indignant, but also weak and open to attack herself. She did not like war and did not want to be part of it, or to have it affect her family. But the war had come to her, right on her own doorstep. The shells could just have easily been fired at the steelworks where her husband and son worked, or at the harbour where Barwise worked; or into the town, and she wondered how the men who fired the guns could do such a thing knowing that there were other humans like them where the shells landed and that they were killing them. Margaret had seen war now; at a distance, but now it was so much more real. However, the war was to bite her much more severely before it was over.

Chapter 8

The Dentist

The summer of 1915 wore on and soon enough it turned to autumn, and a grateful Indian summer, but at first life in Devonshire Street was not much changed, though in Margaret's mind the seed of fear had taken root on 16 July. This was Barwise's birthday and he turned sixteen. If the war lasted another two years then he would be of age to do military service, and even though he would not be eligible to serve abroad until age nineteen, the very idea of it filled her with foreboding. Surely the war could not last another year! That thought seemed to be an outrageous one, because of course a way through would be found by then. It was something she was not comfortable thinking about, and though she prayed for peace every night, she wrapped herself in a cocoon of everyday work and ignored the fact of Barwise's approaching maturity, even in the face of its inevitability. Something would turn up; though in her assumed air of tranquillity, there was an element of brittleness. Even the threat of food shortages at the beginning of the year had retreated.

As the wife of a former farmer, Margaret knew very well that Britain did not produce sufficient food for its needs, but imported 60% of it from abroad. She had heard her husband grumbling enough about unfair competition with his neighbours to know why British farming had been in recession for something like forty years. American wheat had flooded the markets in the 1870s and consequently the need for British farmers to match their prices had kept farm profits and wages low across most of the UK. Being at war against a nation that had made a priority of building submarines was something the government was wary of even at the start of the war and people had been advised of the need to grow their own food where possible so that the nation would not go hungry. In Margaret's case this was not something she could do because the small back yard at 55 Devonshire Street was concreted over; but some of her neighbours had allotments on the open ground by Vulcan lane. At the beginning of the year the Germans had sunk a lot of ships and the price of food had begun to rise, so demand had increased for such plots. The men at the steelworks had been allowed to dig patches of spare ground alongside the railway sidings, but as Tom had found out, he did not have to. All he had to do was let the new vegetable growers have the manure out of Skiddaw's stable to enrich their plots, and he was rewarded with his share of carrots, potatoes, onions and cabbages, not forgetting the copious beans that were grown down at Moss Bay. The advantage of growing produce down there was the distance from the town, and the twenty-four hour shifts with men about all the time, meant that people were deterred from helping themselves. Margaret knew that some of the allotment holders at Brook Street railway sidings were being much irritated by the disappearance of what they had taken trouble to grow, and had fenced around their plots; some had even taken to standing watch overnight. She did not blame anyone who took food to feed their hungry families, but on the other hand it was theft and she did not approve of that.

The sinking of the Lusitania in May had caused such anger in America that the Germans had stopped their unrestricted sinking of any ships they caught around Britain, so thankfully for Margaret's purse the prices had gone back down somewhat, but not quite to levels they had been when the war started.

Once she had been content to shop in the area in her immediate locality but now her expeditions took her further afield, even as far as Station Road in search of the best prices. Like the good household manager she was, she was intent on making the most of what she had and had even mooted the idea to Tom that she might take on a job at least part time. His answer had been what she thought it would be. With so many children and a house to run, the strain it would throw on them all would be enormous. Therefore she stayed at home and maintained the family nest; their island of sanity and refuge from the world. Her shopping expeditions were mostly accompanied by Ettie who would quite happily skip along beside her mother and was in addition very useful because she softened the stallholders and their prices suffered an immediate cut when they saw her. She even garnered quite a lot of free goods as people bestowed apples, pears and other things she might like on her, just to see her smile. If the day was pleasant Margaret liked to set out and go down Oxford Street and start her shopping at Hagg Hill market, as it was the largest one in town. That way she would only be carrying a heavy bag on the way back. With beef at sixpence a pound she could make a good stew that would feed the whole family when she added vegetables and there was sufficient bread. Lamb was eightpence a pound which she thought odd because the fells not so many miles inland probably had more sheep on them than people, and surely beef should be dearer. Fish, thank goodness, was threepence a pound as it came up straight from the docks where it was landed and sold by the men who caught it. When there was no market she preferred Percival's in Fisher Street where the trawler owner's wife ran the shop and sold his catch. Needless to say, the Little family ate a lot of fish, Tom being particularly fond of plaice. General groceries could be had at fair prices in Walter Willson's in Fisher Crescent for Mr Willson had a chain of shops across Cumberland, and bought in bulk, so his prices were low. On the way back from the market Margaret liked to divert to Brayton Street, a longer way home, but she could call in at number 35 and have a cup of tea and talk with Omega, her older sister, if she was in, which she generally was. On this particular day they spoke of Barwise, who had a toothache and would have to go to the dentist, but the main part of the conversation was Nellie.

'So you get the idea she's not very happy since Carlisle?'

'I'm not sure Ommie, because I don't get to see much of her since she came back from Carlisle and the rail crash that she attended. There's something in her mind that's troubling her, and that is not surprising from what I've read about what happened. She spends a lot of time up at the hospital now even when she's supposed to be off.'

'It's not because she's sleeping badly?'

'Not that, no. I think it's the work she's doing.'

'Well, I can't see your Nellie being afraid of hard work!'

'No I didn't mean that. I mean I think she finds it too easy.'

'Nursing easy? Well from what I've heard, that's a new one. Nurses work very hard indeed.'

'Yes I know that, but there's nursing – and then there's nursing isn't there?'

'Well you're going to have to explain that.'

'It's not what she thought it would be when she came back from her course.'

'Now my understanding was that she'd be nursing wounded soldiers.'

'Yes. That's what she's doing, but it's not what she thought. The infirmary has had very few wounded sent to them.'

'Well she's helping them isn't she? What's wrong with the girl?'

'Oh it's that course. She had to deal with badly wounded

men and do stuff.'

'Stuff?'

'That's her word, not mine; she won't tell me exactly what she did, but I think what she's doing now is not enough for her.'

'Not enough?'

'Yes. She was dealing with massive wounds and men who were more or less straight off the battlefield. Now she's dealing with broken legs and the occasional injury from the steelworks and the mines.'

'So is that not enough?'

'I think she wants to help men who have been wounded in the fighting; those who have done their bit on the battlefield.'

'As opposed to them that aren't you mean?'

'I don't think I like that thought, Ommie. I don't think it's that; it's just that she wants to do something to help the actual war effort and what she's actually doing is her normal job as she does in peacetime. I don't think she understands that some people have to carry on just as they always did. If a lot of the men from this town went to war there'd be no war because there'd be no steel. Poor Barwise got handed a white feather last week.'

'What did he do?'

'Oh you know Barwise; nothing like that will knock him down. He handed it back to the silly young flapper who gave it to him, told her that he was sixteen years old and asked her for a kiss in return for the introduction. He also asked if she'd like to meet him under Mandale's clock later and go for a walk.'

'And did she?'

'Apparently not. She was a very fashionably dressed little madam and disappeared up the road towards Stainburn. Probably lives in one of those posh villas up there and her daddy's a manager. Pretty enough I gather.'

'Come back to Nellie; what's she thinking of doing about

her situation?'

'I don't know, but from what I can gather it's just everyday nursing; you know the sort of thing. She spends her time changing dressings on wounds that are mostly healed, emptying bedpans and filling in forms. It's her opinion that it's the sort of work that could be done by the volunteer girls; the problem is that she feels wasted because of the knowledge she now has. She's found something she is very good at and she's not doing it.'

'With her training she probably is very good. Is she thinking of doing something about it?'

'Not at the moment. She wants to qualify as a Sister, but that's by nomination so she must serve her time. I'm getting the feeling that she'll want to move on and I'm thinking she'll want to go to one of the big hospitals and work with the seriously wounded off the trains. Time will tell.'

'Have you heard from Dearham lately? We haven't seen them for months.'

'I had a letter from Mother just yesterday. They're fine. Father's gone back underground though; they are so short of underground workers that he agreed to go back as a marra.'

'Not as an undergoer?'

'I think he takes the view that an undergoer is young man's work Ommie, and rightly so.'

'For heaven's sake, why does he not retire? He's sixty-five now and he's been paying into a pension plan with Pearl Assurance all his working life!'

'He says he'll take his pension at seventy, but that if he was at home now he doesn't know what he'd do all day and Mother says he'd just get under her feet.'

'He's in very good shape for his age.'

'There's no denying that, but none of us goes on forever. Still, the way he's going, he'll outlast us all.'

'He will. Now have you thought about next Thursday?'

Chapter 8 — The Dentist

Some years before, Margaret had felt completely tired out and it did not seem to be getting any better; her friends at church knew about it of course, and among them was Miss Winter whose medical knowledge had suggested not a problem requiring physic, but something more pleasant. Her suggestion had been that Margaret was working too hard and was the only person in her family who never had any time off; she worked all the hours of the day, seven days a week. She needed to set herself some time for recreation; the old adage that all work and no play made Jack a dull boy applied to Jill as well. When she had told Tom this, to her surprise he had agreed and suggested that she and her sister should go out and get away one evening a week; the agreed and most convenient day being Thursdays.

'I have. They're showing some Charlie Chaplin at the Albert Hall; shall we go to that?'

'The very thing I had in mind; that's settled then!'

Workington had five cinemas and it was considered respectable entertainment that women could go to, unaccompanied by men. The interiors were generally salubrious and there were smartly dressed commissionaires in uniform to keep order and deal with any malcontents, whilst efficient usherettes kept watch inside. Margaret and Omega had taken to this new and luxurious form of entertainment like ducks to water; and it did not strain their pockets either.

Eventually Margaret arrived home and prepared dinner, but Tom had some interesting news from work.

'I've seen some Germans today. Apparently it's allowed to make prisoners of war work for you; or rather you can ask them if they want to in return for better treatment, food and such like. They've got a load of lads from the German Army down at Moss Bay doing building work.'

'Aren't you worried they'll do something nasty, Tom? That sounds a bit dangerous to me.'

'Dangerous? No. Most of them look as if they couldn't hurt a fly and anyway they've got lots of our lads down there on guard; don't forget there's a fence round the works. No they're working quite well.'

'Where have they come from?'

'They bring them down from the camp up at Rowrah and take them back there on the train every night.'

'What sort of things are they doing?'

'Digging for the most part. Some are bricklaying and laying foundations for some new furnaces. Others are building a tunnel.'

'A tunnel? What for? To get back to Germany?'

'You've been watching too much at the picture house Margaret. No, it's a water and sewage outlet for all the new stuff they're putting in. Instead of a plank over a hole on the beach we're to have proper toilets among other things.'

'That'll be an improvement. You've been grumbling about that for long enough.'

'Aye well, the union has finally persuaded them to do it. You should try using them as they are now when there's a storm blowing off the sea in winter!'

'No thank you. I don't think I will. Now what are we going to do about Barwise?'

'What about me?'

'That tooth needs seeing to. You've been moaning and whining about it for three days.'

'I'm not going to the dentist!'

'Yes you are young man,' said Tom. 'You might as well get used to the idea, so you can tell Matt Roach you'll be late for work the day after tomorrow, because you're going to.'

'It's not that bad really!'

'And this is the lad that talks of going off to war; scared to go to the dentist? You're going and that's that. Your mam will take you there too. Mr Smith is a fine dentist; you'll not have any trouble there.'

'What do I need mam there for?'

'In case you need gas; you're a minor so she has to be there.'

On the way to the dentist two days later Margaret bought herself a newspaper by way of a treat to read while she waited. In the window of Mr Thexton Smith's dental surgery was a sign:

'Even so small a thing as a tooth has caused:
Generals to lose battles,
Ministers to lose the threads of their discourses,
Philosophers to cease philosophising, and
Poets to write drivel instead of elegaics.'

Mr Smith's surgery was a place that Margaret actually liked because it was in a strange way, very homely. It had the usual dentist kind of smell of course, redolent of mouthwash and toothpowder but it was furnished quite opulently. Her own house had linoleum on the floor throughout, and home made rag rugs where necessary, but this surgery had a nice patterned fitted carpet which made the room nice and cosy. The dentist's chair sat on a rug down one end, and Mr Smith invited Barwise to sit on it. He did so, but with a most palpable look of fear on his face as he moved past the drill with its foot pedal; he had several amalgam fillings already by that drill and he did not like it at all. As the dentist began to look at Barwise's teeth, Margaret looked in the mirror at the other end of the room and checked her hair, then she sat down on the nicely padded high backed chair that waited for her. Unfortunately, the idea that she might have time to read the newspaper was soon dispelled by the dentist telling her that the tooth would have to come out. Mr Smith kept very up to date in the practice of dentistry and with some patients he did use the American method of local anaesthetic for fillings if they wished. However, in common with most British dentists most of the time he used gas; in this case nitrous oxide.

'Mrs Little, I may need some assistance if you do not mind.'

'What sort of assistance Mr Smith?'

'I would just like you to hold your son's hand as I put him under and for him to squeeze it; you must let me know when the pressure relaxes. Now then Mr Dryden, if you please.'

Barwise was not very willing as the dental attendant inserted a speculum and placed the mask over his mouth and nose.

'Now just breathe deeply please and we shall soon have this done.'

Barwise breathed deeply as Mr Dryden filled a leathern bag with gas, and he relaxed into a deep sleep.

'Another bag if you please Mr Dryden, and that should do it. Ah, hold him. Mrs Little as well please. He's a strong chap!'

Margaret saw the real reason why the dentist had asked her to move forward as Barwise began to fight him.

'Barwise! Be still!'

'He can't hear you Mrs Little; he's completely unconscious, but many patients struggle when they are under gas. If you and Mr Dryden can hold him; thank you.'

Mr Smith was very quick, reaching in around the speculum, twisting and pushing the infected tooth, he had it out in a tug. The whole operation took less than 20 seconds.

A few minutes later Barwise began to come round to find Margaret swabbing blood from his mouth with a piece of lint, and she was glad that he did because she found the experience an upsetting one. It was not so much the blood itself that made her feel on edge, but the fact that it was on Barwise and he was uppermost in her fears about the war. Too many mothers had eldest sons fighting in this war, and too much of their blood had been shed. The picture of Barwise with blood down his chin was to haunt her for the next three years and more.

'Thank you Mrs Little; that will be three shillings. Ah, thank you. Good morning to you now.'

'That was not as much as I thought it would be Mam,' said Barwise as he and Margaret made their way down Jane Street and back into town.

'Mr Smith is a good man, Barwise. He has several scales of fees and he charged me what he'll charge any working folk. But if I were Mrs Curwen up at the Hall, or Miss Thompson, then he'd probably charge me a sovereign for having a tooth pulled. That way he can tend to us, and to them, and not make a loss. They all do it, the dentists. Now you might take notice of what I keep telling you. Be canny wid the sugar; it's bad for your teeth.'

'Yes Mam.'

It was not until Margaret got home that she had a chance to read the newspaper and what it told her was worrying. The Prime Minister had indeed appointed Lord Derby to be Director General of Recruiting. That in itself was not surprising because he had the reputation of being one of the best recruiters in the whole country. A speech from him could persuade hundreds of men to join up and go to fight. He was going to run a huge campaign to get men for the Army because they needed all they could get. That was not surprising, considering the numbers of dead and wounded boys whose faces she saw by the hundred in the newspaper casualty pages every week. He did not say how long his campaign was going on for, but the distinct impression she got from the article was that if Derby could not get enough men to volunteer then the government would begin to compel men into the Army.

The great recruiting campaign got off to a flying start in Workington. At least it did not have quite the punch of Lord Lonsdale's recruiting posters of 1914, which had caused some indignation right across Cumberland, but it was effective nonetheless. Cumberland had its own Pals Battalion raised by Lonsdale and his poster had read somewhat controversially.

ARE YOU A MAN
OR
ARE YOU A MOUSE?

Are you a man who will for ever be handed down to posterity as a Gallant Patriot?
OR
Are you to be handed down to posterity as a Rotter and a Coward?

If you are a Man,

NOW

is your opportunity of proving it, and ENLIST at once and go to the nearest Recruiting Officer

REMEMBER

if you can get 15, 30, or 60 of your Comrades to join, you can all ENLIST together, remain, train and fight together.
THE COUNTIES — CUMBERLAND AND WESTMORLAND — HAVE

ALWAYS

BEEN CELEBRATED FOR THE FINEST MEN, THE GREATEST SPORTSMEN, AND THE BEST SOLDIERS.

<u>NOW IS YOUR OPPORTUNITY OF PROVING IT.</u>

HURRY UP!

Please take my humble Advice before it is too late.
THE COUNTRY HAS NEVER BEEN IN GREATER PERIL.

LONSDALE,
Lowther Castle

Lord Derby had a reputation as a good sort, a patriot, and was very popular down Liverpool way where he involved himself so much in local affairs that he had earned himself the nickname 'The uncrowned King of Lancashire'. If he said men were needed, then they were needed; whatever his investigations found, whatever he recommended, people would listen to. If he could not get enough men for the Army, then as far as most folk were concerned, no-one could, and the government would have to bring in conscription. Nobody in their right mind wanted that, because as Lord Kitchener said, one volunteer was worth three pressed men; so it was up to everyone to help Lord Derby get the men the Army needed. Workington, like every town in the land, was going to have a big recruiting event; it would be quite a show, but with a very serious purpose.

Chapter 9

Recruiting

The Derby Scheme began, as far as Workington was concerned, with a body of forty men from the Border Regimental depot at Carlisle castle entraining and arriving at Maryport on Saturday 16 October. Preceded by a band they then marched through the town and then to Flimby and then on to Workington; all the way crowds lined their route to cheer them. Privately many locals had grave reservations about the Derby Scheme, and Tom had spoken of his doubts to Margaret.

'If you think about it, the whole thing is daft as far as Workington is concerned. They want the 'unstarred men' to join up. But Workington is a steel and coal town; there'll be precious few unstarred here I would think.'

'Well yes; it does seem a bit of a waste of time if you put it that way. Why are they doing it then do you think?'

'I think they're just trying to whip up a bit of enthusiasm, but I'd be very surprised if they got many men. It's not that there won't be lads who'll want to go, but if they do, what will happen when the steelworks shuts down? Or the mines? No it's daft. I don't think they've thought it through. Anyway Workington has given a lot of men already.'

'Yes it has! I saw the roll of honour today.'

'At the Carnegie?'

'Mmm. It's huge and it's got nearly 800 names on it; all the men who have enlisted for active service.'

'Aye, I saw that Mr Watts unveiled it. I expect he'll be

making a mayoral speech today. There'll be a lot more names to be added before this war is over I should think.'

'We'll go and listen to the speeches?'

'Oh yes we'll do that; there's no harm in listening, but they won't get many. They got loads when they formed the Lonsdale Pals last year, but there's getting to be a shortage of hands now for all the work. But having a listen does no harm.'

'I'm not sure about that Tom. There's a lot of people have been saying things lately that I have been very surprised to read.'

'You mean those Bishops?'

'Yes, exactly. I never thought that I would see Bishops telling men that they were fighting for the principles of the Christian religion. It just is not Christian to kill, so I don't see how he could say that.'

'The Bishop of London?'

'Yes. When I saw that letter up in the church it made me feel very odd. A lot of the Salvation Army are not happy with Bramwell Booth either, telling people it was noble to go and serve. It might very well be, but it's still sending men off to fight and kill.'

'Well it's not exactly what I think of as Christianity either, but did you see what Ben Tillett said?'

'That he supports our war aims, after years of saying the bosses would try to start a war for their own gain and that we should stop them by going on a general strike and he'd pledge his Dockers Union to join it? The man's a hypocrite and I have no time for him. Ramsay McDonald has kept his principles and I admire him for it. He's warned about the coming war for years and now he's against it. The Labour Party is split down the middle over this, but now I've joined I'll keep up my membership and not go back to the Liberals. McDonald and Arthur Henderson are still talking to each other at least; if not united the Labour Party has not split.'

'Well thank goodness that you are too old to go; it's the only time I've been thankful for aging and I'm sorry if it seems selfish, but I've no mind to be left a widow at my age.'

'I hardly think it will come to that Margaret. It's a matter of luck in war.'

'I'm not so sure of that. You don't get to see many newspapers, but I see the casualty lists in the Carnegie Library and there's thousands of men being killed. I worry for Barwise.'

'Now that's absurd. He's only sixteen and cannot serve abroad until he's nineteen and that will not be until July 1918! The war will be over long before that, my dear.'

Margaret relaxed her mind a little, 'You are right. Of course you are right; I'm being silly aren't I?'

'I think you are. Shall we go up to Central Square and see what's going on?'

Central Square is a grand name for an open space that is not as big as its name implies, but a short trip up John Street brought Tom and Margaret to the edge of the throng crowding round the perimeter of it. Their children were already there; they had been so excited by the idea of seeing a parade that they had gone ahead with their older siblings to try to get places near the front. Oxford Street, Jane Street and out along Washington Street had been decked with bunting. By now it was late afternoon and the original body of Border Regiment men who had marched from Maryport had arrived, their numbers swollen by others, but also with a group of about forty local men who had fallen in behind and even now were attesting at a desk set up in the lobby of the Central Hotel. The attestation process was probably the most popular factor in the Derby Scheme because men did not have to go and fight right away; they simply swore to come when called and their name was put on the list. In exchange for this they were each given an armband embossed with a crown and the letters GR and 'attested" which they could wear at all times to show that they had sworn to serve when called. The armbands were also being given to men who had been 'starred' as an indication that they were ineligible for military service as the job they were doing was deemed vital to the war effort. Tom had been offered one, but by virtue of his grey hair and moustache he did not need it. Younger men without it were apt to be insulted, spat at and offered white feathers on the streets, as life outside the armed forces become simply unbearable for them, though in theory, service was voluntary. However, by wearing an armband they were instant heroes to their community as men who had volunteered, and each man who came out of the hotel lobby was cheered.

Eventually the large first floor window above the glazed canopy of the hotel entrance was opened and a figure was seen; there was to be a speech, and in a very short time Central Square fell into a deathly hush. The speaker was the Earl of Lamplugh, a local aristocrat and coal magnate, much respected for his charity and his interest in local affairs. He had a fine loud voice, helped by the acoustics of the buildings round the square, and he seemed to reach into the heart of everyone there. He started in a fairly usual manner such as the crowd were prepared to hear and had heard from various speakers since the war began. Exhortations about King, country and Empire, the flag and our noble cause against the dreadful enemy were standard fare for recruiting speeches at this time, but as he approached the end of his peroration his words began to take on a different tone.

'My friends and comrades, for so I feel that I may call you in this time of national trial, I am glad to see such a crowd here today for I wish to speak to as many people as possible and to speak plainly as an Englishman to Englishmen. My message must be clear and simple; it is this.

I have only two sons. One is at the front. He has been home

for a few days on leave and went back to the front again on Friday last. What he told me is that they need more men out there if we are to beat the Hun. There are no ifs or buts about this; if we fail then it will be because we do not have enough men. My other son is in the artillery, and when he has completed his training he will go to the front and do his duty for his King and country. If I had twenty sons I should be ashamed if each one of them did not go to the front when his turn came'.

At this point there were murmurs of what seemed mostly agreement across the crowd, and a few cheers.

'England is not going to be unprepared again, and the moment that peace is signed you may make up your mind that England will have, not national service, but conscription and the only men who will have to be trained will be the men who have stayed behind.'

This was met with a mixed reaction. The Earl was a prominent local Tory and was taking his audience much for granted. Many among them were members of the Labour Party, which had been warning for years about the ruling classes staging a war to regiment the workers. The idea of conscription did not sit well with them, and as most of those present knew, the Labour Party and the TUC had held special conferences just a few weeks before and voted overwhelmingly against conscription. In some areas, particularly in South Wales, Clydeside and Sheffield, there had been talk of strikes, even a general strike if the government attempted to force men into the Army. Even his talk of "England" did not go down well with many people who were members of the Labour Party, Socialists and thought of workers more as "British" and united in adversity. The Earl's next point drew some boos.

'When the war is over I intend, as far as I possibly can, to take nobody except men who have done their duty at the front. I go further than that and say that, all things being equal, if two men come to me for a farm, and only one has been at the front, there is no doubt as to who will get the farm.'

This was an alien thing to most of his audience who were composed of steelworkers and coal miners; obviously his Lordship was reprising a speech that he had given in a more rural area. Perhaps that was not so bad, but no man likes to be threatened. There was some cheering as this short address came to an end, but there were a few boos too and many people simply did not react at all. It was as well that he was only the first speaker, but three more came and spoke in better ways. The Mayor, Mr Watts was well received, speaking of the men who had already gone to fight and distinguished themselves. The best speech came from Mr John Randles, chairman of Workington Iron and Steel Company who dwelt on the valuable contribution that the men of Workington were making towards the war effort. He pointed out that in every field of endeavour the nation was involved in during this conflict, they could not accomplish much without steel. This being so, the battle that was being fought in the steel hearths and furnaces of Moss Bay was as deadly to the enemy as an assault on his trenches. He urged his listeners to double, nay treble their efforts to make the steel for shells and guns, and battleships and rifles with which to send the enemy to a hotter place than that inhabited by the Bessemers. This affirmation of how vital the town and its folk were to victory met with rousing cheers, reinforced by the fact that his company was the major employer in town. The spectacle ended with the soldiers parading with the bands down Oxford Street and Station Road to board a train back to Carlisle. There was a lot of cheering as they went, waving of flags and singing of Rule Britannia and Hearts of Oak.

A spark, generated by one of the speakers had settled on Nancy and as she shepherded the smaller members of her family back home, she was thinking hard. The stalwart looking Major from the Lonsdale Pals had said that the whole nation was pulling together in the titanic struggle against the Teutonic invaders and that 56,000 women across the country had given their names in at Labour Exchanges as being willing to engage in war work if they were needed. He paid tribute to the womanhood of Britain and hailed their gallantry and patriotism, worthy of the men they were sending to fight. That did not matter so much to Nancy, but the news about the Labour Exchanges was something she had not heard about. It set her mind in a whirl; the Labour Exchange was in Oxford Street and she resolved that she would pay it a visit during her lunchtime as soon as she could.

Margaret and Tom were slow to leave the square owing to the crowds in the way and they bumped into Joe Johnson, whom they invited back for a cup of tea. Margaret was fascinated by the American and had been since Tom had brought him up to her one day in church and introduced him; since then he had been an occasional and welcome visitor for a cup of tea whenever he strayed into the upper part of town. His long Chicago slow drawl, the darkness of his skin and the sheer size of him were a source of wonder to her, and the younger children could not, apparently, get enough of him. It was his stories more than anything else that endeared him to them because, having travelled so much he told them of all the places he had visited and of the sights he had seen. He was very good with children too, though, or perhaps because of the fact that he had none of his own. Today, at first the talk was of conscription.

'I do not think the country would accept conscription,' said Tom, continuing the theme of conversation started by The Earl of Lamplugh.

'Well I figure you're right about that at this time,' said Joe, 'But things could change mighty quick if the conditions do. I think it would be powerful unwise to try to force men now.'

'You think there would be trouble?'

'Well I tell you Tom, a few years ago I was stoking on a grain boat from New York to Cherbourg and there was an older guy who'd been in New York in '64.'

'That's the year I was born,' said Tom with a grin.

'That right? Well that was the year that Lincoln tried to conscript New Yorkers into the Union Army. You hear about that?'

'I can't say that I have. What happened?'

'Well the people of New York did not wish to be conscripted on the grounds that they were Americans and entitled to Liberty, and they held that the state had no right to compel them to fight.'

'Did they do anything about it?' asked Margaret.

'Yes Ma'am. They took up arms.'

'Took up arms?'

'That's the way I heard it. They took to the streets and rioted in their thousands, swearing they would not be coerced.'

'And did they win?'

'Nope. They did not. The President turned the Army onto the street in Manhattan with fixed bayonets to impose martial law.'

'Did that stop the trouble?'

'No Tom, it did not. The rioters faced the troops in the streets and would not disperse so the soldiers opened fire. They cleared the streets, arrested the ringleaders and threw them into prison, held without trial, and went ahead forcing men into the Army anyway. New York accepted conscription, but not willingly. Now can you imagine that happening here?'

'I can actually. There was a lot of trouble in the coal strikes in '10 and '12. There was a train of gunpowder set alight in South Wales and blown up and troops had to be sent in to restore order.'

'Yep I see; but now the country's at war and folks are all pulling together ain't they?'

'I'm not so sure. You're in the union aren't you, Joe?'

'Sure am. The NUR; I've paid my dues and joined the Labour Party.'

'Then you've met some syndicalists?'

'What's a syndicalist?'

'There are some men, Margaret, who think that the real enemy in this war is not the workers of Germany, but the bosses and rich in this country. If all workers in all unions joined together in one vast syndicate they could hold a general strike and within days the government would collapse and the workers would take over through their unions. Those are syndicalists and there's a lot of them about; more now the war is going on.'

'That's true enough. We had them back in Chicago in the meat packing industry and I hear they have some support in other countries too. Remember the Triple Alliance that was going to call a strike in October last year?'

'Of course! I would have been in it, and so would you. Railwaymen, coal miners and transport workers were all going on strike; it would have brought the government to its knees.'

'But the war stopped it happening?'

'Exactly Margaret, the war. But it's still there; the resentment and the trouble. When this is over the wages will drop and it'll be back to business as normal; and that's when there'll be trouble. Union membership is shooting up like a rocket.'

'Why are more people joining up?'

'Because, Ma'am, men think that if it comes to conscription, the unions will be able to resist better than men on their own.'

'But I thought the TUC is backing the war.'

'True enough, but the same is happening as happened back in the states. If the union leaders will not lead, then the men look to their local reps. The shop stewards will lead the trouble if it comes. And if they try to conscript then it will.'

Chapter 9 — Recruiting

'Mr Johnson!'

'Yes young William; and what may I do for you today?'

'Are you going to tell us a story today?'

'Billy Little! That's bad manners interrupting Mr Johnson while he was talking.'

'That's no matter Ma'am; I like to tell a tale or two, so if my young buddy here wants to hear a yarn then I'll tell him one soon enough. Did I ever tell you about how I nearly won the race? No? Well then, if you kids just sit round quiet, then I'll tell you now.'

Billy, Joe, Ettie and Ommie ranged themselves on the floor in front of Joe Johnson who took a sip of tea from the cup he was holding, and so began:

'Now let me see; I arrived in Workington in a cargo vessel out of the St Lawrence River back in '02 and we docked at 10 o'clock one night, and I was on duty in the stoke hold.'

'What's a stokehold Mr Johnson?'

'It's where the ship has its furnaces Joe; there are fires to make steam to power the ship and I worked there shovelling coal. If we did not do it then the ship would not go anywhere. So there I was, just arrived in this country again, and thinking I'd like to have a little run ashore; I could see there were a few pubs on the dockside and I like British beer, but it was not to be. You see the ship was a little old and as soon as they came into the dock and stopped the engines, the pressure in a steam pipe burst it and I got scalding water and steam all over both my feet.'

'Did it hurt?'

'Well Ettie, I have to say that it did and quite a lot too as a matter of fact. Now don't look so sad honey; it's all healed up now.'

Margaret wiped away a small tear that crept down the side of Ettie's nose.

'They carried me up out of the stokehold and I was hollering quite a bit and put me on a wagon up to Workington Infirmary. When I got there the folks were as kind as any I ever met in my life; they painted my feet with some liquid and dressed it with bandages, then I was in there for weeks. Every day they changed the dressing and painted some more stuff on it and in a few weeks I was healed, though my feet will never look the same again. But you know something that struck me? They didn't charge me a penny. When I said I was not a charity case and would pay my way, they told me that the hospital is funded by contributions from everyone in town and they did not take money from anyone. Now that floored me I can tell you, since I had never seen such a thing or thought it. One of the nurses even arranged for me to have a lodging down on Church Street and an introduction to the folks in St Michael's. Now it may seem strange to you, but I pretty soon decided that I was not going to leave this town where they looked after people and are so friendly. At first I started doing odd jobs to earn my way, like window cleaning and such, but my feet hampered me so I decided to teach them a lesson.'

'How do you teach your feet a lesson?' asked a wondering Ommie.

'Well, little lady, I was trying to walk them into submission, going up to Cuckoo Arch and back as fast as I could, or walking out to Siddick and back, but it was then that I saw a fine idea in the *Cumberland Times*. There's this writer called Cousin Charley, and for all I know that may be his real name…'

'We know Cousin Charley. Mam sometimes gets a paper and he writes the childrens' page.'

'Pree-cisely. Anyway he suggested a walking race from Workington to Cockermouth, then to Maryport and back again to Workington. That's 22 miles and I thought it a great idea, a manly notion in which I would compete, and maybe win the prize.'

'What was the prize?'

'It was cash, money Joe, but I forget how much. Seventy men entered for this and on the day they turned up wearing all sorts of outfits, but because of my feet and how they were still slightly swollen, I wore galoshes.'

'Galoshes for a race!'

'That's right Ommie, galoshes; they were big enough to accommodate my burned feet. There were about 2,000 people turned up to see us off and a whole crowd of cyclists to follow us and off we went. I was the only man of colour there and certainly the only such competitor, but that's where they started shouting at me, "Go on Darky Joe. You show 'em lad!" They were calling me that to egg me on to win and that's why I don't mind them calling me it now, because they meant well by me.'

'I heard they knew your story Joe; about your feet and they admired your pluck. You made a lot of admirers that day, because they thought you were game.'

'That so Tom? That's as maybe. We started at the Low Station, and if we got thirsty or felt we were running out of energy there was a wagon following us with flasks full of that new hot energy drink which I have to say I like very much.'

To the mystified looks of the children he continued, 'It's called Oxo, and it tastes like a beef broth. Being so tall I took the lead and was getting many cheers from hundreds of people lining the route; I'm glad that all I would take from bystanders was the Oxo, because someone handed one poor lad a brandy so big that he soon started falling behind then curled up by the road and went to sleep. I reckon there was something in it to make him sleep. Anyway, I was striding out well and way, way in the lead by the time I got to Cockermouth on account of my long legs, but my feet were paining me. I mean really paining me.'

'Did you carry on Mr Joe?'

'Yep, I sure did Ettie. I went on, but I was getting slower and slower and soon I was being caught up and passed. We came to a place called Dovenby and I knew I had to stop. I never won that race and I had to get back to Workington on the train, but it was worth every ache I got, because I was known round the area and my back was getting sore from people patting me and saying well done. This is my town now and I aim to stay here.'

'Well it's a pity you didn't win. Who did?'

'I agree with you Billy and I would have liked to win, but let me tell you buddy, that's the world we live in and we all have to cope with both winning and losing. The race was won by a man called Billy Kay from Embleton in Northumberland. Billy Mears and Billy Blacklock from Workington came third and fourth'

'Too many Billys round this town I'm thinking! Some of them should be Williams!'

'Yours answers to Billy as well Tom, but we cannot win everything.'

'So is that why you stayed Joe? The hospital and the friendliness of the people?'

'That's mostly it Ma'am.' Joe Johnson thought a long minute, then continued, 'There's something here which you don't get everywhere. Sure I made friends on the race and I go to church and I've met people, but there's something else ain't there? You know what I mean. You moved here too.'

'It's the air, the mood, the atmosphere.'

'Sure; that's what I think too. It's not just because it's a bustling place and there's work so a man can live. There's something to the folk here that goes beyond the friendliness. There's a sort of salty down to earthness about this place. Folks look you right in the eye and tell you what they think. They don't look down on you, but take you for what you are and it doesn't matter about what you do, or believe, or the colour of your skin. You play a straight hand with them and they play fair with you. That's what I like, and that's why I stay here of all the places I've seen.'

'Better than Chicago?'

Joe Johnson laughed a great laugh, 'You just said a mouthful. Oh yes, Ma'am. Better than Chicago. I ain't never going back there, you can bet on that.'

The day moved on into evening and Joe Johnson left to go home. It had been a strange day, but a reassuring one. The British Army was getting to be huge and full of enthusiastic men who would win the war in the coming year. Margaret's boys would never have to go and fight; Nellie was working hard at the Bankfield Hospital and Nancy had been told that she was being promoted from chamber maid to waitress in the Central Hotel. Her fears for Barwise were just bad daymares intruding into her thoughts. She would dismiss them from her mind, for certainly this war, so far, was what happened to other people and with any luck her family would come through it unscathed.

Chapter 10

The Munitionette

Nancy did not 'live in' at the Central Hotel, but worked there from six in the morning until eight at night, or longer if she was required. This was leavened by the fact that she only worked at weekends on Saturday mornings, and every fortnight until two o'clock in the afternoon to help with lunch. Sundays were entirely free for her as the live in girls handled meals for guests, and the restaurant and tearoom where she was a waitress were closed in respect of the Sabbath. Mr and Mrs Hagan, the owners, were good business heads, but took the fourth commandment seriously. It did not hinder their profits because much of Workington shut down on Sundays anyway, and the business people and commercial travellers who made up the bulk of paying guests during the week, were mostly at home with their wives and families. Still, for £18 a year it was hard work, and though she had her lunch and her evening meal in the hotel at no expense to her, she was on her feet most of the day and consequently often found them sore. It was not unknown for her to leave the hotel when she finished work, and take her shoes off to walk home if the weather was dry, which caused some amusement and considerable empathy from the local police sergeant on his rounds as he passed through Central Square. This was Sergeant Wilson, who lived at the police station in Gladstone Street with his wife. He suffered terribly with sore feet, which was particularly painful towards the end of his round supervising the various beats in central Workington; habitually he walked round slowly with his bootlaces very loose. If anyone asked him to come to attend to something that required more haste, he would ask them to 'wait a moment while I do up my whangs,' then he would bend down and tie them up. For this reason he was known locally as 'Paddy Whangs' but held, nonetheless, in great respect. He and Nancy had begun on nodding terms as one sufferer recognising another, but now occasionally had a chat.

Nancy had hoped, before the war, that she would progress up through the ranks so to speak, for she had started in the hotel as a general kitchen maid straight from school at fourteen. As she grew older and gained more strength she had been appointed as a chambermaid and spent her days heaving mattresses, changing linen and cleaning rooms. It was only lately that she had become a waitress for before the war all the staff in the restaurant and tea-room had been male, so when offered a position there, she had seen it as a step up that could get her a similar job anywhere, and had taken it. Of course, it was not the summit of her ambitions, for what she really wished to be was a milliner. There was in her a flair for design and she loved the idea of crafting hats that looked splendid on people, because she had a penchant for a nice head-dress. She was a very realistic girl though, and for someone of her class and background to enter this genteel and ladylike arena was, she thought, very unlikely. If she was pretty, or so her mind ran, then she might have had an entrée, but in her own head, she was not. 'Workmanlike' was how she thought of herself and joked sometimes with her mother that she was of 'solid Cumbrian peasant stock.' Her elder sister Nellie was one she thought of as 'pretty', but although Nancy's hair was of a similar shade, her face was slightly rounder and her eyes did not ordinarily twinkle as did those of her elder sibling; though she did not know it, she was to acquire that in later life. Nancy was inclined to have a more solemn, even a grave expression; the face of someone who took life seriously and who could be counted on in a crisis. At the same time she exuded a maternal quality that led her mother to rely on her more than on her other daughters when dealing with the younger members of the family. Being of a strong mind, she had determined to be, at least for the moment, content with the job she had.

At first she had told herself that she was happy doing what she was doing, but as the war took hold on her consciousness she began, as did many people of her age, to wonder if she was contributing enough. In an age that exalted patriotism and duty, a nagging thought lingered at the back of her mind that she could be doing more, and this feeling, engendered by news from France, had germinated when she watched the Lonsdale volunteers march off to war. As a woman of course she could not join up, pick up a rifle and go to shoot the Germans, but she knew quite a few young women of her own age who wanted to do something for the war, and they mirrored what she was thinking. Nellie at least was doing something worthwhile by nursing wounded soldiers, but the problem for Nancy was the poster; 'that poster' as she thought of it. The Parliamentary Recruiting Committee had put out a poster and it was on the bus stops, hoardings, walls and in the stations. It showed a haunted looking man with his daughter looking at him and asking, 'Daddy, what did you do in the Great War?' The intended effect was obvious, but it had unforeseen echoes in the mind of Nancy, and in this she was sure that she could not be alone. She did not wish her children, if she had any, to ask her in future years, 'Mam; what did you do in the Great War?' She could almost hear the answer 'I served teas and coffees to the gentlemen in the tearoom of the Central Hotel.' Not long before, she had seen a short film in the picture house that showed a young society woman lounging around doing nothing. Her husband had been digging up the lawn to plant potatoes and she would not join him because the work was boring and she did not wish to get her dress dirty. Eventually she had changed her mind, changed her dress and helped to plant the potatoes, a process that she had enjoyed. Nancy thought her a fairly useless piece of fluff who really should have pulled herself together and got on with it well before she did, and herein lay the key to her own reactions. She could not be doing with foolishness; if something needed to be done, then best be getting on with it. In similar fashion, if something needed to be said, then it had to be said, flat out and clear the air. Nancy was as straight as a die, honest and as packed full of conscience as a squirrel's cheeks with nuts. The thought that she might pass the war in an idle everyday job serving tea, or meat and two vegetables to rubicund men with rosy cheeks whilst others helped their country in its time of peril, was irking her more and more. Somewhere in the back of her mind she ascribed this guilty feeling to her mother more than to her father. Margaret had taken great care to instil in all of her children a sense of duty and of hard work, and this in turn had to do with her religiosity. Work was pleasing to God, and especially work that helped and did service to others; work to aid the fight against evil which the whole country was engaged in, was even more so. It was true that she had heard stories that women who did war work earned big money, but this was not the thing that was uppermost in her mind, which was why she had gone to the Labour Exchange in October 1915 and enquired about munitions work. To her surprise, the man behind the desk had not been dismissive, but had taken her name, address and date of birth and told her that she would be hearing from them in due course. Since then, life had gone on in the same rut of sore feet, long hours, small tips and urgent demands for gravy, mustard, sugar and just a little more milk.

In November 1915 Nancy had been clearing up the remains

from a table where four managers from various engineering factories had what appeared to be a lucrative lunch, when she noticed that one of them had left behind a copy of the Manchester Guardian. In large headlines was a call from the Minister of Munitions, Mr Lloyd George and Lord Murray of Elibank, for 40,000 women to come forward for the manufacture of munitions. It set her mind a racing to the thought that surely it could not be long before she was called, and then Elsie made her indignant; she was the other waitress in the tearoom. Elsie's father was a machinist lathe operator at one of the small engineering companies in the harbour area and he got wind that something was afoot down there, though it was the subject of some secrecy. The Drill Hall in Edkin Street was the headquarters of the 2nd Cumberland Battery and ammunition column of part of the Royal Artillery, though they also had a small office where you could enlist in the Lonsdale Pals. With great logic it had been decided to build a national shell factory down on Stanley Street near the harbour. Over 200 women were to be employed there initially and Elsie was one of them. When Nancy enquired how she had got the job, she told her that her father had pulled a few strings, so she served out her notice and went to learn how to use a lathe to smooth shell cases and earn a lot more money. Nancy was not so much jealous as indignant. Being of a very determined mind, she begged half an hour off work and although she did not exactly storm and demand, she went to the Labour Exchange and asked firmly why, since she had put her name down for war work, she had not been called for the new factory. The answer took her aback.

'My dear Miss Little I quite understand why you are unhappy and your frustration will not be allayed when I tell you that there is very little about this that I am allowed to reveal. What I can say is that we have been asked to hold a list of young women in your position for a very special reason, and that you will be called when the time comes. The work will be important; now that really is all I can say and I'm afraid you will have to be patient.'

Nancy could 'do' patient and so she waited, and the days of her life were humdrum, so that she began to believe that nothing would ever happen. The year moved towards its end and the whole country was awash with expectation. When the Derby Recruiting Scheme ended on 12 December thousands of men had joined the Army and Lord Derby was due to present his report to the government. The country hung with bated breath waiting to hear whether or not enough men had volunteered to make up the seventy divisions that Lord Kitchener said were necessary for victory. Just before Christmas it was revealed that although hundreds of thousands had come forward, there were still half a million single men who had not attested that they would come when called. As the year turned into 1916 the government began to process a new law that made all single men between 18 and 41 automatically members of the armed forces unless they were exempt or could demonstrate to a local tribunal that they should not be called. Rumours swept the country that the Army was being readied for a 'big push' and that this attack by the British would be on such a massive scale that the Germans could not possibly stop it. The war would be over soon. None of this affected Nancy in what she did, save that there was a slowing of customers to some extent. In one respect only was her life affected and that was because meat was becoming expensive so at home it was served fewer times than formerly, its place being taken by fish, which was cheap and plentiful, and occasionally by gifts sent down from Edderside in the shape of a fresh rabbit or a bit of mutton. Tom's brother Joe was aware of how high prices were becoming; even potatoes, which before the war had been sixpence a stone were now one shilling and fourpence and were becoming scarce. It was not even possible to make up the bulk of a meal in bread because that was also becoming expensive. The family was getting by, but it was becoming more difficult and Nancy's taking her lunch and dinner at work was a great help to their budget. She saw meat more often than they did, but was not allowed to take it home. It was unfair, she thought, that in the middle of town where people were beginning to struggle to get enough to eat, you could still stuff your face with all you wanted, if you had enough money to pay for it. Some of the men who visited Workington and stayed in the hotel while they went about their business were very well padded and looked as if they were doing nicely out of the war.

If she remembered occasionally that she had given her name in to do war work, she would give a mental shrug and think that the reason she had not heard was simply inefficiency. When she saw Elsie, formerly her colleague, now turning out shell cases, around the town, she saw that her old friend was wearing new clothes and shoes, and looked far better turned out than she once had. It was not in Nancy to be jealous, but it crossed her mind more than once that she too would like to be earning more money.

On Friday 31 March 1916 Nancy trudged home wearily at 9.30pm. It had been a long day and all she wanted to do was get her shoes off and have a cup of tea in the back room, and a good chat to her mother. Margaret met her at the door, 'There's a letter for you Nancy.'

'For me? Whoever is sending me letters? I never get letters.'

'It's got OHMS on it!'

'Whatever does that mean?'

'On His Majesty's Service Nancy. That's very official, government business. Here it is.'

'Oh. Just let me see...' Nancy opened the letter, which was typewritten with blanks for details to be filled in, and read.

'Dear <u>Miss Little</u>, your name has been passed to me as having applied to do war service at <u>Workington Labour Exchange</u>. I commend your wish to serve your country in her hour of need and invite you to meet with me at <u>Workington Labour Exchange</u> on <u>8/04/1916</u> at <u>3 pm</u> in <u>room 20.</u>

Please bring this letter with you and present it at the reception desk.

Yours faithfully

D Gilmour (Factory Management Board)'

'You put your name down for war work? Why?'

'I want to do something Mam. You know why. There's people all over the country doing their bit and I want to do mine.'

'But what are you going to be doing?'

'I don't know. I just put my name down for war work, but that was months ago. This is the first thing I've heard, but it looks like some sort of factory work.'

'But where? Do you think you'll be down Stanley Street?'

'I really don't know Mam. Not until Saturday.'

Nancy had a very bold streak to her nature that meant that unlike many girls of her age, she felt no trepidation on entering the Labour Exchange the following Saturday. On the contrary, she was intrigued, especially when told to go up to room 20, which she did, and found it full of about thirty young women, all sitting in rows on wooden chairs facing the front. Behind a desk was a man of about fifty, shuffling papers and assisted by an older women who appeared to be his secretary, which indeed she was. After a few minutes he began to speak to them about why he was here and why they were there.

'Good afternoon ladies, and thank you for being here this afternoon. As you may gather we chose Saturday afternoon because it is the time when many workers have time off and so we would not impinge on your normal working hours. I apologise for cutting into your time off, but of course the nature of what we are going to talk about makes it necessary. Before I can proceed, Mrs Wemyss, my assistant will pass some forms among you, thank you.'

The forms turned out to be a section of the Official Secrets Act of 1911, which warned that if any person for any purpose prejudicial to the safety of interests of the State obtains or communicates any information which is calculated to be or might be…useful to an enemy, he or she shall be guilty of a felony.

'Before I can proceed further I must ask each of you to come up in turn to sign and date these forms. If you talk about or reveal anything which you hear from now on in this room or where you work, then you may be liable to imprisonment or worse. You must never speak of it to friends, family or anyone else; if you do then you will be arrested. I trust I have made this clear? I do not wish to seem dramatic, but if you feel that you are unable to sign the form in front of you then please feel free to leave now.'

A murmur crossed the room but no-one left; everyone, Nancy included, signed a declaration that they understood this part of the Official Secrets Act and that they would not speak on these matters; and she never did.

'Very well, thank you. I may talk freely. As you may have seen in the local press there has been a great deal of activity in the area surrounding Gretna Green. There is a lot of construction going on up there and the government has commissioned the building of two large factories to produce munitions. We hope to begin production of cordite this August and to do that of course, we need workers. That is where you come in. The work will be pleasant, healthy and not at all dangerous, but it does need some training.'

Mr Gilmour was in the persuasion business and it was

wartime, so he may perhaps be forgiven for his remarks, which were far from accurate, as his listeners were soon to find out. Nonetheless most of what he said was quite correct and very satisfactory to the people listening.

'Now I understand that you don't know how to produce explosives but it's not a hard job from your point of view. You will receive four weeks of training during which time you will get fifteen shillings a week. When that is completed your wages will rise to between £2 and £3 a week depending on the responsibilities you are assigned to.'

This time the noise in the room was not a murmur but excited chatter. This was wealth! Mr Gilmour was evidently well used to having this effect because he smiled slightly, then as the hubbub subsided, he carried on.

'There will be deductions of course for food and lodging, but there will be more money available for those that are prepared to work on Sundays. There are no regular intervals for 'lunch' or tea breaks. You will have those when your supervisor tells you that you may be released; the pay reflects this. I think that it may be best to proceed from this point on with any questions. The fact remains that you may leave this room at any time and not sign up to do this vital work for the war; but you have signed the Official Secrets Act. What do you wish to know? Hands up please.'

A number of hands went up and Gilmour picked one.

'This training. Where would it happen and what would we have to do?'

'The training would take place at Gretna in the new factory and it would be carried out by chemists and technicians who are in overall charge of the processes. Next.'

'Where would we live?'

'At first the work force will be living in wooden huts, but we are going to build some large hostels which will be far more comfortable. The huts will be provided with beds, stoves and a scullery so should be quite comfortable. Next question please.'

'Where would we take our meals?'

'There are already large canteen facilities which we plan to expand. You will be able to purchase good and nourishing food at them; in addition there are plans for further restaurants and even cafes around the site, because it will be very large. There will be thousands of people working and living there; in effect it will be quite a large town that is being created out of farmland.'

'Please Sir, that must mean that there's a lot of building work going on up there!'

'Yes indeed, there are thousands of navvies working round the clock to build the factories and accommodation. Any more questions?'

There were, of course, more questions. Mr Gilmour was evidently used to it and over half an hour he dealt with the provisions of a hospital, cinemas, assembly halls for dances and socials, shops, transport, churches that were being built for different denominations and drunkenness.'

'Yes, I do not deny that there has been a lot of drunkenness, you are quite right young lady, but it was, I fear, only to be expected and I'm sure you have seen many reports in the newspapers about some shocking incidents in Carlisle. There are plans to deal with that I assure you, but on the site there will be no trouble. We have our own police station already built, the sales of liquor are regulated in the immediate area, and the site as a whole is patrolled by soldiers who will stand for no nonsense. You'll be quite safe.'

Eventually the questions ended and Mr Gilmour concluded.

'It is planned that any workers willing to sign on today will start training at Gretna on Monday 29 May. They would travel up on Sunday 28 May and have time to settle into their huts ready for work at 6.00am on the Monday morning. Those who wish to may fill in their employment forms now; you will be accepted, be in no doubt. Those who wish to take the forms home and think it over may do so, posting them to the address at the end, but once again, no talking about what it involves. Thank you ladies, those who wish to leave may do so.'

Nancy began to fill her form in straight away and as she did so, another girl came up and greeted her.

'Gertie! What are you doing here?'

'Same as you I should think. It's a bit of a do isn't it!'

'I should think so. Official Secrets and all. Are you going?'

'What do you think Nancy? Of course I am on that money. It'll be nice to go along together if you like. It's better to have someone you know when you're going to a strange place.'

'That's very true. Alright, we can go up there together and if it's huts we can try and get in together. Where have you been hiding? I haven't seen you since school!'

'Oh you know. Working. I managed to get a job in the Beehive Co-op.'

'Which branch?'

'The big one on Vulcan's Lane.'

'That's handy for where you live; you still there?'

'Oh yes; still in Darcy Street with mam and dad. Never mind, it's not for ever and with all the money we'll be earning, who knows what the future may bring?'

With her form filled in and a guarantee of work Nancy handed in her notice at the Central Hotel, much to the disgust of the manager, and served out her time. It would be hard to replace her because government work was taking so many men and women from their ordinary employments that there was beginning to be a shortage of domestic servants, waiters and maids. However, this was not Nancy's concern and she looked forward to what was coming with a good deal of excitement.

Chapter 11

The Devil's Porridge

Nancy and Gertrude Palmer met at the Low Station on Sunday 28 May and they proceeded at their own expense to Gretna, via Carlisle where they were ushered into a newly built hut close to the station. It had been necessary to obtain her parents' permission for her to go to Gretna because she was under age, but Tom and Margaret had not demurred; their fledgling wanted to spread her wings and that was all there was to it. At Gretna, the new workers waited until a motor-bus arrived and took a large group of them two miles onto the new factory site which covered, so the driver said, twelve square miles. It was raining and out of the window the new factory looked more like a sea of mud with every bit of debris in the world thrown onto it. Everywhere there were huts, half finished brick buildings, enormous shed-like structures, railway lines half laid and apparent chaos. Legions of rough looking men laboured everywhere and the whole place was a hive of activity; it was plain that work was going ahead at frenetic pace. Soon through the rain ahead a double line of long wooden huts came into view and the bus stopped beside one, the driver calling out 'Welcome to Timber Town!' There seemed to be endless rows of black huts stretching into the distance, eighty-five of them in all, so Nancy found out later. A plank ran up from the bus door to a step into the hut. Nancy noticed that similar plank walkways connected the huts, but that away from these the mud was deep and nasty. Dragging her bag into the hut with

Gertie in her wake she found an elderly woman waiting for her.

'I'm the hut matron Mrs Armstrong. You can choose your own cubicle if you move down quickly enough to the far end.' There was a central corridor lit by electric light and on each side, the aforementioned cubicles were ranged and in each cubicle were two bunks. The corner cubicles had already been occupied by the first girls off the bus, but Gertie said she would not have wanted one of them anyway.

'Think about it Nancy. What's it like in the end terrace house in Devonshire Street?'

Nancy had quickly seen the point; the end cubicles had two exterior walls and very exposed in cold weather. She moved down the corridor and found that in the middle of the hut there was a large 'living room' with a stove and cooking facilities, and that the corridor continued after that with more cubicles. She and Gertie occupied the cubicle on the south side of the hut, which had a partition between them and the living room. Mrs Armstrong occupied a larger room with a door on the other side of the living room and a hut maid next to her also had one, but none of the cubicles had doors, just a black curtain across the opening. There were two shelves in each cubicle and each bunk had a lockable cupboard fixed to the wall beside. At one end, fixed to the wall was a wider shelf that could be used as a desk, but on which sat a basin and ewer. A single window to outside kept the pattering rain from soaking the beds, and the planking of the walls was none too thick. The stove in the living room was not giving out too much heat, though it was lit, and Nancy gave a brief moment to hope that she would not be living in the hut by next winter if this was the temperature now.

'We shall be snug in here I think Nancy. You don't snore do you?'

'I don't but I think we might get some that do. Never mind. I daresay we shall sleep soundly enough if we work hard.'

'That's the spirit.'

After half an hour of settling in, a stentorian call from Mrs Armstrong announced that there would be a meeting in the living room and so all the new occupants of the hut filed in and settled onto the hard forms that lined the room and crossed the centre.

'In a few minutes time I shall lead you over to the stores where each of you will be issued with overalls. You will not be wearing your own clothes at work; that is forbidden. You will also receive a cap which you must wear at all times, and absolutely do not wear anything metal in the way of buckles, hairpins, rings or any other items of jewellery. The only permitted item is the "On War Service" badge, which is made of brass and does not spark. Any infringements of this will receive penalties through the docking of pay, and repetitions may lead to dismissal. As you will understand, there are dangers to working with explosives and basic rules of safety have to be maintained. Now the hut rules are very simple. Lights will go out at ten o'clock each night and we will have a rule of silence to allow those on early shift to get their sleep. If you are out after then, you will have to wake me up from bed and I will require some explaining if you do that!'

Some excited comments were made sotto voce about shift work, but Mrs Armstrong caught the gist of them.

'Yes. When the factory gets into full swing there will be twenty-four hour working and it will be done on rotation by hut. Everyone in this hut will always be on the same shift and working together, so it is in your interests to get on with each other. The early shift starts at 7.30 in the morning so it will be up at six o'clock. They work until 2.30 in the afternoon when the middle shift takes over. The night shift will start at 10.30 at night and go through until 7.30am. That's A B and C shifts. This means that there will always be huts where the people are asleep.'

'Mrs Armstrong, what do we do when not working or sleeping?'

'You'll find that there are a lot of things to do and many recreation facilities are being built as I speak. In addition there are frequent trains into Carlisle and other towns nearby. Now as to this hut, which is my province, the rules are very simple. Treat this as if it were home and as if I were your mother.'

This caused some few repressed titters of amusement or disbelief.

'I'm sure that most of you know what I mean. Mr Pearson, the Director wishes this to be not just a place of work but like working with a large family though one with rules. If you have a visitor from another hut, then she must sign in and out. Every time you go out you must sign out in the book by the door and sign in when you come back. No men are allowed in the huts at any time. Be considerate to each other, use your natural good manners and I am sure that we shall all get on. It's important to note that you may wash in your cubicles but you are required to bathe at least once a week and there are bath houses for that purpose at several places round the town; we shall be a sweet smelling hut. We have a hut maid who will clean up while you are out, and change the linen, but try not to make her job too hard. Lastly, although I am hut matron here, my official title is Welfare Worker, which means that I have to look out for you and supervise your wellbeing. If you have any problems at all then you must refer to me for assistance, as I am the official proper channel. Now ladies, if you will please follow me…'

Slowly the group followed her teetering along planks on footwear not designed for such work and eventually arrived at a very large building with the sign "STORES" on the door. Trooping in, they queued up at a counter where two women eyed them up and down, gauging their size; if in doubt they plied a tape measure very quickly and they seized folded clothes from shelves behind them and handed them over to each woman, two of everything. The ensemble consisted of a long sleeved tunic that went on over the head, belted in the middle, with one button up near the neck, and a pair of trousers in a finer material, which caused some comment. They were to wear trousers! For their heads they each had a mob-cap in the same coarse material as the jacket. There were a few exclamations at the colour of the garments which was a reddish kind of khaki that did not promise to flatter anyone. To their great relief, they were then given white cotton blouses with collars that would be worn under the tunic; at least they would not be scratched to distraction. Finally, they had to move further up the counter where each was fitted with a pair of black rubber soled boots and a pair of gum-boots. In none of these items was even a scrap of metal.

Back at the hut there was a very distinguished looking man waiting for them in the uniform of the Royal Army Medical Corps, accompanied by a nurse. Each woman had to go to her particular cubicle and he very quickly came from one to the other with his stethoscope and listened to their chests. Then he held their tongues down with sticks and got them to say 'Aaaaahhhhh' and certified them as fit for work by ticking their names on a form that the nurse carried on a clipboard. Finally each was handed a pass with their name on it by Mrs Armstrong, who told them that they must under no circumstances lose it, along with a book of rules and a hostel pass stating which number hut she lived in. Each morning they would be passing through armed guards at the actual factory gate and would not get in without it and might be arrested. Any passes that were lost must be reported immediately. These formalities being over, the matron led them across the site about a quarter of a mile to a large low brick building which turned out to be an enormous canteen where dinner was served and to many of them, far better than they would have had at home, though of course they were paying for it anyway through deductions from their wages. There was no compulsion to use the canteen of course and if your name were not ticked off the list then no deductions would be made. That said, the prices were so reasonable compared with eating outside, that most workers used the facilities inside the camps. The place was lined with long trestle type tables with benches down both sides. There were literally hundreds, of young women at these eating yet there was almost no talking; and this was only one canteen in a place which would ultimately employ over 12,000 women. Most had arrived only the day before or today, so time would be needed for them to be easy in their new situation. The canteen had its own Matron and she had a staffed kitchen, a scullery, larger facilities for washing, extra toilets and bathing. There was also a staffed laundry where the workers could leave their clothes to be washed. Only the occupants of certain huts were allocated to this canteen to prevent over-crowding and there were many others of various sizes scattered round the factory site.

With dinner over, the girls, for most of them were just that, were free to socialise and most went back to their huts to settle in.

'How old are you Nancy?' asked Gertie.

'Same as you, 19, why?'

'Well did you not notice? Everyone in this hut is the same. In fact I think that we might be among the oldest here.'

'Now I feel old!'

'That might be an advantage. Some of the other girls look pretty rough and there's accents from all over.'

'That doesn't worry me,' announced Nancy. 'I take folk as I find them and if they treat me fair then they'll get the same from me.'

'I mean some of them look as if they might be the sort that like to fight.'

Nancy laughed, 'I'm no lightweight Gertie. As I said, I'm not worried. Let's just be nice to people and they'll be nice to us.'

'You've got a lot of faith in human nature.'

'In general I do. Do as you would be done by, and be done by as you did.'

'Aye we're all Jock Tamson's bairns; you're not wrong there.'

The voice from the door made both girls jump and a figure came through the curtain with her hand stuck out.

'Hello. I'm Janet. I'm just over the corridor so I couldnae help hearing what you were saying.'

'You're Scottish,' said Nancy taking the proffered hand.

'Well dinnae make it sound like an accusation,' smiled the newcomer. 'I cannae help it.'

'No…' sputtered Nancy, 'I didn't mean it that way. It's just I've never met a Scottish person before.'

'Well you have now. Where are you from then?'

'Workington.'

'Well I never met anyone from Workington before. That's a braw accent you have there hen.'

'Yours too. Where are you from?'

'I'm from Wick up in the far far north of Scotland.'

'What are you doing down here?' asked Nancy, somewhat awestruck at the distance from home.

'Och probably same as you. I'm here for the money and so's my pal. Lizzie; come over here and say hello.'

Thus it began, for similar conversations were taking place, or were to take place over the next few days and weeks where the members of this new 'family' began to know each other and to form friendships and relationships that would bind them together in their common task. When Nancy eventually tucked herself into her narrow bed with the cotton sheets and two coarse woollen blankets, she actually felt very optimistic about her new job.

Some of the girls in the hut were evidently not used to getting up at 6.00am, but Nancy was used to rising at five to be at work by then. Looking out through the condensation soaked window at the grey early morning light, with a mist lying low over the site, she shivered, but climbed reluctantly out of bed and began to dress. She had to study the trousers hard to decide which was back and which was front, but eventually a joint decision with Gertie showed which way was correct. It felt very odd to be wearing them for she had never dreamed of doing such a thing and was glad that her mother and father could not see her. When she was dressed she and Gertie looked at each other and laughed.

'May I have the pleasure of this dance Miss?' said Gertie.

'Don't mind if I do,' replied Nancy, and laughing fit to burst they danced out into the narrow corridor and waltzed around the living room. Mrs Armstrong was there but did not chide them.

'Please sit down ladies until all of you are here.'

The hut maid, a quiet girl named Annie, served tea from a large urn and a couple of biscuits to each worker who turned up. Nancy could not resist saying; 'Go canny wid the sugar! And that's 'ot cream'.

'What?' said Gertie.

'Oh it's what my mam says when she's serving tea. I swear she's like a parrot sometimes!'

'Well she's not wrong is she? Things are in short supply. Sounds like your mam's got her head screwed on right to me.'

When all the occupants of the hut had assembled, Mrs Armstrong addressed them briefly once more.

'Now ladies I shall take you over to the canteen where you

will have breakfast. When you are on morning shift there will always be tea and biscuits ready here at six before you go over to breakfast proper. The times that you will eat depends on what shift you are on. We shall all sit together and when you are finished you will be taken by one of our works supervisors to where you will start training for your various jobs.'

Like ducklings following their mother, for the last time they followed her as a group. From this time onwards they would be expected to get themselves up and fed and to arrive at work on their own. Nancy had been used to rather frugal breakfasts at home, pobbies being the norm, but here it was more than adequate, there being a choice of porridge, or scrambled eggs with toast, and there was plenty of it. This would be the last thing they ate until 4.45pm when they would get a full meal with meat; and then at 9.15pm cocoa, soup and bread for supper. When they had eaten they boarded some carriages of a light railway that ran close to their canteen and were taken the best part of half a mile to a small platform by an enormous shed which was filled with hundreds of tubs each about waist high and about a yard in diameter. Waiting for them was a man in a white coat with a bald head, and a woman with a clipboard. The woman called the register of all the names, and then the man began to speak with a soft pure Scottish accent that betrayed a Galloway background.

'Good morning ladies. My name is Mr Spencer and I am the supervisor for this section of the Dornock gun cotton factory. My task is to oversee your work in mixing the Devil's Porridge. Now I see that some of you are looking mystified but do not worry, I shall explain. First of all, is there anyone here who knows what gun cotton is?'

Not a hand went up.

'Very well; is there anyone here who knows what cordite is?'

Nancy, who was not shy with information, threw her hand straight up.

'I think Sir that it's the explosive the Navy uses to fire their shells.'

'That is correct young woman; you do not have to call me Sir though. We are not in school and I am simply Mr Spencer.'

Nancy smiled in a somewhat discomfited way, because it had indeed felt rather like being back in school.'

'Indeed, cordite is a smokeless propellant which is used in naval guns, but may also be used for a variety of purposes including bullets and grenades. It is vital to our war effort and yet in short supply. Our aim is that within a very short time, this establishment will be producing over 800 tons of it every week. That is where you come in. Before you can have cordite, you must have gun cotton, for cordite is made of 65% gun cotton and 30% of nitro-glycerine; ah I see you have heard of that!'

An excited murmur ran round the group with some faces that expressed trepidation.

'You need have no fear ladies. The process that you will be working with is quite safe and nitro-glycerine is not involved. At any rate the dangers associated with it by the popular press are much exaggerated, but it will not be used here. When the gun cotton is made it will be taken up to the cordite works at Mossband and there it will be transformed into a more deadly form. Yes; you with the hand up.'

'There's 5% missing Sir. What is that?'

'Ah I take your point. It's petroleum jelly which is used to keep it plastic, otherwise it would dry out and be difficult to use. They also use acetone up there as a solvent and make it into a kind of dough, which can be extruded into rods and cut up to fit different shell cases. It's a rather more dangerous process, but of course there are safeguards in place. However, that does not concern us, being the end process. You ladies must concentrate on your own work, so let us begin by demonstration.'

Over the next hour or so the supervisor took the new cadre of workers through the process of making gun cotton showing how raw cotton was treated with two parts of concentrated sulphuric acid and one part of nitric acid in water cooled and lead lined vats. After a few minutes the acid was drained off and the treated cotton was washed with copious amounts of water which was stirred around with a long pole. Each girl had to try the pole and it was quite hard work, for all the world like stirring a thick porridge, for this was what it looked like.

'Now at this stage ladies, you will find the only danger in the process. You must of course not allow yourself to be splashed with the acid, which would be most unfortunate, but also you will notice that the pole is a long one. When you stir the mixture, stand well back and do not breathe the fumes in. The cotton has been acidified and must remain damp. In the old days it was found that if it was allowed to dry out, the evaporation of water concentrated the acid in the cotton and caused explosions or fires.'

A ripple of fright went round the group.

'You need have no fear of that. It only happens when the acidified cotton is not washed enough. This gun cotton will never be allowed to be dry, for it will be washed and potched by you and the other shifts that follow you, eight separate times over a period of forty-eight hours. Then, and only then will it be allowed to drain until it resembles a thick dough. At that point it is mixed in sealed tubs with alcohol and sent up to Mossband where it is no longer your concern. Now if you will follow me outside, I have a small demonstration for you.'

Once the group was outside the factory and well away from the building, the supervisor produced from a box that had evidently been placed there previously, what looked like a hank of cotton wool.

'This is our finished product ladies, now just watch what it does.'

Mr Spencer took a yard long stick with a taper tied to the end and made the group stand well back. Lighting the taper with a match he held it to the gun cotton which took flame immediately with a bright yellow-white-red flame, then exploded with a 'whuff'. Some of the group jumped and giggled nervously.

'Now you see if you confine that in a shell or a gun, you have a very powerful explosive and the more we produce of it the better. If we can out-produce the Germans then we shall win this war. I know that I can rely on you to do your best. You will have noticed that we are already in production, but it's rather small scale at the moment. For the next four weeks each of you will be attached to an experienced worker whilst you train. They have been brought up here from the Royal Gunpowder Works at Waltham Abbey so they are a long way from home. They know their business, and in one month's time I expect you to do so as well. Thank you ladies; now to work.'

The lady with the clipboard allocated each new worker to an experienced hand and Nancy found herself working with Lilian who came from Epping Forest in Essex.

'The trouble with you lot is that you all talk funny. I can 'ardly understand a word you say.'

This was delivered in flat vowels in an Essex accent that sounded much like a foreign language to Nancy.

'Well I'm from Workington and we all talk like this.'

'Well Gawd alone knows 'ow you manage to get anyfink done dahlin.'

This was delivered with a friendly grin and Nancy knew that she would have no trouble with her instructor. She was up here simply to do the job she did 'dahn sarf' and was not fond of the idea of staying for long. As soon as her time was up she'd be back to Essex where the weather was better and she could get the train into 'Lahndan' for a good night out. No offence luv but the weather was bloody 'orrible and she couldn't make 'ead nor tale of what people were blabbin' on abaht.

She made Nancy smile, but it was plain theirs would be a short acquaintance; Lil had been paid good money to come up and instruct people, but would be back home as soon as she could.

The work was simple enough. You started with an empty lead tub that you had to examine for any obvious flaws. If there were flaws then you had to send for the lead plumber who would see to it. Then the girls arrived from the cotton storage sheds pushing a heavy cart with bales of the raw material. This was opened and pummelled at the entrance shed to the factory into heaps of loose cotton and put through a fluffer; next it was placed on a cart and trundled to Nancy. These carts had no metal in them, being pegged together and on rubber-tyred wheels. Nancy lifted the cotton into the tub and when it was full to the mark, she signalled to the two men who had charge of the acid cart. They came with their carboys and rubber gloves and aprons, tipped the mixture into the tub, and then they stirred it for a short while with long hardwood poles. After this it was all Nancy's. This part of the process was very short, for two minutes after the acid was poured, Nancy had to open the 'acid outflow valve' at the base of the tub and let it drain. At this moment was the most dangerous part of the process, because the acid reaction with the cotton could flame and explode as it had done when the process was first discovered, but by adjusting the proportions of sulphuric and nitric acid in favour of the former, the process had been made far safer. When she was satisfied that gravity had done its work and sufficient acid had disappeared down the lead pipe, Nancy closed the outlet valve and reached overhead to pull down a water pipe. Opening the valve she flooded gallons of clear water into the tub then took her potching stick, another long hardwood pole and began to stir; as she did so she turned over a tab, one of eight on the tub to indicate that this batch was on its first rinse. It looked for all the world like oats soaking, so she thought that 'Devil's Porridge' was a very good name for it.

For the next five minutes she stirred it then left it to soak as she moved on to begin the process in the next tub; she would return to stir it some more at intervals later. When those were done she would move on to tubs commenced by the previous shift, look at the tabs to indicate which wash they were on, and repeat the entire process. When a rinse was complete, she would open the water outlet valve and let the whole lot drain, but had to keep a close eye on it; before any evaporation took place the next lot of water had to come in.

This was her job, dangerous if her supervisor had understated it, vital to the war effort, repetitive, even boring, but very well paid. It certainly developed the muscles in her arms over a short period of weeks. As she had been told at the Labour Exchange, her pay was indeed fifteen shillings a week during the four-week training period, but her training was now over. Nancy was getting two pounds every week, though she was keeping little of it about her person; there was a Midland bank in the rapidly developing township and her deposit was growing larger all the time; she was even boosting her earnings by volunteering to work on Sundays. She had promised Gertie that at some point in the not too distant future, they would go together to Carlisle on a Saturday afternoon after shift. The shops there were supposed to be as good as any in the country, there were theatres, cinemas and music halls, and if they felt like it, they could eat in a restaurant. It sounded like an excellent idea and she looked forward to it immensely.

Chapter 12

Barwise on War

1916 was the year of 'the big push' and everyone in the country knew it. At some point in the year the Germans would be defeated by a massive attack by the new armies that Lord Kitchener had been building up since 1914. All the eager fit volunteers who had rushed to the colours in a year and a half of patriotic fervour, would be released upon the foe like so many mastiffs to maul him to death. These were the best of British manhood, because they had gone to fight of their own volition and not been forced. The Germans were having a hard enough time holding the forces that were already pitted against them, but when the new armies got to them, the war would be over in weeks. Everybody said so and expected it; indeed how could it be otherwise? Even the vicar said so, and he was a very well educated man and should know. Margaret respected the vicar greatly and there was a particular reason for this; early in January 1916 she had felt the need, as she sometimes did, to pray. It was something that made her feel better in herself and part of the reason why she had gone through the confirmation process in 1913 to become a full communicant. She liked St John's Church, though it was rather gloomy inside and not at all inspiring; the previous vicar Mr Greene had tried to turn it into something, as he put it 'better adapted to public worship' but she thought the effect a bit like a large shed. The building itself was huge, having been built originally to accommodate 2,000 worshippers with a parliamentary grant as an act of thanks for the victory at Waterloo. The reason she liked it was because it was a high church. There was something about the display of the priest in full robes, the large decorated altar, the candlesticks and the nature of the ritual as presented that she felt more suitable to holy things. Today she found the church empty so sat quietly thinking, and then she prayed, silently, for peace.

When she had finished, she stood up to leave, and a voice spoke to her across the church, making her jump slightly.

'Hello Mrs Little. I saw you there but did not wish to disturb you.'

'Oh good morning Reverend. I just popped in for a few minutes; you didn't disturb me.'

'I'm glad. It's nice to see that people like yourself feel able to come in to pray.'

'I do sometimes when I feel the need.'

'Yes, it can be a great comfort. I find it so myself, but I wish that it could be a little more salubrious.'

Margaret was intrigued.

'Salubrious Sir?'

'Yes. Salubrious. It's a good word I think.'

He paused and looked around with a critical eye.

'Am I right in thinking that like me, you prefer high church?'

'Well yes. I came to religion much later in life than some and I like the sacraments and ritual and robes; it just feels right I think.'

'I agree with that Mrs Little. I mean, just take a look around you at this great white-washed shed. That's what it is when all is said and done. It's not exactly crying out the glory of God is it?'

'It is rather plain I think, but the building itself is splendid.'

'It should be a far more fitting place to worship, and as I sense that you would appreciate such things, I want to tell you something.'

Margaret's interest was unfeigned.

'Are you an imaginative person?'

'I think I am.'

'Then imagine this. This great white roof painted blue like the evening sky, and decorated with geometric patterns in white. Imagine the dark wood of the gallery painted white, and the whole thing turned around so that the altar is to the West and not the East. Great electric lights illuminating the whole like day, and the organ pipes set above the great west door in a proscenium with columns. Do you know what a baldacchino is?'

'No Reverend, I'm afraid I don't.'

'It's a great canopy above the altar set on four great pillars twisted like barley-sugar, the whole decorated with gold leaf and patterns, a huge red cloth hung behind the altar with a picture of our Lord in glory. They have one in the Vatican in Rome, but there are few of them in this country.'

'That's what you want to do here? It sounds wonderful. A great improvement.'

'I confess that the vision is not mine. I had an expert along here late last year and consulted him over what may be done with this style of church – a Mr Comper. The vision is his. It would make this one of the most magnificent churches in the north of England.'

Margaret pondered about that for a moment then spoke slowly and with deliberation.

'I think the design is his. And it's a good one. But the vision is yours. That's rather different.'

Mr Croft blinked. 'I hadn't considered that. Thank you for saying it because I won't deny that the thought gives me pleasure.'

'When will it be done Sir?'

'Not yet I fear. It will cost a lot of money, and there is a war to think of first. But it will be done eventually; I have sworn to do it.'

'Then I will give you any help I can towards it, and I'm sure the rest of the congregation will too. They are all very enthusiastic about this place. It's special.'

'I think so too and that's why I want to do it.'

Margaret liked the new vicar; he was a man who thought about things and liked the style of religion that she did. So it was that she made a conscious decision to listen to his sermons far more attentively, because he was worth listening to. This decision was not one that she made alone, for others in the neighbourhood had made the same resolution. It was to have beneficial consequences in the not too distant future.

For the family in 55 Devonshire Street, as for the town, the beginning of 1916 passed without undue excitement save for a great gale that blew in from the West on 16 February. It was the sort of day when men crammed their caps down hard on their heads if they wanted to keep them, and families busied themselves indoors. In the early afternoon flares were seen offshore at Siddick just up the coast and the town was set agog as the maroon was sent up and exploded with a mighty crack overhead. This was the signal for the town Rocket Brigade to assemble, and soon their wagon was tearing along the road northwards to the shore at Siddick, just by the great black spoil heap that dominated the skyline there. A three-masted steamer called the SS Thames carrying grain from Liverpool to Silloth had run ashore and heeled over in the force of the gale. The shores of the Solway are peculiar in that they slope shallowly away from the land and in places are so near to flat that a person may walk out a great distance and still only be up to their knees in water. The Thames was 300 yards from the shore and the crew evidently worried that their lives were in danger; the waves were high and driving hard up to the beach. The Rocket Brigade had practised for this eventuality many times, but although they tried repeatedly to send a line over the ship, the force of the wind would not allow it. Nonetheless, they stayed in attendance, the sea being too rough to launch any kind of boat and as the afternoon wore on the tide began to go out, though slowly for the wind still drove the water up the beach. Eventually, just as the light began to fail, the crew were able to walk ashore to safety. The ship herself was left sitting on the sand, and on the next high tide an old paddle tug from Workington Harbour towed her off and into deeper water.

It was Margaret's particular friend Ethel Kirkbride from a few doors down who drifted in with the news of the shipwreck that evening, but she had a soft chuckle when she related that it was in fact no such thing and that a lot of folks had gotten themselves excited over something that had, very happily, turned out well. Ethel was the wife of Thomas Kirkbride, a local policeman; she was sitting by the range drinking tea when Tom came in from work, and Margaret's husband was not a happy man.

'I tripped over a drunk in the lonning again. That's the third time in the last month.'

'Well I've told you Tom not to use the lonnings to go to and from work. Why don't you go along the pavements like civilised people do?'

'Oh so I'm uncivilised am I?'

'You know very well what I mean Thomas Little, so don't come it. If you don't want to trip over things in the dark why don't you go along the roads?'

'Now we've been here before Margaret. I like the lonnings; they're quiet and that lets me have a think on my way to and from work. I just don't like having to say hello to people at that time of morning and when I'm coming home I can't be bothered, I'm that tired.'

'In that case Tom dear, you mustn't grumble if you trip over things occasionally, even drunks sleeping it off.'

'What I don't understand is why there are so many drunks

in Workington. What do you think Ethel? You've lived here all your life. Did you always get so many drunks everywhere, because I have to say I hadn't noticed it elsewhere. Maryport on Saturday nights can be a bit raw with all the sailors, but this is Wednesday.'

Ethel pondered a moment.

'I think that there probably are more drunks in Workington than you'd get in the average town of this size, but you have to ask yourself why Tom. I know you don't drink, but you used to.'

'Yes well I had good reason to swear off the drink as you well know,' this with a look at Margaret, 'and I'm glad I did. But so many people in one place; and I could smell the whisky on him very strongly.'

'I think it's likely that you've set your finger right on the nail there Tom. There's a lot of whisky drunk in this town, but I'm taking it that you know why?'

Tom was now intrigued.

'No I don't. I mean I used to drink whisky and far too much of it because I liked the taste, but from what you're saying I would gather that there's a reason why people in Workington drink more whisky than in other places?'

'There is. Now let me see, when did you arrive in Workington? I think you said 1903?'

'That's right.'

'Yes I thought so. Then it happened before your time, so I'd better tell you.'

'I'd be interested to know.'

'Well here's the tale as to why there's so much whisky drunk in Workington. It was back in the winter of 1900, so over two years before you moved here, that right?'

'Aye that's right, it is.'

'Well some folk started coming down with a sickness that none of the doctors could make head nor tail of, but there were so many people coming in, mainly men, that they started to call it "Foot and Hand disease." It seems that they got swollen faces and feet, sore eyes, aching legs and then the skin started to peel off their feet and hands.'

'It sounds awful!' interjected Margaret.

'By all accounts Margaret, it was worse than I can describe. It is known that further south in Salford and in Manchester fifty one deaths were reported from this, and there were cases all over the north west.'

'How many in Workington?'

'Not known. The number of deaths and close to death cases were never disclosed to the public.'

'Do you know what caused it and where it came from?'

'Yes I do. It was noticed by the Workington Brewery Company that outbreaks of the illness were taking place near to where they owned pubs.'

'You mean that the brewery company was causing the illness? How?'

'Well as a precaution they sent some of their beer off to be analysed and when the results came back it was full of arsenic.'

'Arsenic! They were being poisoned. How did arsenic get into the beer?'

'That's what they wondered, so they tested the sugar which they used and the fault lay with the highest grade sugar that they bought. The sugar company was supposed to be reputable and had supplied them for years.'

'But how did the arsenic get into the sugar?'

'Now let me see if I can remember it right. The government set up a Royal Commission to look into that and so did the Society of Chemists and they found the cause. It seems that the sugar company had not sent sugar but a form of glucose, which is produced by using sulphuric acid.'

'Good grief! They were putting that in beer?'

'Apparently so Tom; it was cheaper and kept their prices down. But in this case the batch had not been processed properly. As a final act in the making of the glucose they had to remove arsenic from it which is a by product of using sulphuric acid; so the 'sugar' they supplied, which was cheap to make, was full of arsenic and ended up in the beer.'

'So people stopped drinking beer.'

'You're right they did. Wouldn't you?'

'No, but I'm teetotal anyway.'

There was a small pause in the conversation, then Ethel laughed.

'Well of course you are! I know that. I was asking what you might call a rhetorical question.'

'So what you are saying is that people went off beer and stopped drinking it.'

'That's right Tom. They started drinking spirits instead and a lot of them were not used to it. They still aren't some of them, and they still don't trust the beer so there's more whisky drunk in this town than in the average if you take my meaning?'

'I do.'

'So now you know.'

'Were there any prosecutions over this?'

'Thomas told me that there were, but I don't know any details; he's more interested in crime than I am I fear.'

'That's as it should be, I think, with his job.'

As an aside it may be borne in mind that the conversation in the back room of 55 Devonshire Street was probably peculiar to its time and place. Workington was a steel-producing town and its workers were now on wartime wages, which were much higher than in pre-war years. For working class men to have the choice of drinking whisky, not the cheapest of spirits on offer, was perhaps an anomaly when compared with most northern industrial towns.

There are many types of patriotism and much of it is shallow. It is easy to wave a flag, sing 'Rule Britannia' and speak of King and Country without knowing much of what it actually means. Worst of this type is the base patriotism of the sort that Dr Johnson had in mind when he declared that patriotism is the last refuge of the scoundrel, meaning that such a person would use his much advertised love of country to trump all arguments against what they said. In some ways it may be that this type does not know what patriotism is, because what they are actually intent on, is justifying their own arguments, prejudices and opinions in reference to a love of country which in fact is no such thing; it is a justification of a certain sort of self love. Surely it must be that the truest patriot is the person who places country first and feels a deep sense of what is good for the nation and its people that is far above personal interests. Such patriotism is selfless, and probably very rare. It is fortunate that the first type is malleable and may be twisted and bent into all sorts of forms by the skilled propagandist. These forces came into play in Workington once again on 24 May when, war or no war, Empire Day was held.

Tom was at work, as was Nellie. Down at the boiler makers the men had begged a couple of hours off to watch the parade on the condition that they would return to work later and make their time up. Margaret and Ethel took the smaller members of their family up to Washington Street to watch the floats go by, but Barwise was much further along the parade route down Finkle Street with his workmates. Needless to say, the patriotism, which was running at very high levels on any Empire day, was doubled and redoubled by the country being engaged in a great war. Barwise had a very bellicose side to his nature and it bubbled to the fore as he stood with Matt Roach outside the Trinity Methodist Church where the pavement was slightly wider and the marchers came down towards them.

All the shop windows were dressed with flags and bunting, pictures of the King and of prominent national figures such as Kitchener, Mr Asquith and Mr Lloyd George. Strings of flags of the nations criss-crossed the street and everyone who could get one licked an ice-cream from Tognarelli's parlour which was besieged with enthusiastic aficionados of their product and which was draped with large Italian flags. The Tognarellis had arrived in town in 1902 to open their establishment and such was the quality of their product that they had flourished and quickly opened several shops round the area. Since Italy had joined in the war on the British side in May 1915 their popularity had grown to astronomic proportions and their ice cream was consumed in direct ratio to this; no special occasion was complete without a Toggy's cornet. As Barwise licked his white ice the head of the parade came down the street led by the Scout groups from round the area, guidons flying and heads held high, marching in step to the music of the Boy's Brigade Band just behind them.

'Aye well good luck to them,' said Matt Roach. 'They're doing a grand job from what I hear.'

'What? Them lads?'

'Yis. They help the police patrol the lanes in the country here about looking for German spies.'

Barwise laughed. 'Have they caught any?'

'Not that I've heard, but they're out in all weathers. They're doing their bit so in my book they're grand lads.'

'Are we doing our bit, Matt?'

'What do you mean?'

'I mean that we're here doing not a lot for the war. We just get up, go to work, go home, have our dinner and go to sleep, then the same the next day. Are we doing our bit? I mean look at you Matt. You're a strong lad, fit and ready enough with your fists; why have you never joined up?'

'The Army you mean?' Matthew Roach rubbed his chin before replying with some gravity. 'Well I'll tell you Barwise that I thought about it. I thought about it a lot. You know that I'm in a reserved occupation?'

Barwise nodded.

'They've done that for a reason. Did you know that production at our factory slowed down early last year? We had about half a dozen of our lads go off to fight; three of them are dead now. I was tempted to go with them as well. I cannot say that banging rivets day in day out is the most interesting job in the world and they wanted me to go. They saw it as a chance to get away you see, to go abroad, see something of the world, and of course to kill a few Germans. It didn't work out that way for them.'

'So why didn't you go?'

'Because I'm doing better here for this country than I can over there. Just think about it. We make boilers. What happens with no boilers? This country runs on steam power Barwise. It needs steam power to make guns and ammunition and ships and all sorts. A lot of skilled craftsmen went into the Army at the start of the war. Do you know they had to bring thousands of them back, because unless they can keep the Army supplied, then we will lose the war. I think it's a sort of balance between men who are needed over there, and men who are needed here, because without us the ones over there will have nothing to fight with.'

The conversation was interrupted as the tramp of marching feet was replaced by the sound of a very loud and professional adult band.

'Clifton Colliery lot!' shouted Matt. 'By God they're good; just listen to that!'

Then men from Clifton almost swaggered in their professional pride as they led a detachment of convalescents in their bright blue uniforms and glaring red ties down Finkle Street with cheers from the crowd fit to blow the nearby roofs off.

'John Peel. Is there any better march?'

'Would you like to go to war Matt?'

'I'm torn Barwise. Really I am. My brother Arthur's gone out, but of course he's a single man and worked on the roads, not in any reserved occupation. I thought of volunteering though my missis was dead against it. But then I felt guilty; not just because of family, but because I thought I'd be letting the country down. Aye, I know its glamorous to go off and maybe get your head blown off, or to come back covered in glory, but I really do think the country needs me to stay here more than it does for me to go abroad. They confirmed that when they made my job a reserved occupation, and let's not forget, yours too.'

Barwise turned and looked at his friend.

'If the war's still on when my birthday comes round I'm joining up. They'll call me.'

'No they won't Barwise. You're a reserved occupation.'

'I think you'll find I'm not.'

'Yes you are. Metal-worker and riveter. You won't even get a call-up.'

'I'll be called up Matt. Just wait and see. The letter will come.'

Matt Roach looked at Barwise curiously. 'You've done something haven't you?'

Barwise merely smiled, but any putative explanation was cut off by the approach of the Dearham United Brass Band, invited down for the occasion to have the honour of leading the Workington Lifeboat float along the route. They set the crowd to bouncing up and down perceptibly as they gave a lively step along to *A Life on the Ocean Wave*. On the float was the white painted lifeboat itself, the upper strake picked out in blue, and a very large Union Jack flying from the rear. In the boat sat the full crew, brave men all, long white oars held aloft, cork lifebelts in place, with the Coxswain sitting by the tiller. It was led by older crewmen with grey beards dressed in oilskins and sou'westers, and pulled by two magnificent dark shire horses. Alongside in blue uniforms marched the reserve crew; all were older men, the young ones having gone to join the Royal Navy.

'Do you want to fight Barwise? Do you want to kill?'

Barwise thought a minute. 'It's not so much the killing. I think I can do that if I have to. That question they ask conchies; what would you do if a German tried to rape your mother? Well I'd kill the German, and I have no doubt about that. But it's more than that. Here we are in the middle of the biggest thing that this country has ever done, and I'm on the sidelines because I'm not old enough. I'm strong enough and I can fight well enough, but I'm not allowed to fight. That does something inside my head and I just know that if I miss it, then I'm going to regret it all my life, whatever else I do.'

'If you put it that way, then I can see it. If that's how you feel then I can't fault you on it.'

'But it's more than that. It's what they've done. The Germans I mean. And what they are; and who we are. They attacked Belgium.'

'What's that to you? You're not a Belgian.'

'Yes I know. But to me that's bullying. For a small nation to just be attacked and taken over by a big bullying aggressive nation is just not acceptable to me. I think there should be law between countries and we should respect each other. I don't want to live in a world where the strong attack the weak and get away with it. It's not right.'

'A bit like me bullying you when you first started.'

Barwise grinned. 'Aye, exactly like that. I was brought up not to bully and to see right and wrong. My mam's very big on that and so is dad. My mam's best friend Ethel is married to a copper. If there's any bother in our area he goes along and sorts it out because that's what he does. He enforces the law. Now that's us, the British in this case. It's our fight because we want to see law and order in our neighbourhood. Belgium has been assaulted and we should stop it; I want to stop it.'

'Your mam and dad might not let you; all they have to do

is tell the authorities you're in a reserved occupation and you'll be turned down.'

'They'll threaten to I have no doubt, but I've got a trick up my sleeve. When the time comes, I'm going if the war's still on. You see there's something else.'

'More? I think you've already said a mouthful. What more is there?'

'Patriotism.'

'Well that goes without saying; take a look around you.'

'No, I don't mean that.' Barwise waved about him. 'This isn't patriotism; this is just show. This is flag waving and singing and shouting like at a football match. No I mean proper patriotism.'

'What's proper patriotism?'

'It's when you love your country and the people in it; you want your best for them all. You want it to be a good place where people can live a decent life in a spot they are proud to be part of. Where they can earn a respectable wage through their own work; bring up their kids knowing they'll get a good education; a place where the rich don't steal everything and where people aren't selfish, but help each other for the good of all. That's the sort of country I want to see and the Germans are the opposite. I know they've got lots of stuff that we have not, but they don't have elections and the Kaiser is just a dictator. I want the British way, and what we want to see to be the way that wins this war.'

'You've thought a lot about this haven't you? You a Socialist? Ramsay McDonald is against the war.'

'I know that, but Arthur Henderson isn't and he's leader now, not McDonald. I've joined the Labour Party, because I think they're going to do great things here when this war's over. Even my dad thinks that.'

'Nay, he's Liberal isn't he?'

'All his life until a couple of years back, but he's joined

Labour since the war started, and mam too.'

'Well, it's your life.'

Matt Roach stopped speaking for a moment and looked as if he was thinking hard, then continued.

'Look Barwise; all this talk about fighting. I know you're game enough, but so are a lot of lads. You're not all that big a lad though, but that's no handicap if you know how to handle yourself. I hear stuff from my brother. Look, would you like to learn to fight properly?'

'How do you mean?'

'I mean do some proper boxing, so that instead of just slinging punches, you know what you're doing.'

'Why should I? I don't want to be a boxer.'

'Hell, I know that. But you do want to fight and that's a rough game, however it's done. I don't know why exactly, but I think it would be a good idea.'

Barwise thought for a minute or two.

'Aye alright seems like a good idea; you worried about me Matthew?'

The older man looked slightly embarrassed, 'Not exactly, but you're a scrawny little bugger and you and me are marras. I just think it would be a good idea.'

'Fair enough. How do I do it?'

'Do you know Jack Smillie?'

'Works a drill in the plate shop.'

'That's him. He's an amateur boxer and a good lad; he's quite well known. If I ask him to do a bit of sparring with you after work for a bit then he will. He'll show you how to look after yourself.'

'Settled then. I'll do it.'

'Good. I'll get it arranged. Now let's enjoy the rest of the show; here's the Border Regiment coming.'

Chapter 13

The Big Push

Across the other side of town Margaret too had treated her brood to Toggy's and they also had enjoyed the parade. There is no need to reprise more of the magnificent spectacle that Workington was capable of putting on at such occasions, but the children made a real contribution to the war effort before they returned to Devonshire Street. On the broad pavement outside St John's Church was *The Tommie's Organ Grinder Party*, with their barrel organ. This group was composed of teachers and girls from Victoria School from over towards Salterbeck, some of whom were known to Ommie. They were dressed in short skirted costumes of outlandish kinds, made from union flags and stripes and multi-coloured material of all sorts. On their heads were strange headdresses, some shakoes, some of decorated straw, some of mob caps and some of handkerchiefs knotted. They looked more like a band of small female brigands from the Balkans than nice girls from back street Workington. The barrel organ was playing 'Soldiers of the King' and the girls sang it very prettily, but it was not long before they were drowned out when they reached the third verse:

> 'War clouds gather over ev'ry land,
> Our flag is threaten'd east and west.
> Nations that we've shaken by the hand
> Our bold resources try to test
> They thought they found us sleeping

thought us unprepar'd,
Because we have our party wars,
But Englishmen unite when they're call'd to fight
The battle for Old England's common cause,
The battle for Old England's common cause.
So when we say that England's master,
Remember who has made her so.
(Refrain)
It's the Soldiers of the Queen, my lads,
Who've been my lads,
Who've seen my lads,
In the fight for England's glory, lads,
When we have to show them what we mean:
And when we sat we've always won,
And when they ask us how it's done,
We'll proudly point to ev'ry one
Of England's soldiers of the Queen!
It's the Queen!'

A couple of the girls looked slightly disconcerted as the words of the song brought forth a strange kind of growl and then wild cheering as the crowd took up the chorus and utterly drowned the small choir out. The mistress at the barrel organ just smiled and motioned to two small girls behind her instrument who raised a cloth banner between them, which read 'Give us your money!' They were collecting to send comforts to the troops in the trenches, and particularly to the men of the Border Regiment from the town. Everyone in the crowd knew that Victoria School would be sending out hundreds of packets of cigarettes, twists of tobacco, pipes, sweets, socks, and whatever else they thought the men 'out there' would like. They also knew that the men appreciated it, because they kept writing home to the 'Star man' who edited the letters in the local paper, expressing how much they liked getting these small thoughtful gifts from the people back home. It made them feel cared for and not forgotten. Unsurprisingly, the money chinked plentifully into the collection tins; William, Joe and Ettie were each furnished by Margaret with a penny for the tins, whilst Ommie augmented hers and gave threepence. The day served its purpose well and when the parade was done all went home full of high spirits and great hopes for the future; the country would win the war of course, and it would be done this summer.

The high optimism continued across the town and indeed the whole country until Tuesday 6 June when newspaper boys ran through the streets with copies fresh off the press shouting 'Lord Kitchener dead! Lord Kitchener dead!'

The ship taking him to Russia on a top-secret mission, HMS Hampshire, had struck a mine and sunk with almost no survivors.

As the news spread small knots of people gathered in the streets talking in hushed voices and many were in tears as word of the national disaster sank in to them. The status of the Secretary for War was so god-like that all hopes and thoughts of victory were inextricably linked to the myth of his infallibility. In Oxford Street a man shouted hysterically 'We've lost the war!' but one of his friends, a man who had known him all his life, slapped him and told him savagely to 'Shut thee gob or arl lamp thew yan.' All flags stood at half-mast and a miasma of gloom spread and became universal. In the next few days was a national outpouring of sorrow over 'the lost chief' and up at the Bankfield Hospital one of Nellie's fellow nurses told her that she 'knew Britain would win the war while Kitchener was alive, but now he's gone.' Nellie told her not to be so daft, because he was only one man, however great, and that of course we could still win the war. The following day in the newspapers people read that a man in Yorkshire, on hearing the news of K of K's death, had committed suicide. It was a national shock that someone who seemed immortal and invincible with almost superhuman powers, should be gone in such a fashion. There were dark murmurings of conspiracies; others that he was not dead at all, but had gone undercover and would reappear to lead the armies of the Tsar to defeat the Germans, and this was especially popular when no body was recovered. There was no grave for Kitchener of Khartoum and the gloom overspread every household in the land, including that of Tom and Margaret who somehow thought that they had lost something of themselves with this particular death.

In some ways the dreadful news that Britain's greatest soldier had drowned, was of use in overshadowing what would otherwise have been the main centre of public attention. The government extended the Military Service Act so that all married men up to the age of 41 were now automatically deemed to be in the Army unless they could provide grounds for exemption. There were also rumours that before the war was over there would have to be conscription for men of a much more advanced age than this. It was doubtful, however, that things would come to such a pass, because the country now picked itself up out of mourning, as everyone knew that 'the big push' was about to happen. There was no security about it at all and talk of 'The Somme Punch' was all over the place. The need for security was hardly perceived because such a mighty force of British troops was massing for an all out attack that the Germans would never been able to stop it. Just a few more weeks and the war would be over and the beastly Hun would be taught a lesson that he would never forget. On Saturday 1 July the stage was set for the bloody apotheosis of the greatest war in history, and the country waited for news of inevitable victory. On Sunday morning the News of the World screamed out in banner headlines the tidings of greatness:

BRITISH ADVANCE.
16 MILES OF GERMAN FRONT TRENCHES STORMED.
THE DAY GOES WELL FOR OUR HEROIC TROOPS.

Over the course of the next few days it became obvious that whoever wrote this had either lied or been greatly deceived. Slowly the full and horrendous scope of what had happened revealed itself in the casualty lists in the local newspapers and the scale of it was sobering. The 11th battalion of the Border Regiment, the famous Lonsdale Pals, had gone over the top at 7.30am, and, as ordered, had marched towards the German lines. It had been a beautiful clear summer morning and as the men climbed out of their trenches, the guns ceased to fire and all fell silent; even the birds began to sing in the morning sunshine. The men had been told to expect little or no opposition for the terrific week long bombardment would have destroyed the enemy. Some smoked, but all advanced in straight lines, rifles at the high port and reached about halfway across no-man's land. Then the enfilade fire of several machine guns began to criss-cross the battlefield. Some 800 men and 28 officers had walked forwards; they did not turn and run; they knew that Cumbrians do not do such a thing. Instead they seemed almost to hunch forward as if leaning into a hailstorm, and marched doggedly onwards into the face of the German fire as their marras fell around them in swathes. If bravery and stoutness of heart could have brought them to the enemy trenches then they would have won the day. If they had only run straight at the enemy when they left their trenches instead of walking, they would have rewritten history. Duty, courage, and honour kept them advancing, and within fifteen minutes more than 500 of them were either dead or wounded and 25 of the officers; Colonel Machell, their commanding officer was among them, not prepared to let his men do what he would not do himself; men could do no more. Other battalions of the regiment also took part and suffered. Fifteen men from Workington were killed that morning, three from John Street, just around the corner from Tom and Margaret's house. The shock was profound, and mirrored all across Cumberland. Door knockers where the dead men had lived were wrapped in black crepe, wreaths hung at the doors, and the curtains closed. Wives, daughters and sweethearts appeared in black, and older men walked with solemn faces and black armbands. As the days went by it became obvious that the promised victory was not about to happen and that indeed something else was taking place. The nature of the war now hit home and it hit hard; people began to be introspective and thoughtful, perhaps to wonder if it was all worth it; this was slaughter. In church the women gathered round the bereaved mothers, offering what comfort they could, but it was little enough in the face of such loss. Barwise turned seventeen on 16 July and still the battle raged on, and from the tone of the newspapers it was a victory and gained a few square miles from the enemy, but the cost of it was appalling. Stories of men kicking footballs over into no-man's land might have been calculated to foster the idea of war as a sport, or a game that must be played, but in the Little household such tales met with short shrift.

'It's ridiculous. Who do they think they're talking to? Children?'

'I agree Margaret, but a lot of people do think that way.'

'Do you think it's because we've never gone in for any sports Tom? I mean, that we don't understand it. There's men getting killed every day by the hundred, sometimes by the thousands.'

'Well we're a bit older than we were, middle aged in fact, but I can't remember seeing life as a game of football ever. I've always been too busy working; and so have you. Maybe that's why it seems foreign to us. But death is another matter, and on such a scale as we are witnessing. It's not something you'd see down Lonsdale Park on a Saturday afternoon, not that I ever go there; it's more like mass organised murder.'

'Barwise is seventeen, Tom. What if he has to go there?'

'Pah! He won't. He won't be old enough for the Army for another year. It'll be done by then.'

'That's what you said last year, but it isn't. It worries me.'

'Aye lass. It worries me too, but I'm sure it'll be all done by the end of the year.'

'That poor woman in John Street.'

'Oh, now, that was bad. To get a letter saying that he had received a 'blighty wound' was alright and coming home, and then…'

'It was the Chaplain wrote to tell her that he had been killed in action. I hear he was such a nice lad. He was only 25.'

'A lot of them are nice lads. But the Germans don't care. Harold from Moss Bay Road was a real good lad, but he's been missing since 1 July. There's another from Wilson Street missing too.'

'Did you see that letter in the Star?'

'Which one?'

'From the Sergeant.'

'No. I haven't read it all yet.'

'Let me read it to you.'

Margaret riffled through the pages of the *Workington Star and Harrington Guardian* and read:

'... we have had a terrible smashing up; all our officers either killed or wounded. It's been an awful time and Workington has suffered heavily. We were one of the first battalions to go forward and we were mown down like grass. I don't think it will last much longer as the German losses must be terrible and the sooner it is over, the better for everyone. I hope I may never have an experience like it again.'

Tom's face was solemn.

'Workington has suffered heavily. That young chap you've bought stockings off in Jane Street has been killed too.'

Margaret began to cry.

'Why whatever's wrong? I know it's upsetting Margaret, but you've no need to get so worked up. None of ours are touched and none of our friends.'

'It's this bit. Just this bit.'

Tom read, and a tear came in his eye too.

'They were singing *John Peel* as they advanced. Oh dear, oh dear. All brave lads. All brave men I should say. I hope this is all worth what it's costing.'

This question was not unique to the Little household; there

were many many people asking themselves exactly the same thing and the mood of the nation paused to think of its dead sons, and to query why it was happening. This may have lain behind a decision by the government, or rather by the newly appointed Secretary for War, Mr Lloyd George, to release an official film. The War Department had been so confident of victory that they had commissioned a film director called Geoffrey Malins to make a movie record of the battle so that it could be recorded for posterity as a source of national pride. He and his assistant, a Mr McDowell had been given license to go everywhere and film whatever they wanted. The film was now to be released for an invited audience on 10 August and then in the following weeks, the general public could pay to go and see it in their local cinemas. Twenty million people did so, and of course the Littles were among them. They chose to walk down to Hagg Hill on Friday 1 September to where there was a small alleyway with a door between two shops; it looked an innocuous sort of place compared to what lay behind the façade of assorted emporia. Down the alleyway the audience entered the Hippodrome Theatre, which had been a music hall built in 1880 and it really was rather grand. It had been converted into a cinema in 1912, and Margaret and Omega had been there many times, occasionally with Ethel. Outside on the pavement was a large two-sided billboard:

> *The Battle of the Somme*
> *The War Office Official Film*
> *In five reels*
> You see your own flesh and blood, these soldiers who march before you, and there are thousands of faces, each of which will be recognised by someone. You see the shells bursting in rapid succession, within easy walking distance, so near was the camera to the German lines. These pictures were

taken under actual fire. Think what risk the brave men who secured them must have run, in order that we at home might see for ourselves what present-day warfare means. This film will do more to hearten the people and hasten the day of final and complete victory over our enemies than will all the newspapers and all the books ever printed.

The narrow entrance passage meant that it was not the first choice of many people, but they liked the faded grandeur of the interior, the space, which could seat 600 customers, and the fact that it was possible to actually get tickets. Tom, Margaret, Omega and her husband Stephen, Barwise, Jack and Nellie all sat together and watched the film, while a pianist at the front played mood music as she always did, to help interpret the action. She was not to play for long as she had not seen it before and the piano stopped suddenly and did not start again. For the first time in history the war came to the audience at home.

Life behind the trenches no longer had to be imagined as it could be seen with one's own eyes. Battalions of men came into view smiling in great spirits, waving their new tin hats as they went towards the enemy, full of hope and optimism. The spirit was such that men in the audience cheered and women clapped. The huge guns were seen firing their lethal loads at the Germans, and scenes of desolation showed the effects of artillery on the ground where the battles had been fought. Then came a scene where men waited to go over the top, and as the camera whirled, the word was given and the men launched themselves after their officer heading for the foe with bayonets fixed. This was too much to bear and every man in the cinema was on his feet cheering loudly whilst women wept at the courage of the soldiers on the screen. The cheer was choked off immediately as one of the attackers fell back, and though it was not clear if he was dead, the mood fell solemn.

Then came the moment – that moment.

The camera focused on one British soldier and as it did so, women screamed and several fainted.

'My God! He's dead!'

On the screen was what had once been a living, breathing man, but who in a moment had been torn from life and the world by a bullet or by shrapnel. A deep sense of awe hung over the auditorium, such as is more often seen in the presence of death at funerals. This was no voyeurism, but a feeling of respect for a man who had given his life for his country. If anything, what was engendered in the minds of most people who saw it, was a determination that such sacrifice should not be in vain. The overall impression created in the collective mind of the nation was of the sheer optimism and cheerfulness of the men who had been sent overseas to fight. Letting them down was simply unthinkable, and as the films showed, two or three times a day in cinemas up and down the country through August, September and into October, the national mood changed, sobered by the hand of death. It was no longer the naïve and flag waving shallow patriotism of the early days of the war. There awoke a grim determination to see this thing through and by hook or by crook, the war was going to be won.

The impact on Barwise Little was akin to the effect of plunging a white-hot bar of steel into a cold-water bath; the sentiments he had expressed to Matthew Roach were now defended, case-hardened, into absolute determination. He would not tell his parents, but when the day came, if the war still continued until his eighteenth birthday then he was going to join the Border Regiment and neither Hell nor high water was going to stop him. For the moment, several times a week after work he sparred bare-fist with Jack Smillie who taught him well; it was a good outlet for the head of aggression that he felt building up. It was well for Margaret's peace of mind that he told her nothing of this, and would not, unless the necessity arose.

Friday 8 September was a dull day at Moss Bay steelworks and Thomas was following his routine tasks in his habitual and methodical manner. He had just finished making up a small train of wagons for the locomotive to come and take away, and then unhooked Skiddaw to take him back to his stable. Round the end of the last wagon came Mr Harrop, the Works Manager, and he had a strange look on his face that Tom could not interpret. He asked Tom to come with him to his office, but would answer no questions, just that there was someone in the office he needed to see. Once they reached the door to the manager's little room, Mr Harrop stopped.

'No Tom; I won't come in. You go in and see your brother.'

'My brother?'

'Aye.'

Mystified and without time to think, Tom opened the door and went into the office; there was his younger brother William, portly, usually jolly and now standing with a face that spoke of woe and sorrow. Mr Harrop did not follow him.

'Will; what on earth are you doing here?'

'It's Joe, Tom; he's had an accident, a bad one.'

'An accident; what do you mean? What sort of accident?'

To Tom's alarm, tears started in William's eyes and he began to cry.

'He's dead?'

William did not answer but nodded and sat down with his head in his hands. Tom stood for a moment, not knowing what to do. In these situations human beings often do not react as they are supposed to in novels, because in reality they may be told things which bounce straight off their conscious understanding, and they take time to sink in. Blinking hard, his head full of things he could not articulate, Tom sat down beside William and put his arm round his shoulders, comforting.

Chapter 13 — The Big Push

'What's happened Will? How is Joe dead?'

To understand fully what had happened to Joseph Little it is necessary to backtrack a little to 1899 when Barwise Little (the elder) had died at West End Farm in Edderside leaving the farm not to his eldest son, but to his widow Ann, known to Margaret as 'Missis' when she became employed there in 1894. The farm had been quite a prosperous concern and Missis continued to manage it until 1903 when she was well into her 70s and decided to retire. West End farm was, for her, a place where Joe and his wife Agnes, could bring up their children, but Missis wanted a quieter life and went to live with her bachelor son William, a clerk of works, in the small village of Bothel. Some time after Joe had taken over the farm, a scheme had been mounted to build a railway line up the Cumbrian coast between Maryport and Silloth, linking two prosperous docks with Workington and Whitehaven. The proposed route passed through the village of Allonby and right by the bottom of West End farm; it was a sure fire winner and many local people invested money into the projected company. Joe had been so sure of its success that he had mortgaged the farm and put his savings into shares, purchasing the astronomical amount of £11,000 worth. He assured Tom that he was going to be very rich and then he would be able to increase his farm on a grand scale; not only that but he would buy Tom another place and re-establish him as a farmer. The scheme had failed; the money was eaten up in surveyors' and lawyers' fees, and the investments collapsed. Joe lost everything and the farm was repossessed by the bank; he was reduced to supporting himself and his family as a farm labourer. This was why he had been carrying out a task he would formerly have delegated to an employee. Now he was dead at only 56.

'It was a horse Tom. He got on the horse, but it took fright and bolted; somehow he fell off and got dragged some distance, and died right away.'

'My God!' said Tom appalled. 'How's poor Aggie?'

'That's the thing Tom; it's like she's made of wood. She hasn't cried or anything like that, but sits expressionless and staring; she won't talk to anyone.'

'Where is she now?'

'She's gone to be with her mam and dad at Edderside with the children as well.'

'Horses don't just bolt Will. What happened?'

'Apparently Joe was riding the horse down the road to a lower field and an automobile went past; the engine backfired and the horse just took off. It's a young horse only recently trained; the Army has taken all the best ones for France.'

'So an accident. A stupid, stupid accident.'

'Are you alright?'

'Aye; I am. I won't be when it sinks in, but I am. We'd best let Mr Harrop have his office back. Come on Will.'

When Tom opened the door Mr Harrop was still there waiting.

'I'm sorry for your loss Tom.' Then he became slightly awkward in manner, but determined to speak. 'Look Tom I know what it's like to lose a brother. I don't want to see you here today and in fact I don't want to see you here next week. I'll see thee a week Monday and you won't lose by it. I'll see to't horse. Go home Tom and see to what needs doing.'

It was then that it hit Tom and he doubled over sobbing and it was William's turn to comfort him. After a few minutes Tom recollected himself and knew that he could not walk back home weeping. In this society men were not supposed to cry in public; he did that with Margaret in the front room at Devonshire Street whilst William spent the night on a shakey-down in the back. The next morning the two brothers went back to Edderside to settle Joe's small affairs and to arrange his funeral. It was a weeping overcast day in the churchyard at Holme St Cuthbert and the grave lay open for its final occupant when Joe joined his parents to rest until the end of the world. The Littles were there in force except the very young ones who had been left at home with Ommie. John Adams and Nancy came up from Dearham as did Margaret's brothers Thomas and Johnny. Annie Eleanor and her husband John Metcalfe came from Maryport. Margaret, dressed in black, comforted Agnes who was inconsolable and sobbing; a widow while yet young. She would now have to stay with her parents in their tied cottage and bring up her children in even more reduced circumstances whilst she resumed the profession which she was very good at when Margaret met her, and went back to being a milkmaid. Strangely enough she was able to command a good wage for this, because so many local women had flocked to the munitions factories that there was a shortage of farm servants. This cut the last ties that the Littles had with Edderside, though it remained their spiritual home for many years. Agnes though was to find that time is a great healer and three years later married a good man, for thankfully such are not rare on the Solway Plain. There would be no more rabbits sent down from the farm to Devonshire Street though; and the time was coming when that would matter; food was getting very expensive and sometimes hard to find.

Chapter 14

The Red Cross

It was not exactly that Nellie was bored, because her work at Workington Infirmary kept her very busy. Her problem, which niggled at the back of her mind all the time, and especially in the wee small hours of the morning, was that it was too easy. That is perhaps the wrong description for a nurse's work, but it was not so much the work as the *type* of work. Miss Winter was quite aware that Nellie was feeling under-used, although privately she thought that she was doing a good full time job of nursing where she was. Being of a flexible mind, however, she did understand the younger woman's wish to play a more significant part in the war effort. At the beginning of December 1916 she received an official request from number 4 VAD Unit, which had been organised to cover this area of West Cumberland. Mrs Florence Wilson from Stainburn had a lot of powerful friends in the area and she had been approached by one of them, Mr FW Iredale, who owned Bankside Mansion, just along from the Infirmary, and he had offered the use of it to the Red Cross Organisation as an auxiliary hospital. They were prepared to take it on, but in partnership with the VAD, to supply the numbers of staff required. It was not one house but two rather magnificent semi-detached houses that looked like a mansion, which had been built some years before by rich ironmasters. Mr Iredale, whose interests lay in brewing rather than in iron, no longer needed such a large establishment and resolved that its best use was in helping to take care of wounded men from France. Mrs Wilson was to be the Commandant of the new hospital and act as her own Matron; there would be two trained Red Cross nurses and other paid staff, but this was where the letter to Miss Winter became relevant. When she had read the letter, Miss Winter thought for a few minutes then sent for Nellie. Once she had arrived, she told her to sit down and got straight to the point.

'There's a plan to make Bankfield Mansion down the road into an auxiliary hospital. There'll be fifty beds and other facilities, and they hope to open this coming February. That is where you come in, because I've been asked to supply a local trained nurse on secondment to make up their complement. There are a lot of young ladies volunteering to do what they think of as nursing work, but who don't know a bedpan from a broom handle, however good their hearts might be and they'll need guiding. There will be two Red Cross nurses there full time but they will need help to start with. I have been asked to supply one trained nurse to help instruct all the volunteers they will be having, because the permanent two will be overwhelmed. I want you there.'

'May I ask why me Matron?'

'Certainly you may; it's because I think highly of you; I also think highly of your mother and I know you'll do a good job and not let me down, or the infirmary. Your standards are high and sometimes Nellie, you make the job look easy.'

Nellie smiled, 'It's not easy though Matron; it never is, I think.'

'No it never is,' said the older woman ruefully, 'but perhaps that's age speaking. You'd have to live in at the hospital, but I don't suppose you'd mind that. You would not have to share with your sisters any more.'

'I don't mind that Matron; it's cosy, but I know what you mean. I am getting a bit old to be sharing with them. Anyway I think my mother will be glad to get some space.'

'You may be right there. Anyway the placement starts in January, before any patients arrive, so you'll be able to help train the volunteers well in advance. The period of the secondment will be six months initially, though it may be extended if they need you. Your job will always be open here. Would you like to do this thing?'

'I would Matron; yes please.'

'I thought you might. You've been chafing at the bit since Carlisle and I know you want to do more. This is your opportunity. One more thing.'

'Yes Matron?'

'You'll be working for the Red Cross, but you belong here; you'll wear your own uniform; they're organised on much more military lines than us, so if you're not dressed like them they might be less inclined to browbeat you; if they do.'

Nellie smiled, 'Thank you Matron.'

'And thank you Nellie. I know you won't let me down. However, I'm not quite finished. You've been here now since you were fourteen, I think?'

'Yes Matron, I started as a probationer when I left school.'

'Now you're 21 and have passed your exams. You also have letters of commendation from a surgeon up in Carlisle…'

'Yes, Mr Edwards.'

'I had forgotten him. Yes, from Mr Edwards and a Mr Plugg; also from the Commandant of Murrell Hill, Mrs Bennet-Brown. In addition to this you have a certificate stating that you passed a course in wound treatment with credit, and to this I must add a recommendation from myself.'

'A recommendation Matron?'

'Yes Nellie. I put this to the hospital board yesterday and they agreed that in war conditions it would be absurd not to make you up a grade, so let me congratulate you Sister Little. You have performed very well Nellie and done this place a lot of credit.'

Thanks are never superfluous and Nellie was quite overcome with her promotion, her immediate reaction being to cry, such a surprise as it was, but the tears were of pleasure. Margaret had entrusted the training of her daughter to Matron Winter and she had done her proud. So it was that in January 1917 Nellie started work in the fledgling auxiliary hospital that was taking shape in Upper Workington. She moved into a small room up in the attic, formerly a servant's bedchamber, where there were two beds; she no longer lived at home though it was just down the road. Men were all over the place banging and sawing, building, putting in partitions and bringing in all sorts and shapes of donated beds whilst supplies of all kinds were being brought in by the ton and carried to where they had to be. The whole place was like an ants' nest with occupants rushing hither and thither in a frenetic rush to get the establishment ready to receive its first patients in mid February. Nellie had no time to think of anything but work as she stayed long hours at the task of getting beds and equipment ready and instructing the new VAD girls in the same. Then there was the instruction side of things where they had to be shown how to change bandages, how to give bed washes, and how to try to maintain a professional distance between themselves and their patients who might get too attached to them. The strangest part of it for Nellie was where she undertook the compulsory showing of photographs of some very nasty wounds to the trainee nurses. Even though black and white these images caused some of the girls to blench and feel sick, which made her to wonder how they were ever going to cope with real injuries and huge open wounds. She need not have worried for she was under a misapprehension as she was to find out before too long. Until the patients arrived she worked until she almost dropped with fatigue and positively fell into bed each night, only to get up and start the same thing next day.

Bankfield was not a true military hospital; it was an auxiliary hospital organised and run by the Red Cross. It was this that made quite a difference to how Nellie saw her role in the war. It had been clear from the first major battles that there were not enough hospital facilities in the UK to cope with the numbers of wounded coming back from France and so the government had asked the Red Cross and the St John's Ambulance people to set up auxiliary hospitals in Britain. They had done this quickly but effectively. Each auxiliary hospital had a Commandant, often a local woman of influence who organised the administration of everything save medical and nursing matters. Under her were usually a Quartermaster who saw to supplies, a Matron who organised the nurses, and then the doctors who organised themselves; sometimes the Commandant, if she was a ball of energy, acted as her own Matron as in the case of Bankfield. The nursing staff were, at least initially, a thin sprinkling of trained nurses who were seconded or transferred from local hospitals, which was where Nellie came in, and the members of the local VAD who were trained in first aid and home nursing. Many of the people who worked with Nellie were local women who volunteered the hours they could commit to away from their day jobs or looking after their families. There were dozens and dozens of them, enthusiastic, patriotic and well meaning. There was one paid cook for the hospital, but the kitchen was always stuffed with volunteers helping out, whilst the hospital itself was kept spotless by a small army of women who came in to clean. It is well said that many hands make light work and this was very true with the bringing to readiness of this new facility. Bankfield was ready for its patients two days before they were due to be, and so the Commandant proudly informed the Commanding Officer of Fusehill Military Hospital in Carlisle. There were operations ongoing at the Somme where the British army was attempting to consolidate some advantages they had gained on the heights above the River Ancre so the flow of wounded to the acute hospitals was steady and Fusehill was glad to transfer some of their convalescents out. The first batch of recovering men arrived on Thursday 8 February, and this was when Nellie's mind again began to be troubled.

Not being a military hospital, the soldiers who came to recover from their wounds were not under military discipline, and not surprisingly they grew very attached to the place and the people. In Nellie's mind there was no problem with any of this, and she was quite comfortable in her little room and happy with her room mate, Alice Burnett, who was lovely and easy to get on with.

Nellie's patients did not have life-threatening injuries; they were past that. They might have lost an arm or leg or received a bad wound, but that was dealt with in one of the big acute military hospitals that had sprung up like mushrooms around the country; Bankfield was a satellite of the hospitals in Carlisle. Once the patients were out of danger in the acute hospitals they were occupying beds that were badly needed for critically wounded men; this was where places like Bankfield came in. The atmosphere was safe, homely and there was plenty of good food, recreational facilities and a town which welcomed the wounded soldiers with open hearts and arms. In their bright blue uniforms they were conspicuous in the town when recovered enough to go out and were treated like heroes, which undoubtedly they were. As far as Nellie was concerned, she changed bed linen, gave blanket baths, took temperatures, changed bandages, sat up with patients who needed observation, and very occasionally acted as a theatre nurse in the one operating room that was not much in use and only there for emergency. Much of what she did could be done by the VADs and immediately some of them came into her mind. Take Dinah Brown from Marsh Side; she was intelligent, articulate, and very able. During the day she worked in a shop in Station Road, but every second week, every day she left work at five o'clock with the blessing of her boss and put in four hours of work at the hospital. She was not a trained nurse, but she did a neat bandage and could make a bed fit for Matron's approval as well as Nellie. Then there was Mary Lister whom Nellie knew through friends. By day she was a kitchen maid in a hotel. By night she gave up three hours of her own time to be a kitchen maid at the hospital. They were people of great heart and noble mind, prepared to put themselves out to give what help they could to soldiers in need and wanted nothing in return save the knowledge that they had made a difference; that they had contributed. In her mind Nellie almost felt guilty at her own feelings, for she knew that she had misunderstood the purpose of Bankfield; she had wanted to care for wounded soldiers, but her sense of mission goaded her to do more. As a Sister she had considerable authority over the VAD volunteers though many of them knew her, because her ability was recognised and respected. Sometimes she felt as though she were there more for reassurances than anything else; the presence of nursing Sisters made the men feel cared for, but simple tasks like the fomentation of an eye were sufficient to bring the feeling that she had done something extraordinary that day, though she knew she had not.

There were fifty men in the hospital at any one time and as varied a group of people as may be found anywhere. The only thing that united them was their loathing of the garish blue uniform that they had to wear with its splayed white lapels and bright red tie. The uniform itself was just about tolerable until it was washed, then the colour ran and became patchy, and the material, being a sort of flannelette, shrank away from its lining when washed and formed some grotesque contours which made them look ungainly and downright comic when required to parade. Parades were occasionally held in the grounds of the mansion, but not very often, which was probably as well considering that when it first happened in February the men had looked round at each other and someone had remarked what a bunch of clowns they looked like, then somebody else had started to sing:

'We are Fred Karno's army
The ragtime infantry
We cannot shoot we cannot fight
What ruddy use are we
And when we get to Berlin
The Kaiser he will say
Achtung! mein gott!
What a ruddy fine lot
Are the ragtime infantry
We fought in many trenches
From Calais to Rangoon
Made love to many wenches
Some white, some black, some broon
And when we're back in blighty
On merry old England's shore
We'll go to Piccadilly
And find another bore.'

With fifty of them roaring it out with broad grins there was not much that could be done to stop them, but it did make plain why the Army preferred military discipline in their hospitals. As these men healed and recovered from loss of blood it was necessary to look after them, to help them regain strength, to begin rehabilitation, and often give them some kind of therapy to help their physical recovery. To this end the hospital employed the services of a full time masseuse, Mrs McKusker, whose dedication was not in question, but whose approach was dreaded by those she served; she laid them out on an altar to Lupe, the muse of pain, and their sacrifices were agonising. The nights were worse, for when the men were asleep their unquiet minds would roam across the sea to France and Belgium and screams would echo down the corridor of Bankfield Mansion. The cries were unsettling, some of them shouting at friends to keep their heads down, some for help, and others for their mothers. All that the night nurses and volunteers could do was to rush to the bedside of the man having the nightmare and rouse him soothingly, releasing him from the horrors he was experiencing, and allowing him to wake up and let the shaking stop. The aspect of this that Nellie found most hard to bear was their shame that in their sleep they had 'let the side down' for they most assuredly had not, and she learned to tell them so until they could go back to sleep holding a human hand for comfort.

There was, of course, a constant round of bed making and linen changing, cleaning, stump dressing, bandage winding and unwinding. Then the men had to be kept busy and even entertained with sports such as croquet, billiards, tennis, film showings and even concerts from local groups of volunteers. From somewhere a donated motor charabanc appeared, so Bankfield had its own full time and unpaid Chauffeuse, Miss Heather Hamilton. She drove them to the beach to frolic at St Bees or Allonby, to museums, to the Lakes, and of course to concerts in local theatres and music halls where the seats, for them, were free. Nellie was engaged in a worthy task, and having committed to Matron Winter that she would do it for six months, she set to do it as well as she could. At night her thoughts made her head feel as if it was in need of a safety valve ready to blow off surplus steam, or to explode. In the coming months she had cause to congratulate herself on sparing her family the need to provide for her, for at a government approved hospital she at least had the benefit of three square meals a day.

The opening of the Bankfield Hospital was not the biggest aspect of the war that affected Workington, or indeed Britain, in February 1917. On 1 February 1917 by order of the Kaiser, Germany resumed the unrestricted submarine warfare that had been stopped back in 1915 after the sinking of the Lusitania. They had 105 submarines ready for action and in the first month they sank 500,000 tons of shipping, the same in March then 860,000 tons in April. Soon a quarter of all ships heading for Britain were being sunk. The effect on food supplies was almost immediate as prices shot up. Not unnaturally, great indignation was caused by this, because the government had set up, under the Defence of the Realm Act, a list of official prices that should be paid for various goods. In Maryport at the Christmas Market in 1916 farmers had raised the price of geese to the ridiculous level of 1/3d per pound. The official price was supposed to be nine pence a pound and a group of housewives got together and loudly declared that they would not touch it at that price; word had spread and the boycott became general. The farmers, defeated, gave in and sold the meat at the price that it should have been; a sixty percent reduction. In the case of potatoes, however, the matter was more serious. Bread consumption had been going down because most wheat was imported from the USA and ships were being sunk carrying a lot of it. Potatoes were now the staple diet of the poor and all sorts of people had been putting out booklets and even films to show people how to make nourishing meals from potatoes. Margaret and Omega had been amused one night in the Carnegie cinema by the antics of one Mary Noggs who spied on her neighbour to ascertain how she managed to put such huge dumplings in front of her husband every night for dinner. It was a great puzzle until she found some potato peelings and spied through her neighbour's window as she grated some spuds and flour into a bowl and mixed it up with egg to make a huge dumpling. Omega thought Mary a great ignoramus for not knowing how to make a potato dumpling in the first place, and Margaret was of firm opinion that all she had to do was ask. Anyway if the neighbour had been spying through the window like that she'd have seen her and asked her to come in for a cup of tea.

Part of a letter from Nancy Adams to her daughter in January made clear that the incident at Christmas had emboldened some of the women in Maryport and made them realise their power. She had gone down to the market on Thursday 18 January to see what she could find, food being in short supply in Dearham too, and was obviously much taken by what she had seen. The first part of the letter was routine enquiries after family and health, but then Margaret's mother went on:

'…then I went to the John Street market to buy a few things and especially to see if I could get some potatoes but I found that the farmers were asking 2/- a stone! I mean the official price is supposed to be 1/- and last week it was 1/9d, so I just stood looking at the price ticket wondering what to do when a woman began to argue with the farmer about his price. He wouldn't budge but neither would she. A lot of other women came along and started shouting that they had families to feed and that he was greedy because the legal price was a shilling; well they used some language I won't repeat but I'm sure you can imagine what I mean. Then somebody saw the town crier Pattinson Lowther standing on the corner of Curzon Street and they had a word with him; I mean he must have agreed with them because he started going round shouting,

"*Oyez Oyez! Mothers and wives of soldiers! You are requested not to pay anything like 2/- a stone for potatoes while your husbands and sons are fighting for King and Country."*

The farmers did not like it at all but they could not stop him and some decided to sell at 1/- a lb and the women accepted that and they quickly sold out. But most of the farmers decided that they were going to take their potatoes home and that was when the trouble started. There was some more screaming and shouting and some men got involved and a fight started. Stalls were overturned and people helped themselves to potatoes. There were boys stuffing their pockets and running off and girls with hatfuls heading for home shrieking like little demons. The police arrived and everyone dispersed but there were quite a few bloody faces...

...here in Dearham a farmer, whom I will not name though you probably can guess, left his potatoes in the fields and when he was asked why he did not lift them for sale he declared that he could not get any labourers to do the job as they were all asking too much so he would let them rot in the field. That was a bit much for many of us and we told him that if this was the case we would lift them for him, so we did. There were dozens of people from the village all digging potatoes but he called the police. They have a job to do of course and we did not blame them but there's no police station here, and being decent men they told us that they knocked off at dusk and there'd be no-one watching at night for rotting potatoes. If anything there were more people out at night because they had children holding bicycle lamps while they dug; and there were quite a few hot potato suppers held round the village I can tell you. Your father does not regard it as theft because the farmer had said they could rot, so in this case, the Lord helps those who help themselves.'

Quite obviously the housewives of Maryport were not going to accept what they saw as war profiteering by the farmers, and news of their stand, and the 'Maryport potato riots' spread until there were similar scenes at Carlisle and Keswick markets the following week. The serious side to the affair now was that some soldiers joined in on the side of the housewives, farmers were assaulted and the contents of their stalls were looted. It might have made the government all the more nervous because on the other side of Europe, in St Petersburg, similar scenes were being played out by hungry people and the consequences were much more dire. In the case of Dearham it did not go so far, but encouraged by their success with potatoes declared redundant, they extended their activities to fields where the farmers had not abandoned their crops and began to steal, even enlisting the help of the local scout troop to keep watch. This, of course, was a different matter which the police could not ignore. Driving up quickly from Maryport in an automobile they got past the scout cordon in the dark and captured four villagers who were not quick enough to get away. Thankfully Margaret's parents were not among them as they did not approve of stealing; the captured felons appeared at Maryport Magistrate's Court and were fined ten shillings each which was both understanding and fair for hungry people; theft when hungry is still theft and the law is the law. The 1916 potato harvest had been very poor indeed, so they were in short supply, as was the supply of food in the whole country. Hunger began to bite across the land, although the worst effects were held off by the fact that spring came quickly and the growing season began early. The U-boat campaign bit deeply and although the people did not know it, the government did; there were about six weeks of food left in Britain by the end of February 1917. The price might be regulated, but getting food was expensive, and difficult.

Margaret was having trouble feeding her family, but managing to scrape by because Tom earned enough and was still receiving vegetables in exchange for manure. Nancy was at Gretna and Nellie was at the hospital so there were two less mouths to feed. Barwise was earning his keep, as was Jack, which left only Ommie, Ettie, William and Joe as non-productive; their combined income was enough to support the inhabitants of number 55 Devonshire Street even at wartime prices. It was much harder on households where there were only the mother and father and a number of small children. The Reverend Croft knew this too and on Sunday 25 February he preached a sermon that made an impression on Margaret and on all who heard it. He told them that he might have the cure of souls for his parish, but he knew that souls have bodies too, and bodies must eat if they were to survive. This was a problem that Jesus had faced and the solution that he found was to be read by all in the Bible.

'You will find this in Matthew 14, 14–21, though it is in all the four gospels:

> [14] *And Jesus went forth, and saw a great multitude, and was moved with compassion toward them, and he healed their sick.*
> [15] *And when it was evening, his disciples came to him, saying, This is a desert place, and the time is now past; send the multitude away, that they may go into the villages, and buy themselves victuals.*
> [16] *But Jesus said unto them, They need not depart; give ye them to eat.*
> [17] *And they say unto him, We have here but five loaves, and two fishes.*
> [18] *He said, Bring them hither to me.*
> [19] *And he commanded the multitude to sit down on the grass, and took the five loaves, and the two fishes, and looking up to heaven, he blessed, and brake, and gave the loaves to his disciples, and the disciples to the multitude.*
> [20] *And they did all eat, and were filled: and they took up of the fragments that remained twelve baskets full.*
> [21] *And they that had eaten were about five thousand men, beside women and children.*

It seems quite clear to me and I am not telling you what

to do. You are being directed what to do as indeed am I. I shall be opening a soup kitchen here at the church and taking contributions of money and food from wherever they may be found. It is not for me to command, but many of you are hungry. There are people out there in our community who are close to starving. It lies in our power, because we are a community, exactly that, to stop this from happening. I think I have no need to say more; let us pray....'

Margaret believed in community and this particular one had been in difficulties before during the coal strike of five years previously. She also had a great respect for Reverend Croft and this determined what she did next; others may contribute to the soup kitchen but she was going to open her own. She walked home with a determined air and told Barwise to come into the yard and particularly into the old scullery, which stood unused.

'Barwise I want you and Jack to clear all the stuff out of there and find other places for it or get rid of it. Then I want you to get to work on that old set pot until it's so clean that I can almost see my face in it.'

'Oh Mam why don't you do it? I've got work in the morning.'

'Never you mind that. I have my reasons; I'm going to talk with your father now. Just get on with it and let me know when it's done.'

Then she went into the house and asked Tom to come into the front room where they slept, so that they could be alone.

'I've seen the doctor and there's no doubt; I'm having a baby Tom. From my calculations I think it's due some time in November.'

'But you're 42! It's been seven years since the last one.'

'I don't think that's got a lot to do with it Master Thomas. I think that using the womb veil has helped, but they are not infallible so number nine is on the way.'

'You seem remarkably matter of fact about it.'

'It's a baby Tom. We will do what we always do and bring it up well with lots of love and manners.'

'Of course we will. I know that. Well done my dear; it makes me pleased that we'll have another. I'm founding my own tribe; my dad would have been happy.'

'I think he would,' said Margaret, thinking back to how glad old Barwise Little had been to welcome his first grandchildren. 'Now I want to talk about something far more serious.'

'More serious than having a baby. It must be a matter of great weight.' This was said in a vaguely mocking manner, but Margaret kept a straight face and serious mien so Tom also became serious.

'Food's short Tom.'

'I know it is, but we're coping.'

'Yes, we are but there's others who are not and down our street too.'

'You want to do what we did in 1912?'

'I do.'

'Well I think you're right, so you'd better do it. This is a fine place to live and I don't want our neighbours suffering when we have it in our power to help. There'll be others of course?'

'Like last time. Mrs Beeby and Mrs Smith will pitch in and a few more when word gets round.'

'Happily I like soup.'

It was an exaggeration because the family would get more than soup. If there was meat available then Margaret would place it into a muslin bag and hang it from a hook into the set pot. Anyone else along the street was free to do the same; that way her family got the meat, which she saw as fair enough, but the juices formed a broth. Into the main part of the pot went salt, pepper, water and whatever vegetables people could lay hands on. The usual result was a tasty 'soup' that her family had with the meat and a slice of bread or extra potatoes. If there happened to be stale bread, which was unlikely, it could be broken up and used to thicken the mixture. In times when meat was expensive or in short supply Margaret would use fish, but that was not bagged; she simply cut it up and threw it into the pot with the vegetables. Had she but known it, she was in fact preparing pottage, the staple food of the English and Lowland Scots for centuries down through the Middle Ages. Anyone else in the immediate vicinity was free to bring a pan along and take what they needed to feed the people in their house. This happened once a day, each evening, so that people got at least one meal a day; any that was not taken away was added to the next day's pot. It was not good to mix meat and fish of course, but all Margaret had to do was send word round that she was doing fish, and all sorts of fish could turn up to go into the pot. Similarly if she was doing meat, then beef-bones from the butchers might turn up, pork fat, pig's tails and trotters, all going into the same broth. The results varied, but the strange thing was that the differing tastes added appeal; the aroma from the set pot, especially after onions were added, was like all the flavours of the world steaming out. Nor was she alone in her endeavour. All over Workington the community grouped together and helped each other, communal set pots springing up like beneficent measles dotting the town. Some could not contribute food because they had next to none, but every day the hatch of the coalhole would be heard opening and a rattle of smush or dug coal would be heard and a voice might say 'For the pot Margaret.' To which she would reply 'Aye thanks Tommy,' or Billy, or Joe or whoever it happened to be out there at the time. The strange thing was that Margaret never felt that she was doing anything special and nor did any of the other women. This was community. This was what people did. Their men worked together, dug coal together, made steel together. Many of them had marched off to war together. Now they faced shortages of food and hunger, and they faced it together. The sense of togetherness and of community was so close and so intense that it seeped into the very bricks of the houses, the slabs of the pavements and into the quality of the air. Any other way was unthinkable. In various places in the North of England during those months, some people died of malnutrition, but not one in Workington.

On 4 April Tom and Jack were late home from work which was not usual, but they were late by an hour and that was. They did not drink and did not frequent any pubs, so Margaret was thinking of going to look for them when they finally walked in.

'Where have you been? I've been holding dinner back for ages and the children are hungry.'

'Couldn't help it Margaret. We were coming along Harrington Road when we saw a small crowd of people on the pavement and when we got close we saw Joe Johnson lying on the ground. The people round him were nearly as drunk as he was and were shouting things like "Good old Yanks."'

'Why were they shouting that?'

'Have you not been out today?'

'Not this afternoon anyway.'

'You've not seen that America has come into the war?'

'Have they? On our side?'

'Of course on our side! I can't say I blame them the way the Jerries have been sinking their ships out there. But I think they've been ready to go since that Zimmerman business in January.'

'You're talking stuff I don't know about Tom.'

'You must remember; the German Foreign Minister, Zimmerman sent a telegram offering part of the USA to Mexico if they invaded them. They offered them Texas and other places; some of the Yanks have been up in arms about it.'

'As you are well aware I have little interest in politics Tom and I have rather a lot on my mind at the moment. What has this to do with Joe?'

'Well as far as I know he's the only Yank in town, and tonight he's the most popular man. There's people been queuing up to buy him drinks though it is illegal; he's as drunk as a Lord and fell over asleep. He's lucky he didn't bang his head when he went down.'

'I'm surprised at Mr Johnson doing that!'

'So was I, but a few of us carried him back to his house, though his landlady wasn't too pleased. He's usually a sober man and all he kept doing was apologising to me in a slurred voice and saying "It was free Tom. It was all free."'

'It's being free is a pretty poor excuse.'

'Oh exercise a little charity Margaret. If the man is offered all the drink that he can hold, with no charge, and he's a drinking man, then the temptation must have been appalling. I've never seen him drunk before and I think he's allowed to kick over the traces sometimes. He'll be himself tomorrow.'

Margaret softened. 'Well he is a lovely man and a friend to us. I expect I'll forgive him for letting himself down this time.'

'You're a hard woman Margaret Little.'

'And your dinner's getting cold. Eat! There's a cup of tea…'

'And be canny wid the sugar… I know,' said Tom. 'All the same, with America in the war we can't lose I think. It'll be over soon.'

'Do you know Tom, I'm fed up hearing you say that…'

The situation with food did improve after 24 May 1917. Some within the Admiralty had been advocating that a large part of the U-boat problem was self-inflicted because Britain was allowing ships to cross the Atlantic on their own, trusting to luck and speed to outrun U-boats. The solution was to group them together in convoys surrounded by destroyers equipped with 'underwater sound detectors' or hydrophones. These were awkward devices to use because a ship had to stop its own engines to be able to hear underwater noises, but they did work up to a range of three to four miles, accurate to a bearing up to fifteen or twenty degrees. The convoy proposal was very similar to that employed during the Napoleonic wars against French raiders, so it was seen as old fashioned and out of date. Many of the senior admirals were aghast at this suggestion, seeing the U-Boats as 'wolves of the sea'; if the Allies gathered all their ships in one place they would simply be herding the sheep in for the slaughter. The argument was settled when the new Prime Minister, Lloyd George, stepped in and told the Admiralty to organise the use of convoys. The first of these crossed the Atlantic from the US beginning 24 May 1917. They lost not a ship save one straggler that fell behind and was torpedoed. Over the next month losses fell to ten percent of unconvoyed vessels, so the Germans began to sink outward-bound empty ships. In response, the British began convoying outward-bound ships; the losses fell. The success of the convoy system meant that the danger of Britain starving receded, though food was still short and Margaret kept her set pot going.

Chapter 15

Paddy to the Rescue

For Nancy, the winter of 1916–17 was one she ever after remembered as 'cold'. The weather had been bitter on the flat lands by the Solway and the huts had proven to be not altogether waterproof nor windproof. In the cubicle shared by her and Gertie the rain lashing on the outside of the one plank thick wall had not penetrated through as it did in some, but there were strong draughts of cold air and the atmosphere was bitterly cold. As the weather turned to frost and a dusting of snow fell the temperature became appalling as the worst winter within living memory took the land in an iron grip. When the hut maid came round to mop the floors free of the persistent mud that would keep finding its way in, despite the doorscrapers and boot-racks at the entrance, the water would freeze on the floor boards and the girls moving about had to be careful not to fall over on it. The only privacy was in the cubicles, but in order to socialise they sat around muffling themselves up in blankets and trying not to let their teeth chatter. It is true that there was a stove in the 'living room', but it was unequal to the task and there was little joy to be had sitting on hard benches chatting in a room where the chill was barely taken away because of the complete lack of insulation, and the fact that water streamed down the weather side corner where a joint had not been properly sealed. Nancy thought of herself as almost leading a lady's life in some aspects. Her laundry was done and her home was cleaned, her bed changed and her food cooked for her; she just wished she could get a little warmer. The method by which food was served was a long queue and no heated cabinets for it, so often it was cold by the time you got it. Nonetheless it was plentiful and eaten greedily.

'Home' was a space six feet by nine feet by eight feet with two bunk beds one above the other. Nellie and Gertie had put up some pictures and photographs and coloured curtains, which made the cubicle look more comfortable, but that was just a visual trick of the mind when the overwhelming chill made them shiver to the bones. The milk in the small scullery where tea was made would freeze and towels used to wash faces the night before would be stiff in the morning and had to be thawed out near the stove before they could be used. It was forbidden to keep even small amounts of food in cubicles and it all had to be locked away because the whole factory site had stimulated the local rat population which had exploded. The trolley girls who pushed their small wagons between buildings complained that on night shifts rats were sometimes running about their very feet as they heaved their loads along.

At work it was better because the temperature in the factory had to be controlled. The making of gun cotton would not be possible if the water being used to wash the acidified cotton froze, so the water passed through devices that heated it in winter and cooled it in summer to a constant temperature which had to be maintained. Even then you had to be careful; the amounts of water being used meant that often the floor was awash with it and quite slippery, so gum-boots were worn inside as well. Outside the buildings the air was raw, especially at night, and the only compensation was that in the hard frosts at least there were times when the mud froze solid and the girls did not have to wade through it; the gum boots they had been issued were very necessary. Another disadvantage for Nancy was that she came from a clean home, but many of the migrant women did not and their standards of hygiene were not the same as those of many others. She personally was always glad to make her way to one of the bath huts once a week, but some did not until the Welfare Officer began to dock their pay sixpence for each bath they missed. The close fitting munitions cap was something she was careful to wear at all times as there was a severe outbreak of nits which was brought under control by a regulation that every worker had to go to the medical hut once a month. At night it was best to stay in as far as Nancy was concerned because the huge munitions works was nowhere near completed and thousands of navvies were still working on the building of many installations and housings for hundreds of purposes. They were highly paid, flush with cash, and when they were not working, many of them were very drunk. Ordinary labourers were earning £7 a week and a rumour was going around that some took home as much as £20. The area around the contractor's huts where the men slept when not at work, was like the Wild West and the police could barely contain the misbehaviour. It was little wonder that the Army patrolled the area inside the actual factory fences to prevent crimes occurring near such vital sites.

Nancy and Gertie had taken a trip into Carlisle one Saturday shortly after arriving at Gretna in early July of 1916, but the experience had not been one she cared to repeat very often; Carlisle was not as it used to be in peacetime. They had chosen for their excursion the exact time that the navvies, released from their labours, flooded into the town. The girls had thought it would be nice to go and, look at some shops, have a decent meal instead of camp food, have a quiet glass of sherry in a city pub, watch a film, then come home. This was rather daring, as it was not considered respectable in their families for women to go into pubs alone, but the 'munitionettes' as they were becoming known as, were pushing the boundaries of what was acceptable. For Nancy it was even more daring as she had been brought up in a teetotal house, but Gertie had not taken long after their arrival in Gretna to persuade her to try the demon drink in the shape of a nice glass of sweet sherry. Although hesitant at first, Nancy had decided that she liked it because it made her feel relaxed.

Influenced by the films both girls had begun to wear lipstick and a little powder, though they would not dare wear it at home; Mother would not approve. Gertie had taken to smoking small cigarettes in public, but that did not raise many eyebrows because so many munitionettes had started doing it. They caught a train at Gretna station after catching the first bus they could get to after finishing their shift and changing; their carriage was full of young women on a similar mission, chatting excitedly at having some time off, purses full of money, and looking forward to seeing the city. On this first excursion they did not know it, but behind them a tidal wave of men was heading for the buses and stations along a well-trodden road in search of drink. Many of them were from Ireland and their chosen favourite was whisky. When their train arrived at the Citadel station Nancy and Gertie decided to have their sherry in a pub in Botchergate where it was evident that women coming in on their own was no innovation. The pub was empty apart from themselves, having just opened at 6.30 pm, and the girls were chatting about workmates, home and many other matters so they were too engaged in their minds to notice anything unusual; they were not used to pubs anyway. They settled in a quiet corner with their sweet sherry to enjoy their time off, the novelty of what they were doing, and never gave a moment's thought to what was happening behind the bar. On the shelves under the great mirrors the landlord and his staff were pouring dozens and dozens of glasses of whisky. Nancy and Gertie were completely oblivious to the wall of sound that came down from the direction of the station, hundreds of masculine voices, excited yells, and to the sound of feet pounding down the pavements in the hurry to be first. Then the door flew open and the accents of Tyneside, Glasgow, Ireland, Wales and Pandemonium filled the air. Whisky was demanded, shouted for, gulped and shouted for again; the first glasses did not touch the sides; the second was to be more considered. Men crammed into the public bar like sardines and had they not been sitting the girls would have been squashed against the wall. Not being invisible they were, of course, noticed.

'Well hello there girls. How are you doing?'

The accent was Geordie, the smell was rank for he had not bothered to change his clothes or to wash.

'Very well thank you,' Nancy replied, wishing he would go away.

'Can I buy you a drink pet?'

'No thank you, I have already got one.'

'Well I could get you another one, and my pal here could get your friend one.'

'No thank you; we only wanted one.'

In ordinary society, in polite circles, even in Workington, the starchy nature of these replies would have been enough, but on this occasion it was not. Society was evolving more quickly for women than it was for men. To these men, or rather to these traditional working class men, only one sort of girl went on her own or with a friend into a pub, and they were fair game. Pubs were male territory unless someone took his wife or best girl into one, and then into the saloon bar. Nancy and Gertie were in the public bar. Unused to young women exercising the freedom to have a quiet drink and a chat, it did not occur to the navvies that this was their sole purpose. They had to be there to pick up men and were in that trade.

'Well there's no need to act so high and mighty Miss. We've

just been paid, we're flush and can show you a good time. Will you go for a little walk with us?'

'No thank you. We just want to sit quietly and be left alone.'

'Well you won't get quiet in here petal,' said the man's friend. He had a face like a weasel and teeth that stuck out in front.

'I can see that,' said Nancy. 'Come on Gertie, let's go.' She got up to leave.

'Oh now ladies, don't be like that. We can pay for your time…'

Nancy's face flared red.

'If my brothers heard you talk like that you'd regret it.'

She and Gertie were on their feet by now trying to pass towards the door. Thankfully most of the men were not very much in drink by this time and the girls managed to gain the exit, but as they left Nancy saw the two unwelcome and persistent navvies edging out to follow them.

'Quickly Gertie, let's walk quickly and get away from them.'

A shout of 'Oi!' from behind them told them that the men had not given up and were walking rapidly after them. Ahead on the pavement a man and a woman were walking in the same direction as them, and Nancy thought she recognised the man because he was very big indeed. As she drew abreast of the couple strolling arm in arm she grabbed the man's arm and said loudly, 'Father, there you are,' to his complete astonishment and the woman's disbelief. It was Paddy Whangs, the police sergeant from Workington, though he was not in uniform; he looked round, saw the two men and took in the situation immediately.

'Ah there you are my dear,' so saying he looked at his wife. 'Now give your mother a kiss because it's been a while since she's seen you, and let's be on our way.'

Nancy kissed Mrs Wilson who looked even more boggle-eyed, especially as Gertie did the same, then she saw that the two undesirable followers were going back through the pub door, to her great relief.

'Thank you Mr Wilson. They were following us and we did not want them to.'

'I could see that Nancy; an unsavoury pair, but that's the trouble with Carlisle at the moment. It's not safe for nice lasses to be out on their own. What are you doing here?'

'We're making explosives at Gretna Mr Wilson, and it's hard work. We just fancied a bit of time off is all.'

Sergeant Wilson laughed.

'Well that's why we are here too. We can't really go shopping or let our guard down in Workington, because a policeman is always a policeman if everyone knows who you are. Once in a while my missis and me like to come up to Carlisle for a show and some shopping where nobody knows us, so here we are.'

He introduced Nancy to his wife as 'the young lady in Central Square with the sore feet who I've told you about.' Then they all went up into the city centre where they parted with thanks at the Market Cross. Nancy and Gertie went for a small meal at an eating-house just near the Market Hall and then to a picture house to see some Charlie Chaplin which would cheer them up. The one that stuck in both their minds forever was *The Floorwalker,* because it had a moving staircase in it and they had never seen or imagined such a thing. They fell about screaming with laughter as Chaplin ran down the up moving staircase being chased by a large man, Eric Campbell, with a huge black beard and they ran on the spot in hilarious fashion. Gertie said that the store was nothing like the Co-op in Workington where she had worked. Similarly the scene where Chaplin pretends to be someone's image in a mirror was so perfectly done that they were in stitches of laugher and admiration at the art of it. In all they had a wonderful time, and it was not until 8.15 pm that they came out of the picture house and headed for the station; they would be in trouble if they were not back at their hut by ten o'clock.

The sights they saw reminded Nancy forever afterwards of Sodom and Gomorrah. There were drunks everywhere, reeling from one place to another. Men vomited, women shrieked and all inhibitions seemed to have been removed. From the pubs came voices roaring filthy songs and down the alleyways there were couples doing things, some of a sexual nature. Nancy noted that some of the women were as drunk as the men and that some of them were obviously from Gretna, though she could see no-one they knew. Many of the women were plainly dressed for dancing and had gone deliberately in search of men, a process which though not unheard of in Workington, was not thought respectable.

On the way back to the station Gertie and Nancy hurried on their way as on the other side of the street a gang of drunks were fighting with a group of policemen who had their truncheons drawn and were laying about them in an effort to control the situation which was ugly. Beside them was a shop front with a broken window and heading for the station were quite a few young women the worse for drink. Thankfully the train journey back to Gretna was uneventful because the labouring men, who lived in contractor huts away from the female huts, were not under the same curfew as those contracted to work in the factories. There was a lot of loud talking and shrieking laughter to be heard, and some girls were sick in the carriages, but there was no violence. Nancy and Gertie reached their hut in good time, but both felt shocked by what they had seen; it had been nice in some aspects, but in others they felt like they had returned from a bad place such as you read of in novels and had no desire to go back there at any time soon. They had reached this conclusion even before Freda Jones arrived home at 10.20pm and had a row with Mrs Armstrong who asked her why she was late. Freda told Mrs Armstrong that she was an interfering old biddy and who did she think she was? Mrs Armstrong could mind her own bloody business; and see that river over there? There was a short jetty just by it and Mrs Armstrong could take a long walk off it for all Miss Jones cared.

Contrition is one thing; wilfulness is another. HM Gretna had authorities and they in turn had methods of dealing with those whom they deemed undesirable. Freda Jones was not sacked, but the very next afternoon she received a note informing her that she was being transferred to another hut, having been assigned to the outdoor gang. Like many others she would work outside, pushing trucks of materials from one building to another, a human beast of burden in the sunshine and the open air. In the bright days of summer when the sun was high and the air full of champagne bubbles there was envy to be had at what they did. Then when the cold, the wind and the rain came; when the girls pushing the trucks round in the freezing winter dark had rats running between their feet in the tracks, the tune was different. No-one was jealous of Freda then.

It is only fair to note that Nancy and Gertie had seen Carlisle in its wild state; the city fathers and the national government had also seen what was going on. Drastic action was taken very shortly afterwards to take a bad situation in hand. In similar fashion the work went on apace at HM Gretna itself to build the amenities necessary so that munitionettes could live more comfortably and that they could find employment for their leisure nearer to home than Carlisle. That lay in the future, and Nancy, lying in her bunk on Saturday nights reading, had to content herself for the moment, with the thought that she was at least saving money.

Chapter 16

A Bit of a Kick About

In national factories such as Gretna, concern for welfare made the government contract for the building of works canteens and it was in these, the white-hot forge of change, that the revolution was born.

When Nancy had arrived at Gretna, the silence in the canteen where she had her first evening meal was deafening. Young women from all over Britain had sat down awkwardly at table with perfect strangers and had sat in prim uncomfortable shyness, muted by the novelty of it all. That had changed. Girls from the huts got to know each other; then of course girls from other huts had been assigned to the same shifts and acquaintance had spread. Mealtimes were no longer silent, for the new friends all talked; and they talked of everything. Men, money, family, politics, religion, what they had done, what they were going to do, what they were allowed to do and what they wanted to do; all was grist to this mill. An impartial observer might have seen that something else hovered over the scene like a miasma, intangible, perceptible only to those who looked for it and charged with a power almost infinite in its possibilities. Nowhere in British history had such large groups of young women come together in such numbers to work, eat and play together. In previous centuries, for large gatherings of females of all ages, one might have looked in a nunnery, but HM Gretna was no nunnery, and these women were young, fresh of mind, and open to learning new things. The miasma was a group consciousness, an awareness of commonalty, a sense of power and togetherness and once it had planted itself in this fertile soil beside the Solway, it grew like a great tree and could not be stopped. It would be no exaggeration to term it a kind of university of the possibilities for women. Under its tutelage, confidence grew, an awareness of what could be done; that collectively they were strong and that much depended on them. They knew that without them the war could not be won; that men and women were fighting in different ways, but that they were equal in importance to the defeat of Germany. These new universities spread their message wherever there was a munitions factory and a works canteen.

Then there was the question of why they were fighting; a better world free of militarism. A world where there was more freedom, including for women. Economically they were transformed. They wore trousers, at least at work. In their pockets was more cash than they had ever possessed, and they spent it freely. The shopkeepers changed their tune, altering their stock to please Miss and Madame if they wished to stay in business; a situation exacerbated by the fact that millions of men were abroad fighting and money from their pay was being allocated to their wives who now had spending power. The daughters in munitions factories had mothers who were now head of the household because their men were fighting in France and Belgium, or Mesopotamia, or other far-flung theatres. The world had changed and it was palpable; Nancy had seen it in the faces of the soldiers who had come home and in the way they behaved towards these 'new' women. Waiting for a bus into Gretna to visit a shop she had been standing beside some garrison soldiers who had evidently been posted from service abroad, perhaps as a 'rest'. When the bus, a double-decker with an open top, had arrived it was almost full of munitionettes from Moss Band, girls who worked with danger every day, and they had conquered fear. This is logical for their work was more dangerous than Nancy's own, which was perilous enough. If you deal every day with materials which could kill you at any moment, and which exposure to could give you life-threatening conditions, then it affects your mind. You have to either get over the fear and live with it, or be in a blue funk of fright that makes you useless; there was very little that these girls were afraid of now, and men were not on the list. The bus stopped and Nancy got on, but the soldiers did not. The bus full of girls began to laugh and call encouragement.

'Come on darling; we don't bite.'

'Got a light soldier?'

'There's a seat beside me blondie – yes you with the Corporal's stripe.'

'Come on boys and say hello.'

One of them was obviously deterred by the raucous calls, but plucked up his courage and stepped onto the platform until he realised that none of his mates had followed him. Their faces were a picture and could be read like so many books; girls did not behave like this and when faced with it, they did not know how to react. Some registered awe, some smiled in a half disbelieving way and others just looked terribly uncertain; all were clearly intimidated. The soldier on the platform got off and chaffed a friend to join him and tried to pull him forward. He resisted physically, pulling back saying audibly, 'No; I daren't. Not with them.' When the bus drove off, there was not one man aboard and the girls cheered at them in a half jeering ironic way that spoke more of how the balance of power had shifted in their absence than whole volumes of script could express.

By December 1916 life at HM Gretna was getting better, at least when Nancy and Gertie were off duty. The 'hub' of the new settlement, worked on round the clock for the last few months, was now complete. There were brick houses for the senior staff and managers, a staff club that was enormous, a hospital, a whole row of shops and encouragingly, a growing number of brick hostels into which Nancy and Gertie hoped to move very soon. Best of all there was a cinema which Nancy loved dearly; it was her favourite form of entertainment though perhaps this awareness on her part might have been due to the fact that the cinema was very well heated, unlike her hut. To be more accurate there were two cinemas which catered for the workers, one holding 700 which was used for dances and a second one which held between three and four hundred. Here she could bask in the literal glow of scenes from all over the world, be shocked, surprised, saddened and warmed; she could see changing fashion, how people lived and all sorts of behaviour that she had never dreamed of. She and her friend would now often go into Carlisle because after the trauma of what she had seen in early July, the government had clamped down on the area with an iron hand. All pubs in the district had been taken over by the state, as had the brewery in Carlisle; the sale of whisky or other spirits in these establishments had simply been banned. In the same way the amount of alcohol in beer had been reduced, and the amount of drunkenness had dropped to below pre-war levels. The police had been reinforced and Carlisle was safe for decent girls again. This is not to say that there were no shenanigans because there were, but the outrageous and promiscuous debauchery of the early months of 1916 was tamed and caged. Because some of the male police officers had difficulty talking to munitionettes and had no wish to deal with them as they dealt with male offenders, Carlisle police had been reinforced by the recruitment of a number of women police and they patrolled the streets and the station keeping order. Rumour said that there were to be women police in Gretna in the New Year, but Nancy had no news to either confirm or deny that.

Nancy lay on her bunk on 1 December 1916; it had been quite a day. She had been going about her quotidian tasks in a fairly efficient fashion for she did not allow herself to get 'bored' as many girls complained about. Her view was that she was being paid well to work, even if it was repetitive; whether it was boring or interesting was neither here nor there, so she got on with doing the job well and was potching yet another tub of acidified cotton on its fifth rinse when a group of men appeared at the door near her and she recognised KB Quinan by sight, though she had never spoken to him. This quiet American had been brought in by Lloyd George when the Minister of Munitions had decided to build the biggest ammunition factory in the world at Gretna. He had designed and built the place, even down to the last details and the American style welfare management systems; he was ubiquitous as his creation took shape, so his face was familiar to most of the people on site. With him was a cloud of men in coveralls who were supervisors and managers, but there was one very distinguished looking man perhaps in his late fifties in a dark suit, overcoat and hat, whom she did not recognise. His face was shrewd and dominated by a large pair of round spectacles and a fierce, somewhat overgrown moustache; rather overweight, he spoke with a soft Scottish brogue. He had, it seemed, a mind of his own because he did not wait for the men attending him to speak, but walked straight up to Nancy.

'Young woman, would you mind explaining to me what you are doing here?'

Nancy was trained not to speak of her work so she looked at Mr Quinan and he nodded, so she explained what she was about.

'So basically you spend all your time rinsing this hotchpotch of acid and cotton until it is free of acid. That must be why they call you a potcher!'

Nancy had not thought of that. 'Yes Sir.'

'So what name do you give it, this gun cotton mess?'

Nancy hesitated, not wishing to be thought flippant.

'Well Sir, we call it the Devil's Porridge in here.'

'Ah yes; I can see why porridge; it looks just like porridge, but I have to say not a very appetising pot. Why Devil's?'

'If you burn it Sir it glows like....' She tailed off and the man laughed.

'Like the fires of Hell you mean?'

'Yes Sir; then it blows up.'

'So that's gun cotton eh? Devil's Porridge. I like that. What's your name girl?'

'Nancy Sir.'

'I like that description Nancy. Devil's Porridge; it's very apt. Do you mind if I use it?'

'Not at all Sir; I did not make it up Sir, and I don't know who did; it's just what we call it among ourselves.'

'I see. Well it's very descriptive and I think even evocative of what happens here; I shall use it and thank you. Now when you have finished with it, what happens to it next?'

'I can show you that Sir Arthur if you'll kindly follow me.'

'Very well Mr Quinan, lead on and thank you Nancy.'

He put out his hand and shook Nancy's own surprised fingers, then she did something she had not done for a very long time and gave the gentleman a curtsey. He was a Sir, and that was worth a show of respect to. One of the supervisors hung back a moment.

'Do you know who that was? That was Conan Doyle. You did well.'

Nancy's jaw nearly hit the floor.

'Sherlock Holmes?'

'The very same. Well done.'

Now as she lay on her bed thinking it over, it had sunk into her that she had met one of the most famous men in the empire, even the world and he had spoken to her. Her grandfather John Adams idolised Sherlock Holmes; she must write him a letter and tell him. Shift had finished at 2.30pm and the sun was going down in the West in spectacular Solway fashion though it was very cold. The ground outside lay stiff with frost and the temperature in the hut was only slightly above freezing. She had changed her clothes and wore a home-knitted jumper that her mother had made for her and a thick warm skirt, but she was still cold. The curtain to the cubicle whipped open and a pink flushed face looked in at Gertie and Nancy; it was Janet from over the corridor.

'Come on you two – we are going to have a kick about.'
'A kick about? What do you mean?'
'A kick about. Football. Come on. Move yourselves.'
'It's cold out there. Anyway women don't play football.'
'I know. Nowhere near as cold as Caithness, but cold enough. Come on; it's just what you need to warm you up. Don't funk or show yellow; get up put your coat on and let's play. It's us against the next hut. These women are going to play some fitba!'

The mention of the next hut was what did it, because all the girls in Nancy's hut worked at the Eastriggs Factory of HM Gretna. The inhabitants of the next hut worked at the Mossband Factory up on 'Nitro-Glycerine Hill', where the gun cotton was taken to be made into cordite. Their wages were a bit higher because of the danger of their work, which was not grudged, but rumour said that they considered themselves a cut above, so the chance to beat them at football was an appealing novelty. A stretch of more or less flat frozen mud had been marked out by the placing of some wooden boxes at four corners, and two goals were delineated by the same method. The area was nowhere near as big as a full sized pitch, but big enough for a recreational game. At the toss a tall girl from the next hut called Anna Riddell won and they kicked off. Nancy had no idea what she was doing and ran about vigorously, but eventually the heavy leather ball came towards her and she aimed a foot at it and kicked. It can be a hampering thing to run round a pitch in a floor length skirt, but kicking a ball in one proved to be rather more of a handicap.

In addition to this Nancy kicked the ball with the front of her foot. The ball shot off almost at right angles to where she had intended it to go, to the groans of her hut-mates; then Nancy sat down on the floor clutching her foot and grimacing in pain. In no way were her shoes equal to the task set.

'Are you alright hen? You know you're supposed to kick the ball with the side of your foot?'

'No Janet, I am not alright. But I will be in five minutes. I'll be straight back.'

Nancy tore off into the hut and quickly changed her skirt for the trousers of her uniform. Then she pulled on the heavy boots that she wore in the factory and dashed outside. The difference was apparent and immediate. She was faster than anyone else on the field and kicking the ball with the side of her foot, however inexpertly, was a thousand times better than with the point of her foot. She grew warm from her exertions and began to enjoy herself. The game could not be called a display of excellence by any stretch of the imagination. None of them had ever played before. The gathering of a group of navvies who evidently thought it the funniest thing they had ever seen did not help their efforts, but at least all they did was watch. Janet proved to be very nimble on her feet, which she said was down to her being a trained highland dancer, and before too long this faculty enabled her to score a goal. It was not a good goal; it was inept and fumbled, but it was this that stepped up the mood. The girls from the next hut did not like being down a goal and play grew more vigorous; and then it grew more aggressive as people were pushed off balls. Half time came and all were flushed and warm, but so were tempers. Every woman except Nancy disappeared into the huts and came back a few minutes later in trousers and boots. The next half was going to be serious. It was at this point that the match changed from a kick about into something with an edge; now that everyone was in trousers the Mossband girls quickly showed that however inexpert they might be, their team overall was much more adept at controlling the ball than were the inhabitants of Nancy's hut. Anna Riddell, a girl from Galashiels, was particularly outstanding and could almost run rings round most people on the pitch. Even the tone of the navvies changed to shouts of encouragement and though the game ended with Nancy on the losing side, she had enjoyed the running about and the warming up effect very much.

Football swept through the factories as an epidemic craze as huts began to play against each other, and eventually Dornock factory girls played against Mossband girls. It was well known that the new fashion for football among women had spread to Carlisle, but it was not at first realised that it had gone further. All throughout Cumberland, southern Scotland and the north of England young women were beginning to use their leisure time to do something that was once the sole province of men. It had to be curtailed somewhat as December progressed, because of the weather.

Chapter 17

Of Football and of Danger

The winter of 1916/17 had been fairly average despite the hard frosts that had frozen the mud, but as the month progressed it bit hard as several large falls of snow covered the ground in a blanket of white. The factory had to be kept open of course, so the snow was cleared from the roads and track-ways, but the huts where the workers lived were shrouded in it and uninsulated. Nancy was allowed to go home for two days for Christmas, but when she returned the conditions in the huts were appalling; it was so bad that workers were quitting and leaving, beaten not by work, but by weather. Nancy and Gertie sat shivering next to the stove in their hut as the New Year approached and their teeth chattered. Most of the other girls were off shift, but not in the living room; it was too cold to go outside and they lay in their bunks swaddled in their day clothes, wrapped in all the blankets they could find, and their breath came out of a breathing hole so that they looked like so many woolly seals. Outside, a blizzard raged and the snow stood five feet deep; Gertie was weeping because try as she might, she could not get warm.

'I can't take much more of this Nancy. It just isn't decent to live like this. I don't mind the work, though it's cold enough there, but this is worse than animals are kept. At least they've got warm straw and thick stone walled barns. I'd be warm at home.'

'I was just thinking of the back room at home. My mam will have the range going and it'll be lovely in there. It was so nice over Christmas with all the family round the table, and so warm.'

'I've forgotten what being warm is. I've a good mind to chuck it and go.'

'Well there's a good many have done it already.'

'Why do we stay Nancy? It's freezing here: much colder and we'd die of it.'

'I know. I don't like it any more than you do.'

'So why stay?'

'Duty I think. And the money of course; but I don't like giving up Gertie. I came here to do my bit. Anyway, think what it's like in the trenches right now. Think what the men have to put up with. I read that they're not allowed any kind of stove in case it shows the enemy where they are and just invites a shell.'

'Imagine that!'

'I know, not that this stove is doing a lot of good. There's no snow on the roof you know. The heat is going straight out.'

'You'd think they would have padded it or at least put a ceiling to keep the heat in instead of being straight up to the rafters.'

'Stick it out Gertie; the weather can't last for ever.'

'I know that, but it's so cold I don't want to go out of the door even for the canteen or the cinema.'

Neither of them noticed the telephone ringing in Mrs Armstrong's room because it was such a common occurrence that it was part of the background noise; nonetheless it was about to change their lives for them. The matron came out of her door and came over to them.

'Now then Nancy and Gertie, I'd like to see you in my room now please, and Janet and Lizzie too if one of you could fetch them along.'

Soon all four of them were with Mrs Armstrong, she sitting on her bed and they ranged round her wondering what this was all about.

'You must be aware that you are very closely watched at all times, are you not ladies?'

They affirmed that they were.

'You may not realise just how closely; Mr Quinan, who designed this whole establishment set in place certain procedures which are intended to look after the welfare of everyone here. Not unnaturally, these procedures allow us to keep a very close record of your work rate, your punctuality and especially your conduct.'

This last piece of information caused some puzzled frowns but Mrs Armstrong smiled and continued.

'Have no fear ladies; your records are excellent and your conduct exemplary, which is why I have called you in here. As you may have realised, these huts are very basic and they were put up very quickly to house our first workers early in the year; they have never been intended as permanent accommodation. You will be leaving here very shortly, as will all the other girls to live in a much better place. This hut will still be used, but it will serve to house workers who are perhaps not so skilled or as well behaved as the current tenants. I shall be calling a hut meeting in the living room to announce that a move will be made to a modern and well equipped hostel building tomorrow.'

Nancy was still puzzled; 'But Mrs Armstrong, why are you telling us this?'

'Ah, now that is because not all of you ladies will be moving to a hostel. You may have noticed that a large number of small bungalows have been built?'

There were a few nods.

'I have been offered one as matron. Again this is one of Mr Quinan's ideas. He thinks that workers would be happier in a more domestic situation, as if they were living at home, so I have been allocated a bungalow in which I shall live, and there are four other bedrooms. That is where you come in and why I have asked you here. I am allowed to choose four girls from my hut to come with me to that bungalow; naturally I went straight to the list to find those with the best records. That is you four. So my question is, would you like to live in the bungalow and continue with me as matron, or would you prefer to go into a hostel with a larger group?'

The silence was slightly stunning, but it was as one who in a desert catches sight of an oasis with palm trees and water.

'In fairness I ought to say that since the quality of accommodation will be so much better, your living costs will rise; if you earn £2 a week you will find that board, lodging and service fees for such as laundry and the other amenities will reduce your wage to £1/2/- a week, though many might see that as quite a good offer. You are of course free to seek places to live outside the official premises, and many are doing just that, but I do not see such lodgings as advantageous as these are; it's you who must decide. If you need time to consider it then I quite understand, but I have been asked to give an answer as soon as possible…'

There were quite a few workers who had opted out of the hostel system and found lodgings close by HM Gretna in nearby villages and towns like Annan; some had even secured rooms in Carlisle, but of course they had to travel to work and pay the costs. Their food also had to be paid for and was perhaps not as plentiful or as varied as within the factory area; the Ministry of Munitions looked after its people in that way, and even after all the deductions the take-home pay was still munificent to those formerly used to receiving £5 for the half year. There was also the consideration that they felt rather honoured to be offered the chance of a bungalow because the number who could be accommodated in such a way was limited; they had earned a privilege. It did not require much thought. They all tried to speak at once, 'Count me in Matron…', 'I want to come to the bungalow…', 'yes please', and it all came out in a grateful, excited gabble of affirmation.

Mrs Armstrong looked at them, smiled, and said, 'Very good. I am pleased that life will be so pleasant. Annie will be coming too to look after you and I'm sure that you will feel a lot better after this cold place. The move will take place tomorrow when you come off shift in the afternoon so you might wish to begin getting ready. Now I shall call a hut meeting and tell the other girls they will be moving into Collingwood hostel tomorrow where there is central heating; unless of course they choose to make their own arrangements.'

The quality of life improved out of all proportion to that in the huts; the bungalows were designed to be converted very easily into civilian use after the war and were laid out with six small rooms and a living space; accommodation for four workers, one matron and one maid. Each room had its own fireplace and it was the maid's responsibility to see to them. Now that time not at work was cosy, snug and homely, Nancy and the other workers became far happier in what they were doing. Many of the amenities which had been under construction during 1916 were now coming into use, so Nancy watched a lot of films at the cinema in Annan, a short bus ride away; occasionally she and Gertie went to dances organised by the Social and Athletic Association in the club which were attended by local men and soldiers. They even ventured into Carlisle as the weather improved and found it much tamed, a nicer place to spend their leisure hours and for shopping than formerly.

As the winter tailed away, the snow melted and the cold gave way to watery spring sunshine, the areas between the huts were transformed; at first they were roped off then gangs of workers brought in cartloads of turf from the Silloth area and laid it over where the mud had been the previous year.

Chapter 17 — Of Football and of Danger

Between the bungalows and huts they formed flowerbeds and the establishment round the hub began to look rather nice. It was some weeks before anyone was allowed onto the grass areas but when they were, the kickabouts began again, and some of the women were getting very good at it. Anna Riddell was so fast on the ball that people began to refer to her by the nickname 'Swifty' which she grinned at and rather enjoyed. There were others who were nearly as good as her; Margaret McAdo for example could run down the wing like the wind, whilst anyone who got in the way of Edith Wilson should look out for themselves; she took no prisoners in a tackle. At first they played in trousers, but as the months went by some of them got very serious about their football and purchased knickerbockers with knee length socks and proper football boots. It was all rather informal and not recognised officially by the authorities, but nonetheless proper matches were taking place between hostels, between factories and there were some comic matches for fun with teams of men dressed up as women where spectators contributed to the Soldiers' Comforts fund. As the men did not always win, some real matches were organised; and they did not win all of those either. With spring the vogue for women's football swept back in the munitions factories like wildfire. On 23 April Nancy received a letter from Nellie who had attended a football match at the Lonsdale Stadium in Workington on Saturday 21 April. She had gone there as nurse in attendance to a group of convalescents from the Bankfield Hospital as part of their entertainment programme. As she read Nancy caught her breath then read part of it out aloud to the girls in their sitting room:

'We heard that there was to be a football match at the Lonsdale Stadium because a group of local businessmen wanted to raise money for the smokes fund. They got a group of girls together from the Shell Factory who like football and they sent

a challenge to Carlisle Munition girls that they would beat them hollow. Of course everyone took it as a joke because there have been joke matches before, but Nancy this was no joke! I've never been one for football; what woman is (or perhaps I should say "has been"?) I went with my patients into one of the stands and of course they were exactly that. I was a little anxious about some of them having to stand for so long, but they did not seem to mind; they are all aficionados I think. There was quite a party atmosphere I can tell you, and everyone thought it a great wheeze to have an all women football match, so there was a lot of laughing as the band marched up and down just like at a regular match I was told.

Anyway the teams came on and the crowd started hooting with laughter; I don't know how those girls stood it in front of so many people, mostly men but with a fair few women too. Carlisle came on in khaki jerseys and black skirts; then Workington came on and a huge gasp went round the stadium. They were wearing red jerseys and blue skirts but their skirts were calf-length; I never thought I'd see such a thing. Of course the men loved it; you should have heard the wolf whistles and cat-calling, and then the match started. For the first 15 minutes or so the crowd still treated it as a comic match, but then the players really got into their stride; you could see Workington's feet and the footwork was, so one of my patients said "Impressive". I should probably put that in capital letters. There was one Workington player called Miss Watchorn, I don't know her first name; she was twinkling along with the ball as if she had been born with it at her feet. She simply outmanoeuvred anyone who came close to her and belted the ball into the Carlisle net where there was nothing their keeper could do.

It was then that the whole atmosphere changed because it was no longer a comic match; there were a fair few people down from Carlisle and they began to cheer their people on. The Workington crowd was going mad with fervour for their team, they just had to win. The Carlisle people could not outrun Workington and some tried so hard that they tripped over their own skirts and fell headlong which really provided the only comic moments for the rest of the game. Their Captain, Miss Raine, did manage to score back and equalise which sent Carlisle supporters into a frenzy of shouting delight, but overall the short skirts won out because Workington ran rings round the Carlisle girls and beat them 4–1. I should think that normal skirts for football will not be seen again. Apparently Workington staged a trial game on 6 April and found long skirts far too impractical so decided to innovate in quite a daring fashion. I'm told this was the first properly arranged football match ever between two female teams in a regular stadium. I did enjoy it. If women's football takes off then I imagine that I shall attend more games; if it remains a male preserve then I probably shall not, but based on the reaction of this crowd I think that women's football is here to stay....'

Nellie was more right than she might have thought. Workington soon had two teams; the munition girls from the Shell Factory and another called 'Workington Combine' which was mostly from the steelworks. They played Whitehaven ladies, and Derwent Mills in Cockermouth, and many others that were mushrooming into existence. Nancy took her letter and went in search of Anna Riddell to let her read it.

'Yes, I saw that. I think we should have our own team here. What do you think Nancy? Would you want to be in it?'

'No. I'm not good enough. I like kicking the ball about and I like taking part in the matches between the huts, but I know there's loads better than me. I just thought you'd like to see this.'

Anna smiled. 'I've already been considering it and I do appreciate your honesty. You are right; if I put a team together then I want them to be the very best we have. And in the interests of inter-factory competition I'm inclined to make it a Mossband team. If Dornock wanted to form their own then it would be difficult to have girls from both.'

'That makes sense. We'll come and support you anyway if you play against other places.'

'I know you will. You know I'm going to do it.'

'What will you call your team?'

'I don't know. Mossband Rangers perhaps? Rovers? United?'

'I'm sure you can do something more original than that Swifty; they all sound like men's teams.'

'That's true and we can't have that. What do you suggest?'

'I think they've already got a name...Swifty...'

'Swifts?'

'Yes.'

'Mossband Swifts. I like that; it's different and describes us quite well. Why not? I'll ask the others, but I don't see why not. It's good.'

As the year progressed the Mossband Swifts went from strength to strength; playing in knickerbockers, they won quite a few of their matches, but as the trend spread and other teams abandoned skirts, the matches became far more even. Mossband acquired a reputation for fast aggressive play, but they were not unbeatable. On 9 June they were humiliated by a Carlisle team in skirts at Brunton Park and went down 4–1; evidently sartorial choice did not always make the difference. Later in the year in the rematch they could only manage a draw, so perhaps superior ball skills had the final say, at least in that year's season. Or perhaps it was the mud, since the rain came pouring down just before half-time and everyone was soaked through and covered from head to foot. They came back to the changing rooms singing to the tune of *What a friend we have in Jesus*;

*'Only one more football practice
Only one more tram to catch.*

*Only one more goal to score
Then we've won this football match.
When this rotten match is over.
Oh! How happy I shall be.
When I get my blouse and skirt on
No more footballing for me.'*

If it stiffened their resolve, it had no visible effect; at least in a draw there was no shame.

It must not be imagined that the lives of the workers were as mundane as might appear because the materials they were using were intrinsically fraught with danger. With more than 12,000 young women working in two factories and on a large number of processes, there were bound to be problems. Up at Mossband, or 'Nitroglycerine Hill' as it was commonly called, the workers had a more hazardous employment than at Dornock gun cotton manufactory. A lot of nitric acid was used there and it was harder to avoid exposure to the fumes of it than where Nancy worked. She heard tales of girls whose gums had become so bad from the effects of this that they had to have all their teeth removed; it was also a regular sight to see girls coming into hostels straight from working, reeling as though drunk. With some of them it was so bad that they had to go to the hospital where they could sleep it off, but Nancy thought that would not do them a lot of good. Even though the pay was much higher she was happy to remain where she was. Potching might not be the most interesting of jobs, but occasionally she had splashed small drops of acid from the mix onto her hand and did not like the pins and needles effect of the stinging that came with that; happily there was abundant water on tap to rinse as soon as that happened, so she never got a serious burn. The story of Emily Hubble made her shudder, though it had no after effects. It seemed that she had been working in the place where the nitro-glycerine was made and a pipe had ruptured spilling the explosive all over the floor. Every person in the shed ran for their lives except Emily who grabbed some sponges that were there and put them onto the pipe, tying them with string to try to stop the leak. She had been covered from head to foot in the stuff which made her skin all red and stinging, even for days after she had submerged herself in a bath and washed it all off. Although she had been promoted to charge hand for this, Nancy thought it the bravest thing she had ever heard of and that she deserved a medal.

She also thought the same about Maud in her own shed. When the nitro-cotton that Nancy potched had its final rinse, she had to remove it, a damp doughy-like mass, and heave it into a trolley before it was taken away. The next stage in the process was that it had to be dried, a careful slow procedure with a substance that became more volatile, the drier it became. Usually some girls brought the trolley down from the drying sheds and it was they who took it back to the drying racks where they would spread it. One of these was Maud Bruce from County Durham, and Nancy knew her as a quiet unassuming sort of girl who was always up for a few minutes chat as they emptied a tub, then took it away. As the cotton dried on the racks it formed a dry mass that then had to be fluffed, but a particular batch of gun cotton did not get that far. The evaporation process must have concentrated acid remaining in the fibres, and it combusted spontaneously. The first Nancy knew of it was when a crowd of girls came screaming at her to get out. As they did so the fire-bells went off and almost paralysed her with the fear of what she had been dreading for months; a fire in the factory.

'The whole place is going to blow; run for your life.'

She needed no second telling, as she knew what gun cotton could do. As she ran towards the door she asked 'What's happened?'

There's a fire on the drying racks; it's going to go sky high any minute!'

In the distance she heard more bells as Gretna's fire engines approached and she pelted for the exit. Reaching the grass outside she ran across it for a good two hundred yards as fast as her legs could carry her then stopped, turned round and the factory was still there. Above the drying sheds was a plume of smoke, but was it her imagination, or was it dissipating? Firemen run towards what others run away from. The men in helmets went into the factory dragging a hose, but they were only in there a few minutes before they came out with a girl between them who was crying. There are many reasons why women cry, as all women know, but many men do not; this crying was a release. Maud Bruce had been near the fire as the panic spread, but it did not seize her in the same natural way that it did others. There was a hose near her and Maud took it up, turned the valve on and jetted water at the fire, half expecting to be blown to pieces or incinerated at any second. To her great relief, though she was shaking with fear, the fire began to die, so she persevered and kept pouring water onto it until it went out. It is sheer raw courage to do such a thing when every fibre of your being screams at you to run away. When the firemen arrived they stood for a moment looking at the weeping girl, then one of them put his arm round her shoulder.

'Well done lass, I've seen some brave things in my time, but I think you've just about knocked them all for six. Come on out of here now and we'll finish up.'

Nancy, and indeed every girl at the plant was as pleased as punch when the King awarded Maud the new medal just instituted in June 1917 and she joined the Order of the British Empire for her courage. Nancy's friend Janet received the same honour, and how she got it underlined to all the girls on their shift the perils they were working next to. Janet was a potcher, just the same as Nancy, and worked further up the same shed. A new batch of cotton had been placed in one of her tubs and the acid had been poured over it; the acid men had gone away. Janet was waiting out the two minutes before draining the acid but she noticed something that made her thrill with horror. A kind of fizzing was going on in the cotton which did not usually happen, and it was giving off heat. It might have been natural to run, but without waiting any more time she opened the acid drain valve and then flooded the tub with a deluge of water whilst calling for help. The supervising chemist came along and ordered the acid to be analysed and it was found that somehow the acid manufactory had made a mistake; the proportions of sulphuric and nitric acid had been transposed and the whole tub could have exploded killing everyone around and destroying the shed. Janet may have had a medal for what she did, but for some time she slept badly and cried out in her sleep.

Nancy and her friends did not feel that they were doing

anything extraordinary; they were earning good money; that much they knew, and they felt satisfied. There was something else though. The government had put out propaganda posters showing a munitionette handing ammunition to soldiers in the trenches. That was Nancy's job and that of her friends. They felt a direct link to the war and they were playing their part. The feeling was one of fulfilment, a patriotic justification of all the danger, the cold, the horrible conditions and the uprooting from home. The girls up the hill with bad gums from acid fumes, burns on their skin, the breathing difficulties all had a role in winning the war and in a real sense they sometimes felt that they too were at their own front line, and if their efforts failed then their country would lose the war. By the middle of 1917 HM Gretna was producing its target figure of 800 tons of cordite a week and the girls knew it. They took home their pay every week with a sense of worth and a job well done.

Chapter 18

The Royal Wink

On 12 May 1917 Barwise sat on a bollard not far from the entrance to Workington Harbour; he was on the south side almost as far as he could go and not too far from the small Billy Bumley house, though he had not taken himself as far as the small lighthouse at the end. The conical shape of the Tidewatcher's hut reminded people of the traditional beeskep though the larger Billy Bumley house up on the cliffs was the original of the name. It looked just like the sort of place that bumblebees called home, but no-one knew its original purpose. The reason he was there was because he liked it; the remoteness of it and the panorama spread out in front of him made him think. The evening was fine and the water a blue grey stretching in choppy wavelets to the far horizon where the dark hills of Southern Scotland rose like distant sea creatures looming at him. It was about 8.30 in the evening and the sun was going down towards the western horizon, the light over the Solway clear, and with a lambent magic quality that made newcomers catch their breath at the sheer beauty of it. Barwise was used to this of course, and watched the sunset often, but he never tired of it. He had eaten his dinner at home then made his way down here to ask himself a question; was he afraid?

The particular stimulus for this train of thought was the newspapers that he had been reading avidly when he could and he had taken to haunting the Carnegie reading rooms for that reason. The Battle of Arras was raging in France and

Belgium and last month the Canadians had taken Vimy Ridge, a piece of news that had been treated as a great triumph in the newspapers and something which stirred Barwise's instincts greatly. He so badly wanted to be part of this thing that it made his stomach churn with a kind of impatience that he just could not go immediately. So many men from Workington had gone and as the months went by he felt more and more left out; he had to be in it before it was over. On the other hand, the battle was ongoing and had been for several weeks and though the British forces were advancing, there was no disguising the stark fact that the casualty figures were enormous. Stirring at the back of his head was an enemy he did not want to fight; his own fear. A battle raged in his mind at night when he lay awake as the armies of his own will fought against those of his instincts. What if he was killed? What if he were injured, wounded, gassed? What would it be like; what would it be like to be dead? Do people who are killed fighting for their country go to Heaven? There were no sophisticated answers to be had for his fears; he was seventeen and his powers of abstract thought, though good for his age, had a long way to go. He wanted to come to terms with the war in his head because he missed his calmness; outwardly he still was as controlled as ever, but in less than two months he would be eighteen. He had set his own course and on 16 July he would hit the tape towards which his life had been running. Never having been away from Workington except for day trips out to the Lakes with his family, he was simmering with ideas of what it would be like to be in barracks; to leave home and go far away. The marching and the training were things he had heard so much about from men on leave and he wondered constantly if he would be up to it.

His mother was quite aware that something was not right with her eldest son, but whenever Margaret tried to ask him what was troubling him, he shrugged it off by telling her it was 'Nothing Mam', and she put it down to his age. The resting expression of his face had taken on a new form, something between worry and puzzlement. Matt Roach was not much use as a confidant in this business and kept on trying to allay Barwise's anticipatory fears by pushing him jokingly and telling him, perhaps to cheer him up, that it would be a 'grand lark'. So Barwise, full of turmoil, gazed towards the West, and the blood red orb of the sun, painting the western clouds with a sanguine and holy glory, sank into the sea and gave him no answers. In the end he looked his last as the glow faded and made his way homewards as, to the right of him, the steelworks furnaces glared out a different kind of light.

Five days later the King and Queen came to Workington. Their purpose was to inspect the great steelworks, but a royal visit is never as simple as that. The royal train arrived at the station, a travelling palace, and King George V and Queen Mary were met by the Mayor of Workington between three and four o'clock in the afternoon. All concerns not engaged in war work had given their employees the half-day off, and all the schools closed to bring their pupils to the Station Road to see Their Majesties. Even before they arrived the display of finery from the dignitaries of the town was an impressive pageant. The Mayor, Alderman Fred Hall, was there looking anxious to show off his home town to the best; the Earl of Lonsdale as Lord Lieutenant of Cumberland, with his wife, the Countess, was there but looked far more at ease as he knew the royal couple anyway. Sir John Randles the MP was also at ease, for as he held a high position in the Workington Iron and Steel Company he knew his brief very well. The King and Queen were coming up from Barrow Shipyards and all along the route people had lined the railway to cheer their progress. They had slowed and stopped near St Bees to the great delight of hundreds of boys

Chapter 18 — The Royal Wink

from the school there who had given them a rousing cheer three times three. There were ceremonies to observe of course; bows to be given, the mace-bearer to precede the royal party out of the station and a large-windowed automobile for the monarch to sit in with his wife. The crowds round the station needed no barriers or control, but maintained a respectful distance from the people of importance. The King wore a field Marshal's uniform with lots of gold braid, and the Queen a very sensible coat with a broad fur collar and a hat which looked a bit warm for the May sunshine. There were murmurs of approval as the King was seen to offer his arm to his wife and helped her into the car, very gentlemanlike. As they drove off the crowd broke into a spontaneous and very heart felt rendition of God Save the King. This was wartime and they meant every word. The King expected, of course, to see and be seen so the route of the royal car went up Station Road and into Oxford Street taking the long way down Harrington Road to circle round to Moss Bay. Margaret and her children were on Harrington Road opposite the cemetery gates and cheered themselves hoarse as the King and Queen went past.

'He looked right at me,' said Ettie.

'No he was looking at me,' retorted Ommie. 'And he winked at me.'

'What would the King wink at you for?' demanded Billy.

'I don't know. Maybe he liked the look of me.'

'I can't see why. You look pretty lumpy to me.'

'Don't be horrible; I'm going to give you a smack for that.'

'No you're not,' said Margaret putting her foot down.

'The King did not wink at anybody. He looked at everybody including you and you all waved and cheered. That's what happened here, so let's have no smacking or bad words about this. Now you'll have something to tell your father when he gets home. It's not every day you see a King.'

'Why was he not wearing a crown?'

'Well Ettie I think they're a bit heavy and uncomfortable to wear all the time. I think he saves wearing it for special occasions.'

'Well I think he should wear it when he comes here. This is a special occasion and he's a King isn't he? Kings wear crowns. If they don't wear a crown, how can they be a proper King?'

The logic of children is sometimes unanswerable; Margaret contented herself with ushering her brood home like Mother Duck; they looked forward to telling their father later what they had seen. It is in the way of things that sometimes what is special is unintentionally outdone by events and fortune. Both of these were in full play on this particular afternoon. At first the royal visit went exactly to plan. Sir John Randles, expert man of steel conducted the King and Queen through all the stages of steel making, to their great interest. The King had wished to know how shells were made, so they showed him, beginning with crude ore, which he picked up and weighed in his hand. He saw the furnaces smelting the ore and watched it being poured into troughs to form pig iron. Then he was led to a Bessemer though at a safe distance, and they put on a 'blow' for him. He watched as the inferno was blasted through with air and oxygen and a wave of heat suffused the whole party accompanied by a deafening roar, at which he did not flinch, though Queen Mary looked slightly apprehensive. When the foreman judged that the batch was done they turned off the blowers and the shower of molten sparks subsided as they poured out the purified metal into moulds. The Queen opted to spend a prolonged time in the laboratories where she was fascinated by a chemist explaining the various processes going on in a range of bubbling tubes and apparatus. The managers led the King onto where the great ingots of white hot metal were rolled into bar steel in lengths suitable for the making of shells, which were then carted away to the National Shell Factory in Stanley Street and to others around the country.

When the demonstration was over the King and Queen met officials and selected workmen with whom they chatted, asking many questions about their hours of work, the conditions of their labour and any general inquiries they wished to ask. The little daughter of the Works Manager, in a pretty dress and matching hat, presented the Queen with a bouquet with a nice little curtsey. She charmed both of the Royals. The King was looking tired by now. The visit was about to end and the royal party were headed back to their car when his Majesty looked across the sidings and saw a man with a horse; it had his attention immediately and put new life into him. Without further ado he looked up and down the railway lines and there was no traffic in sight, it all having been halted for the royal visit; so he stepped across the sidings and approached the man with the horse who was now coupling it to the side of a wagon with a chain.

'What are you doing here?'

Tom had not been selected to meet the King and since the visit was virtually over he had decided to get on with the task he had to finish before he knocked off work. When George V came over he was not quite dumbstruck, but certainly surprised. Not certain as to how to behave, he settled for whipping off his cap and answering the question he had been asked.

'Shunting... err... Your Majesty.'

The King was well used to embarrassed workmen, 'With a horse? I thought you used engines for that...'

'Well we do Sir, but sometimes there's only a few wagons to shift and a horse is more convenient than calling an engine for such a small task.'

'I see; I had not realised that. He's a full bred Clydesdale isn't he?'

'Yes Sir.'

'What's his name.'

'Skiddaw Sir.'

'A good name for a Cumbrian horse; he's certainly big enough. My, but you're a fine fellow.'

So saying the King came forward and stroked Skiddaw's muzzle.

'Magnificent animal. If I had a treat for you I'd give you it.'

Tom felt in his pocket and rather bashfully pulled out an apple.

'He likes these Sir.'

'By Jove I should think he does. Thank you. What is your name?'

'Thomas Little, Your Majesty.'

George V fed the apple to Skiddaw who slobbered most appreciatively over the royal glove as Tom squirmed, though the King did not seem to mind at all and laughed as he patted the horse's neck.

'You know horses don't you, Sir?'

The King's eyes twinkled, 'You're not supposed to ask me questions you know; that's my job. You'd better not let them hear.' He nodded over towards the rest of his party who were picking their way over the lines towards him. Then to Tom's utter disbelief, he winked.

'But yes. I know horses and have done all my life. You too I think?'

'Yes Sir. All my life too.'

'I shouldn't right now because one of them rolled over on me and broke my pelvis two years ago, but you know what you have to do then.'

'Yes Sir; you have to get back on one as soon as possible,' replied Tom, wondering how a horse had injured the King in such a manner.'

'Exactly what I did as soon as I could,' said the King, almost as if the episode had been humorous. Poor thing was startled when some troops cheered me; never mind, such is life. Well then Mr Little, show me a sight I have never seen and shunt these wagons.'

As the royal party all watched Tom led Skiddaw on and as the huge horse strained into his collar the great railway wagon began to move down the track a hundred yards to where it slowly contacted onto the buffers of a waiting line of others. Then Tom uncoupled the chain and led his horse back to collect another wagon.

'Nicely done,' said the King. 'I enjoyed watching that. Thank you. I must go now, but I wish a very good day to you.'

'Thank you Your Majesty and a very good day to you too Sir.'

Tom bowed slightly, the King smiled, and then he moved away back to his car. As they drove off Mr Harrop, Tom's boss sidled up to him.

'Hell Tom, that man was as happy as Larry. The bosses are well pleased. There'll be a few bob extra in your packet this week. All that steel, but he was bowled over by a hoss!'

At the dinner table that night Ommie was positive that the King had winked at her from his car and Tom knew that he was a winking man, so he had to allow that if His Majesty had winked at one then he may very well have winked at the other.

'I have to say that I liked the man. He knows about horses for sure, but there didn't seem to be any side to him.'

'Well he's the King Tom, and an Emperor. You can't get much higher than that.'

'Yes I know, but I had the impression that I was dealing with an ordinary man.'

'What do you mean ordinary? Can a King be ordinary?'

'I think he can. When you're with someone clever you know it. You just feel that intelligence sort of glowing off them. You know what I mean.'

'True. I do. Like the Vicar; or the Headmaster at St John's.'

'Well, he didn't have that. I got the impression that I was talking to a very ordinary man, not of great intelligence, but with a lot of plain common sense. He struck me as down to earth.'

'Well maybe that's the sort of King we need. A clever one gets too many ideas. If he's ordinary then he's more likely to understand the rest of us than someone with too many brains. Anyway I'm glad he was nice to you. That's what counts.'

Barwise did not meet or see the King that day. As a metal worker he was, as were the rest of his workmates, intent on getting on with their work and what they were doing was particularly important. They were working on some strange shapes that were to be part of something bigger; like large metal boxes of boiler-plate; they had to be well riveted together yet with one of the faces curved. They also had to be made in sets of four.

'What did you say these things are called again Matt. Sponsors?'

'Nay you daft larl radgee. "Sponsons" was the word; get it

in your head,' was the semi-affectionate reply.

'And they're for tanks?'

'Yes. This is war work Barwise and that's what I was saying to you. Without us doing this there'd be no tanks. Now these go into the side of the tanks; you've seen pictures of them with little turrets sticking out the sides?'

'Yes of course I have.'

'Well that's what these are. These little holes tell me that these sponsons are going to a female tank.'

There was a moment's silence.

'Now you're going to ask me what's the difference between a man tank and a woman tank aren't you?'

'Yis.'

'I thought you might. A male tank is armed with two six pounder guns sticking out each side and four machine guns. A female tank has only machine guns.'

'So why do they call them male and female then?'

'I thought you had some brains Barwise! Let's put it this way, they say the first tank was called Little Willie and the next was called Big Willie. Got it now?'

'No. That's the Kaiser and his son.'

'No, it ain't you great tapper! The big gun is like a willie – get it now?'

'Oh. Yes. Yes I do.' Barwise turned pink.

'Well thank God for small mercies. You're doing good work here; vital work. You still going to join up?'

'When I'm called, yes. I will. I know what you're saying Matt; I have heard you going on about it a few times, but it's what I want to do.'

'I know that lad, but I'd be sorry if you got your head blown off.'

Barwise grinned. 'Not as sorry as I'd be.'

'True enough. Tell you what; you can't fight for another

year and you'll be training for that year.'

'That's the way I see it.'

'They'll send you on home leave if and when you have to go to France. Hopefully the war will be over before you have to go, but I want you to promise me something.'

'What's that?'

'When you get leave and before you go, you come and see me.'

'Aye alright. I will. Why though?'

'Oh it's something my brother said; I'll have something for you. Just come and see me. You've promised.'

A promise is a promise and Barwise always kept his promises. It was not until 3 July 1917 that the bolt arrived from the blue, at least as far as his parents were concerned. That Tuesday he got home from work to find, as Nancy had before him, a brown envelope with OHMS on it waiting for him. His mother was looking very puzzled about it, but he knew instantly what it was. Without opening it he went upstairs to his bedroom where, thankfully he found none of his brothers in residence. Heart pounding, he ripped the letter open and several pieces of paper fell out. It was headed 'Military Service Acts; Enlistment notice.' It was a standard letter with date stamps, but his name and address handwritten in a box near the top. Underneath he read that he was, under the terms of the Military Service Acts of 1916, called upon for service in the Army. He was required to present himself at the Headquarters of the Border Regiment at Carlisle Castle on Tuesday 17 July. This was the day after his eighteenth birthday. A travel warrant was enclosed and a postal order for four shillings, being his first service pay. It was quite clear that there was no procedure to be gone through; as of 18 July he was deemed to be a member of the Armed forces and had received his first pay. The letter ended that upon receipt of this notice he should immediately inform his employer of the date on which he was required to report for service. He saw no point in delaying the inevitable; Barwise was a straight down the line person and this matter needed no delay. Staring for a few minutes into space and gathering his resolve, he made his way downstairs and into the back room where Margaret and Tom were already present, she preparing the evening meal. In response to his father's questioning look Barwise put the letter down on the table and sat down without saying anything. Tom took up the letter and read.

'Well it's a mistake. You're a metal worker doing war work. That's a reserved occupation as well they know. We'll tell them it's a mistake and get this cancelled.'

'It's not a mistake Dad. I'm joining up.'

'Of course it's a mistake. You filled in the National Register just as everyone else did. They know you are a riveter and that makes you a starred man.'

'I'm not a starred man, Dad.'

'Of course you are. You do vital war work.'

'Nevertheless Dad, I'm not starred.'

Margaret came and sat down beside him, worry written large on her face.

'What have you done Barwise?'

'I've done nothing Mam. But I'm not starred.'

'But you must be on the National Register…' her voice tailed off and then she continued, 'What did you say your job was? On the Register I mean.'

Barwise looked at her with a dead straight face; 'I put down that I was an apprentice, which is what I am.'

'You did not say apprentice riveter. Oh Barwise!'

Tom's face showed fury as he banged his hand on the table. 'So you did it; and you did it on purpose!'

'I did and I have no regrets about it either Dad.'

'No regrets? We'll see about that my lad. You are a metal

worker and reserved. You are also under 21 and I am your father and I say you are not going.'

'Yes. I am going.'

'You damned well are not. I'll be down at that tribunal in the Town Hall tomorrow and tell them what's what and you will do as you are told.'

'No Dad. I won't. I'm going and that's all there is to it.'

'But Barwise, why? When you don't have to? There's hundreds of men from Workington have been killed. Why should you run the risk of that?'

'That's why Mam. You said it. How can I look myself in the mirror in future and know that I stayed at home when I wanted to go, and let other people go and get killed in a war that I should have been in but shirked?'

'But you're not shirking. The work you do is needed; it's vital.'

'I know that, but there's lots of people can train as riveters. It's not exactly the most skilled of jobs. The point is that I want to go and do my bit. This is the biggest thing in my life; the biggest war ever. How can I not be in it?'

'But you have a choice.'

'Exactly Mam. I have a choice, but everyone has to make it themselves; I have thought about it a lot and I want to go. I don't mind those who stay at home and work on war stuff. They are doing their bit too, but we all have our own answer; I have to fight. It's what I want.'

'Aye well it's not what your mam and me want,' growled Tom. 'You can get it into your head that you're not going and so I shall tell the tribunal tomorrow.'

'You do that Dad and you won't be seeing me again.'

The two men sat, the son looking directly into his father's eyes, the older man glaring, not used to defiance. A hostile silence suffused the room for the better part of a minute as

Margaret looked desperately from one to the other. Her mind flew to Dearham, and she wished that her father were here; she had often described him as the wisest man she knew, and now she wondered what he would do. Suddenly it came to her that she knew.

'Barwise; I need to speak to your father about this; would you leave us alone now please?'

Face perfectly set like a mask of determination, Barwise got up and left the room in silence.

'Tom, I think we need to stop and think about this.'

'I have thought about it. He's not going and that's that.'

'But who are you?'

'Me? I'm his father that's who I am.'

'I know that, and he couldn't ask for a better one.'

'Try telling him that just now; the attitude of him, that cheeky young pup.'

'But that's just it Tom. He isn't.'

'How do you mean?'

'He's not a young pup. He's going to be 18 on the sixteenth of this month.'

'He's still under age.'

'Oh you can say that, but look at him Tom. He's been earning a wage for four years. He's a young man and a very fine one too. Don't tell me you're not proud of him.'

'Well yes I am, but that tells me even more that I don't want to let him go and get his head blown off.'

'Your dad was a wonderful man Tom, but he kept you working on the farm milking cows for years. Did you want to do that?'

'You know I didn't. I wanted to get out and branch out for myself.'

'Well that's Barwise too, Tom. You're doing what your dad did.'

This brought silence and thinking. A few minutes went by.

'You want him to go?'

'What I want is not important.'

'He might get killed.'

'He might.'

'Do you want him to get killed? There's a very good chance of it.'

'I know that Tom. I know that and I don't want him to go.'

'So what are you saying?'

'It's not my decision Tom.'

'And it's not mine either?'

Again there was silence.

'He's a man Tom; a young one, but the decision is his. Even if he gets killed it's still his decision. God knows I don't want him to go and if anything happens to him I don't know how I'll bear it any more than any other poor woman in this town. But he's eighteen. He can't go abroad until he's 19. I think we have to stand aside Tom and let him have his way.'

Tom stared at her.

'He's a man. Let him be a grown up.'

Tom stood as if frozen for an unending second; then he walked to the door and opened it.

'Barwise. Come down here.'

His son came down the stairs slowly and re-entered the room with the same fixed and stubborn look that he had left with.

'You have made up your mind?'

'You know I have.'

'I know. Your mother and I will not stand in your way.'

The tension dropped from the air with a palpable release of springs and Barwise smiled; not gladly because he was not glad. There were a few lines of Rudyard Kipling that kept running through his head, for like many of his generation he did not wish to go, but at the same time he did because he felt he must:

'And now the hugely bullets
Come pecking through the dust
And no-one wants to face 'em,
But every beggar must.
So like a man in irons,
Which isn't glad to go,
They moves 'em up in companies,
Uncommon stiff and slow.'

This surely is where true courage lies; in the sure and certain knowledge that one is going willingly into a situation where one may easily die, however much instinct says not to. Barwise Little, like all other young men of his age, faced up to something alien, life-threatening and unavoidable with doubt in his mind, fear firmly tamped down in the back of his brain and the unquenchable hope that each human has, that whatever faces us, somehow we will come through it in the end. His birthday meal with his family was cheerful in a brittle sort of way and his luggage, upstairs, was light for he would not be needing much from home. On the morning of 17 July, although he did not want them to, his parents insisted on accompanying him to the station and he had to watch Margaret weeping as his train pulled out. Her boy was not going to war; he was gone for a soldier; just before lunch Barwise presented himself to the sentries at the gates of Carlisle Castle and was directed to the receiving hut on the flat ground to the North of the castle where the barracks stood. Shortly after that he was ferried out to the expanded garrison accommodation at Carlisle race course. He was on the road to war.

Chapter 19

Saving Lives

Margaret's pregnancy was quite pronounced by late July 1917 though it did not slow her down much as yet. It was her tenth pregnancy and if it went to full term as hoped then it would be her ninth child. The doctor thought it was due sometime around mid November, but since she was always active, her routine had not yet varied. She knew that she would slow down for about a month before the birth, but in the meantime it was something she was well used to, and there was a house to run children to care for, and meals to cook. She was perhaps feeling a little more tired than she normally would, but then of course she was now 42 and some fatigue was to be expected. At least Alpha Omega was very helpful and a responsible person to trust with jobs, whilst even Ettie was going out of her way to do all she could to help her mam. The boys could be relied on to chop wood, carry buckets, work the mangle and bring coal, so much of the heavy work could be taken from her. Around the set pot where the communal broth was prepared, there were other women from the street who pitched in and helped and were well aware of her condition, so were very willing to do all they could.

'Many hands make light work' was the repeated motto of Mrs Smith from over the road and she was right, though Margaret wished she would not repeat it quite so often. The departure of Barwise for the Army and training disturbed her a little, but not as much as if he had been going on active service.

His age meant that he could not leave the country for another year and she was sure that the war would be over by then. He would be able to come home with honour and at least be able to say that he had been willing to do his bit, but hostilities had ended before he could be posted abroad. She hated the war and what it was doing; she hated the killing and the suffering, the hunger and the violence of it all. Her morals, her religion and her instinct all told her that it was wrong, yet she could not voice it outside her own bedroom where she expressed it to her husband. Tom was in broad agreement with her, but they did not speak of it in front of their children in case the neighbours heard through them. The mood of many people was so set on fighting to the bitter end that to make any anti-war remarks was to invite trouble of a sort they did not want.

'Did you hear about that disturbance in Whitehaven, Tom?'

'Wellington Pit? Aye, I did. That'll hit them hard for a while, but they'll get it back working in six weeks or so I should think.'

'I didn't mean the pit. What's happened there?'

'Oh, it's on fire apparently; there's a huge underground fire and they've had to close the whole pit and wall it off to starve the fire. They think it should burn out in a few weeks.'

'That's terrible; what'll they live on without work?'

'National Insurance Margaret. That's something to thank Lloyd George for anyway. Nobody'll starve.

'That's true. Anyway it's not that I was talking about. It was Mr Richardson.'

'The MP? No, I've heard nothing about him. What happened?'

'Well apparently he tried to have an anti-war meeting in Whitehaven Market Place.'

'Ha! I bet he didn't get many to that. It wouldn't make him popular.'

'No it didn't. There was a riot.'

'Really? It's in the paper? Let's see it.'

'Here you are. Apparently he and his agent had just started to speak when they were attacked by a mob.'

'Oh yes, I see it. They were pelted with mud and stones and took refuge in the house of a mine agent nearby. Good grief! The mob smashed the windows and forced their way in, assaulted the police superintendent who tried to stop them and broke the door down. I see he escaped out the back with his constituency agent. Just as well. They'd have probably hung him from a lamp post.'

'Yes' said Margaret, but that's not the worst of it. Read what happened at the court.'

'They were all charged with unlawful conduct so as to cause a breach of the peace and with wilful damage; and the magistrates dismissed all the charges to loud cheering. That's a bit off. To assault an MP is one thing, but Superintendent Hogg and damage to a house is another. Whatever else, it's still breaking the law.'

'That's what so worrying Tom. You can't say what you think any more. It's like people have gone mad. If you say anything at all against the war they fly at you like some lunatic; you dare not even mention the idea of making peace. It's like a dog that's tasted raw meat and wants more; they don't want peace; they want victory and they don't mind any cost to get it. I don't know what's happened to people. Once they would have been nice and normal and not said boo to a goose. But this was like a pack of wolves. You can't even talk about peace in church.'

'These are the times we live in Margaret. There's nothing we can do about it as ordinary folk, so I suggest we keep our heads down. I don't want bricks through the window or our children assaulted; and I do wish to stay on good terms with our neighbours. There's no need for us to be jingos, but sometimes it's best to go with the flow. What we cannot alter, we must bear.'

How widespread this view was will never be known. President Wilson's suggestion of peace talks in early 1917 was not widely known of and the scale of national effort in this year was such that all people could think of was total war and winning it. The war had taken on a life of its own, consumed all in its path like wildfire and none could withstand it.

In Bankfield Hospital it burned in Nellie's head even harder than ever. By the end of June 1917 she had been working at the auxiliary hospital for six months and had been found so useful that the Commandant had asked her to stay on for a few more months. It had seemed a logical thing to do because the Infirmary was managing well enough without her, but Nellie's head was not at ease. In her own mind she was simply drifting and she was not at all clear what she wanted to do about that.

It is often the case with human beings that they float through periods of their lives, uncertain of where their destination may be and unsure of their purpose. Of course it may well be that there is no purpose and that the point of life is simply to live it, but Nellie, being human, liked to think that there was reason behind what she did; that she had a place and a point to her life. Whatever it was, she knew it had something to do with the war, but it eluded her. Saul, on the road to Damascus had one of those moments that come to human beings rarely during their lifetimes when what has been dim becomes as clear as crystal. Nellie's moment came on 28 August towards the end of her shift when she seized a few minutes to tidy up some of the debris left on the tables in the gardens of Bankfield Mansion, and picked up a *Daily Mirror*.

It could be said in all fairness that The Daily Mirror may not often be viewed as a source of inspiration to people though it is useful as an organ of news. Nellie had not read a newspaper for several days so tucked it under her arm, and since she had finished for the day she went to her room, lay down on her bed, and began to leaf through it in a desultory kind of way until she got to page six. The page header was, as usual, sensationalist to a degree, '*A silhouette from the front – Fritz gets a hammering.*' A line of soldiers was outlined black against the sky on a distant hillock whilst a huge artillery piece loomed in the foreground. Then her eye was drawn to the bottom of the page by the recognition of her own name, for there was printed '*Nellie*'. Naturally it captured her attention so she gave it her concentration. It was a picture of a nurse.

Nellie sat up in bed, her eyes on the picture which showed a round faced girl in her twenties with short hair, glasses and a nurse's cap and read, '*Hospital bombed. Miss Nellie Spindler formerly of Leeds Infirmary, who was killed when German airmen bombed a hospital in France.*' Her mind whirled, but this was not enough for her. She needed to know more, so she literally jumped off her bed and went down to the lounge where there would be more newspapers. In the local she found a syndicated article with more detail. It appeared that Nurse Spindler, aged 26 and daughter of a Chief Inspector of Police, was killed during an artillery bombardment. Something happened in Nellie's head and tears pricked at her eyes. There were women under the enemy's guns at the front line. What on earth was she doing here? With her knowledge and her skills, why was she here in Workington emptying bedpans? Her shoulders began to shake as great emotion swayed her, and what she had been keeping down in her unconscious mind came out; but in the end no actual tears came. Instead she went back to her room to compose herself and to think. For a long time she sat like a statue on her bed, just staring at the wall, then all at once she stood up and walked out of the room. On the ground floor she walked to the door of the Commandant's office and knocked firmly on it twice.

'Come in,' said the voice of Mrs Wilson and Nellie opened and walked in, closing the door behind her.

'Sister Little, what can I do for you?'

'I wish to apply for transfer to the Red Cross Organisation Matron; as soon as possible.'

Mrs Wilson leaned back in her chair and looked hard at Nellie.

'I'm sure that can be arranged, but have you talked to Miss Winter about this? She'll be wanting you back at the Infirmary surely?'

'I'm absolutely certain of it ma'am. I want to transfer to the Red Cross.'

'Well it is of course entirely possible; the organization would be glad to have another trained Sister I know, but I'm not sure that they would allow you to stay here. You'd probably be transferred somewhere else.'

'That's what I want ma'am. I want to be transferred somewhere else.'

'I see. May I ask where exactly?'

'To a base hospital Matron. I want to work at a base hospital or a Casualty Clearing Station.'

Mrs Wilson's face took on a look of concern.

'But my dear girl; do you know what you are wishing for? Why there was a poor girl killed just yesterday. You might die.'

'I know ma'am. That's why I have to go.'

'What do you mean?'

'It's in my head Matron, but it's in my heart too. I know that I have to go there. If I don't go there my head will never be quiet about it for the rest of my life. I know it. I'll never be at peace as long as I live. I have to go.'

There was a pause.

'So tell me why it is there, Sister. You say it's in your head and your heart. Can you tell me why it's there?'

Nellie's answer was almost ripped out of her soul;

'Because I can't stand idly here safe on the shore when I can be of service over the sea.'

Mrs Wilson's face jerked up at her with a most odd expression, 'What did you say Sister?'

'I can't stand idle when I can be of use over there where I'm needed.'

Mrs Wilson looked at her, then reached into her desk drawer, pulling out a well thumbed book which she opened and looked through. Finally, finding the page she wanted she read,

'Rather, ten times die in the surf, heralding the way to a new world than stand idly on the shore.'

'Almost the same metaphor. Do you know who said that?'

'No ma'am.'

'It was Florence Nightingale'.

There was a pause.

'Now I know that I'm an old fogey and some of you young things think I'm a dragon, but I know a calling when I see one.

I will not stand in your way and will help you all I can. There are some forms you have to fill in and you can do them now. You are right of course; they need all the trained nurses they can get out there. I know you have some training in wounds, but you'll need more. I imagine you'll be in Carlisle before long for that, but not every girl wants to go where you will be; two or three months I should think, and you'll be there.'

'Thank you ma'am; I am very grateful to you.'

'Well let's hope you think that in six months time. Now just fill these in and welcome to the Red Cross.'

Half an hour later Nellie had done her paperwork and emerged rather dazed at what she had done, yet in her mind clearer of purpose than she had been for months; she could see her way through the mist around her on a road paved with certainty. She trod lightly. Now she had to tell her parents.

They were not happy, of course, but they had let Barwise go and now they had to let her go. They knew Nellie for a determined person and she would be twenty-one and her own mistress in a few short months. Anyway, she was not going to fight, but be at a base hospital, so she said, behind the lines with lots of other girls; that would be quite safe. The article about Nellie Spindler had been small, they had not seen it, and Nellie chose not to draw their attention to it. Margaret's reaction was not so much of fear, but of apprehension and a certain amount of pride; her little girl, her first-born was going to the war. Moreover she was going to do good; to engage in something which Margaret admired. It all happened quickly too; the Red Cross did not hang about when it came to the provision of nursing personnel because they were sorely needed. On Monday 24 September 1917 she received instructions and a travel warrant which told her to report on Thursday at Fusehill Hospital, the huge military establishment in Carlisle, to serve some time there and for more intensive training. Once again

Margaret wept in a mixture of fear and pride because one of her children was going away to serve her country. Her worries were, for the moment at any rate, misplaced, because it was to be months before Nellie would be sent abroad. First she had to put her time in at Fusehill and work within the confines of a huge hospital under military discipline.

Margaret was particularly emotional at the departure of another of her children because the next one was about to arrive. Seven months of pregnancy during the hot summer had left her feeling tired and fraught, although it was in her nature to manage her house as best she could at all times. Alpha Omega was a blessing and a boon during the long summer holiday from school, but when she had to go back in September the weight of the house and shopping fell again onto Margaret, at least during the day. She had not found it easy and had to fight off the urge to sleep much of the time. When her friends told her to go slower she replied that being with child was not an illness and there was work to be done. No matter how much of her load they tried to lighten, she was still putting in a lot more hours than perhaps she should have done; despite this she was, on the face of things, quite well and the doctor assured her that all was coming along quite nicely. Nellie told her that she would get leave before being sent abroad and would of course come down to see her new brother or sister before she left.

Nellie arrived at Carlisle Station feeling quite an old hand in the city after her stay there two years previously. To a newcomer the place must have looked like pandemonium because it was busier than it had ever been in history. The normal traffic was bad enough; troop trains and loads of ammunition, coal, iron, steel, stone and all the commodities of war passed north and south on the line between Western Scotland and England, feeding the engines of destruction. However, one of the bloodiest battles ever fought was going on even as she arrived in the city and the word 'Passchendaele' was engraving itself indelibly on the national psyche and the hospital trains ran round the clock. This was literally the case, because the trains that transported men and materiel to the various fronts had priority over trains of wounded, so they were not whisked to medical care as fast as possible, but when gaps in the traffic would allow. From a clearing station behind the lines to a base hospital could take three or four days on a hospital train, but the base hospitals were overwhelmed and kept men only as long as they needed to. Hundreds, thousands of men were shipped home and onto other hospital trains to be taken all over the country. Each carriage contained perhaps thirty to forty bunks and one nurse who did all that she could, but in reality could attend to basic comfort only. These girls were worked off their feet, washing and feeding, administering medicine and brandy, giving hypodermic injections, drinks, cleaning floors and toilets, attending to bedpans and bottles and changing dressings. The trains smelled of mud and chlorine, of blood and faeces, of urine, smoke and stale breath all underpinned by a thick unhealthy fug of an atmosphere that men lived in for days. They arrived at places like Fusehill, many at the end of endurance, the place they came to live or to die. Red Cross volunteers and a few nurses were very much in evidence, because as trains arrived they would move onto them dispensing drinks, sandwiches and other necessities to men who were fagged out, dirty and fed up. Many of them were still caked in mud, lousy and with their wounds hastily dressed, just as they had left France and the battles a few days before.

The Medical Officer of Health for Carlisle would receive a phone call from Southampton, where many of the wounded were brought ashore, to tell him that a hospital train would be passing through on its way to Scotland or stopping at Carlisle if there were enough beds available. In either case it would have to be dealt with at the station and more likely as not in the middle of the night when there was less war goods traffic about. It was the ones who stayed that would concern Nellie for this stage of her career.

It was a short walk from the station, as Nellie knew, and her bag was not heavy, so she had no difficulty finding her way to what had once been the Carlisle Workhouse, but which had been converted into a 400 bed hospital, opened in April 1917. As the year progressed it had taken over buildings in nearby Brook Street and the Newtown School so now possessed 861 patient beds. Soon she was walking between the impressive red brick piles that made up what was virtually a campus, and in through the main door between the mock Jacobean cupolas of the façade where she reported at the reception desk. Having been directed and reported to the office of the Commandant, an officer in the Royal Army Medical Corps, she learned he was very respectfully known as 'Mr' FitzGerald. He was very distinguished in his field so had no need to observe military punctilio in a hospital setting. No doubt his day would have been lightened by conversation with Nellie, but it was to his outer office she went, and found herself in a brisk and mostly one-sided conversation with one of the Commandant's secretaries. In short order she was allocated a bed in a double room in the nurse's hostel, hospital identity cards, a meal card for use in the canteen and a docket to draw fresh uniforms from the stores. Equipped with these she then trotted off down the maze of corridors to the office of Miss Graham the Matron. This place was evidently very different to the small hospitals she had worked in up until now; administration was firmly in the hands of the commandant but the nursing staff were Matron's and she ran a tight ship. There was no time to waste on a lowly newcomer, so after a cursory inspection Miss Graham told Nellie to report to her immediate superior on the second floor in Ward four to let her know that she had arrived. She would find out her duties and when to commence, then she could locate her room and settle in.

Nellie was beginning to feel weary of dragging her bag around this vast building by the time she reached the door of Ward 4 and found that there was an office just outside it bearing the name, "Sister Lydia Taylor."

Hoping that this was the last port of call in her bureaucratic round, she knocked, not too loudly, and a voice on the other side said, 'Come in'. Nellie went through the door, and, not sure how to begin, simply said,

'Good afternoon Sister; I was told to report to you because I've been assigned to your ward.'

'Ah yes. Good afternoon to you also Sister Little; I've been expecting you. I must say it's nice to get a new nurse with some decent training. I see you've worked in two hospitals and were made up to Sister a few months ago.'

'Yes, Sister Taylor. Less than a year ago.'

'You've done well I think and it indicates some ability that you've had the step up so young. I understand that you want to serve in France ultimately?'

'That's right, Sister Taylor.'

'Well let's start out right shall we; use my name so much and you'll wear it out. I know who you're talking to and you know who I'm talking to, so let us call each other plain 'Sister'. This is a military hospital, but we are both nurses; I was formerly Matron at a sanatorium before volunteering for war work, but there's only one Matron in this establishment, which is how it should be. This ward is in my charge as is Ward 5 over the passageway. In each ward are thirty beds so I have the oversight of more patients than in many civilian hospitals. You are here to train so that when you are sent to France you will be fully prepared for what you have to do out there. Your training is partly my responsibility; I would imagine that if you prove satisfactory you should be ready for the transfer you seek around about next March, but we shall see how you get on. Just remember that although we are both Sister, I have oversight of you and you act on my instructions.'

'Yes Sister.'

'I have placed you on a rota commencing tomorrow, but have given you some time to settle in. Morning shift starts at 7.00am, but you will not be on it. Report to Ward 4 at 2.30pm tomorrow; the shift starts at three o'clock, but there will be some introductory talk to do before you start work. That shift will run until eleven o'clock when the night shift will take over. You will have to serve your turn on that, but not yet. Have you done that before?'

'Yes Sister; at Bankfield in Workington.'

'Yes; they are a convalescent hospital I recall. We have more acute cases here and often have to deal with emergencies so you'll have to be very competent to do the night shift. In time we shall see. Needless to say, you may be called on at other times; if we get a train in then the shift system goes by the board and it's all hands to the pumps until the work is done. I hope you are prepared to work hard?'

'I am Sister; that's what I want to do.'

The older woman's face creased into a faint smile, 'I know you do. I was young and an idealist once. I'm sure you'll do very well. Now take yourself up to the third floor up the main stairs and turn left; not right because that is another ward. That's where you'll find the nurses' accommodation; we live over the shop you see. You're sharing with another young woman who has much the same ambitions as you. Room 7 is where we have put you.'

Sure enough, when Nellie climbed the stairs she found herself in a long corridor with a green linoleum floor and lit by regularly spaced electric lights with green metal shades which stretched down to the far end of the building where there was a window. The lights were necessary because at the end furthest from the window it was quite dark. She did not wait at the room 7 door because it was her own room, but knocked and walked right in to where a dark haired girl was unpacking a bag into a three drawer lockable cupboard beside one of two bunks. As Nellie entered she stood up.

'Hello; I'm May Hollister.'

'Nellie Little.'

For a moment they looked at each other, and Nellie relaxed. May had nice dark brown eyes and they were gentle and caring. Her face was quite broad and her lips were rather thin; her hair was black and straight and there was an almost wistful far away look to her. Nellie liked her on sight and knew instantly that there would be no problems with her room mate.

'Where are you from?' enquired Nellie.

'From Whitehaven. I've been at the Infirmary there for five years now. And you?'

'Workington Infirmary; and more or less the same.'

May's father was a coal miner at Wellington pit; she had three brothers and three sisters and lived in an old terrace of miners' cottages overlooking the town called Granby Terrace. The way she described her life was rather like life at 55 Devonshire Street would sound; Nellie thanked her lucky stars that she was sharing with someone she had things in common with. It would have been so easy to end up with a middle class miss from somewhere like Harrogate with whom she would be chalk and cheese. To her great pleasure she found that May had volunteered to serve in France for just the same reasons as she had; a sense of wanting to do more. Her feeling that she was in the wrong place she found echoed in May who had concluded that she had been given a mission that she simply had to follow.

Nellie had been brought up to observe her religion, but May much more so; she knew that nurses could not actually serve in the front line, but wanted to do her bit as close to where the action was as she could.

The best thing about May was that she was a good companion; she talked freely of her own life and had lots of stories, but she also listened. They explored the canteen together, ate their supper and passed a pleasant evening of conversation, at the end of which Nellie felt that she was beginning to know her. The best bit was that when night came and they went to bed, May did not snore any more than she herself did. Both of them passed a peaceful night and woke shortly before seven o'clock. With a certain pride and apprehension about the course they were embarking on, both put on their new uniforms and went down to have breakfast reasonably early. It was a good job that they did so because as they finished an orderly came into the room and called out in a stentorian voice;

'All supervising nurses to Matron's Office immediately please. All supervising nurses, immediately.'

Nellie and May were unaware of events in France of course, but the Battle of the Menin Road Ridge had been in progress for several days now and the British army took over 20,000 casualties in five days, something like 3,000 of them being killed. The shattered and bleeding remnants of the rest were crammed onto hospital trains and immediately overwhelmed the resources of the hospitals further south. Thousands of men straight off the boat were packed onto northbound trains and by the morning of 28 September Carlisle was being asked to accept its share. A huge flurry of activity took place as men were moved out of Fusehill and away to convalescent establishments to make room for what was coming. Carlisle was a hospital city and like a well-oiled machine its parts moved into action. A small army of nurses and helpers waited on the station armed with refreshments, brandy, cigarettes etc as the VAD swarmed in from all over the area. Doctors and nurses waited to examine labels on men and to assess urgency as they were unloaded. The city's large fleet of ambulances waited on the station forecourt and down the surrounding streets whilst people with private cars who had permits to do so also waited to ferry walking wounded. Carlisle cared, had been in the forefront of setting up its own military hospitals, and had gained itself a name for efficient care of the wounded. Just after 10.00am the signal box told the station-master that the hospital train was about thirty minutes away and word was relayed to the hospitals. Every nurse, every orderly, every doctor was on standby; the operating theatres prepared and the world hung on a breath until the locomotive came in sight and slowly puffed its way into the station. The doors opened and men flooded on; a few seconds later and the first blanket-covered forms began to be carried out and deposited onto the platform, surrounded by medical attendants. It looked like chaos, but in the calling out and the shouting, the scurrying and the ant like activity was a smooth and practiced order. The killing was done; now it was time for the healers. Soon the ambulance bells rang out all round the hospital city as men, hurt and maimed, cut and battered by war, were ferried to caring hands, surgical help, to life-savers, and to cool clean sheets.

Chapter 20

The Soldier

The hut was of wood, painted black outside and with a roof of corrugated iron; it contained thirty bunks lined up, fifteen to each side. This was because it was home to a training platoon that comprised thirty recruits, whereas ultimately they would be joining fighting platoons at the front that held anything up to fifty men. At the far end of the hut were two small rooms that housed the Sergeant and his assistant, a Corporal. Carlisle race-course would not be holding any equine events for quite some time to come, as these buildings and others covered much of its vast expanse of grass; the whole was surrounded by a wire fence which was patrolled by armed sentries. Barwise had arrived in the back of a Crosley tender with a handful of other lads of his age and had been ordered into the hut by a sergeant who read their names off a clipboard and allocated them to various huts. Although he had made a few attempts at conversation in the back of the lorry they had mostly fallen on stony ground as his companions were in various stages of excitement, shyness and shock at leaving their normal lives behind. Now in hut 6 he was told to dump his bag onto an empty bunk and wait there for instructions. Looking around he saw more strange faces, but directly opposite him, to his pleasure he saw a face he thought that he knew. He could not put a name to it, but he was sure that he had seen the lad somewhere before. For the moment he did not have time to think about it as his new Sergeant appeared at the far end and yelled at the recruits to stand by their beds. When they did so, hauling themselves up into what they thought looked like 'Attention', the Corporal called the register.

The Sergeant was a fierce looking man in his late forties who stood ramrod straight with a small rattan cane under his arm and he spoke to his charges with no ceremony at all.

'Right you men; look at me! Look at me well.'

They duly looked and when they did so, a fascination set in. Sergeant Grieve had no right hand, but a hook in its place. He also had a patch over his right eye, and when he moved he walked with a limp.

'That's right. That's me. The gammy leg is from Colenso and the eye is from the Boxer Rebellion. The arm and the hand I lost on the Somme. I've been there my lads; and that means you are very, very lucky.'

There were of course some very puzzled looks occasioned by this last remark, though a certain awe was sparked by the Sergeant's having been at such legendary battles. He was evidently something of a hero and probably to be feared.

'So can any of you young geniuses tell me why you are lucky?'

The lad whose face Barwise thought he knew ventured to put his hand up, not without a rather worried expression.

'You're not in school lad. The way to do it is to stand to attention with a slight stamp to draw attention and say "Permission to speak Sergeant".'

'Yes Sir, sorry Sir.'

'I thought you were a bright lad; I can see you're not. I'm not a Sir; that's for officers. I'm a Sergeant, and Corporal Simonini is a Corporal do you understand?'

'Yes Sergeant.'

'Good; I'm glad that's settled then. Now tell me why you are lucky.'

'Because you are here Sergeant, and can train us properly.'

'Almost. Very nearly; in fact I might revise my opinion and think you have a brain after all. Yes. I'm here and I can train you properly. But most important it means that I survived so I can train you to survive; I'm lucky and if you are lucky then my type of luck will rub off on you. What's your name Private?'

'Holliday Sergeant. Bill Holliday.'

'Right Holliday; you and your pals can get outside now and we'll go for a little run to the stores. You look like a bunch of scruffy civvy oiks to me, and my platoon is going to at least look like soldiers. Then I might be able to turn you into proper ones. Think of it as making steel in a crucible. Here we take in the plain iron and we melt it and add stuff, and make it into the proper stuff to smash Jerry with. Now jump to it!'

When he said 'run' it was exactly what he meant. The thirty new lads found that he expected them to run everywhere when not marching. The Sergeant and the Corporal had them go 'at the double' at all times as part of their regime to get their charges fit. The stores were over the other side of the race course and many were puffed out when they got there. Before long Barwise was in uniform, but it did not look quite as he had imagined. The blue collarless shirt with the white neck-band was well enough, but the breeches were a problem. Like everyone else there he had worn them before, but always with long stockings. Now he stood looking vaguely ridiculous in his socks and a long length of hairy leg between where the breeches ended and the socks began. He knew that he was supposed to wrap the seven foot long strip of khaki cloth round his leg, but never having worn puttees before, he did not know how to begin and a few young men had already tried and failed. Strangely enough this served to break the ice with this group and there was a lot of good-humoured laughter as the strange piece of clothing fell repeatedly round peoples' ankles in a limp heap. Apparently

Chapter 20 — The Soldier

this was not unexpected because Corporal Simonini appeared after a few minutes and told them to gather round; he had one bare leg.

'Right men. Begin at the bottom and tuck the corner of the strip round. Now wrap it round the join between sock and boot, quite tightly. Do that.'

This they did, in silence because of his presence and with a lot of concentration and in some cases, effort.

'Now you simply wrap it round spiraling upwards to below the knee, like this.'

They followed suit.

'Now wrap the last bit of it firmly round the junction between your breeches and your leg and wind the binding tape round three times. Now tie a simple knot like so; and that's it.'

When the Corporal looked round he saw that all of the platoon had more or less managed it.

'You'd better practice doing it. Scruffy puttees on duty and especially on parade will get your name taken and maybe put on a charge. Any questions?'

'Yes Corporal,' ventured one lad. 'What do we do with our own clothes?'

'Under your bed you'll find a cardboard box; this is a normal procedure and a present to you from His Majesty's government. Put your clothes in there, seal it with your home address on, and your effects will be delivered gratis, courtesy of a grateful nation. That's the last favour you'll get, as you will learn in the next few weeks.'

He looked around and produced a cardboard box and pulled from it a list.

Right; answer your names when I call you. Armstrong...'

As each man answered the Corporal gave him a set of identity discs to hang round his neck. The discs were printed with each man's surname, initial, army number, B.Regt. and religion. Barwise's read CE. One was red and the other was green. The green one had eight sides and was to be removed if the soldier became a casualty and showed anyone attending him that he had been recognized as wounded and was being seen to.

'Yes, they're made of cardboard because they're more comfortable to wear in hot countries. They do damage easily and they do rot in the ground. So if you're killed and you want people to know whose body it is, I recommend you get a metal one done privately. That's up to you, of course, and quite unofficial. Best thing of all to do is…' they hung on his words, 'not to get killed.'

When the Corporal had gone, Bill Holliday looked at Barwise and said, 'I think I know your face. Where are you from?'

'I think I know yours too. I'm from Workington.'

'Me too; I live down on the Marsh.'

'Devonshire Street, but I work at the boiler factory.'

'You'd pass me on the way to work then. I mend boots in a shop down there.'

'Ah now that clicked! I've bought segs from you before.'

'That'll be it. We sell a few clogs, but not many, though we do stock the segs. Kids get through a lot of them.'

Barwise grinned, 'Aye well, we all did that,' which brought an answering smile. It was one of the commonest things that children got into trouble for in Workington. The metal segs or caulkers on the bottom of a pair of clogs would make terrific showers of sparks if you kicked your feet along the cobbles and younger children regarded it as great fun to see who could make the most rewarding display. It also wore out the segs very quickly and new ones had to be bought; many fathers kept their own cobbler's last at home for the purpose of hammering these on, but it meant time had to be spent doing it.

'What's your name?'

'Barwise Little.'

'You think we're the only two from Workington here?'

'Well I don't see any more I recognize.'

As it turned out they were indeed the only ones from Workington in this particular batch of recruits and so they formed a bond from which would grow a strong friendship. One of its first effects was seen in Barwise's brown B5 ankle boots, standard issue hobnails for all British soldiers. They were brand new and dull; but a cobbler is a handy person to know in such a circumstance. Bill Holliday pulled a small bottle of oil from his bag, set to with a long rag, and soon had boots that gleamed.

'Look after your boots and your boots will look after you. My dad was a soldier and he taught me that.'

Then he did Barwise's; the comradeship cemented in tangible form.

'Never mind what anyone tells you Barwise – don't piss in your boots to wear them in. It's a myth and all you'll get is stinking boots.'

'I never even thought of doing that! Who would do such a thing?'

'There's some old soldiers will tell you it helps shape the boots to your feet so you won't get blisters on a long march, but it's rubbish; take it from me.'

'Why do they do it then?'

'I think it's an old soldier's joke they play on new recruits, you know, a bit like sending someone for a pint of elbow grease.'

'But that's just daft.'

'Aye, but it gives them a laugh I suppose. Oh and don't leave them under your bed at night. Put them in your locker.'

'Why?'

'Because if you don't someone might use them instead of

going out to the latrines.'

'You're pulling my leg!'

'Not from what I hear. They'll smile to your face during the day, but on a cold rainy night your boots are fair game as a piss-pot if they don't want to go out.'

'That's disgusting.'

'Maybe, but it's done. In the same way, keep anything you value either locked up or close to you if you don't want it to go walkies.'

'Thieves? Surely not.'

'You're a bit innocent I think; there's all sorts here Barwise; rich men, poor men, beggarmen and thieves. I think living down on the Marshside has made me a bit more cynical than most of you Uppies; not that I'm saying bad things about my neighbours; there's a lot of good folk among them, but some rum ones as well if you take my meaning. Just because they've got the same uniform as you it doesn't mean they won't have the shirt off your back if you let them. Believe me, some of the stories I've heard would stand your hair on end. If you lose or damage kit you get charged for it, so write or scratch your name on everything to stop people pinching it to replace their own. Trust your marras and no-one else.'

Barwise paid special attention to the stoutness of his locker; it was very sound. In the rest of their equipment they were not so lucky. The excellent lightweight 1908 webbing equipment was in short supply in wartime, so they had to make do with the 1914 leather equipment which was much heavier. Over their khaki tunics they had a wide waist belt and two braces on left and right. On this were a bayonet frog and an attachment for an entrenching handle, with a pouch for an entrenching head. There were pouches on either side, each to contain seventy-five rounds of ammunition, and a water bottle carrier. At one side hung a small haversack and on the back was a large pack, each of canvas. The haversack held personal items and a knife, as well as rations. The large pack carried a greatcoat and a blanket. In all their webbing and packs weighed over 70lbs and that was before they attached their bayonet and carried a rifle. Then there was the Brodie helmet which, when first worn, appeared to weigh a ton, but which they soon got so used to that they could not bear to be outside without it. It gave a false impression of safety that the uniform cap they also had, did not. At least they did not have to parade with full kit at first. Before that day came there was much to do and the first six months was basic training.

The start of the day was not so bad because Barwise was among the majority of young men who got up early to go to work. There were a few from the softer classes who did not labour with their bodies but sat at desks all day, and they found things hard, but when Reveille sounded at 5.30am Barwise was always ready as if to go to the boiler works.

He liked Reveille, partly because the Border Regiment bugler played the long version which was tuneful and nice to wake up to. Someone said that the short Reveille had words which meant *'Get out of bed, get out of bed you lazy buggers.'* But it was not in use at Carlisle. Later he was to hear it played as 'Rouse' to summon men to 'stand to' in the trenches and did not mind it so much; it told the enemy that you were awake and discouraged him from trying any dirty surprises.

When the men were up they commenced cleaning, tidying and laying out their kit for inspection. As they did this, two were detailed off on a rota to go to the canteen and bring back the heavy urn containing the morning 'brew'. This came as hot tea, milky and sweet with condensed milk and if you did not like it that way, then tough. Each man had his own one-pint enamel tin mug which he also had to keep clean. At 6.15am the Corporal would shout 'Stand by your beds!' and Sergeant

Grieve would enter the room to inspect men and kit which had to be spick and span. If it was not, as they learned very quickly, then later in the day they would have the pleasure of running round the edge of the parade ground in full kit while the Sergeant shouted personal insults at them; a process which none of them relished.

When the Sergeant had expressed his delight with the display of personal and environmental splendour in front of them, his mood would change and he would order the platoon outside in their shirtsleeves; it did not matter whether it rained or shone. Whatever the weather he had them outside and stood, apparently unmoved by cold or downpours as Corporal Simonini put the recruits through a regular routine of PT.

Much of it consisted of running, jumping, press-ups and other things the lads had never done unless their schools were particularly enlightened, but there were some innovations to promote teamwork. Some telegraph poles were kept at the side of the parade ground and teams of ten men had to lift them and hold them above their heads. Then they had to throw it to be caught by another team. As the weeks went on the Corporal progressed them to standing on each other's shoulders in human pyramids, which they found great fun, although at first they were clumsy at it. The session always ended just before eight o'clock after a run round the parade ground, when they were allowed back into barracks to put on their tunics and caps.

At eight o'clock (Ack Emma in Army slang) the bugle sounded again, and though the Sergeant frowned upon them singing *'Come to the cookhouse door'* to the tune, it meant their breakfast was ready. The British Army had taken advice from experts on what they should feed their men and they aimed for at least 4,000 calories a day, though in many cases men received 4,600. The quality of what was served to them was not always good, but there was at least plenty of it; everyone got the same, at least among the rankers. The officers' mess served better quality food, but Barwise thought that his breakfasts were more varied than he got at home. It was always one dish; ham, brawn or fish served with a chunk of bread and either tea or coffee. As he chewed his way through the gristle and rind of his gamey tasting ham, or fished the pig bristles out of his brawn, he might have reflected on the joys of a bowl of pobbies, but he did not.

From nine o'clock to midday the whole platoon was on the parade ground, for the first three weeks without their equipment. They were not given rifles because the Sergeant told them they hadn't yet earned them. Instead they were given wooden staves and with these they learned to drill; the first time they did this was downright embarrassing. Corporal Simonini demonstrated how to stand 'at ease' with the stave resting on the ground beside him then on his command 'To your front' they had to brace or stiffen themselves in readiness for what came next.

'Platoon!...' shouted the Corporal and though he did not

say the word, they had to come to attention. Then came the awful part as he commanded them to 'Present arms' and eleven of the men dropped their staves. Simonini appeared to swell up to twice his normal size and went berserk. There was no attempt to discriminate between those who had dropped their staves and those who had not. As far as Simonini was concerned he was training a unit and if one got it wrong then they all got it wrong. This was convenient for him because it meant that he did not have to devise particular punishments for individuals; he simply punished them all. This was, of course, quite deliberate because clumsy individual soldiers who got their mates into trouble because of their own faults, would find themselves unpopular and under unbearable peer pressure to get it right. The Corporal could swear like no-one that Barwise had ever come across, and with where he worked he had heard his fair share of bad language. It was prolific and profane enough to sear paint; he insulted their fathers and mothers, did unspeakable things to their sisters and had the most inventive imagination for what he could do to various parts of their bodies if they messed up like that again. When he was finished he made them run round the parade ground perimeter lashing out at the last man with a cane that he carried; and he did not spare the force of it either. He was not a big man, indeed rather small and wiry, but it was quite clear that he was a top soldier and his eye was mean and cruel; he reminded Barwise of a weasel and he did not wish to be the rabbit in his sights. The drill was learned by fear and it was not too long before the platoon could present arms even to Simonini's precise standards. The fear, however, was tempered by respect; Simonini at first sight would have been thought to be best placed in the front line in France, killing Germans, but Sergeant Grieve had taken the opportunity to inform the platoon of why he was not.

'Your Corporal hates being here, so you want to be careful

and not get his dander up. He'd rather be in his old platoon doing nasty things to Fritz, but he's not allowed to. You want to know why he's not allowed to?'

They did.

'Because he was in the original British Expeditionary Force in 1914 during the great retreat. You might have heard how the BEF turned round at a little place called Le Cateau and taught the Jerries a lesson in musketry they'll never forget. Well Corporal Simonini took two machine gun bullets through his chest that day.'

The Sergeant paused to let this fact sink in.

'He's a walking miracle and by all rights, he should not be alive at all, since he lost a lung and two ribs though you would not know it from his fitness. He'd love to be out there paying them back for that, but he's not allowed. And he does not like that one little bit; so don't you go crossing him. He wants the best, so that you'll kill more Jerries; so you be the best you can and stay on his good side.'

The overawed recruits took due notice. After a month or so they were seamless, able to 'Order arms', 'Shoulder arms', 'March', 'About turn', and 'Wheel' with a practiced efficiency which satisfied even Sergeant Grieve. He usually came along towards the end of the drill when Simonini would call his charges to a halt and yell 'Officer on Parade' when they had all to turn to their right and stand to attention. After that they were dismissed at about 12.15pm when they had to go for lunch. At two o'clock sharp they had to back on the parade ground for yet more drill until 4.15pm when they were dismissed. This went on for four weeks and the boring but exacting routine pounded into them the habit of instant obedience.

Once dismissed a soldier's time was, in theory, his own. In practice much of the time was spent in shining boots, laundering clothes, ironing and pressing, shining buttons and cap badges because a scruffy soldier would incur wrath from on high. Sometimes a small group might head into Carlisle on the short bus ride to find a pub, but the government control of public houses and the watering of beer in the Carlisle area had lessened the attraction of drinking expeditions. Barwise was never much of a drinker anyway and he, like his friends in the platoon, was not exactly flush with cash. The weak local beer was also served in the camp canteen, so occasionally a group would set up a table in there and smoke and play cards. There were other attractions in Carlisle of course, in the shape of music halls, cinemas and girls, but the authorities knew this and had taken steps to diminish the numbers of men partaking of these things. Venereal disease was very common among troops at the Western Front and affected the fighting quality of those who had it, as well as straining the medical resources available. Accordingly the recruits, who were nominally on a shilling a day, did not receive cash in the normal run of events. Each of them had a pay book which had to be produced at a 'pay parade' when an officer would give out the amount of money that each had earned, but these events were few and far between. This was quite deliberate because the War Office believed that soldiers on active service should not have too much ready money. Every man guarded his pay book jealously because without it he would get no money; if lost then he had to report the loss and he would receive no pay for every day he delayed in reporting it. Some regiments even deferred pay parade indefinitely until the end of the war and men subsisted entirely on what the unit provided for their meat and drink.

In a garrison town like Carlisle, young men without money held few attractions for local business ladies when there were thousands of well paid war workers around who were much more lucrative. Thus, there was induced in the bashful boy recruits, a certain embarrassment that whispered to them that there was little point in going into town, finding a nice girl and being utterly unable to 'treat' her because your pockets were empty except for fluff. Even in those who might have been inclined to go in the hope of being treated themselves, there was a wariness of being seen as a 'ponce', a low sort of man who relied on women for money. Finally, there were the repeated and graphic compulsory lectures which assured them that if they did stray into encounters with unknown women, then they could catch horrible things that not only would make their private parts turn black and drop off, but would make them unable to be fathers. The usual rumours circulated about the authorities putting bromide in the water to calm down soldierly urges, but the lack of enthusiasm felt in the pursuit of female company was probably more likely explained by the lack of cash, shyness, fear, and finally, utter exhaustion caused by the rigours of military training. Boy soldiers tended to stay in camp. Barwise was lucky in one sense that he had a sister working at Gretna which was not too far away; he met Nancy for tea a couple of times when they could arrange a time that synchronized their off duty hours at a café in English Street, but this was hardly painting the town red. They chatted mostly of family matters and letters from their mother, which were quite frequent. Nancy would give her little brother a few shillings so that his pockets were not completely empty, but during his training, Barwise was not to remember Carlisle as a place where he was able to have a good social life.

Five weeks into their training the platoon members were issued with what they had been waiting for.

'This is a short magazine Lee Enfield mark lll rifle and you will care for it as if it were a baby. If you do not then you will answer to me.'

Simonini looked round the thirty young men gathered round him and licked his lips almost as if he relished the thought of what he would do to anyone with a dirty rifle.

'It's got a ten round magazine in two rows which you change by pulling it out and shoving another in. It's so easy even you village idiots could do it; and if you get good at it you can fire between twenty and thirty rounds a minute. You might even be able to do half as well as my hero did in 1914.'

Seeing the expectant eyes wanting to know more, he continued.

'My hero, Sergeant Snoxall, placed 36 hits on a 48 inch target at 300 yards in 1914. That's shooting!'

Simonini looked round expecting to see approbation and saw it in their eyes.

'Not that I expect any of you horrid little men to come anywhere near that standard. Regulations are content if you can fire fifteen into the target from a lying position by the end of your training. And you'll do that; you'll do it for two reasons. Firstly because a trained rifleman will get sixpence a day more on their pay. Secondly because if you don't do it, you'll make your Corporal look incompetent, and you would not like that would you?'

He did not need an answer, for he knew they would not. What he had described was the standard British Army practice known as 'the mad minute' where a group of riflemen would send more aimed metal at an enemy than any other soldiers in the world. This was seen demonstrated to perfection at Mons in 1914 where the Germans thought that every man on the British side must have a machine gun because so many of them were being mown down.

Barwise and his companions were not allowed to actually fire their weapons yet of course; that was a much more specialized activity which would come later. Simonini was far more concerned with cleanliness and marched them into a lecture hut where each man had to lay his rifle down on a bench. The Corporal then showed them how to strip down and clean a Lee Enfield, a remarkably simple operation that involved removing the bolt which was the easy part. In the butt was a small brass oil can and a pull through cord with a weight. This was inserted into the void where the breech had been and allowed gravity to carry the cylindrical attached weight through to the mouth of the barrel. Then the cord could be used to give the inside of the barrel a vigorous clean. All dirt must be removed from chamber, barrel, breech and magazine or they would be placed on Defaulters' Parade the following morning where a range of penalties would be incurred. Since no-one wished to lose pay, be confined to barracks, do extra sentry duty or have more kitchen fatigues, peeling potatoes, rifles were usually cleaned well. Having learned how to handle and maintain their weapons over a period of weeks, the platoon now had to learn how to fire them.

Lying down in the firing position on the range was Sergeant Grieve who was waiting there when Simonini marched his men in for their first practice. The Sergeant fired his weapon, using his hook on the trigger, and placed a shot directly into the bullseye; they were duly impressed.

At first most of the platoon were fairly hopeless, but one stood out. Barwise learned immediately that he had to treat his weapon with respect because having aimed it at his target, he pulled the trigger and the butt slammed back into his shoulder with a jolt that made him groan with pain, and nor was he the only one.

'Not so simple is it? Perhaps I should have told you? Your weapon has an effective range of five hundred yards and will still kill at almost two miles. That means that it has a kick like a mule. Right, Little; do it again and this time tuck it back firmly into your shoulder; brace against it and don't let it kick you.'

Barwise sent a bullet straight into the middle of the target three hundred yards away. Sergeant Grieve breathed in hard through his nose and said, 'Do that again lad.' Barwise took aim and once more fired into the centre circle of the target.

'Well now, fire off the rest of your magazine and let's see what you can do.'

Barwise fired the remaining eight bullets in his magazine and hit the target with each one, though not all were central.

'You seem to have a knack there Private. Have you ever used any sort of firearm before?'

'No, Sergeant.'

'I see. Well there's some men are just natural marksmen and it may well be that you are one. You keep that up and we'll make a sniper of you. Very useful.'

As it turned out Barwise was quite easily the best shot in his unit and even when it came to the mad minute he could place twenty-one shots into the target whilst most of his mates could manage eighteen or nineteen; he had found something he was very good at. Not all were. Back in their hut and off duty the first task was to clean their rifles. Barwise was cleaning his well enough and chatting and joking with Bill Holliday, Joseph Longcake and Fred Stronach when there was a loud bang, yells of surprise and the lower end of the hut filled with black smoke.

Grieve burst into the hut followed by Simonini.

'What the Hell was that?'

The young man who was the cause of the incident was Jack Alderson from Whitehaven and he was almost in tears looking at a hole in the hut wall where he had very narrowly missed a lad from Egremont who was pale and shaking.

'I'm sorry Sergeant; it was me. I was cleaning it and it just went off.'

'Sorry won't do it boy. This is a court martial offence and you are under arrest. Rifles don't just go off; you've been stupid and now it's up to Lieutenant Ball. Follow me.'

Lieutenant Ball was duty officer and he listened carefully as the Sergeant related what had happened.

'You left a round in the magazine. How did that happen?'

Alderson was shaking and replied, 'I thought I'd fired them all Sir; I miscounted. I'm sorry Sir.'

'That won't do Alderson. You've been negligent and almost shot somebody. There are penalties for serious offences that are not covered by normal sanctions. You now have a choice and I advise you to think carefully as you make it. You can elect to be tried by court martial or you can accept the punishment that I give you. A skilful plea in court might get you off, but I doubt it and you'd probably end up in the glasshouse.'

At the mention of the dreaded military prison system Alderson gulped.

'I'd rather accept your punishment Sir.'

'I think that wise.' The Lieutenant stood up and placed his cap on his head, as the prisoner and the NCOs replaced theirs. 'Sergeant; this man will have Field Punishment number one for twenty-eight days with loss of pay and kitchen duty; to be marked on his record.'

'Sir! Prisoner about turn! Quick march.'

Justice was summary but effective. The sight of poor Alderson with his back to a fence for two hours every day, his feet tied together and his hands tied to the fence as he stood at attention, was an object lesson in not being careless.

The weather was bad too and the offender did not have an easy time of it. In the kitchen they worked him hard and he had no leisure time left by the time all the dish washing was done. He still had to do all the training that the others had to do in addition to his punishment, but on the whole was thankful to still be with them. He apologized profusely to the lad he had nearly shot, who accepted this with a good will and expressed the hope that Jerry would make no better job of doing it than Jack had.

Simonini it was who did them the greatest favour they would have during basic training, though they did not know it. On the face of it stabbing with a bayonet is an easy enough thing to do. The Corporal took the platoon into a lecture hut again and showed them film of a Sergeant demonstrating how to stab a bag of straw with a bayonet. As he watched the film he looked dubious and sucked his teeth. Then he took them out onto the range and allowed them all to attack straw sacks as they yelled savagely and with glee, having the time of their lives. Then he gathered them round and asked them;

'Did you like that film?'

Several replied that they did, upon which Simonini snarled and spat on the floor.

'The Sergeant in that film is a bloody criminal.'

They stared at him.

'You want to know why? Can you tell me why?'

No-one could.

'Right; you, Pearson. I don't like you and you don't like me. Get that broom handle and try to stab me with it. Just do it you nasty little animal.'

Stung by the remark Pearson, did exactly what he had been ordered to do, but his broom handle never reached Simonini who parried it to one side and rammed his stick hard into the young man's belly.

'You're dead Pearson. Why are you dead?'

The soldier got up off the floor, gagging his breath back.

'Cos you fought back Corporal.'

'That's right Pearson. I fought back and I'm not a bloody bag of straw. What will Jerry do?'

'He'll fight back Corporal.'

'Exactly so. Damn right he will, and he'll rip your guts out if he can. Now you lot, pick up them broom sticks. I want to see thrust and parry. I want to see you fence and dance with them sticks, so when you face Jerry you'll kill him instead of him killing you. Now get on with it.'

The recruits had a theory that when Simonini was feeling a little tired, which they knew was an unlikely event, Sergeant Grieve took over. The Sergeant liked to dig; he told them so.

'I love digging. I really do, I love it. Can you think why?'

He would wave an entrenching spade at the group, but they all knew why he liked it by now; he had told them the first time he made them dig a trench.

'January 1900 I was laid up after getting a Mauser bullet through my leg at Colenso. Billy Boer was a crack shot and he chewed us up bad that day my boys, very bad indeed. But he did me a favour because most of my mates went on the following month to a place called Spion Kop. You might have heard of it?'

Most of them had indeed heard of the place where the Boers had handed the British army yet another bloody defeat.

'It's a hill and my regiment was one of those that stormed it, only to find that what we thought was the summit, was not. The real summit was above us and Billy Boer was on top, hundreds of them. They started shooting our men down by the dozen and the officers told them to dig in. So they did. The soil was about a foot to eighteen inches deep and they could not scrape them any deeper so they were slaughtered. I lost many good mates that day.'

Here the Sergeant paused for dramatic effect, then he waved the entrenching spade at them again.

'This here is your best friend my lads, because it digs an 'ole. And an 'ole, as you will find, is what keeps you alive more than anything else. This is a war of 'oles and if you've got any sense more than you were born with, you'll learn to love digging, appreciate a good comfy hole and keep your head down in it, apart from when you are going to give Jerry a bad time of it. Now I want a trench, with fire step dug from here to here and if it's not done by half past four then you stay until it is. Snap to it!'

Barwise did wonder if Carlisle race course would ever be the same again and one day, whilst heaving earth out of yet another trench and the platoon just having finished it, asked Corporal Simonini if the authorities would not be unhappy at their course being so spoiled. The Corporal looked thoughtful about this then said,

'You know son, you're absolutely correct. Right you nasty little men; fill that 'ole back in again sharpish before I dismiss any of you.'

Since it was 4.25pm Barwise was the object of much muttering and unpopularity, which was vented later in their hut, but they filled the trench in that they had just dug; and the next day Sergeant Grieve made them dig it out again. This time Barwise kept his mouth shut.

Sundays being a day of 'rest' the normal routine of drilling, digging, firing and so on, did not apply. Instead the platoon would line up with the other training platoons and form a column. Then, with officers on horseback to the front and rear they would set off on a route march, normally of about twenty miles, but sometimes more. In column of march they were not expected to keep in step unless they came to a settlement. Then they had to march in true soldierly fashion whilst the inhabitants came out to cheer. This was sometimes painful as the Army issue brown boots caused blisters and sore toes. Men who had not done much walking would take their boots off at one of their rest stops, but would find, through their pain and despair that it was hard to get them back on again. The pain had to be walked through and strengthened resolve and will in the process. Some men had pissed in their boots to help the fit; it did not work. Bill Holliday did more good for himself and his marras with a small bottle of Neatsfoot oil rubbed into the right places to soften them up than any old soldiers so called tricks.

Six months of basic training, marching, digging and hard effort left a hardened and lean group of young men proficient in drill, with the knowledge of how to use their rifles and bayonets and able to carry out orders without question. Sergeant Grieve gave them twelve hours notice in December 1917 that their time at Carlisle was done. A new platoon of recruits would be coming in and they were to march to the station and head south to the training camp at Ripon in Yorkshire, though their destination was not revealed to them. They had learned the basics of soldiering; now they had to learn how to make war. They would not be going home for Christmas for the country was at war and their training must go on; neither did they expect to. They were young men training for combat and however much home leave was desired they accepted that it was not practicable. They had only been in the Army for less than six months and there were men in France who had not been home for far longer than that. Even a brief telegram from home on 13 November that announced that he had a new brother, Thomas Henry – known as Harry, born that day was not sufficient reason for Barwise to be allowed home. His mother and new sibling were doing well, but there was a war on. He would see both in due course; the platoon trained on. Their last column route march took them down the Blackwell road, marching in step with the inexorable tramping crash of hobnail boots as they turned onto the rounded cobbles of Botchergate with a small group of Border Regiment bandmen playing *Light of Foot*. Leading them to the station on horseback was Lieutenant Ball, proud as a peacock to be leading such a fine bunch. All along the line of march the people of Carlisle turned out to cheer, to wave flags and yell encouragement at them, though they might not have cheered quite as loud if they had realized the march was a German one:

'Give Kaiser Bill a bashing lads.'
'Show them Germans where to get off marras!'
'Well done lads, well done!'

As the column neared the station the musicians broke into the regimental quick march and as *John Peel* lifted their hearts there were many people moved even to tears. They did not know it, but as the hearts of the men they yelled praise at swelled with pride, they also knew that they would not be doing what the crowd wanted; not yet anyway. Most of them were still eighteen years old. It would be another seven months before Barwise would be allowed overseas, and in some cases, more than that. Carlisle was a patriotic town though; they always gave their men a good sendoff and this was no exception. The train rattled southwards as they wondered where they were going. Wherever it was they knew one thing; it would be hard work.

Chapter 21

A Time out of War

Much had happened to Barwise between July and December 1917, but for all the men who march away there are people left behind. Retreading our steps back to the period just after he left Workington serves to illustrate that the impact of his leaving was considerable. The departure of her eldest son for the Army had an effect on Margaret that might well have been expected. Her mood fell into a depression that was underlain by a fear that she might not see him again. She told herself that it was nonsense of course; he had not gone to war and would not for another year. By that time it could all be over. The Germans were now fighting against the United States as well and surely they could not hold out for long against the combined might of all the powers against them? The Russians had won a great victory at the end of July and pushed the Germans back over 200 miles, but though this had made her think that they were done for, they had rallied and smashed the Russians right back to where they had come from. Still, that Mr Kerensky was now in charge and he seemed a very determined man. When he got going the Russian steamroller would finish the Germans off properly. All he needed was time. Her problem, and she knew it well, was that no woman with children can switch off being a mother. She was aware that she was far from alone in what she was feeling, because she knew women all across town who had sons at the front and to her mind that was far from where Barwise was. Really, she thought, she should be counting her lucky stars, because if he had to do military service, at least he was where there were no Germans firing bullets at him. But then of course there were other dangers; accidents in training and all sorts of perils that a young man was exposed to, all alone, on his first time away from home. She knew she should let go and let him get on with living the life he had chosen, but that's no easy thing at three in the morning when the spectres of dread roamed her mind, keeping her awake and paralysing her reason with fear for her chick. During waking hours she could at least rationalize them away, but she grew tired, hollow round the eyes, and fretful.

Tom was well aware of his wife's troubled mind and as with most men, he sought a solution to her problems, it being unthinkable that there is no remedy for some things. What Margaret needed, he reasoned, was something to take her away from the usual and put her on a more cheerful track; in short she needed a holiday. As the weeks went by and July turned to August, his conviction grew that there was great merit in his thinking. It may be well understood that 'holiday' meant exactly that; a day away to do something linked with leisure activities. The middle classes might well be able to afford to go away to some fashionable resort like Lytham St Annes, or Harrogate for a week, but the average steelworker or miner in Workington could not afford such extravagances. Occasionally though, a 'holy day' was something that they could afford, especially if it did not cut into their earning of a wage. With many families in Workington this took the form of a day's enjoyment in the Lakes and was a type of excursion that the family had done on many occasions before, it being so handy and cheap. So it was that he suggested a day in Keswick.

'But there's a ban on travel like that now isn't there?'

'No my love; there's no ban. The government has asked everyone not to travel unless necessary, for fairly obvious reasons.'

'Well there you are then. It's not necessary.'

'I don't agree. It is necessary and I think in this case it's not Mr Lloyd George's decision to take. It's our family and we decide. You need a break away from the house; we all do.'

'That might be true, but it seems a bit selfish.'

'No, it's not even that. Remember that vicar who's a poet?'

'Yes I do. They read some of his poems out in church and I don't like them much; he's a bit of a jingo.'

'Reverend Rawnsley; well he wrote a letter to the paper last year saying that folk in the Lakes are in trouble. Shopkeepers, hoteliers, café owners and so on, because no one is coming. Without at least the day-trippers some of them have gone broke and many are in difficulties. So if people go and buy an ice cream or a drink it helps them keep their livings. Now surely that's not so selfish?'

Margaret had to admit that put in that light an excursion would do good to other people.

'Then of course there's the children. They play a lot in the street Margaret, but they are not as lucky as we were to grow up among fields and lanes, trees and clean water.'

That settled the matter and she agreed to a family day out at Keswick.

'But when Tom? When will you get any time off and not lose pay?'

'Oh, that's easy enough. We'll go next Sunday, the Glorious Twelfth.'

'After church?'

'No; service does not start until half past ten and after that the day will be too short. I had in mind to start about nine o'clock in the morning and get to Keswick about ten. We'd have the whole day if the weather is nice.'

'But you know I don't like missing church Tom; are we

going to St John's again?'

'Aye I know that, but it doesn't matter which church does it, so I think we shall go to Crosthwaite in Keswick. We've seen it from outside, so let's go there and add a new experience to our day. Nancy can come too.'

'Nancy? She'll be at work.'

'No,' Tom smiled and reached into his pocket. 'This came this morning when you were at the shops. She's coming home Saturday night and is not back on shift till Monday afternoon. Now don't tell me that doesn't please you a bit.'

So it was that on a bright sunny day that promised a full and proper summer warmth Tom and Margaret with Nancy, Joe, Ommie, William and Esther caught a train just after nine o'clock from Workington Central Station. Sitting on the hard slats of a third class carriage, the family filled a compartment by themselves; there was no corridor or access to a toilet so the children had been strictly enjoined that they had to 'go' before they set off. With them Tom carried a bag containing their lunch, and Nancy carried a small overnight bag as she would not be returning to the house, but going straight to Gretna. As the train turned up the River Derwent, its waters blue in the sun, glinting at the start of a beautiful day, Margaret knew that it was the right thing to be doing. Barwise and Nellie were far away doing their bit, living their lives as they wished, but it was partly because of who they were and their sense of duty. This was not there by accident, for in part she had put it there; she missed them, but at the same time felt proud of them. In the shining river some men fished, but she wondered if it was for sport or for food in these straitened times. Crossing and re-crossing the river between fields of an almost impossible green, the train chuffed its way along, gathering speed into the heart of the hills ahead. The mass of the Skiddaw range could be seen, not shrouded in cloud as it so often was, but clear in morning light, sharp and revivifying. As the train passed, wildflowers of pink and white tossed and danced in the airstream.

At each station more Sunday trippers got on, perhaps most at Marron junction where a train had just pulled in from Egremont, Cleator, and Whitehaven. Her lingering guilt at any unnec-essary travel vanished as it was clear that many people were determined that enjoying such a day was necessary to them, and probably in the national interest in keeping them content.

Past Cockermouth the scenery closed in and the land rolled more the further the train went as the foothills of the Lake District showed a countryside of a very different type than nearer the coast. The track here was single line working and Thomas had seen their guard take the looped 'token' that meant that their train was the only one allowed on this section of track; there would be no collisions today. The Lake District Fells loomed ahead now, overshadowing and seemingly impassable and then the train came to a halt in a place where thick trees pressed almost to the line, where a platform sign read 'Bassenthwaite Lake.' Ahead the gates of a level crossing were opening to let them through and the children strained out of the window to be the first to glimpse the water.

'There it is!' shouted William and sure enough the vast expanse of the lake opened up in front of and beside them, placid and lovely, surely one of the best views from a train in the whole country. Over the lake Skiddaw loured at them as if to say 'Climb me if you dare.' They would not be climbing any mountains this day, but they had done it before. Skiddaw is a smooth mountain, once as big as Everest, but now worn down to a stump, a big hill, easy to walk up and a nice stroll for any Keswickians who felt like a stiff walk. The other Lake District peaks are a very different proposition, but like an old tabby cat Skiddaw looked far fiercer than it was. The train skirted the very edge of the water, blue as lapis lazuli, studded with the occasional boat and it almost seemed as if they too were in a boat speeding through it. Through Braithwaite Station, packed with flowers in bloom in carefully tended profusion, the train curved round across the flat land between Bassenthwaite and Derwentwater.

'Soon be there,' said Tom, 'and then to church.' Sure enough, within a few minutes they arrived at the impressively canopied platform of Keswick Station and Tom marshaled the children near the exit, getting their tickets ready to present.

'This is a station that's a bit special Ettie,' Margaret informed her younger daughter. 'The old Queen came here many years ago to stay and they didn't want her to get wet in the rain so they built this and a covered way up to the door of her hotel next door.'

'Just to stop her getting wet? That's a lot of trouble to go to just for that. Couldn't they have got an umbrella? It would have been a lot cheaper.'

Sometimes children can bring you up short and Margaret could not think of an immediate response to her eight year old's very cogent point.

'Well you see Ettie – she was a Queen and that's what they get. Queens get the best of everything.'

'Why?'

'Because they do. Now stop chattering about Queens with your mother; she's got enough to do and let's get along.'

In these situations fathers must be obeyed, but Margaret knew that Ettie would think about it; she would talk to her later at bedtime and explain why Queens had such things done for them. First of all she had to think of some reasons for herself. Nonetheless, the family all gawked at the huge Keswick Hotel, fit for royalty and wondered who on earth had enough money to stay in a place like that; they certainly did not.

'The Kaiser stayed there a few years back,' said Tom. 'Funny to think of that, and now we're fighting him. Him and Lord Lonsdale were marras and now Lonsdale hates his guts and raised a battalion to fight him.'

'Will Barwise be in it?' asked William.

'He might. The Lonsdales are the local battalion and they are the Eleventh Battalion of the Border Regiment. Barwise is in that regiment. He might be put into one of the other battalions though.'

Tom now led the way down Station Road to Bank Street, down Main Street past the pencil factory, and out to Great Crosthwaite. There was of course a temptation to stop and look in shop windows and the children all wanted to go into the pencil shop, but he briskly informed them that they had better put their best foot forward if they did not want to miss the start of the service. It was less than a mile and by marching his family at a brisk pace Tom got them to St Kentigern's Church at 10.26am and had plenty of time to get them settled into rear pews before the Vicar started; the church was crowded. To Tom's great chagrin a young man mounted the pulpit and began to give the service. Looking like a man taken aback by disappointment he leaned over to his neighbour, 'Psst. Where's t'vicar?'

'That is him. He's not been here long but he's very good, as you'll see if you listen.'

'Oh. A new vicar. What happened to t'old vicar?'

'He retired this last Easter and went to live in Grasmere. His wife died last December and he felt he could not carry on here without her.'

Tom sat back with his expression so plainly put out that the man took pity on him.

'You're in luck though. He's here today. He did not want to cut all his ties, so he comes back quite often to see folk and one of his friends drove him. If you look right to the front you can see his bald head. That's Mr Rawnsley and next to him are his friends, Mr and Mrs Heelis.'

Tom thanked him quietly, but his eyes shone with quiet satisfaction. When the service was over he hustled the family outside and lined them along the path as the Vicar took his station by the door speaking to people as they came out.

'Now I've brought you here for a special reason.'

'I thought you had something in mind, Tom Little; I know you too well not to know when you're scheming. Now I know why we didn't go to St John's where we've been before. What is it?'

'Hardwicke Rawnsley's here. He'll be out in a few minutes so you can get a good look at a famous poet; after what you said I thought it a good idea for you and the children to get a look at him.'

Margaret was singularly not thrilled, 'Well I shall have a look at him, but he's a bit too much in favour of this war for me to really like him. I'm never sure about vicars who support notions of death and glory, especially when people like my own son are concerned.'

Nancy was much in favour of the idea though. 'Well I saw Conan Doyle last year; I wonder if I can manage to see one famous person a year from now on.'

'That's more like it!' said Tom. 'Now at least someone appreciates my efforts to show them someone unusual.'

'Of course I appreciate your efforts,' exclaimed Margaret. 'Don't be daft. I like to see a famous person as much as the next woman, it's just I'm not over keen on this one, that's all.'

They all stood in silence among the other people waiting along the path and soon the domed bald head and impressive full set beard of Canon Rawnsley, founder member of the National Trust, poet, priest, and man of influence came into view. Tom positively beamed at standing so near to one of Cumberland's greats; Margaret merely looked. With Rawnsley was a stoutish lady dressed in what looked like the Sunday best of a well to do farmer's wife; with her was a man, evidently her husband, and as they all came out of the door the Canon introduced his friends to the Vicar. What he said was indistinct, but the Vicar was facing towards Margaret and she heard his words clearly.

'I'm very pleased to meet you Mrs Heelis.'

Margaret's eyes widened and her mouth opened with astonishment. Recovering herself she bent down and whispered into Ettie's ear; in her turn the little girl's eyes widened in surprise, 'Is it really?'

'Yes it is; now I'll pick you up so you can get a good look with all these people around.'

The young may not be contained. Where an adult maintains a discretion and a polite silence, being content merely to look and be close to, children will speak. As Mrs Heelis passed down the path towards the gate Ettie spoke up,

'Are you really Beatrix Potter?'

William and Joseph knew that name and stopped also to stare; the world was silent and still as the lady turned to look at Ettie; Margaret flushed and wished she was not there. Without a pause Mrs Heelis replied, 'Yes I am. And you are?'

'My name's Esther Little, but everyone calls me Ettie.'

'Well I was called Miss Potter before I got married, but now people call me Mrs Heelis.'

'And you wrote Peter Rabbit?'

'Yes I did. Have you read it?'

'Yes. Mam got it from the library for me. I've read all your books; or at least mam has read them all to me when I was littler.'

Mrs Heelis's eyes twinkled. 'Your mam has excellent taste,' and she smiled at Margaret who flushed again.

'Is Peter in your car?' asked Ettie, pointing towards the vehicle at the gate.

'No I left him at home. They are not really fond of having rabbits in church.'

'That's a shame. I would have liked to have seen him.'

'I wish you could have seen him too. I have a suggestion instead. You are a nice little girl; not all girls are nice; some are horrid, but I keep a few things for nice little girls in my car. Come down to the gate with me and I shall give you something from Peter.'

Margaret put Ettie down and she reached up without hesitation and took Beatrix Potter's hand and together they walked to the car. The famous writer's intention had been anticipated and her husband was ready, smiling and placed something into her hand.

'Now this is for you from Peter; I shall tell him that I met such a nice little girl and he will be very happy that I gave you a model of himself to keep.'

Ettie took the Peter Rabbit doll with great delight in her eyes; 'OOOh thank you! Thank you! I love it!'

'That makes me glad dear; glad that you are so happy.'

Mrs Heelis bent down and kissed the little girl's forehead. 'It was nice meeting you Ettie. Goodbye now.'

'Goodbye Beatrix Potter. Thank you.'

With a wave the car was gone and Tom stood looking rather agog at what had happened.

'Well there's a turn-up for the book! I wasn't expecting that!'

'No I don't suppose you were' replied Margaret. 'But I'm so glad it happened. I've seen Beatrix Potter; what a nice nice woman. Just how I thought she might be. Let me see Ettie.'

All clustered round the little girl to see her new toy; Peter Rabbit did not seem to mind; he had a new family and from that moment he never left Ettie's side.

'Where shall we go now?' asked Nancy.

'Pencil shop I think. This lot all want new pencils.'

'I wonder how much longer it'll be open on Sundays.'

'How do you mean Nancy?'

'Well it's like in Carlisle. Most of the shops are still open on Sundays, but some are starting to shut. It's a bit inconvenient if you run out of something.'

'I know what you mean. All my life we've had shops open on Sundays and Christmas day and all the holidays, but now, just when people need them to be open because they're not at work, more of them are shutting. They give religion as a reason, but the Sabbath was made for man, not man for the Sabbath. Never mind; the pencil shop is open so they can have their wish.'

'I suppose they make pencils here because there's loads of lead mines around,' said Ommie.

'Now there, my girl, you'd be wrong. There is no lead in pencils.'

'But my teacher tells us not to suck our pencils because we'll get lead poisoning.'

'You might get a black mouth, but not poisoning. The black stuff in your pencil is not lead; it's Borrowdale Plumbago. They call it black lead but it's not. It's actually a kind of coal and it's not dangerous to you. It's only found one place in the world and that's why Keswick pencils are the best you'll find anywhere.'

In the centre of Keswick most of the shops were indeed open, the Sunday closing habit not having caught on yet. The place bustled; there were numbers of day-trippers like themselves, but most of the crowd was composed of locals, many of them miners. The town was a hub of importance for the war effort and legions of tough wiry men earned their livings in the lead and zinc mines round Threlkeld and Thornthwaite, the copper mine at Goldscrape and the barytes mine at Force Crag. Uneconomic and closed in peacetime, these mines were essential to the manufacture of munitions and other materiel of war so they thrived in the closed monopoly market of a UK surrounded by U-Boats.

The lane down to Derwentwater was crowded, but that

was no surprise. The air was balmy and full of the smells of summer. The waters of the lake danced in summer sunshine and a light breeze moderated the heat of the day to a pleasant caress. Men walked with their jackets off and their shirt collars open whilst women guarded their complexions with wide straw hats. Children did not mind the sun and ran about the grass chasing each other; the family found a space to sit down and eat lunch which was mostly sandwiches of jam and of cheese although Margaret felt very pleased at her children's reactions when she pulled out a special treat just for them, procured from Porky Haigh's.

'Pig's trotters!'

There were four, one each for Ommie, William, Joe and Esther; hard to get in wartime, but she had queued for them early and succeeded. After food the three young ones went for a paddle while their parents and elder siblings lay back on dry grass and relaxed.

'You haven't told us much about the factory this trip, Nancy,' commented Ommie. 'What's new up there?'

'Oh I wasn't going to talk about that, because I'm a bit fashed about it.'

'Oh? What's got your goat then?'

'I got fined the other day.'

'Who fined you and for what?' asked her father.

'I got stopped at the factory gate by one of the new lady police.'

'Lady police?'

'Yes Mam; we've had them for a while now because some of the men police didn't like dealing with girls. They're over keen though and over hard.'

'What did you do to cross them?'

'I was told to take my tunic off and I was wearing a non regulation blouse with buttons under it.'

'Is that a crime?'

'Well it is now. They worry that the buttons will fall off and get into the explosive so we're supposed to wear these pull over blouses without buttons; it's just that my own was ever so much more comfortable so I was wearing that. Everyone does it, or used to. Not any more.'

'And they fined you for that? How much?'

'Sixpence.'

'That's a bit steep for just having buttons,' said Tom.

'I thought that, but it was worse because she cut all the buttons off me before I could go in.'

'They have the power to do that?'

'Yes Mam they do.'

'Well that's a bit of a nerve! Did you get them back?'

'No, because I wasn't supposed to have them.'

'It sounds to me like a recipe for some of them to get bigger than their boots.'

'Oh they all are. They're very full of themselves and there's quite a bit of trouble between them and the girls; fights and such like. They have to go round in twos and threes now, or accompanied by a man constable.'

'Women police! I hope it doesn't catch on in Workington. I don't think it'd go down very well.'

'Not down the Marshside on a Saturday night for sure,' growled Tom. 'They'd get eaten alive. Anyway enough of that. How much are those rowing boats?'

'They're a shilling an hour Dad, not cheap,' said Nancy, 'But this is a holiday and it's my treat. I'm a bit flush right now so I'm paying for the boats and no arguments!'

'Boats? I was thinking of one boat.'

'There's a bit too many of us for that; we're a tribe we Littles, just look.'

The rowing skiffs held four people and they were seven so

without more ado Nancy ushered Joe and William, along with Ommie into one boat with her in charge.

'You and Mam go in that one with Ettie; I've got two strong lads to pull me round so I'll have a nice time.'

Out on the water Margaret lay back on the cushions against the back board. Ettie dabbled her hand in the water whilst Tom slowly sculled out into the lake; across the water could be seen the grounds of Lingholm, a peacetime residence of Lord and Lady Rochdale, now a VAD staffed convalescent hospital for officers. On the green lawns running to the water she saw nurses going about their business and small groups of men in their bright blue uniforms out enjoying the summer sun and air. Gnats danced in the brightness and along the shores patches of wild flowers added their gaiety to the scene.

Cries of other people in boats or onshore were distant and she felt sleepy. The scene sparked her to wonder what Nellie was up to and why her daughter had not chosen to keep a safe post such as she saw across the lake; she could be sent somewhere dangerous, but had not been yet, thank goodness. Barwise at least had no choice in what he did. Momentarily she felt herself on the edge of tears, but then pulled herself together; there really was no point in remaining upset at Barwise having been called up. There was nothing she could do about it and she would just have to accept what she could not alter. At any rate he might never have to fight. This last thought she clung to still, as if to a liferaft, though she knew that what happened to him would be down to chance – and sometimes to his own prudence. She was always prudent and she hoped that her son had inherited sufficient of that to keep his head down when the need arose. She must go and visit her father and mother soon in Dearham. Her spirits rose at the thought of talking her fears over with John Adams; he was always so grounded, so sensible and so wise. She knew well that he would say more or less what she was already thinking, but it would be comforting to hear him say it. In the meantime here was a moment to lie back in the heat, listen to the water chuckling under the boat and enjoy time out of war and away from the world of home and work. Times like this did not come very often.

The rocking of the boat appeared to have an effect on the baby in her womb and he gave a series of hard kicks that turned her mind to wondering about what it would be; a boy or a girl? At least this one would not have to go to war like Barwise. This one she could keep safe. With one of those irrational twists of mind that mothers-to-be fall foul of, she was utterly convinced in her mind it would be a boy, largely because it just felt that way. The size of her bump and the vigour of the kicks confirmed her belief and she occasionally pulled herself up and admitted that it would be quite a surprise if the baby turned out to be a girl. What would this unborn son be like? Confident, outgoing and fearless like Barwise? Or would he be shy like little Joe? Maybe he'd be robust, solid and reliable as William was; already people were calling him 'Big Bill' and he was certainly large for his age. Or could he turn out quiet, soft-spoken but determined like John? Dreaming about the future of one's children is a mother's prerogative, but as she reflected she knew one thing well; this baby would be his own person. All her children were and she encouraged this in them; to say what they thought, to talk things over and think things through; not to judge quickly or to act in haste and place their faith in God whom she taught them to believe in with absolute certainty. So her mind wandered in that circle and she smiled to herself; what would he be like? She'd start finding out in November when he arrived.

A splash of water came over the gunwale to bring her thoughts back to the present. Before Tom could react one of the group of Brigham School boys in a boat which had just missed them called 'Sorry Mister; we didn't mean to do that. It was an accident.'

Tom looked across at them thrashing their oars about inexpertly and replied, 'Aye I can see that lads, but it was my wife you splashed. I think you need to get a bit more practice at boating, don't you?'

'Yes Mister. Sorry Missis; we didn't mean to.'

Margaret smiled, 'Apology accepted, but try not to splash me again.'

They duly promised with all schoolboy earnestness that they would take care not to. As she watched them row away she thought them so very very young and hoped that they would never have to go to war. Nancy and the boys were far away over the lake; their idea of a good time on the water was to dig their oars in as hard as they could. Nancy of course knew this and had allowed them to blow themselves out; now she and Ommie had the oars and were pulling back at a slow and relaxed pace. As they drew closer Margaret could see that the boys were red faced and puffed out with heat. There would be no trouble from them for the rest of the day and they'd fall asleep on the train back. Time to row back to the shore and go for a stroll along the lake.

The path was busy and various stalls had been put up selling cakes or lemonade, parasols and hats, but one caught the eye and that was a small stand with a red black and gold Belgian flag hanging limply beside it. On a table was a portrait of King Albert in his uniform and trench helmet, a man Margaret really admired. In this she was far from alone, as the warrior King was a hero to all on the allied side, but he was particularly popular among women, being a handsome and dashing sort of chap. Tom knew of her penchant for the King and sometimes teased her that if she met him, she'd run off with him, which she never denied though it made her laugh. Belgian people holding collecting tins, some of them in Belgian national costume, surrounded the stall. Of course the girls stopped to admire the long puffed and banded sleeves, the laced bodice, the full dark purple skirt and the nice little pillbox hats perched on top.

'It would almost be worth being Belgian to wear that,' said Ommie, 'And dad would look quite good in that.'

Tom looked at the ample black trousers and red piped black jacket with silver buttons and allowed that it was a nice looking sort of get-up, but he didn't think it would play well down Oxford Street in Workington.

'Unless I was a Belgian of course, but I'm not, so they would just think I was daft.'

The children were supplied with a penny each for the collection boxes, for which they were thanked gravely and the family continued their walk through the pastureland in the glow of mid to late afternoon. They walked down by the Lake, the children paddling again, until level with Rampsholme Island, and then they sat for a while. Up the hill in the field they could hear the shouts of girls where a group of the Women's Land Army were urging their horses on to plough up a field that had only been used for sheep for centuries.

'I never thought to see women ploughing the land in my lifetime.'

'Times change Tom and we are at war. We need all the food we can get.'

'Aye, but that land's never been ploughed. It's not really for growing stuff. I suppose they can put potatoes on it, but it probably won't be much of a crop. It's too wet round here.'

'There's a shortage of potatoes Tom. Even if they only grow a few it might avoid the riots they had last winter. They had one in Keswick too you remember.'

'Anyway Dad,' interjected Nancy, 'I would have thought you were used to women doing things that they've never done before; just take a look at me.'

'True enough. I never thought to see the day when my little girl would be making things to blow up Germans with.'

'Exactly. It doesn't matter what sex a pair of hands are in times of emergency so long as they can get the job done.'

'I admit they do seem to be doing that rather well. That lass has ploughed a very straight furrow. Mind, after the war I hope the lad that used to do it gets his job back.'

Nancy looked at him with a sly little slantendicular expression, 'But you just said yourself that land had never been ploughed, so there's no lad involved.'

Thunderstruck, Tom looked at his daughter.

Margaret laughed, 'Oh she's got you fair and square there, Master Thomas.'

'Hmph. Smart women. What's it all coming to?'

Then he joined in the general family laugh as they began the walk back towards the station and home. It had been a lovely day out, one to mark in the memory with a 'special' notice to savour, to remember and to mull over as a good time to treasure. In the midst of war people do not stop being people. They still have to go to work, to labour even harder than they did before. They still need their time out, their leisure, their time to recreate their minds and bodies in the open air and sunlight. Margaret and Tom had taken their family to a place where they could pause and from whence they could move forward. It was a prelude to a difficult time and the day became something to recall and give them strength to face what was to come. Over in France the guns thundered away; one of their number was training to face them. It comforted Margaret to know that Nellie was at a safe hospital and not within range of any German artillery. It was a good job she could not read her daughter's mind at a distance, for if she had her own thoughts would not have been as calm as they were this evening. Back then, home to the terraced houses of Workington, and Nancy back to Gretna; escape from reality is ever a temporary respite, but life may not be avoided for long.

There was a grace note to the day when they arrived home, because as the family sat round their table Tom went out and came back carrying a box.

'We have a present for you, my love, just to say thank you for looking after us all.'

Margaret looked around the table at her children, then back to her husband.

'You don't have to buy me things to say that; I'd do it anyway... what is it?'

They all laughed.

'You have to open it and see Mam,' said Joe.

Wondering, she began to open the box.

'Careful you don't smash it!' cried William.

Margaret proceeded with more care, then lifted out a teapot and set it on the table. This was followed by a sugar bowl and a cream jug. They were of a white-based clay with blue and brown decoration in an abstract pattern, clearly of local manufacture; the teapot had written on it *'Margaret Little.'* When she saw the sugar bowl she burst out laughing and any black clouds that might have lingered in her mind were chased away by hilarity as the family joined in. '*Be canny wid the sugar,*' it read.

'Oh my,' said Margaret. 'I do say that, don't I?'

'You do Mam,' said Ommie, 'A lot. Now look at the cream jug.'

'*That's 'Ot cream.*'

'Well it usually is all the cream!'

'Aye,' said Tom. 'And you always tell us so!'

'Oh dear, am I that bad?'

'No Mam,' said Jack, placing his arms round her. 'We all

have things we say all the time and those are two of yours and we love you for it.'

'Oh that's a nice thing to say. They're beautiful and thank you all. A lovely end to a lovely day.'

Margaret was lifted, secure in the love of her family and her mood lightened in the days and weeks left before the birth of her new baby. He would be born into a world at war but hopefully the world he would live in would be the better for it.

Chapter 22

Special Service

Nellie received exactly the same telegram as Barwise did on 13 November 1917. 'YOU HAVE A NEW BROTHER STOP THOMAS HENRY STOP HARRY STOP MOTHER SAFE STOP BABY DOING WELL.' Once again it was not a sufficient reason to be allowed home; her conditions of service stated quite clearly that she was due a week's leave after six months, but she had not yet completed that much time with the Red Cross. Even then leave was only given if circumstances allowed. She did not mind so much, being used to births in her family. If mother or child had been close to death she could have asked for compassionate leave, but this was not the case. Nurses were needed at their posts, day and night. It would be lovely to see her new brother, but the exigencies of wartime meant that her meeting with him would have to be delayed; so much more would she savour it when the time came. She regretted that she could not keep her word to her mother to go and see the new baby straight away, but the matter was not in her power. For the moment she had something more immediate in her mind that would affect her own future in a very big way and this was the day that she had an appointment with the Matron of Fusehill Hospital.

Matron Graham's face was grave as she looked at Nellie.

'You do realize what this means, don't you.'

'Yes Matron, I do.'

'You will be in range of the enemy's guns and could be killed. In addition, you will be very close to the line. If the enemy broke through you could easily be made prisoner and all that might involve.'

'I know that Matron.'

'And yet you still want to do this?'

'Yes Matron.'

'I suppose you are aware that Nurse Hollister has also applied for special service? Yes of course you are; silly question. You and she are good friends are you not?'

'Yes Matron.'

'Normally, Sister, a nurse like yourself who wanted to do work overseas would be sent to one of the big base hospitals in somewhere like Calais or Boulogne. That's where the Red Cross has some hospitals. But this; have you any idea what a Casualty Clearing Station is like?'

'A vague idea I think Matron, but whatever they are like they need trained nurses.'

'That is true; the Army used to only allow their own nurses to do service at a CCS, but as the war has gone on there are not enough of those. There are many of our nurses in them now, but they don't allow just anyone. You'll have to go before a selection panel and they will decide.'

There was a pause that seemed interminable.

'Well obviously I'm not going to stand in your way. I'll say the same to Hollister when I see her in a few minutes. I will put your name forward and I imagine that you will be gone from here in a very short time. You'll have to go to London to appear in front of the panel, but I think you'll get your wish. You are aware of the current situation.'

'I think so Matron.'

'The Russians have more or less surrendered; it will be any day now. Over a million German soldiers will suddenly have no enemy to fight and they are shipping them westwards now. The battles in the spring will be gigantic; there will be many casualties.'

'Yes Matron.'

'But you know all this well enough I think. You see it as your duty and you feel that you must help. I wish you luck, Sister Little; you will be informed in due course if the selection panel wishes to see you, but I don't think they'll stand in your way; they even have some VADs in the CCS's now. You may go now. Please send Hollister in on your way out.'

Nellie turned to go.

'Sister.'

Nellie stopped.

'God go with you.'

Nellie smiled, 'I'm sure he will Matron. Thank you.'

Their summons arrived in due course and on 5 December, early in the morning Nellie and May caught the train from Carlisle to London. Travel was third class for nurses, but Nellie and May did not mind. They were both heading for the same place and the instructions were clear enough. They would be transients, so had been accommodated at a house owned by the Red Cross at College Road in Dulwich. If they passed for service abroad then they would not be making a return journey; each had made it clear that they wished to be posted as soon as possible if selected. Both women had written letters home, but did not want to visit; it would be too emotional and yet another delay that neither of them wished for. They were to report at the hostel when they arrived that evening, but they would go before the selection panel singly, the following morning. There was only one overwhelming thought that nagged at their minds all the way down.

'Whitehaven Infirmary's only got thirty-two beds. I mean they've expanded it, but Howgill Street is a bit hemmed in, so they've never had enough space for a bigger hospital. That's not enough beds really. Do you think they'll stretch the rules?'

'I hope so May. If they don't then we've come a long way for nothing. Workington Infirmary doesn't have fifty beds either and neither does Bankfield.'

'Yes, but Fusehill does.'

'And we've been there longer than two months, so that's alright.'

'It's just the certificate we haven't got. For that you have to have served three years in a general hospital of at least fifty beds. Neither of us has that.'

'Look,' said Nellie, 'Matron Graham told me that those rules were drawn up before the war. Lots of things have changed. I don't think they're going to turn their noses up at us; and anyway if they do they're daft. We can do nothing about it. It's up to them, so whatever happens tomorrow we just have to accept.'

'You're so much better at that sort of thing than me. I get so worked up about it and I know it's silly. I can face any number of people with horrible wounds, but this sort of uncertainty just puts me on edge all the time. I shall not sleep well tonight I know.'

'You probably won't sleep well anyway. Another strange bed. I wonder what the place is like.'

'Well it sounds nice enough. College Road, Dulwich. Posh sounding; let's hope it is.'

'Well May, so long as the bed is comfortable I'll sleep on it; it's a big day tomorrow.'

Being strangers to London the two nurses found their arrival rather disorientating. Their uniforms disposed people to be helpful, so within the hour they had found their way through the underground to Victoria Station from whence they had to take another train out to Sydenham Hill. Emerging from that station they had no idea where they were. It was so cold that they did not wish to waste time looking around, so accosted a passerby, an elderly man with a moustache.

'Oh you're looking for the Red Cross place on College Road; just go down that lane there and it goes sharp down hill and turns into a footpath. It brings you out on College Hill. Turn left and keep going about half a mile or so and you'll see it. You can't miss it; there's a big Red Cross out front.'

By now thoroughly weary, the two nurses were glad to arrive at a very large house set back off the road with a double entrance and what had evidently been some sort of porter's lodge at the gate. Here they reported to the caretaker, Mr Cowie, who soon showed them to their rooms.

'You'll find there's a division here, ladies, between the women's rooms and the men's. We get a lot of Red Cross people needing to stay in London, but far more nurses than male employees. There are a few rooms for men, but they enter by a separate door. It's forbidden to entertain members of the opposite sex in the womens' area and vice versa; but I am sure you will not be doing that.'

'Of course not!' said May.

'I have to say that we have had some strange ones through here in the past.'

'Not too many I hope?'

'Oh just the odd one; most nurses have seen a lot of life and are very sensible on the whole, but we do get a few flippertigibbets.'

'I love that word,' said May. 'It's so evocative and makes you see exactly what it means. I've met a few of them in my time.'

'So have I,' replied Nellie. "My mam fairly spits it out about some of the louder girls in our area.'

'Mrs Cowie does not hold back if she comes across young ladies who misbehave, and especially at the moment. Our niece Edith is staying with us and she's only thirteen, so she's very down on those who think they're here for a party.'

Chapter 22 — Special Service

'You won't get any trouble of that sort from us.'

'I'm very glad to hear it. Now there's a canteen on the ground floor and as you might have gathered you are bed and board, courtesy of the society. You take what you get though, this being wartime, and dinner's at seven o'clock. Don't be late.'

Having assured him that they would not dream of being late, Nellie and May, having washed, sat in Nellie's room, a random choice, for both were nicely warm, benefiting from that luxury seldom seen outside institutions or the homes of the better off; central heating. Outside a frost was forming already and a thick rime was gathering on the branches of trees; the oncoming night was extraordinarily cold. Predictable it might have been, but the two nurses spent the time between settling in and dinner quizzing each other on the sort of questions they might face in front of the panel. It had been a long day and all they had had to eat had been a hasty breakfast and some cheese sandwiches on the train, so it was not surprising that they were down in the canteen at 7.00pm sharp, and savouring a large plate of a stew. It was mostly vegetables, but did have a small amount of meat in it. This was the only thing on offer, but they did not mind that as it was very tasty and piping hot, particularly welcome on an evening like this. They had been sitting for a few minutes and the large room gradually filled up with other Red Cross women who were staying at the hostel, but as with dining rooms throughout the land and throughout the years, people tended to be shy of each other. There were a few cursory nods and polite smiles, but individuals or pairs of friends tended to steer away from other people and sit, if possible, in isolation from each other. The large table next to Nellie and May remained unoccupied for a good twenty minutes until two men came and sat down with their plates. This caused no great reaction among the diners as one wore a dog collar and the other was older with grey hair. One wore the uniform of a chaplain and the other that of a colonel in the Royal Army Medical Corps. The colonel in particular had a large salt and pepper moustache which Nellie, who was facing him, tried very hard not to look at, because it was so bushy she was sure he was straining his food through it, a thought which almost made her giggle.

The temptation to laugh though was stifled when the two men continued a conversation they had evidently been having before they started their meal. It was the chaplain who spoke first.

'I tell you, Fearghal, there was nothing your chaps could do, and he would not let me do a thing. He was a fine looking lad nearly six feet tall and he walked into the CCS under his own steam. At first the medics thought he must be walking wounded and they had more urgent cases to attend to. He just sat on a bench there staring at the wall with a most soulful expression on his face and looked so desperately civilized. He was just the sort of young chap you'd want to see as your son-in-law.'

'I know what you mean, Julian. I've seen a lot of those in this war. Such a desperate waste.'

'I agree, but especially in this case. I took little notice of him at first; I'd had three men die in front of me in half an hour so walking wounded could wait, but then one of the nurses went over and looked at him more closely. Ye gods but the control that girl had! The front of his coat was soaked in blood and she opened it and she didn't turn a hair at what she saw. How she did that I shall never know.'

'Bad wound?'

'That's an understatement. She'd seen bad wounds before and so had I. No. You could see the wall Fearghal. There was a hole right through him and you could see the wall behind him. I don't know how on earth he had been standing.'

'Nor do I. What did she do?'

'There was nothing she could do. She went and got one of the doctors and he had a look. When he saw it he patted the man's shoulder and he smiled back, ever such a sweet smile, as if from another world. The doctor asked if he was in pain and he said that it was nothing to speak of. Then I went over to him.'

'Good Lord, Julian. What do you say to someone in such a situation?'

'I don't know; I still don't know. I didn't have to. Before I could say a word he spoke to me. He said "It's all right Padre, I know." So I said, "what do you know?" And he said, "It's all up with me and there's nothing you or anyone can do".'

'And you replied?'

'Is there nothing I can do?' And he said, "No Padre. I'm finished. You could go and comfort that poor chap over there though."

Some injured fellow was moaning on a stretcher and begging for help. Anyway I asked if he was at peace, whatever that means. God knows why I asked him that; it's meaningless, but he answered me and what he said I shall never forget.'

'What did he say?'

'He said "Peace? Oh I'm at peace Padre and that's not just Mother Morphine speaking. You see all this? None of this matters; not one atom. Live or die, it's all the same and changes nothing in the universe."'

'That's rather deep for a man in his situation.'

'I don't think so. I asked him if he believed in God then, and in the life hereafter and he smiled and said, "I fancy I shall know the answer you seek in rather a short time. What you really mean to ask is am I afraid? Well Padre the answer is no. We all end and it really does not matter when. The person you have to square accounts with is only yourself. The matter is whether or not you live well, and die well. God? I don't know, any more than you do. No bravado I'm afraid, just an incident that marks the end of me. You know what I really want?"'

The colonel hung on his friends words, 'What did he want?'

'He wanted a cigarette. That's all he wanted so I gave him one. Then I went off to tend the poor fellow on the stretcher. When I looked up a few minutes later he'd gone so I went to look for him. He was sitting on a bench against the wall outside with his face to the sun and the cigarette hanging out of his mouth, quite dead. There was a strange half smile on his face as if he found the whole thing rather droll.'

'He died peacefully?'

'Oh I know he did that. The troubled one is me, because I think of him sometimes and it keeps me awake. I wonder; I really do wonder at him, and even envy him that peace of mind.'

'A brave lad then.'

'Yes; certainly that.'

The chaplain looked sideways, 'Oh I am sorry ladies; I did not intend to put you off your dinner; I do apologise.'

A small tear was making its way down May's cheek, so it was Nellie who replied.

'No Sir; you have not put us off our dinners. But that was a moving story and it sort of made dinner a poor second to listening. I'm sorry if we eavesdropped on your private conversation. It was not intentional.'

'I understand; I should have been more careful about whose ears were near. Please don't be upset by my tale.'

'There are many such tales I'm sure,' replied Nellie, 'and many such incidents. A nurse must be able to bear them and worse. We are not upset Sir, but you tell a fairly riveting story I must admit.'

The chaplain laughed; 'Well I've been told so much before I do confess.' Then he held out his hand and introduced himself.

'Captain Julian Bickersteth at your service, army sky pilot.'

Seeing their puzzled looks he explained with a chuckle 'That's what they call priests in the front line, not without a certain accuracy. Anyway I'm a ready ear and spiritual helper to all and sundry, so if you need my services please do not hesitate to ask. This is Colonel Fearghal McDonald, an old friend of mine.'

The colonel, wary of fraternizing with lesser beings grunted a genial acknowledgement, but the conversation did not continue. After a few pleasant and nondescript remarks the nurses finished their meal and disappeared up to their rooms. They did not stay up late because the following day was going to be rather busy and very important. Their beds were comfortable enough for both girls to be well off to sleep before 11.00pm and even the gurgling and knocking of the central heating system did not keep them awake.

About five o'clock in the morning Nellie woke up with a start and lay in the pre-dawn dark wondering why she was not still asleep. It was unlike her to wake so early and it would not begin to be light for another two hours or so. There it was again; the thing that had woken her was a dull kind of thud in the distance. What was it? Getting out of bed, she looked out of the window, but could see nothing except the outline of trees at the front of the building. More curious now she went out into the corridor to find May and several other nurses at the end facing north where there was a better view of the night sky over London.

'What is it? What's going on?'

'Gothas. It's an air raid; the pigs are here again and dropping bombs on the city; look.'

In the blackness the frosty night air was crystal clear and the sky was a huge vault of stars and constellations. Climbing up towards them Nellie could see about ten thin pencils of light probing upwards. Searchlights! A dull sort of whine could be heard as the heavy Maybach engines of the bombers made their presence known. A series of dull thuds impacted on the window making it shake slightly.

'Anti-aircraft gun,' said one of the other nurses. 'Our boys will get them.'

'Can they reach them?'

'Oh yes, they can get them. Our planes can't get high enough, but the guns can shoot the swine down, and they do.'

'What sort of creatures can fly over a city and drop bombs on people? Women and children and old people?'

'Monsters and inhuman devils. Hanging's too good for them if you ask me.'

'I can't hear too many big explosions,' said Nellie. 'Do they drop many bombs?'

'They only drop a few explosive ones, but they drop a lot of firebombs. They're bad enough and they cause damage, but they do kill people. It's the blast bombs that kill more though. We should be alright here; it's the docks they're after most likely.'

There was a certain fascination watching the beams of light sway to and fro in the night sky looking for the enemy who did not wish to be seen. For a good quarter of an hour they stood watching the show and could even see a couple of red glares in the distance where fires had been started.

'Good God! Look at that.'

High in the sky like a huge moth, a silver coloured plane was caught in the searchlights. The anti aircraft guns pounded forth an absolute fury of rounds at it, but as the girls watched it seemed to them that the explosions were far below the height of the plane.

'That's not a Gotha. That's one of those Flying Giants. They don't have so many of those, but we haven't managed to shoot down one of them; they fly too high for our guns to reach.'

'Have they shot down any Gothas?'

'Oh yes, but they are smaller I understand and they don't carry so many bombs. My brother's in the RFC and he tells us loads of stories.'

For a while longer they watched and the giant plane vanished into cloud and the dark; ten minutes more they persevered, thinking it would be seen again, but it did not return.

Then one of the girls shivered.

'It's cold. They must turn the heating off at night. I'm going back to bed; maybe I can have a bit of a doze before it's really time to get up.'

'Good idea. I don't see why Jerry should deprive me of my sleep.'

Some stayed, like May who could not tear her eyes off the searchlights. Nellie, perhaps a more pragmatic personality, yawned, reflected that she had a selection panel to pass, and headed for her room. She was perhaps three feet from her door when there was a sharp 'whoof', a very loud explosion and the sound of a lot of material hitting the other side of it. She immediately flung herself to the floor, not knowing what to think or do; there was a moment of silence before the screams started. Lifting her head she saw that the air was full of dust and that May, poor May, was running in a panic towards her.

'Nellie; Nellie are you alright?'

'I'm fine May, really. What on earth has happened?'

'I think a bomb has dropped very near, but I don't know where.'

Nellie got to her feet and very cautiously tried to open her door. It did open, but there was some resistance so she pushed harder and the shards of glass that had fallen on the floor inside it gave way to her pressure. The window glass was all gone, blown inwards; if she had been in the room or had walked through the door a few seconds before, then she would have been cut to pieces. The bomb must have hit the street; crossing to the window she looked out, took in her breath sharply and grabbed her coat from a chair. Shaking splinters of glass from it she said,

'Get your coat and shoes May and quickly; they've hit the Lodge.'

'Mr and Mrs Cowie's house?'

Running down the stairs and out of the door Nellie and May were the first on the scene. The back of the house had walls that stood, but the roof was completely gone. The front was a mass of debris and furniture thrown about as if by a lunatic with the strength of a giant. The flare of a ruptured gas-pipe in the back room dimly lighted the whole, or where it had been. A huge gap had been blown in the front wall and Nellie went straight for it.

'Mr Cowie! Mrs Cowie are you alright?'

She was not sure what to expect, but spotted a human foot poking out from under a table lying at an angle against a pile of shattered wall bricks.

'Give me a hand May. Let's get those bricks off.'

Shifting bricks in semi darkness and freezing cold in a nightdress is perhaps not the easiest of tasks for a nurse but frantic pulling and heaving managed to clear the weight from the table.

'Right, you get that end and I'll do this. Heave!'

They could not shift it. Then a man came through the gap in the wall.

'I saw you run in here so I followed.'

It was Colonel MacDonald, who took in at a glance what was happening and grabbed hold of the end of the table with May, so they all heaved again. The heavy piece of furniture came free and underneath was Mr Cowie, groggy, bruised, lacerated cuts on several parts of him, but alive. Nellie took charge.

'May; you stay with the patient. Colonel, you are a doctor are you not?'

'I am.'

'You'll have your bag in your room?'

'I do young woman and I'll go and get it now; have no fears for this man. He'll live.'

'Blankets.'

'For shock. Yes, I'll bring those. What are you going to do?'

'There's a woman and child missing.'

'I'll get some more help. I don't think that everyone in the main building has understood what's happened yet.'

They hadn't. The hostel was full of frightened people, some crying, some comforting and unaware what had happened to the lodge house. When the Colonel informed them, help was soon on the way. Nellie had by then found Mrs Cowie and her niece; both were dead, lying like rag dolls, flung over a bush and a wall, and there was nothing she could do for them. It was then that for the first time in her life she lost her composure and shrieked at the sky shaking her fists in a scream that was almost primal.

'Is this what it's about? Is this what you do? You rotten bastards; you've just killed a woman and child who had done nothing to you. Are you proud of this you big men? I hope our boys make you pay for this. You bloody swine.'

This is perhaps to put too much sense to her words, which were really an outpouring of rage, and fury that was, for the most part, incoherent and impotent, like a minnow raging against a shark. She was shaking with the force of her anger, tears of pure wrath pouring down her cheeks, but she was Annie Eleanor Little, and soon her upbringing asserted itself as her personality imposed calm; she put herself into the 'deal with it' mode.

As best she could make out the bomb had exploded in the back room of the lodge and it must have blown them out through the roof, the thick walls acting to contain the explosion and direct it upwards. By the time help came Nellie was crouched down beside two still forms on the grass of the back lawn, having laid them out as decently as she could. She was back in control of herself. The colonel arrived with a group of men and saw her, so put a consoling hand on her shoulder.

'I'm sorry you had to see this my girl; very sorry.'

'I'm sorry too,' said Nellie.

She got up, and brushed away a small tear wondering if he had heard her screaming at the bombers. 'I've seen a lot worse,' she said, and walked away not wishing to say more. He did not try to stop her.

May and Nellie returned into the main building; it would be impossible to stay there because most of the windows in the front of the building were gone. In their rooms they gathered up their clothes and their belongings, shaking dust and broken glass with splinters of wood out of them and as soon as it was light made their way into Central London and Victoria Station. Here was a cafeteria where they were able to have a much-needed breakfast with tea, which put new heart into them.

'There was no point in staying there Nellie. They've got enough on their plates.'

'I know. I daresay they'll manage to sort things out eventually, but we were only booked in there for the one night. I must say that I don't feel much like a selection board after what just happened. but we've got to go through with it.'

'I'm a bit shaken myself, but for better or worse I want to serve in France; anything to help beat these rotters. We might not feel like it Nellie, but it's got to be done.'

'I know. Come on, let's go and find the place. The directions start from Bond Street underground station.'

Soon they stood outside number 3 Vere Street, Headquarters of the College of Ambulance, and reported at the reception desk where a chalked notice announced that selections would begin at 10.30am. Since neither of them had an appointment time they simply had to kick their heels waiting in a large room with a small crowd of other earnest young women, and wait for their turn to be called. The interviews were delayed in starting for some reason that was not explained to the waiting nurses. Nellie was called at 11.45am and she made her way along a marble floored corridor and into a room through a dark paneled and perfectly huge door. Nervousness seized her and she barely saw that a group of two women dressed as Red Cross Matrons and three men in RAMC uniform were sat on the opposite side of a long table in front of her. One of the men told her to come forward and take a seat facing them, so she obeyed and sat down. The chairman of the panel had been writing on his notes and had not taken much notice of yet another candidate. Now he looked up and recognition was mutual.

'Good Heavens!' said Colonel MacDonald. 'It's the girl who runs towards danger!'

Nellie said nothing.

One of the women in Matron's uniform said; 'Do you mean to say that this is the young woman you told us about earlier? The one who ran into the bombed out building?'

'The very same. What is your name young lady? I have been regretting not asking you before now.'

'Nellie Little, Sir,' was her reply, her head full of confusion.

'You are probably wondering if I heard you shouting in the garden of the lodge this morning.'

'Yes, Sir.'

'I did my girl; and I felt exactly the same so have no fears on that score. You were rather loud and the sentiments heartfelt. I call it a very human reaction. Now we must ask you some questions you understand; just routine stuff so answer as best you can.'

What followed was twenty minutes of questions about nursing; how she would deal with suppurating wounds; how to best dress a burn; how to deal with gas poisoning and so on. She was practiced and her answers were automatic, though her mind was whirling. At the end of the session the panel conferred among themselves then Colonel MacDonald addressed her again.

'In the garden this morning as we left that poor woman and child, you said that you'd seen worse. That remark has stayed with me; I know you have not been to the front; may I ask where you saw worse than what you saw this morning?'

'I was one of the nurses called out to the Quintinshill disaster Sir.'

The silence could almost have been cut with a knife.

'I see. Now I know what you meant.'

Again, there was a pause. 'I had a nephew on the troop train.'

'I'm sorry Sir.'

'Don't be. He survived due to good nursing.'

The panel members put their heads together and murmured among themselves, an interlude that ended with Colonel MacDonald nodding his head; then he turned back to Nellie.

'We are in no doubt as to your suitability for service abroad. What I saw this morning was as eloquent a statement of your fitness as anything I may wish to see. I was very impressed my girl; very impressed indeed. Tell me, are you in the habit of giving instructions to senior surgeons?'

Nellie looked up at him, 'I'm sorry Sir. I did not intend such a presumption. You must think me a fool.'

He grew serious, 'Not at all Sister Little. You found a situation; you were first on the scene. You dealt with it admirably and, as the person in best possession of the facts you issued logical and rational instructions to the people next on the scene. I find your behaviour under pressure to be most admirable, as I did that of your friend. What was her name?'

'May Hollister Sir.'

He scanned the list in front of him.

'Ah yes, I see her name; we'll have her next I think. Now I want you both to wait for me in the waiting room. We will not finish our session until about three this afternoon I think, so avail yourself of the canteen and get some lunch when Miss Hollister comes out, but I want to see you at the end of this meeting.'

Mystified, but under orders, Nellie waited whilst May went through her turn at being questioned, and they followed the Colonel's instructions. At ten past three he emerged from the selection panel which had now concluded its business.

'I should not do this because it's usual to inform candidates by letter, but I have no hesitation in telling you that you've both passed for foreign service. There was some demur as to the length of your service in larger hospitals, but your actions this morning just swept that away; I hope this makes you glad.'

'It does Sir, very glad, but what do we do now? Go back to Carlisle?'

'Is that what you want?'

'No Sir. That's a long journey. We came to serve and that's what we would like.'

'That's what I thought. Well you can't go back to College Road; that place is out of action for a while. Now give me a few minutes and I'm going to write a note for your board and lodging at another Red Cross Hostel. You must go there for a few days for the paperwork to catch up with all this, but I can assure you that you will be posted abroad very soon. Satisfied? That what you wanted?'

'Yes Sir; very satisfied.'

'That's exactly what we wanted Sir; thank you.'

A few minutes later they had a letter from him addressed to the Matron in charge of Tredegar House, a hostel for probationary Red Cross nurses at 99 Bow Road, just a short walk from Mile End station. It was early evening when they got there and the Matron was not too impressed, but glad to see them.

'It's highly irregular because this place is supposed to be for probationers and you are not. You're only here for a few days and this is not a hotel. However, Colonel MacDonald wishes it so, and that is how it shall be.'

She paused for a moment, then continued,

'My girls are under a lot of strain. We had air raids early this morning you know?'

'Yes Matron, we heard about that.'

May and Nellie exchanged a small smile.

'Yes well, they dropped a lot of incendiaries all over our areas so we've been dealing with minor to serious burns and injuries caused mostly to firemen all day. My teams are tired; I won't put you on a rota, but I would greatly appreciate it if you could help out in the wards for the time you are here?'

'Of course we will Matron. Which hospital please?'

'It's the London Hospital. Thank you ladies; I am grateful.'

For the next five days Nellie and May lived in the Bow hostel and served shifts together in the wards of the London Hospital. Finally, the first post on the morning of Wednesday 12 December brought each of them a thick letter marked OHMS. They knew what it was of course, but it did not lessen the excitement as they tore the envelopes open. They were identical apart from the names. They were both to report to Number 53 Casualty Clearing Station on or before Wednesday 2 January 1918. The unit was currently to be found at Bailleul, not far from the Flanders front, where it had been since July 1917.

'That's more or less right on the Western Front Nellie. Bailleul!'

Nellie knew the name too; she had read of it many times in the newspapers and heard it from patients in Carlisle. They were going to the battle area. A full list of travel instructions was enclosed for each girl together with a list of equipment that they must have. Each had a docket which entitled them to report to the headquarters of the Red Cross at Devonshire House Piccadilly and draw what they needed from the central stores.

'Just listen to this Nellie! One bag, six foot by three foot to be filled with straw on arrival, one pillow or pillow bag, two blankets.'

'A Macintosh rug is useful. I bet it is!'

'One enamel washing basin and a piece of soap.'

'Shall we share a basin?'

'Yes – it'll save weight.'

'Two towels; one for bathing; well that's sensible.'

'Enamel plates, two, two tea cloths, a brush for boots and a bicycle lantern or candle lamp.'

'Yes, but all your other stuff is on top – the uniforms and so on.'

'Fairly usual things I think. Better go shopping for a few necessities before we go.'

'I agree May, but I'll tell you what. It says here to allow three days of travel. See what that means?'

'We'll be here over Christmas.'

'Exactly. So let's enjoy it before we go. We've both got what we want so let's take in a few shows before we head off; let's have a good time.'

'I'm all for that. I haven't been spending any money for weeks and it would be nice to see a few theatres and what's going on.'

'Then let's do it. We're going off to the front May; let's eat, drink and be merry.'

'I don't like the end of that saying, but I am in total agreement with my honourable friend. Time to paint the town a bit red!'

This is exactly what they did; living life while they had it, and all the time each hour brought more trains rumbling through Germany round the clock carrying one million German troops westwards. They had beaten the Russians; now, flushed with victory they were ready to smash the British and French. They were the storm and Nellie and May had volunteered to go straight into the middle of it.

Chapter 23

Ripon North Camp

'Right you lot; out now. Don't hang about. I want every man lined up on that platform in one minute flat.'

Sergeant Grieve's stentorian bellow filled the carriage and the thirty men in his platoon did not hang about. Within the specified time they were lined up with rifle and pack facing the train they had just left. It was hard not to shiver in the intense cold.

'Tenshun!' bellowed Grieve, as he was joined by another Sergeant, a stranger to the men, and another Corporal. They held a brief conversation and Grieve produced a piece of paper from his pocket on which the two newcomers signed their names. Then Grieve turned once more to the platoon.

'Stand easy. Now men, this is where Corporal Simonini and I say goodbye; we're going back to Carlisle to train some more oiks. I'm happy with what we've done and you are about half way to being proper soldiers now. This is your new instructor, Sergeant Telford. He will take the iron that Corporal Simonini and I have forged and turn it into an instrument of steel for killing Germans. Good luck, and try to stay alive.'

'Attention!' shouted the new Sergeant. 'Present arms.'

Sergeant Grieve and Corporal Simonini almost looked moved at the compliment, usually reserved for officers; they snapped to attention, saluted, then walked away.

'Now,' said Sergeant Telford. 'This is Corporal Brough, who you will be seeing a lot of. Just do as you are told by us and do it well and we shall get along just fine. Carry on Corporal.'

'Slope arms! About turn! Stand at ease! Now board the carriage in front of you at the double.'

The platoon saw a narrow gauge train in front of them with small carriages and wooden seats. Once aboard they were free to talk. All along the length of the platform other men from other carriages were doing the same

'Where the devil are we?'

'I don't know Barwise. There's a signal box over there with Littlethorpe written on it, but that leaves me none the wiser.'

'I daresay we'll find out soon enough.'

The little train rattled off at a steady pace; night was approaching so the oncoming darkness prevented them from seeing much of the countryside they were passing through. It was only about twenty minutes before they came to a halt and a voice shouted, 'All Border Regiment personnel alight here. All Border personnel alight here.'

'Does tha think they're gonna set us on fire then?' asked Bill Holliday.

'What the Hell are you on about you daft bugger?'

'Alight…'

'It's not funny and it wasn't when Noah telt the animals to get out of the Ark; now shift your carcass onto yon platform and get out of my way. That new man looks a proper stickler.'

'Hell Wath.'

'What?'

'Hell Wath. It's the name of where we are at. Look.'

'Funny sort of name for a spot.'

'Aye, well Barwise, you know what they say; Hell Wath no fury like a woman scorned…'

'That's it; one more crack like that and I'm going to lamp thew yan just to keep my sanity.'

'You men stop yakking like a bunch of old crows. Platoon

will form column of threes; shoulder arms; quick march!'

Ten minutes of marching brought the platoon to the realization that they were in a vast area of huts, served by its own station and that there must be thousands of men here. It was in fact, though they did not know it, the largest training camp in the UK, accommodating over 30,000 men at any one time. To the north and west were infantrymen and to the south cavalry and artillery. To the southeast was the headquarters of 76 Squadron RFC, so service personnel far outnumbered the population of the small market town of Ripon which they almost surrounded. The Riponians did not mind though, because the town boomed with the spending power of so many men which it had been estimated pumped over £9,000 a month into the local economy; a considerable sum which would have been far more if the junior soldiers had all received pay.

At last, breath clouding round them in the bitter cold, the platoon was told that they had arrived at hut F76, that it was their home from home, and they were dismissed. There were no windows at the ends of the wooden hut, but the ends were clad in corrugated iron. They crowded in and saw that the Sergeant was accommodated in a cabin at one end with the Corporal at the other. In between were two rows of trestle beds, three eight inch planks wide with straw mattresses, cotton sheets and wool blankets folded neatly on top of them. Opposite the Sergeant's cabin was a row of three lavatory cubicles, and opposite the Corporal's, a washroom with five sinks; it would be crowded for ablutions. Folded against the wall were three plank tables and thirty canvas backed wooden chairs. They were allowed a few minutes to choose their beds and take off their packs. In the middle of the floor halfway down the hut was a pot bellied stove that was already alight, so the hut was at least warm, and the NCOs had stoves of their own in their cabins.

'Stand by your beds!' Corporal Brough allowed them a few

seconds to obey, then when each man was standing at the foot of his bed he addressed them.

'Things will probably be a little different to what you're used to in Carlisle, so listen carefully and I will tell you what you need to know. This camp is run along the same lines as those of the Army in France; we have no canteen.'

No-one moved, but the question hung in the air and the Corporal, a florid looking man quite unlike the sinister and lean Simonini, continued,

'You will take your meals in here. The food comes from the cookhouse, but it don't get here by magic.'

He paused to let that sink in.

'There are thirty of you and three tables; each table makes up a mess. Each mess is responsible for sending two men to the cookhouse; by each table you will observe four dixies.'

Eyes clicked round to look at the metal-lidded buckets.

'One's for tea, another for meat; one for vegetables and one for pud. Eat from your mess-tins and wash 'em yourself at the sinks. Dixies to be scrubbed out at the end of each meal. Make sure it's done, for the mess that does not will find itself with extra duties. We will feed you well, for you will work hard. We will make soldiers of you; and what does an army march on?'

Here he picked on Arthur Beattie, a shy young chap from Frizington.

'I don't know Corporal. Sorry.'

'Where was you brought up you ignorant little man? Does anyone know?'

'Its stomach Corporal.'

'Quite right; its stomach. Thank the good God that we have someone in this morbid looking bunch with the rudiments of some form of education. Name?'

'Bill Holliday, Corporal.'

'Well you won't find this no holiday, Holliday.'

The Corporal seemed very pleased with his show of wit.

'You won't be doing no laundry either. Nothing but the best for his majesty's armed forces. Dirty clothes will be left in that box at the end of the hut and taken into Ripon by cart every Friday. They are hand washed by fair young maidens in their own homes and brought back to you clean and ironed, you lucky, lucky blighters. The powers that be think that you have better things to do, though God knows what that might be.'

Here he looked round at his charges with a skeptical glance.

'As to the rest; you shares the washbasins and keeps the hut tidy and swept. Baths once a week on Sundays at the bathouse. There's a YMCA hut, Church Army place and enough to keep you busy in the unlikely event you find yourself getting bored. Now I'll come back in five minutes and I want two men from each table to bring your dixies. I'll show you lot where you have to queue for the cookhouse, then it's up to you.'

He turned to go, then changed his mind.

'One more thing. You might be old enough to serve his Majesty and to fight and die. But don't get any ideas over that. You are underage for alcohol; any of you get drunk then you are not only in breach of regulations but of the law. I won't come down on you like a ton of bricks; it'll be like ten tons of shit. Don't do it.'

When it arrived, the food was lukewarm as the queue outside the cookhouse had been long and the night cold, but there was plenty of it. It was the perennial army favourite, curry with overdone rice in the second Dixie. The third was full of sweet milky tea and in the last swam a lake of sweetened semolina pudding though there was no jam or anything else to put in it.

Their training now took on a new purpose. After the usual PT the following morning they were marched off to a place called Wormald Green and filed into a trench. Facing them was a series of targets that appeared to stretch into the distance and indeed there were hundreds of men engaged in musketry practice. What was new to them was having to stand on a fire-step and shoot from over a parapet of sandbags. That made it all rather more realistic than it had been up till now. They also found that the 'messes' they had been divided into became more formal; each mess was now officially called a 'section'. In France a platoon of trained men was divided into sections of ten to twelve men, each commanded by a Corporal. Three of the platoon were nominated at random by Sergeant Telford to act as Corporal for nine men each – provided they did not get ideas above their station in life. Their elevation to greatness was temporary and solely for the convenience of Sergeant Telford and Corporal Brough who was a real Corporal and therefore only second to Telford before God.

What followed was worse. On their third day at Ripon they were ordered by Brough to parade at dusk with rifles and full packs and marched to a supply depot. No warning had been given and they had thought they were snug for the night. At the supply huts they had to load up with 'trench supplies' and their own rations. They also had to remove their boots as they were issued with waders; the boots were laced together and slung over their packs. Almost staggering under the load of barbed wire coils, distress rockets, telephone wire and even a rum jar that they would not be given any of, they then walked in pouring rain to a place where a thin trench had been dug in the ground. Sergeant Telford was waiting for them.

'Right you men. We are carrying out a practice night relief. There's a platoon of lucky lads from the Durham Light Infantry in there at the moment and they've been there since last night. Now it's your turn. Yes, Natrass?'

'Are we going to be in the trench all night and tomorrow as well please Sergeant?'

'You certainly are Natrass. That's what happens in France with the only difference being that in the real battle areas it's longer. You have a problem Natrass, from the expression on your face?'

'But it's raining Sergeant.'

'It's raining in France as well Natrass where lads a little older than you spend four to six days in the front lines before they are relieved. All weather; snow, rain and ice. Think yourself lucky Natrass; you've only got to do twenty-four hours. If you are really lucky then the war might be over before you have to do it for real, but for the meantime, jump to it!'

The platoon began to file into the narrow trench and slosh through the mud and water, slipping on the wooden duckboards which paved the floor of it and which the rain was swamping. They had gone quarter of a mile and a shot sounded as a bullet whizzed over their heads. The Sergeant, at the head of the line turned and shouted; 'Oh yes, I forgot. Just to make it fun for you we've got a sniper out there. He'll try not to kill you, but if he sees you then he'll put a bullet right next to you. Of course accidents happen sometimes. Better keep your heads down…'

As the platoon got closer to the 'battle area' the trench

stopped being more or less straight and began to zig-zag. Three quarters of a mile after they had entered it, the Sergeant made contact with the first men from the DLI who were being 'relieved'. It was immediately apparent that the word applied in more than one sense for the relief on their faces at seeing the Border Regiment badge was palpable. No sooner had they made contact than the DLI men began to leave their front line trench, pushing past in their eagerness to get out. Men stumbled, bumped into each other and a couple fell over in the mud.

'Section one; sentry duty. Get your sorry selves up on that firestep, keep your heads down and your ears open. If you hear anything then let me know. Sections two and three get your heads down. Section two will relieve section one in four hours.'

Bill Holliday had found a cubby hole.

'Look Barwise; we can be right cosy in here; come on.'

'Oh, I don't believe so,' came a drawl from behind them. 'I rather think that's mine.'

Turning round to look at the speaker Bill and Barwise snapped to attention 'Sir!'

'I think you'd better learn the difference between an officer's dugout and "other ranks" accommodation, don't you?'

'Yes Sir.'

The newcomer wore the uniform of a Subaltern or Second Lieutenant.

'You've been training without the presence of an officer so far, haven't you?'

'Yes Sir.'

'I thought so; it shows. Sloppy soldiers I cannot abide. Straighten yourselves up. Now salute. Too slow. Do it again. Now get out of my sight; you make me feel nauseous.'

They fled. They had met Lieutenant Tinian, newly promoted and assigned *pro tem* to the training camp. The rest of their section were strung out in different lengths of the zig-zag trenches and had curled up into 'scrapes' in the rear walls, each just about big enough to hold a man. Wrapped up in their blankets and covered in their Mark VII waterproof groundsheets, they attempted to stay dry and get some sleep. The ingenious garment could be used as a cape or even as a small 'tent' but did not make up for the discomfort of their situation. Barwise and Bill managed to find two unoccupied scrapes and dozed. They did not sleep and neither did anyone else; it was far too cold. After a few minutes they had achieved some sort of warmth when their attempts at slumber were rudely interrupted by a noise like an express train going overhead and a loud explosion, followed by several more. Two artillery pieces were adding their contribution to the realism of the trainee's experience.

'Bloody Hell! That was a shell; a real one.'

Out front a flurry of explosions now took place and the sentries yelled out for the Sergeant.

'Out now! Stand to arms.'

For the next hour the entire platoon stood in the trench with fixed bayonets, an exercise only mitigated by the fact that the rain had stopped.

'What's so sloppy about us?' demanded Bill of Barwise.

'Nowt; I just think he was taking it out on us.'

'Taking what out on us?'

'The fact that he has to do this. I bet he doesn't like it any more than we do. Who would? Trying to get some sleep in a hole in the ground in the middle of a field in winter.'

'Silence in the ranks; no talking. Watch to your front.'

At the end of the hour section two were detailed for sentry duty whilst the others slept, or tried to.

At three thirty precisely a series of loud explosions was heard out front and whistles blowing, accompanied by loud shouts. Lieutenant Tinian arrived fairly quickly from his dugout.

'Very well, Sergeant; send up a flare.'

The parachute flare lit up the area to the front of the trench where the figures of men could be seen.

'Man the firing step; set sights for 300 yards. Make ready; aim; fire at will.'

Everyone knew the figures were dummies, but they blazed away at them all the same; two of them even fell over. Firing their rifles was still sufficient of a novelty for them to enjoy it. Eventually they were stood down and were thankful until they were again called at sunrise and stood to for another hour, this being standard practice in every front line trench.

The whole of the next day all was quiet and the problem they faced was boredom. Some of the men had packs of cards and those not on sentry duty played, but without gambling, which was strictly forbidden; at least if it was seen. Just after three in the afternoon Cyril Nesbit was so fed up that he decided to have a look out into 'no-man's land' and moved the piece of canvas that provided a screen to one of the embrasures. Within seconds a bullet hit the sandbag beside him.

''You stupid excuse for a soldier! What were you told to do with your head Nesbit?'

'To keep it down Corporal; sorry Corporal.'

'Oh you will be Nesbit. You will be.'

'Corporal?'

'You're dead Nesbit. You just got shot through the head; I have no place for a dead man in my trench. Now get your kit and get the Hell out of here. Report to the cookhouse and you tell them from me that you will be peeling spuds for them for the next week every night when the others are finished for the day. They're going to love you Nesbit; but you won't like it.'

The rain had stopped altogether at some point in the morning and since then Lieutenant Tinian had made his presence felt on several occasions. None of them had been pleasant.

'Corporal; that man's puttees are dirty. Take his name.'
'Sir!'
He saw no incongruity in telling a man off for having muddy puttees in a muddy trench.

'Sergeant, that soldier has a button loose on his left shoulder.'

'Show me your bayonet. I thought so; it's rusty. Sergeant, deal with this man…'

If he thought that he was displaying the firm stamp of leadership by such displays, or trying to impress the platoon that he was a martinet, then he failed. After a few such acidulated interventions he was cordially despised and regarded as just another discomfort to add to their misery like the rain, the cold and the mud. The finale to this scene came shortly before dusk when Percy Natrass was returning from the latrine trench in a hurry to get back to his section. Unfortunately, he came round a zig-zag at the same time as Tinian and bumped into the officer. He immediately stepped back and snapped to attention, saluting impeccably.

'Sorry Sir. Accident Sir.'

'Clumsy oaf; why don't you look where you're going?'

'Sorry Sir. My fault Sir.'

In point of fact it was both their faults and just one of those accidents, but Tinian did not mind that.

'You're damned right it was and I'll make sure that you don't repeat it. Sergeant Telford. This man; field punishment number two for three days.'

Percy Natrass lost three days pay and had to march wearing handcuffs and fetters for three days. He could still function as a trainee, but with great difficulty; his marras helped him. Sergeant Telford could have made the punishment more severe by adding hard labour; he did not. Corporal Brough who had taken to one of the men acting as a section leader who was from Alston, his own hometown, revealed the reason for this in a lapse of discipline.

'He was a ranker you know, no better than us. His dad's a bank manager or something down near Ulverston; he went to Grammar school and they're making a lot of those types officers these days. He thinks he's got to be strict to impress, but I've seen his type in the line. They ain't popular.'

Word, of course, went round. Thankfully Tinian was not a conscientious officer and they did not see much of him save at weekly inspections or on parade where his purpose appeared to be nitpicking. This introduction to the trenches was a mere taster for what went on later. Towards the end of their training they were being required to man their trench in the middle of Yorkshire for four days in a row before being relieved. During this time they were expected to carry out a range of tasks for which they were not yet trained after their first time. Their inexperience gradually wore off because the training they were receiving was admirably realistic.

They learned a lot from their first casualty and it was the unfortunate Arthur Beattie who taught them the lesson. They were being shown how to throw bombs; for the more technically minded, they were working with Mills grenades. The grenades they had were not dummies, but a rather sophisticated toy with a small charge in them, equivalent to that found in a small squib on bonfire night. The initial step was simple enough; they had to brace themselves, one foot in front of the other, pull the pin and count one, two three and throw it like a cricketer bowling a ball. It had to be thrown on 'two' at the latest as real grenades exploded after four seconds. Originally it had been seven seconds, but it was found that the enemy had time to throw them back so there was no room for delay. Beattie was a bit slow on the uptake and the dummy went off in his hand, blowing his little finger off and making a mess of the rest. He stood there looking at his hand and his eyes boggled as he stared at it in disbelief. It was only then that he began to yell, not in pain it seemed, but in shock. The bomb instructor produced a field dressing and clapped it round the hand whilst one of his marras wrapped a blanket round him. Nearby, in Studley Roger, was a 670 bed military hospital where the surgeons took care of him. Shortly afterwards he was sent home to recover, his training interrupted. He would not be going to war for a while.

The men of Barwise's platoon did get time off, but the same conditions applied to them in Ripon as applied in Carlisle; they were not paid. They were still boy soldiers and up till age nineteen their pay would be held for them unless they applied for a payment. This is not to say that they had no amusements; they did, for a grateful society went out of its way to provide comforts and diversions for their brave lads. The YMCA hut was a pleasant place where tea and sandwiches were provided gratis, and home baked cakes made by matronly local ladies who also staffed the establishment. There were newspapers, a gramophone with records and a visiting vicar who was a jolly and encouraging soul quite clearly intent on spreading goodwill. There were even card tables with gambling strictly forbidden, dominoes and a darts board. It did tend to get rather crowded and in such a large camp the organization had provided several such huts, as had indeed the Church Army. Not all men wished to avail themselves of places staffed by 'Holy Joes' though, and amused themselves off duty in other ways. Many had been farm labourers or even gardeners and the Army encouraged them to cultivate the large areas between the huts. Thus large 'beds' of cabbages, potatoes, marrows, carrots, beets and so on were carefully tended and supplied to the cookhouse to help feed the 30,000. Such men received a 'payment' in addition to their pay in return for a docket from the head cook.

Back home in Workington, Barwise had often swum in the

Yearl where he had learned how one summer long ago. When he was eight his father had taken him down to the weir that formed the pool there and he had stripped off for a paddle and mess about in the water. Tom had picked him up with a laugh and thrown him in. When he surfaced, coughing and spluttering, blinking water from his eyes his father had laughed again and told him to swim back. It was only about six feet and he doggy paddled it. Tom said he was a good lad, gave him a penny and told him if he could do it again he'd give him another; so he had. After that he had often gone down there with pals; for Workington lads it was probably the most popular destination on hot days and cost nothing at all. Not far from the barrack hut was the River Ure and some genius had erected a wooden tripod offshore that acted as the support for what was effectively a cantilever diving board in the shape of a long thick plank that projected upwards and outwards over a wide deep part of the water. You could run up the plank, give a loud yell and bounce into the air to land with a mighty splash in the Ure; great fun and Barwise did it often in the warmer months.

There was of course a lot of football and it was compulsory, with a camp league running fixtures several times a week. It has to be said that our trainees were not that good, especially when it was borne in mind that the Army drew its members from all strands of society, including professional footballers and those who would have been if they had not been called up. There were some platoons that could run rings round others so enthusiasm for the game varied across the camp according to which hut you were in. Barwise played, but never felt that he had a horse in the race; his father did not attend Workington football matches, nor in fact Workington Town rugby matches. Brought up in the country, on a farm, he had no tradition of going to games or showing interest in them, and this was mirrored in his sons. To Barwise it was a necessary chore and he'd rather be doing something else. To him the Uppies and the Doonies were proper football; the rest was dull. There was another amusement that he preferred rather more and he was not alone in this.

Across a field separating the two camps, was the Headquarters of 76 Squadron RFC. Planes were still a novelty though the lads from West Cumberland had seen some before the war. Workington's annual sports day in 1913 had included a visit to the town by Gustave Hamel, the celebrated aviator, which was to feature flights in his plane for those who could afford the fee. Fourteen thousand people turned up, the Little family among them, just to see the plane. It was a blustery Saturday in August and Hamel had cancelled the pleasure flights for safety reasons. So as not to disappoint the spectators he did take off along with his mechanic for one circuit so that the plane could be seen in action, but when he came in to land, Lonsdale Park was so crowded that he could not set down so overshot and the side wind blew him into the sea. He and his mechanic waded ashore and dozens of fascinated spectators, a young Barwise among them, ran into the water and manhandled the plane safely onto the beach.

Consequently, Barwise was fascinated by aircraft and it was pleasant to wander over the field at the end of a sunny day if he heard the engines roaring and just sit and watch the planes.

It was on the third occasion when he was leaning on a gate watching a DH4 take off that he was aware of a figure approaching him. The DH4 was virtually obsolete in 1918 but 76 Squadron, a home defence outfit unlikely to see action, was equipped with older aircraft which were outmoded for use in France.

'Hello. I've seen you here before.'
'Yes Sergeant; I just like watching the planes.'
'Well yes, I gathered that or you wouldn't keep coming back.'

'I'm not doing any harm Sarge.'

'I know that. Don't worry I'm not here to have a pop at you. Border Regiment eh? Where are you from?'

'Workington Sarge.'

'Well I'm from Aspatria, but I won't call you marra because I've got three stripes and you've got none.'

'Not yet Sarge.'

'That's the spirit. I'm John Edmondson, sometime butcher and now Sergeant Pilot in His Majesty's Royal Flying Corps.'

'Barwise Little, Sergeant.'

'You can probably guess why I've come over to speak to you.'

'No Sarge I can't.'

'Well the RFC is always on the lookout for likely recruits. Have you ever thought of serving in the air?'

The thought was a novel one to Barwise.

'I can't say that I have, Sergeant.'

'Any mechanical skills at all?'

'Afraid not Sarge. I was an apprentice hammerer but that don't count really does it?'

'It might. We need ground crew to repair aircraft that are damaged. You'd be trained. Would you consider transferring?'

'Never thought about it Sarge.'

'Well think about it now. You like planes, so why not?'

'Dunno Sarge. I'd like to think about it.'

'You do that; I'll expect an answer in due course, but don't leave it too long.'

Barwise walked off with his mind awhirl with ideas. Sergeant Edmondson, he knew, was the sort of man that his sisters would probably find very attractive. His face was fine featured, the eyes dark and twinkling, and his manner intense with a focused enthusiasm; and what an enthusiasm! It was quite an infectious air that he projected. To work with planes. Not to have to sleep in a trench. Perhaps he should request transfer? He decided to ask Bill Holliday.

'It's an idea Barwise. You want to have a good think about that. Mind you I wouldn't even consider it if it meant going into the air.'

'Why not? I've always fancied flying in one of those things.'

'Aye well the word is that your life expectancy over there if you're in the air is about ten days. They send you over and ten days later you're dead. So stay out of the air.'

'Yis, but he wasn't talking about actually flying. He was on about ground crew; repairing planes and that lark.'

'I wouldn't ever trust a Sergeant trying to get me to do something. I'd be looking for the catch.'

'You've got a point there.'

'Anyway Barwise, I'd miss you and so would the others. You've got marras in this platoon. Folk to back you up and you go to war with the blokes you trained with.'

'That's true as well. Look Bill I'll think on it.'

'You do that and think on it hard.'

It happened that Bill and Barwise were on cookhouse duty that same evening and, as often occurred, the queue got out of order and places got lost. Bill was holding his two dixies waiting his turn when he was shoved to one side and a larger man behind him moved forward.

'Hey watch it pal; that's my place you're taking.'

'Oh is it?' said the larger man who wore the uniform of the Durham Light Infantry.

'Aye it is.'

'I don't see your name on it, so I think I'll keep it.'

'That's not fair; you've got no right.'

'Oh, I have. I've got these. What you going to do about it?' The DLI man shoved his fists under Bill's nose while an expectant buzz went down the queue. Bill gulped; although aggressive with his rifle and bayonet he couldn't use his fists for toffee, which Barwise well knew. Barwise slapped the Durham man hard on his cheek and a gasp went up. Barwise put his own fists up.

'We can do it here if you like and end up on a charge or you can meet me in an hour by the diving board. Which is it to be?'

The DLI man looked at him; Barwise was smaller.

'I'll be happy to oblige at the diving spot, though I don't see what it's to do with you.'

'There's two of us and you pinched my place too. You can keep it for now, but in one hour you're going to pay me for it.'

'Cocky little bugger ain't ya?' He grinned nastily. 'Aye; I'll keep the place and in an hour I'll knock your block off for dessert.'

On the way back to the hut Bill remonstrated, 'I don't need you to fight my battles for me Barwise. You should have let me look after myself.'

'Ah, go on with you; he'd have had you for dinner; he's bigger than you and a lot stronger. You're not a fighter either in that way, though if you could use a bayonet you'd murder him.'

'But he's bigger than you too.'

'Yis he is. I noticed that.'

'Well are you not worried by it?'

Barwise grinned, and it was full of relish.

'Not a bit. I'd say it's just what I need.'

'What? To get lamped by a bruiser from Durham?'

'We'll see about that won't we?'

Of course the rest of the platoon were agog with expectation and strongly advised that Barwise should not eat a dinner; that he would be weakened with a full belly. Barwise simply told them that he was hungry and that anyway the great gowk had first to hit his belly. He ate his dinner and made his way, surrounded by friends to the place appointed. There was quite a crowd, but no officers or NCOs. Technically what they were doing was a disciplinary offence, but soldiers' fights to settle quarrels amongst themselves, although not sanctioned, were ignored if run properly. It released harmful tensions. A larger and older man came forward to where Barwise and his opponent stood facing each other.

'You'll be wanting to do this properly, so if you wish I'll officiate. I have a certain experience in fisticuffs so I'll see fair play. Is it a fair fight you want or dirty?'

This was delivered in a pithy Liverpudlian accent.

Both men wanted a fair fight so the newly appointed referee began.

'Right. Youse all form a square. You go to that corner and you to that one. No kicking, no gouging and no punching below the belt. Do that and I'll lay you out myself. Rounds to last three minutes.'

Barwise called over to his opponent, 'Have you ever met a man called Smillie from Workington?'

'I have not and I don't want to if he's owt like you.'

'Good,' said Barwise. 'Then let's get on with it.'

'Gentlemen, please commence.'

The DLI man came out of his corner and met Barwise in the middle. He swung a mighty blow that, had it connected, would have knocked Barwise's head off. Barwise hit him hard in the midriff and as he folded hit him again on the chin. He crumpled like a sheet of paper and was out like a light on the floor. There was a stunned silence and a low moan of disappointment which someone voiced as,

'I thought we came to see a fight.'

'And so you did,' said the referee. 'And he's finished it proper so you've seen what you came to see.'

The cause for the discontent became obvious when several people were seen handing money out; the odds had been very much in the larger man's favour. The referee threw a steel helmet full of water over the unconscious man and slapped his face until he came round; his mates took him away. Then the Liverpudlian came over to Barwise.

'I've seen Jack Smillie in action. He's good. Did he teach you?'

'Just some of the basics.'

'Well them basics was good enough. My name's MacManee. If you see Jack give him my best and tell him that I said you'd got a future in the ring if you're so minded.'

'Summat I'd not thought of.'

'Aye well you want to think on it if we get through this war in one piece. If you do we'll meet again I'm sure. Well done mate and good luck.'

Shaking the Liverpudlian's hand Barwise turned to find his platoon waiting for him with expressions varying from awe to glee; they carried him shoulder high back to their hut. He knew then that he would not be leaving to join the RFC. These were his marras; if he was to fight for his life then these were the people he wanted beside him. Intensive training lay ahead; he'd make the most of it and survive; he was determined.

The following Sunday he saw Sergeant Edmondson who was philosophic about his refusal.

'Ah well, don't blame me for trying; we need good and interested young men and we are a new service eager for fresh talent.'

'No Sarge. I do appreciate the offer and I thank you for it, but you know?'

'Yes I do know. Shake hands on it and if you're ever up Aspatria way, then look me up; Edmondson's butchers in West Street; you can't miss us.'

'I'll do that Sarge if I get through this; I will.'

'God willing we both will. Good luck to you'

Barwise had set his course and there would be no more wavering. He would now set out to be the best at soldiering that he could be, to learn the craft and come through safely. The only badge of success at the end of the process would be getting home alive; he knew that every man on the Western Front thought exactly the same thing. And like every other man on the Western Front his mind numbered himself among the saved.

Chapter 24

Defence in Depth

'Now then listen carefully,' demanded Sergeant Telford.

'You men have all been trained in the use of the rifle and bayonet as is standard army practice. However, now is the time to know that not all of you will be going into battle with the aforesaid weapons.'

It is hardly surprising that such an announcement caused a ripple of surprise among the twenty-nine men listening.

'Times have changed and the Army likes to keep up with them. Nowadays every platoon has a Lewis gun section of eight men. These eight men have care of two Lewis guns and one man fires the weapon, so a section is two four man teams. One man in each team fires the weapon so carries no rifle. With him is an assistant whose job it is to change the magazines and the other two are heavy mob.'

'What do the heavy mob do Sergeant?'

'Good question Ostle. Exactly what is implied. They carry heavy stuff – in other words they carry as many drums of ammunition as they can in addition to their rifles. It's their job to protect the gunner in close quarter action…Gather round.'

The trainees duly gathered round the Sergeant in a semi-circle in the bay of the trench they occupied. The Lewis gun, a circular magazine already in place on top of it, poked its wicked looking nozzle out towards the targets a hundred yards away.

'What you are looking at men, is firepower.' The Sergeant hung on the last word. 'Firepower! We used to have Vickers guns, but they were too heavy to carry into battle and they've all been handed over to the machine gun corps. But this beauty; every platoon has two of them. Every battalion is four platoons so that's sixteen machine guns plus four spares whenever you go into action. Used properly they are devastating. You will use them properly. Now watch this.'

The Sergeant took aim at the butts where dummy figures had been set up, and fired riddling one with bullets and emptying the whole magazine.

'Now what was that?'

'Good shooting Sarge.'

'No! It was bloody bad shooting. It was abysmal shooting. It was the worst possible shooting. Why?'

Silence.

'A whole magazine for one man! Talk about a sledgehammer to crack a nut. This thing can fire singles, short bursts or all at once. Short bursts is best. It only takes one bullet to kill a man. Don't use it as a rifle; it's a machine gun. Now watch this.'

Corporal Brough had changed the magazine whilst Telford was talking and the Sergeant squinted through the sights again. This time he was more energetic and in a series of short bursts swiftly knocked over ten dummies.

'There. I just destroyed an entire section of Jerries and I've still got plenty of rounds left. Try doing that with a rifle. No disrespect; the Lee Enfield is a fine weapon; but it can't do that. Now it's your turn.'

Some of the platoon were impressed enough to volunteer for intensive Lewis gun training, but Barwise and Bill Holliday were not among them, although Barwise proved to be very good with it. Part of the training they had, in case they ever had to do it in the field, was to disassemble the Lewis gun and put it back together. It was a beast of a weapon in that regard; in addition each forty-seven round pan shaped magazine had to be reloaded with .303 bullets by the gunners after each use and it was fiddly, one round at a time. Barwise knew full well what he wanted to do and that was to be a rifleman in the bombing section. The 1917 infantry instruction manual required a platoon to be composed of an Officer, a Sergeant and three Corporals. The private soldiers would be divided into the Lewis gun section, rifle grenade section, bombing section and the rifle section. It was the bombing section that Barwise was interested in because he saw them as the cutting edge of an attack and that was where he wished to be. The bombing section comprised two bombers who threw grenades over zig-zags into the next section of enemy trench. They carried pistols and were accompanied by two strong men who carried bags of bombs. Beside these were two riflemen and two bayonet men. It was their job to wait until the thrown bomb had exploded then rush round to finish the enemy off. This would probably involve hand-to-hand fighting and Barwise saw it as real soldiering.

The British Army had come of age by 1918; they were no longer a mob of barely trained civilians. Each man had to be able to slot into any section where necessary; as well as being trained in close combat with bayonet and rifle, they were able, to serve in any section as well as their own. This type of articulated force had not been seen in so specialized a form since the days of the Romans legions; the only problem was that the German Army had evolved in similar fashion. Barwise disliked the Lewis gun for its awkwardness and did not wish to look after one, however well he might shoot it. His degree of proficiency with the weapon was so advanced that he found himself entered into the inter-platoon contest that was held at the end of the course. He was the man who shot the gun and his team carried off the small silver shield that was awarded to the winners. Though he received it with a smile and a handshake from the camp commandant, it did not endear the Lewis gun to him enough to wish to specialize in it.

The rifle grenade he found a fiddly weapon to use and not very accurate. Of course he could use it; every man could, but he found that he was a bit of a purist; sticking a steel rod down the barrel of a perfectly good rifle like the Lee Enfield offended him on some level. Firing a blank cartridge to propel the grenade on the end of the rod at the enemy, he did not find as satisfying as shooting at them from long range. His instincts, he knew, were to be a sniper, but for that training you needed experience, and thus far he had none. He would have to serve his time and learn his chosen specialism; rifleman.

The next few weeks were a maelstrom of activity as Sergeant Telford and Corporal Brough put them through a series of learning processes and then made them repeat them all. They attended lectures by specialists in grenades, in gas attacks, use of the flamethrower, hygiene and how to cope with rats. This last one left them hooting with laughter as the rat expert brought with him a number of stuffed specimens which got progressively bigger as he pulled them out one by one. The last one was as big as a small dog and larger than most cats, puffed out to enormous size and the sight of it brought the house down. The laughter was just dying away when an unidentifiable falsetto voice called out 'Looks like Tinian' and the occupants of the hut became helpless. It was impossible for Sergeant Telford to restore order for three minutes as red-faced young men lost control of their limbs, weak with laughing. Needless to say, the aforementioned officer was not present; he never was.

On 21 March 1918 news went round the camp like wildfire. The long expected attack in France had come. Seventy-two full strength German divisions took maximum advantage of morning fog to throw themselves in overwhelming force at twenty-six British divisions. Not surprisingly they broke through, as the British commanders had known they would.

'I know we're only eighteen Sergeant, but we can shoot. We're better trained than the men they sent over in 1916. We're needed over there; why won't they let us go?'

'Ours not to reason why, Little,' replied Sergeant Telford. 'There's a lot of us feel the same way, but we have to wait for orders. This is the Army.'

'But this place is packed full of men and the other camps are the same. There's enough of us to see them off.'

'That's as may be, Ostle, but you still ain't old enough. You go when they let you go.'

Such remonstrations were common throughout the military camps of the UK over the next few weeks. The General Reserve of 120,000 men was waiting for orders to move to France, which did not come, and something in the order of 400,000 partly trained conscripts, though many were still eighteen, could have been sent by a very quick change in the law prompted by impending disaster. For a couple of weeks a sense of gloom settled over the platoon hut as it would with men who want to do something, to take action, but who may not. Perhaps nowhere in human beings is fury more repressed and concentrated than in those who are utterly impotent in the face of events they know they can affect, but are not permitted to. Training went on regardless; the atmosphere improved after 5 April when the German attack halted, but it was a temporary respite.

Having been assured by Sergeant Telford that the platoon was ready to mount a practice assault Lieutenant Tinian, who was generally of too exalted a station to bother himself with such details, met them at the artillery range near South Camp at 3.30am.

'Sunrise is at 05.41 Sergeant; zero hour. That's when the barrage will start. We will be observed of course from zero hour and I don't want any cock-ups. Clear?'

'Clear as crystal Sir.'

'Good. You know the drill; carry on.'

Telford was a good NCO; there was an hour before anything had to be done by the men and the reason they were here so early was to get their eyes accustomed to the dark and their minds to the trenches.

'Alright men. Get your heads down for an hour. In a real assault you would not be posting sentries; it would be the platoon assigned to the front line.'

At 4.30am he went round the bays where men were, shaking them into activity with a whisper.

'Come on boys; we go in ten minutes.'

Dragging themselves out of their scrapes, cold in the morning dew, they tried to get some life back into their limbs and stood by the small ladders that led out over the top. All was quiet and no-one spoke. Each man was wearing his groundsheet and carrying no pack except those charged with carrying bombs or ammunition. The days of the Somme when men carried eighty pound packs into battle were long gone. Lieutenant Tinian appeared from his dug-out; nothing distinguished him from the men and he also wore a groundsheet. At 4.40am he whispered to go forward and section one left the trench walking without a sound and treading carefully. Twenty seconds later section two followed, then section three. It was hard to see in the dark, but their way was guided by white tapes that a working party from another platoon had laid across the ground earlier in the night. Not a man spoke; they had been told that if they did then they would receive Field Punishment number one. Barwise and Bill, riflemen for number two bombing section, dared not speak a word. The platoon advanced one hundred yards into no-man's land and then lay down flat; there they would lie, out in the open, for the next hour. In front of them was wire – their own, and in front of that, the 'German's'. Both had been cut earlier in the evening by men from the same platoon that laid the tapes. The 'enemy' trench was two hundred yards ahead.

Although there was silence most of the men had noticed; Lieutenant Tinian was not there. Seeing no need to lie on the ground for an hour in the dark, he was in his dugout with a candle, a book and a hip flask. At 5.30am, when it was still dark and any observers still could not see across no-mans land, he strolled over, located Sergeant Telford and lay down beside him. Neither spoke; Telford did not wish to. A professional soldier, he had no good opinion of Tinian, which Tinian knew, but did not care about. Telford would not say anything and it amused Tinian to think that he was powerless. Punctilious and outwardly efficient to his superiors, the Lieutenant viewed his subordinates rather as badly trained servants who needed bringing up sharp. There was little point in having power over men if one were not free to abuse it occasionally; the privilege of rank.

The sky was turning light as day arrived and at 5.50am two guns of number 62 Reserve Battery of the Royal Field Artillery commenced firing over their heads. The shells landed on the empty enemy trenches and at the first explosion number one section of Barwise's platoon rose and walked forward one hundred yards. Two minutes later number two section followed and two minutes after them number three section did likewise. There was no rush; men who rushed would walk into their own barrage and no-one wanted to do that. They came to the enemy wire and lay down. The Sergeant looked at his watch. Three minutes to go; and sure enough at the end of that time the guns shifted their aim, creeping forward one hundred yards on to the enemy reserve trenches. All eyes were on him and he punched the air; battle language which everyone knew. Number one section aimed their Lewis guns at the German parapets and fired; the non-existent enemy kept their heads down. Number three section lay on their backs and fired rifle grenades at the trench; the Sergeant punched the air again and number two section dashed forward; the bombers threw live full strength grenades into the nearest section of trench and straight away Barwise, Bill and two bayonet men ran across and jumped into the trench. Some wag had placed a picture of the Kaiser's face on a dummy that confronted Barwise, so he shot it. One of the bayonet men gave it four inches of cold steel for good measure; 'Cop that you bugger!' he said with a wink at Barwise as he withdrew his weapon. The bomb men arrived; one turned right and the other turned left; they each threw a bomb over into the next bay and a rifleman and bayonet man immediately rushed in following the explosion. A dugout was there and as soon as he arrived the bomber threw a grenade into it, all standing aside from the entrance as it went off. The rest of the platoon now arrived piling into the trench in an eager hurry like a pack of fox-hounds. Lewis guns were set up pointing both ways to defend what they had taken and now all that remained was to bomb their way along all the zigs and zags to take the rest of the enemy position. The creeping barrage fire of the Royal Artillery guns now also stopped; they were trainees and could not go back to barracks. It was great fun and made up for all the discomfort of lying out in the cold. The platoon had done well, with no messing about and they knew it; by the standards of most recruits, first time on a live firing exercise, it was slick and polished. It was also heavily spiced with danger by the use of live ammunition; accidents were common in these exercises but not this night. Much smiling and joking was evident. They held the trench for two hours, then a Colonel arrived to mark the end of their practice. He came striding down across no-mans land and looked down into the 'captured' trench.

'Well done Tinian; absolutely textbook. That's how it

should be done. You've done a good job here with these men. I congratulate you.'

Tinian knew better than to actually smirk, but his reply did it far better.

'Thank you Sir. I always insist on the highest standards; they have to be as good as we can make them.'

To say that the expression on Sergeant Telford's face was thunderstruck would be something of a euphemism. Tinian's character as an officer was made quite clear in this response; he was authoritarian, snobbish, a nitpicking bully and quite happy to take credit for what other men did.

'Quite agree. Quite agree. Ah well, you can send them back now; I daresay they need some sleep.'

What the men really wanted was their breakfast and Sergeant Telford, a very decent man, made sure they got it. Then they were allowed to sleep for four hours; no longer because the Army wished them to be back to a normal routine as soon as possible. This being a Saturday and a field exercise just having been completed, they were woken at 1.00pm and had to turn out to attend a lecture at three o'clock. The lecture did more to raise their spirits than anything else could; it was entitled 'Defence in Depth' and they came out of the hut buzzing about it.

'So Jerry thinks he's winning, but he's not!'

'That's the way it looks, Barwise.'

The speaker was Joe Gibson from Distington.

'We have hardly anyone in our front line, so when Jerry attacks he goes through like a paper bag and we let him. It looks as if he's going a long way, but we are letting him have land of no value.'

'And we hold the high ground, heavily fortified or any areas which are easy to defend and Jerry has to fight for every one of them.'

'Aye, so when all the newspapers are saying he's advanced

forty miles he has, but he's got a lot of our lot behind him and he's got to take them or leave strong British forces in his rear. He must be losing one Hell of a lot of men! It doesn't look that way in the papers, but I'm glad to see real method in what I thought was madness.'

Although Joe Gibson did not know it, he was right. The British had lost 255,000 men to the German attack from 21 March to 5 April and the Germans 239,000. The Germans, however, had outnumbered the British by more than two to one and they should have broken through. That they had not done so showed that the British now had the tactics to stop the Germans. Moreover the Germans had lost men they could not replace. Britain had over 400,000 fresh troops in the UK. Although they had not yet won the war, the men in Barwise's platoon were right to be optimistic; many of them itched to be over there to finish the job. They were not allowed to as yet so had little choice but to put the matter to the back of their minds in the face of more immediate concerns. The most important of these was the Ripon Camp sports day, an inter-regimental contest held every year since a Scots regiment had initiated it in 1915. This year it fell on Saturday 25 May.

It would be an understatement to say that some of the sports were rather esoteric. Not everyone wanted to enter the bomb throwing contest, because everyone knew someone in their platoon who could hurl a grenade further than they could. Percy Natrass was the best bomber, but he did not win; a tall chap from the King's Own Yorkshire Light Infantry was better, so Percy had to settle for second. Barwise entered for the bayonet race. This involved charging across a field stabbing six straw dummies on the way whilst emitting ferocious yells intended to paralyse the enemy with fear. His yell was not very impressive, for he doubted if it would work, and he was not placed. As he remarked afterwards, 'If some idiot ran across a field at me with a fixed bayonet shouting at the top of his voice, I'd shoot the bugger.' The sentiment was shared by most of the platoon, though not all; some of them still believed the old drill Sergeants who described the bayonet as the Queen of the battlefield. The recruits knew it was not – it was the machine gun, and artillery was King.

There was a sufficient variety of more usual events; the skittles matches were very popular, as was throwing the hoop, but the unquestioned favourites were all the events where women took part. There was a considerable cadre of nurses at the large base hospital, but they were by no means all. The Army had finally seen sense in 1917 and founded the Women's Royal Army Corps and now there were many in uniform carrying out a whole range of duties formerly done by men; they were drivers, orderlies, store women and cooks for the most part, but their role was expanding. The egg and spoon races between them caused uproarious support, whilst archery, seen as a most female pursuit, was never so vocally popular. Bill Holliday fancied his chances at the fence-jumping contest, but fell over and squashed his nose like a tomato on the floor; it was not broken, but it did bleed a lot and all his marras fell about laughing. It is a strange thing in humans that they often as not react to people hurting themselves in silly ways by uproarious laughter.

The best days, if they were not involved in a military exercise such as manning a trench, from which there was no release, were Sundays because religious pressure had modified army routine so that men had more time off. The morning routine of PT was continued as it was every day, but then there was compulsory Church Parade. Of course, if men were Jewish or Catholic or had some other denominational provision, they were excused to go to their own places for worship. Most men marched onto the football fields, formed a large square and

Chapter 24 — Defence in Depth

listened or tried to listen to an Army Chaplain or a visiting vicar who, much of the time, they could not hear. The best bit was the hymn singing, because they all knew the hymns and everyone liked a good sing song. After church parade they were dismissed and their time was their own. On Sunday 26 May 1918 Barwise and Bill Holliday decided that the Sabbath was made for man and that they were going to have some time off. It was prompted by the fact that the weather was bright, dry and above all, warm with early summer sun.

'Let's go for a walk,' suggested Barwise. 'Let's just get out of this place for a few hours.'

'Aye alright, but where? And just us two?'

'I think so; unless you want to ask Perce to tag along; he's a good marra even though he is a long streak of Cumberland bacon.'

Three of them set out and headed along country lanes towards a place they had heard much of that was only about three miles away, and that was Fountains Abbey. They did not march, but strolled, taking pleasure in the feel of the sun, the smell of the grass and trees and the flitting of birds. They did not have a penny between them and no food or drink. Being young and free of cares about this sort of thing, they had decided to skip lunch, but be back for evening meal with their mess. It did not take them very long even at a stroll and in just over an hour of walking, talking, joking and messing about, they reached the Abbey. For a moment the sheer beauty of the setting and the place stunned them into silence. It was Barwise who broke it.

'Well I have to say that if it had a roof on it'd knock St Michael's in Wukiton into a cocked hat.'

'It does anyway you daft gowk,' was Bill's reply.

'Well,' ventured Percy Natrass, 'St Nicholas in Whitehaven is pretty good, but even Carlisle Cathedral is tiny compared to this spot.'

They wandered about the great Cistercian ruin goggling at the size of the pillars in the nave, open to the heavens; the fan vaulted cloisters and drank in the magnificence of the sights. Being young men, however, this was not enough. Activity was necessary and the Abbey was completely deserted; the war had evidently dried up monastic tourism. The valley of the River Skell was wide and flat with grassy banks sloping gently down to its slow and deep black flow. It was completely irresistible and before long their uniforms were on the grass and they swam, skylarking in the water for about forty-five minutes without a soul to disturb them and no-one to hear their shouts and calls.

Afterwards they lay on the grass in the sun talking about life in general

'I'm telling you they had no idea about shirt-tails. Some of them had never had a shirt to their name, let alone one with tails until they joined the Army. They didn't know what to do with them.'

'Are you serious, Perce?'

'I swear blind Bill; they were that poor they'd never seen one.'

'So what did they do with them?'

'Well there was one bloke, an absolute genius, thought the shirt tail was a handy device for wiping your backside on when he'd been for a shit. So that's what he did and before the Corporal found out, half the platoon were doing it.'

'Chuffing Norah, that must have been a sight to see. Londoners you say?'

'That's right; they knew nothing about using a toothbrush; a lot of them had rotten teeth and lost half of them to the dentist and instead of going to the toilet they'd nip outside the hut and piss up against the wall.'

'Phew! Makes me glad to be in a decent Cumbrian Regiment; I'd not like any of that! I mean we're not exactly well off; there's nobody in our street is, but at least we know better than that. Workington sounds like paradise compared to that spot; what was it called?'

'Bethnal Green I think it was.'

The afternoon was wearing on and they wished to be back for food, so shortly after four o'clock, they began to make their way towards camp. The warmth of the day was beginning to give way to evening cool and they had decided to go through the centre of Ripon as it was more direct. Eventually they came to a place where a footbridge crossed the River Skell, just outside the town, and they turned right to follow it towards the tower of the cathedral, which they could see in the distance. A road sign informed them that they were in Borrage Lane. It was Bill Holliday who broke the silence as they trudged along.

'I'm as dry as a bone; I wish we had summat to drink.'

'Well we don't, so you'll just have to do without.'

'Thanks Perce – for nowt.'

'If you don't ask then you don't get.'

'What do you mean Barwise?'

'I mean there's a chap over there I'm going to ask if we can have some water.'

'Good idea! Why not? Can't do any harm. Soldiers in uniform; who knows? He might even give us a beer.'

'Fat chance!'

Set back from the road was an ordinary enough cottage, one of a pair with a dividing wall, and in no way distinguished at all. The late afternoon sun was shining off its whitewashed walls, and in the front garden was a man sitting at a table taking advantage of the warmth. He was not basking though, but thinking and beside him were some papers on which he occasionally wrote with a pencil.

'Good afternoon,' said Barwise. 'I'm sorry to bother you but my friends and I are very thirsty and I was wondering if I might trouble you for a glass of water?'

The man looked up and Barwise saw that he was a little older than himself, perhaps twenty-five or so; he was in shirt sleeves, dark trousers with the collar undone, and a rather incongruous pair of carpet slippers in a very bright shade of red. He had dark hair, parted in the middle and eyes that looked at him dully at first, then with interest; or was it amusement? Later, Barwise was to think that those eyes had looked right inside him, past the surface and the thought made him slightly uneasy.

'Of course,' said the man. 'Why not? Everyone gets thirsty; come in.'

Getting up from his seat the man led the way round to the back of the cottage; as they passed by his table Barwise glanced down and saw a piece of paper with many crossings out on it, but headlined 'Futility'. It looked like a poem of some sort, but he did not have time to look properly. Barwise was expecting a pump, but the cottage was close enough to the town to be connected to the water supply. A rear door entered into a scullery where there was a tap and the man produced some cups. With great relief the soldiers drank their fill of cool clear water.

'Thank you,' said Barwise. 'That's very good of you; we needed that.'

The other two also thanked him. He seemed to struggle in how to address them, but after an awkward pause he replied, 'No trouble at all. I'm quite sure that if you'd asked at any house you'd have got the same.'

'Because we're soldiers?'

'Yes of course. Soldiers are in fashion at the moment; had you not noticed?'

'I had that,' smiled Barwise, 'but a lot of us would rather it was not so and that the war was over.'

'I think I might be of that number,' said his new acquaintance.

It was his voice that broke through to Barwise's brain, because it was clipped and posh; it spoke of an education rather beyond St John's Workington or even the Grammar School. A cautious bell began to ring in his head.

'Have you been a soldier?'

The reaction was a singular one for the man looked taken aback for a moment.

'Have I been a soldier? I suppose that's a question of our time. Yes, I've been a soldier and was until last year. I got blown up and I've been in hospital for a while.'

'Sounds like you've done your bit,' said Percy. 'At least you're through with it.'

'Let's hope that the War Office are of the same opinion,' said the man.

It was Bill who asked the obvious question, though Barwise darted him a furious glance for doing so.

'We all wonder what it's like out there; you've been so you're an obvious bloke to ask. What's it like?'

A curious look came over the man's face.

'A friend of mine described it as a Hell where youth and beauty go.'

'That doesn't sound too good,' said Percy Natrass.

'No,' agreed the man. 'There's nothing good about it. I can do better if you really want to know.'

Alarms bells rang in Barwise's head, 'No thanks. It's probably best we find out for ourselves. You might put us off.'

'I might indeed. I have some photographs which are very graphic in showing what it's really like. Do you want to see them?'

'No,' said Barwise. 'I don't think it's a good idea. If they're as bad as you say they might knock the heart out of us and we've got to go anyway, photographs or no photographs. There's no choice, so it profits us none.'

'I think I'd like to,' said Percy.

'No you wouldn't,' said Barwise. 'You're nowt but a radgee who bowks at the sight of blood. Look at pictures like that and you'll be waking me up yelling in your sleep. Am I right?'

'Aye you're right. I won't look then.'

'I see that you are something of a leader of men,' said the householder with a slightly amused tone to his voice.

'Me? No, just an ordinary private and nowt special.'

'You underestimate yourself I fear. Most people are held back not because of lack of ability, but modesty. Don't be too modest would be my advice to you.'

'And I'll probably take it; it sounds like something my Dad would say; but you're not much older than me.'

I think I have a few years on you. What does your father do?'

'Oh he works in a steelworks, but he didn't always. He was a farmer once.'

'Ah. Do you take after him?'

'How do you mean?'

'I mean, do you know anything about growing things?'

'A bit but not as much as him.'

'Do you know anything about roses?'

'Not a lot; but I can look.'

'Well have a look at this one will you?'

'What about it?

'It's not doing very well; it was here in this pot when I moved in and I like the colour and smell of it. I rent this place you see. The trouble is that it looks rather sickly and I was wondering if I could do anything to perk it up.'

'I suggest moving it into the sun.'

'Really? Just that?'

'Yes. This is the shady side of the house. If you want it to do better then just move it into the kind old sun and it'll be right as rain.'

'Say that again.'

'Which bit?'

'About the sun.'

'I said if you move it into the sun…'

'No, that's not what you said. Your exact words were…'

'The kind old sun. That's what my mam says, but I know she got it from her father; my grandfather, John Adams, used to say when he came up from a shift down the mine that he was glad to see the kind old sun again.'

'He had a good way with words I think. May I use it? It's a good expression.'

'Feel free marra; the language costs nothing and I think he'd be pleased you liked it.'

'Marra?'

Barwise collected himself; he was not talking to a Cumbrian. He held out his hand, 'It's how we talk where we come from. It means pal; I'm Barwise Little from Workington.'

A definite social awkwardness now presented itself, as the man hesitated, some sort of barrier rising between them, but then he did hold out his hand.

'Hello; my name's Owen. I'm from Shropshire….'

He might have said more, but the tentative moves towards further acquaintance were halted abruptly by a force of nature in the shape of a Captain in the uniform of the Royal Welch Fusiliers. His arrival round the corner of the cottage had something of the effect of a cat thrown among pigeons. Captains were creatures from the stratosphere, as far above a lowly private as the angels above the creatures of the pit. This one had ears that stuck out a bit, piercing brown eyes and just radiated an unquestionable authority. His presence was devastating and Barwise snapped into a salute, closely followed by Percy and Bill. The newcomer returned the salute.

'What are you men doing here?'

'Just came to ask for a glass of water Sir.'

'And you've had your water?'

'Yes Sir, thank you Sir.'

'Then its time you were off, I think.'

They needed no second telling and hastened down the path, round the corner and onto Borrage Lane. Barwise, the last in line heard the beginnings of a conversation.

'Playing with the Privates Wilfred?'

'Just being mischievous Seigfried; they had not realized I was an officer.'

'Just leave the lower ranks alone; you'll get into trouble.'

'A bit of fun is all; and you've spoiled it.'

Barwise waited no longer; Wilfred Owen was an officer and hadn't told them. Now he told the others and they were dismayed.

'Well, how were we to know? He wasn't in uniform.'

'Are we in trouble, do you think?'

'No,' said Barwise. 'I don't think we are. He seemed a decent enough sort and he gave us water though he could have told us to get lost. No; I think we'll be alright.'

They were alright. Two days after the Borrage Lane encounter the platoon was engaged in one of the never-ending drills on the parade ground. Various officers were wandering around casting a professional or critical eye over the performance of various units. Barwise, stood at attention in the afternoon sun saw Wilfred Owen in the uniform of a Second Lieutenant and groaned to himself, 'I should have known he was an officer.' He had nothing to worry about. Owen walked over and eyed the platoon. In the front rank were Percy Natrass, Bill Holliday and Barwise. He looked at each in turn with his eyes as deadpan as a fish. When he came to Barwise he looked at him and a faint smile just curled the corner of his lips. With an almost imperceptible nod he walked away. Barwise had been right. He was a decent sort.

The days and the weeks wore on as the summer progressed. Over in France the Germans continued to attack and it seemed that every three weeks there was a new offensive aimed at capturing Amiens, the railway hub that served the entire British sector of the Western Front. It would be a military disaster for the Western Allies if they got it; the Germans kept taking more and more territory but somehow they never got anywhere near Amiens. Barwise was intelligent enough to wonder if they were being allowed to thrash out their strength by bashing against a brick wall. Soon he would be nineteen and would be seeing for himself; he did not have long to wait. On Sunday 30 June Sergeant Telford went round the platoon and handed each man an envelope. In it were posting details; the platoon was being broken up and sent to different units of the Border Regiment on the Western Front. The letter told them where to report to for the ferry across the Channel, enclosed a travel warrant and gave them one week's embarkation leave so that they could see their families before they left. Every man got an envelope except Barwise. On his asking Sergeant Telford why, the Sergeant was quite clear.

'There's been some sort of clerical mix-up, Little. I did ask Captain Gillibrand why there was no letter for you and he told me you were born on 16 July.'

'And so Sarge?'

'This lot are all in the class born between the beginning of January 1899 and 30 June 1899. You shouldn't be here.'

'What do you mean Sarge?'

'I means you're two weeks too young to be going out with this lot. Don't take it hard; you'll be sent out in the New Year if the war is still going on.'

Barwise's mind whirred. His marras were going to war and he would not be with them.

'Permission to speak to Captain Gillibrand Sarge.'

'I thought you might say that. Alright lad, follow me.'

Captain Gillibrand had also been expecting a visit.

'These are the regulations Private. There's nothing I can do about it.'

Barwise could almost have thought he imagined the slight emphasis on the word 'I'. Standing stiffly at attention in front of the Captain's desk, he asked permission to speak.

'May I ask Sir if anyone has the power to do something about it?'

A slight and small weary smile crossed the Captain's face.

'You may Private. That would be Colonel Nicholson; I take it you'd like to see him?'

On Barwise's assurance that he would, Gillibrand picked up the telephone and two minutes later Barwise was being marched to see Colonel Nicholson.

'You are eighteen years old. Regulations say you cannot serve overseas until you are nineteen. You want me to stretch the rule for you?'

'No Sir.'

'Then why are you here?'

'The system of classes Sir; it runs out on 30 June.'

'What of it?'

'The platoon does not ship out for France until Saturday 20 July. My birthday is on Tuesday 16 July Sir.'

'Oh, I see. So you will be nineteen by the time they go. Now that is a point well made.'

'Yes Sir.'

'And you want to serve with your friends.'

'Yes Sir.'

'Quite right. I would too; I completely understand.'

The pause seemed interminable, but in the end Colonel Nicholson spoke, 'They need every man they can get out there. You are a strong young man, keen and want to serve. I'm not going to let some pettifogging regulation stand in your way; you'll be old enough when you go and that's good enough for me.'

After half an hour's wait in the clerk's office Barwise found himself in possession of a travel warrant home commencing Wednesday 10 July. He was posted, he found to his pleasure, to 7 Battalion The Border Regiment, the same as Bill Holliday and Percy Natrass. The brightest news was that Lieutenant Tinian had been posted to another regiment in need of officers and would not be coming with them when they left England. When Barwise's embarkation leave was over he had to return to Ripon Camp by no later than 6.00pm on Thursday 18 July. He would have his nineteenth birthday at home. Four days after that he would be on a ferry across The Channel, his destination, the Western Front.

Chapter 25

At the Front

Nellie found the jolting of the bus along the hard cobbles of the *pave* roads of Northern France very jarring and in more ways than one. They had never been designed to take modern traffic and though the authorities tried to keep them in a useable condition, potholes and bumps were common. It was particularly bad on this journey because it was cold and patches of ice made the solid rubber of the wheels slide into potholes and the suspension was none too good. The bumpy ride was compounded by the fact that, although it was bitter cold outside, it was scarcely much better inside. Both girls were wrapped up as best they could, but could still see their breath in clouds; the soldiers riding upstairs on the open top must have been frozen stiff. Nonetheless, she had to laugh at May, who was singing to herself yet again.

'What's so funny?'

'You are.'

'Why? What have I done that tickles your funny bone?'

'It's the singing May, just the singing.'

'Don't you like me singing?'

'Oh yes, I like you singing well enough, but it does get a little wearing at times you know?'

'Wearing? If you like it, why is it wearing?'

Nellie laughed again and answered by bursting into song:

'A bachelor gay am I,
 Though I suffer from Cupid's dart
 But never I vow will I say die
 In spite of an aching heart
 For a man who has loved a girl or two
 Though the fact must be confessed
 He always swears the whole way through
 To every girl he tries to woo
 That he loves her far the best:
 At seventeen he falls in love quite madly
 With eyes of tender blue.'

'I'm sure I don't know what's so amusing,' said May. 'Don't you like the song?'

'It's a nice song May, but that's about the twentieth time you've sung it today. It's like a broken record!'

'Oh, I see what you mean. I have been singing it a lot, haven't I?'

'Well – yes. You could try singing something else. That would be nice. Perhaps from another show? Or another song.'

The two nurses had made the most of their time in London before setting off for their posting. They had seen *'The Maid of the Mountains'*, *'The Bing Girls are Here'*, and *'Yes, Uncle'*, and it had done them the world of good. All these shows were completely escapist and as far from the war as one could possibly get, with light and enthusiastic music, dialogue and acting. The one May kept singing was from *'The Maid of the Mountains'* that was a splendid confection about brigands, booty and beauty. They had been to St Paul's, Westminster Abbey, seen Nelson on his column, visited the National Gallery and taken refreshment in the John Lyons teashop on the edge of Trafalgar Square, among other distractions in their off duty time. On the morning of 30 December they had taken the train down to Folkestone and crossed the Channel, landing that evening at Boulogne. The last day of 1917 had been spent in a nurses' hostel that was quite comfortable, being a seafront hotel converted to wartime purposes. There they found that the morning would bring a bus that would take them to number 53 Casualty Clearing Station presently located at Bailleul, near the front in Flanders. Much to their amusement, their transport turned out to be an open topped vehicle which still had '*Manchester Corporation*' written on the side. Nurses and officers went inside; other ranks upstairs and open to the weather. Though cold, everyone was thankful that it was not raining.

Nellie's eyes now squinched in mischief and she began singing, taking up the song where May had left off…

> '*At seventeen he falls in love quite madly*
> *With eyes of tender blue*
> *At 24 he gets it rather badly*
> *With eyes of a different hue,*
> *At 35 you'll find him flirting sadly*
> *With two or three or more,*
> *But it's when he thinks he's past love,*
> *That is when he meets his last love,*
> *And he loves her like he's never loved before…*'

It was, of course a highly popular show and she should not have been surprised when some of the men on the bus took up the song and it spread upstairs as the bus bowled along through St Omer, bringing smiles and waves from people passing by. The road was busy with traffic, both motorised and horse drawn, heading towards the front and away from it. No doubt it would have been busier, but here and there it was obvious that the area was well served with narrow gauge railways, for the British government had scraped and salvaged every mineral line that it could to construct a network to supply the needs of their armies here. The noise of the engine of course masked the sound of anything external, but eventually they stopped on the outskirts of St Omer and the driver turned off the ignition. It was then that they noticed the rumbling; an army chaplain sitting on the other side of the aisle was obviously very observant, for he leaned over to them and interpreted what they were thinking.

'It's the guns, ladies. It never stops, day or night.'

'Never?'

'Yes, never. The front runs from the Channel coast all the way down to the Swiss frontier and someone, somewhere, is always firing. It will only stop when the war is over.'

'I hope that is soon; it seems to be going on for ever as well.'

'To that thought I say "Amen." I'm sure we all want that. Where are you ladies heading?'

'We're not supposed to say.'

'Indeed you are not; I might be an enemy spy.' The Chaplain laughed, 'On this road I would say you are heading for Bailleul and either CCS number 8 or number 53.'

Their faces were an open book.

'I take it that it is your first time out here. Don't worry; I'm no spy and there are enough people on this bus who can vouch for me.' Here he looked around.

A weary looking Captain spoke, 'Don't worry ladies. The Reverend Clayton is well known to all of us. You can trust him.'

He looked trustworthy; he was small and wore glasses on a face which was open and which radiated frankness, understanding and, Nellie noticed, full of compassion. Here was a human being who really cared about others.

'Where are you going Sir?' she asked.

'Up to Pop; that's where I have my house.'

To her unasked question he responded, 'Poperinghe. My apologies, but we all call it "Pop" up here, but you are new. Yes

I have a house there.'

'It's a strange place to have a house Sir, so close to the front.'

'Yes I suppose it is, but that's where it's needed. It's a kind of rest house. If you ever get to Pop, though I do not recommend it, come and have a cup of tea with us if you wish. It's called Talbot House and it's in Gasthuisstraat.'

Nellie smiled, 'I'm sure we will Sir; it's not every day we get offered a cup of tea, but why do you not recommend it?'

'Ah well Pop is well in range of the enemy guns; we get shelled regularly, though some sort of normal life is carried on.'

'Is Bailleul in range of the guns as well?' asked May.

'I'm rather afraid that it is. If the Germans get it into their heads they do shell the back areas, but Bailleul has not been hard hit for a long time now. It's generally safe.'

'That's nice to know Sir, but I imagine we will have to take our chances with everyone else. We volunteered for this posting and knew what we were getting into.'

'Did you? Did you, I wonder? Well you are brave ladies both and I should particularly like to offer you tea if you do come.'

'Particularly?'

'Yes. Particularly. British women are a welcome sight out here; and I don't mean for the obvious reason.'

May ventured, 'I don't suppose the men see many girls near the fighting?'

'You'd be surprised. There are a lot of French and Belgian girls living in the area; they live here you see so they carry on with their lives as best they can. No, your value is much more because you are British. And nurses. You are a visible sign of caring you see.'

To their mystified looks, he continued, 'Why do men fight if not for home, for wives, family, best girls, children? To see British girls in the fighting area is a reminder that this is a national struggle as well as a sign of what they will protect if they can. But it's even more than that. If a man fights he knows he will run a great risk of being killed, but the greater risk is that he will be wounded. Now I ask you, which man fights harder? The man who knows he is on his own, or the man who knows that if he is hurt, then he will be well cared for?'

'Well obviously the second one,' said May.

'Exactly. So if he falls in the mud, wounded and in pain, he knows that he will be whisked away to a hospital, the best we have; that doctors and starched clean nurses will do their utmost to look after him. The nation cares enough in doing this and he will fight the harder for it. It might seem a small point, but I assure you that it makes quite a difference in men's minds. That is partly why I run my rest house.'

The conversation continued for miles along the road with the Chaplain setting out what he did in his house which he called 'Toc H' which was signallers' jargon for Talbot House and Nellie resolved that she would try and visit 'Pop.' Her curiosity was aroused. He left the bus at Steenworde, his road to Poperinghe requiring him to change transport. They continued south and east towards Bailleul where eventually they stopped outside a large and institutional looking building with Red Crosses all over it.

'Here you are ladies. This is the madhouse,' said the driver.

To their querying look, he laughed and said, 'CCS number 53 is housed in the old local asylum. Don't worry all the loonies are gone; probably fighting each other down the road. Just go in there and report; they'll take care of you after that. Good luck.'

With that he revved up his engine, put the old bus into gear and lurched off to his turn around point; he would go no further. Lugging their bags into the entry hall of the old asylum they found that all was quiet and dark wood with a bright fire blazing on a large hearth. They basked in front of this with pleasure for the bitter cold outside was kept at bay by

Chapter 25 — At the Front

its glowing radiance, which started at the door.

'Now then, you'll be Hollister and Little; but which is which?'

They introduced themselves.

'Well I'm glad to see you, though not as glad as I would have been three months ago when we were swamped. I'm Matron Wilson by the way, in charge of all nurses here; Major Ure commands the unit and is senior surgeon.'

'Was that Passchendaele, Matron?' asked Nellie.

'Yes Sister Little, it certainly was,' replied the newcomer in a matron's uniform of the Queen Alexandra's Imperial Military Nursing Service (QAIMNS), the Army's nurses. 'We were overwhelmed by the sheer number of casualties and working eighteen hours a day. It's a lot quieter now of course, being winter, but we know that the Boches are planning a big attack. I doubt it will be quiet for much longer. Now come with me and I'll show you your rooms.'

The nurses were accommodated very well in small rooms at the ends of the very large wards. The beds were compact and comfortable and each nurse had her own room with a radiator and a lock on the door. This was one wing of what had been an extremely large mental institution before the war, and as it turned out, part of it was still being used for that purpose. There were extensive bathrooms in the civilian wing which the nurses were allowed to use, and all seemed well on the way to being a home from home, until the Matron's next remark.

'Well now ladies, I suppose you must be hungry after such a journey.' In response to their keen nods she continued, 'Follow me please; ah no; do not take your coats off. No, not the hats or gloves either.'

Her face stayed perfectly straight and, exchanging puzzled glances Nellie and May followed her down the stairs and out through a back door onto a lawn. The nurses' mess was a single skinned marquee with trestle tables and food was being served from a side table where it had been brought from the kitchen indoors in large dixies. The food was lukewarm and the tent was freezing cold; peoples' breath hung in clouds over the scene and ice covered the tables and walls of the marquee. Over to one side was an opening that led through to a smaller marquee with armchairs in it; no-one was there. It was badly lit throughout and in the centre was a small stove where frozen girls perched briefly as they wolfed their food down as quickly as possible so that they could get back indoors.

'This is the nurses' canteen and ante-room for social life.'

Something in the Matron's manner made May ask as her teeth began to chatter; 'But where are the men?'

'Ah, they have different arrangements,' replied the Matron.

'They have a nice big hut with its own scullery, canteen and ante-room each with a big open blazing fireplace.'

Nellie's mouth fell open; 'But that's...'

'Exceptional, Sister. The word you want is "exceptional". In no other CCS will you find a situation like this. Never mind, I can practically guarantee that there will be a big change in the very near future. No, don't ask me how. Let us just say that there are forces in nature against which no man may stand.'

The two girls exchanged more puzzled looks, but the Matron would not be drawn any further. Like all the other women they ate their food as fast as they could and got into the main building to unpack in their rooms. The CCS was practically empty as there had been no major actions in the last few weeks and there were only a few patients left who were too sick to move. This was of course the purpose of a CCS; to take the wounded men who flooded off the battlefield in their hundreds and thousands, and to patch them up. The first job of the nurses was to take a man who had been stretchered in straight from the battlefields of the Ypres Salient and clean him up. Their uniforms would be thick with the clay mud of the liquid swamps they had been fighting and living in, and uniform and mud had to be removed by the simple method of cutting it all off. The same had to happen with lice and ticks except that this happened with water and carbolic. If a man was lightly wounded then the cleaning was not such an involved process; that could be done later at a base hospital or even back in the UK. The more serious cases needed to be completely clean at the CCS because they had to be operated on right away. The CCS had several operating theatres housed in Nissen huts, painted white and kept scrupulously clean, but they could not handle sophisticated operations. They also did not have a lot of time to dedicate to an individual, because of the sheer numbers needing treatment.

When the patient was clean the nurses could set about the second phase of the job. Filthy and blood-soaked field dressings applied at regimental aid posts could be removed, wounds swabbed with Lysol or Dakins solution, if necessary, stitched and then re-dressed. Once done the next patient could be seen. It was not the function of the CCS to provide any sort of long-term care; the job was to stabilise their patients so that they could be shipped out as quickly as possible. By providing a more immediate care this intermediate stage of treatment saved countless lives and this was really why Nellie, May and thousands of other young women wanted to be here and not anywhere else. Even nurses who had served their six months and been sent to a safer place like a base hospital often wanted to come back to a CCS because this was the cutting edge of their profession. They were the shock troops of nursing and they fought the grim reaper with tenacity and determination, cheating him of his prey, snatching men from under his scythe wherever they could. Their lives exactly mirrored those of the troops in the field. There were periods of boredom and inactivity when nothing was happening. Then there were the battles when exhausted women were often on their feet for twenty-four hours, cleaning, bandaging, stitching and comforting all they could until the three hundred or so wounded men the CCS had tended in that time were shipped off on a train or a lorry convoy.

In the salient, of course, there were routine casualties so they might receive six to ten men a day hurt in accidents, explosions of shells, winged by snipers. In quiet times these men stayed longer at the CCS and there were five when Nellie and May arrived. Three were intestinal injuries; the operating team had removed sections of their guts that had been destroyed by bullets or shell fragments. They were very skilled at stitching back together, but these men were unlikely to survive; infection would carry them off in a few days. Certainly they were not fit to travel. The nurses knew this and also knew that they could not keep septicaemia at bay, so their time was spent in keeping these men comfortable and towards the end warding off their pain with morphine. They eased them gently out of the world, encouraging them to write home before it was too late, reading to them from letters sent from their families and comforting them. The other two casualties were fascinating and Nellie could scarcely stop herself from staring at one of them. He had been shot in the forehead by a sniper and lived. Usually that would have been the end of him; even if he had lived he would have arrived with brain matter visible and would have died delirious or raving shortly afterwards. But he had been seen by a Medical Officer who had extracted two fragments of lead from the wound and left it. The rest of the bullet was somewhere deep in his forehead and no-one wanted to go probing for it. The wound itself had all but healed leaving a dent about an inch and a half deep and the appearance of it was astonishing. The man himself was quite hale and hearty about it, walking around avowing that he'd always been an ugly bugger and his wife was no oil painting so she'd be glad to see him even with an 'ole in his head as it made no difference to her so long as he was alive. All he wanted to do was to get back to his shop and he was soon to ship out back to 'Blighty' discharged on medical grounds. The MO told him that the bullet would either kill him in its own good time, or stay in there and do nothing. It would be a brave doctor who attempted to remove it. However, if the patient were very, very lucky then it might just work its way out over many years.

The other man was fascinating for a different reason. He had no big toe on his left foot, because he had shot it off. At first he said that he had done it by accident while cleaning his gun, but later he had changed his story and said that his pal had shot it off whilst he was cleaning his own rifle. There was little doubt what the outcome of this episode was going to be. He would be taken to the Town Hall at Poperinghe and tried for cowardice; at ground level there were two cells where men found guilty spent their last nights on earth. Just outside in the yard was a wooden post, against which he would be shot at dawn. He was a man heading for middle age with a wife and three children at home; he had volunteered and been out for three years and had probably just had enough. Nellie knew this and tried to treat him as just another patient, but it was hard when she knew very well that all they did was in vain. Their orders were to keep him pending trial and as soon as he could walk he would be gone.

It was on 6 January that the girls found out what Matron Wilson had meant when she spoke of a force of nature. Both were being employed in basic cleaning of wards that appeared to be already spotless, when a large and expensive car drew up outside and a man stepped out in a Major's uniform. This was not so very unusual, but he turned out to be escorting a personage who was very singular. She stepped out of the car and drew herself up like a Queen in scarlet and grey uniform and cloak; on her breast she wore the Royal Red Cross, the highest accolade a nurse could receive. She did not flinch in the bitterly cold air, but crunched across the ice of the courtyard to be greeted by Matron Wilson like the relieving force of a besieged battalion.

'Wilson; it's good to see you again. How are you?'

'I am well ma'am thank you. I am very happy to see you here today, very happy indeed; particularly so in this weather.'

The august looking lady cast a keen glance at the Matron,

'It's not every Matron is keen to see the Matron-in-Chief I have to say. I take it that your happiness stems from a particular reason?'

'I am glad that we are to be inspected, Ma'am.'

'Now that is probably unique!' said the lady and uttered a short little laugh with a touch of grimness to it. 'I see you will not be drawn, but I have eyes. Let us proceed.'

With a smile and a twinkle Matron Wilson led the way into the hospital building where the Chief Medical Officer, Major Ure, stood waiting. The visitor, as far as he was concerned, was here to inspect the nurses and he was not answerable to her. Army nurses do not, as a rule, salute though Major Fuller and Major Ure exchanged them. Major Ure was a square faced sort of man with little time for women. A good surgeon, a domineering husband and an authoritarian father, he was here to meet this lady as a matter of required courtesy because of her importance. It was Matron Wilson who made the introductions.

'Major Ure, may I present Matron-in-Chief of the BEF, Maud McCarthy? Miss McCarthy, Major Ure.'

The usual pleasantries were exchanged, then Miss McCarthy was escorted by Matron Wilson around the wards and the nurses' quarters. She was highly satisfied with all that she saw. The nurses were clean and well turned out, the wards were spotless and the accommodation more than satisfactory. The Matron-in-Chief was in a very good mood as they finished their tour of the building.

'Now I'd like to see the nurses' canteen and anteroom. A good life off duty is very important if we are to maintain the highest standards of nursing in places like this.'

Matron Wilson took Miss McCarthy outside and into the marquee where some half frozen girls were beginning to line up for their lunch. Already prepared was a table for the Matron in Chief where she was invited to sit down and sample the food. It had been cleaned recently and ice twinkled where water had frozen.

'I'm damned if I will. Where's the ante-room?'

On being shown the frigid canvas tent where nurses were expected to spend their off duty time she did not 'hit the roof'. She was not that sort of person being small, warm, but with a core of steel and one of the most efficient people in the senior ranks of the British Expeditionary Force. Nonetheless, it was evident that she was under some emotional strain, for a very slight Australian accent crept into her speech.

'I assume Wilson, that you have raised this matter with Major Ure?'

'Many times Ma'am.'

'I want to see where the Medical Officers have their canteen.'

On being shown she swept into the well-lit and beautifully warm hut and found Major Ure eating a nice hot meal. Stopping in front of him she said just a few words.

'In the course of my long career in army nursing I have met many officers and gentlemen; you may be the first, but you are most certainly not the second.'

'But what on earth...?'

'That you don't know what I'm talking about merely confirms my opinion. It is obviously not worth my time talking to you because you would not comprehend what I would say; you have not the mind for it. You will understand in a very short time.'

There was no drama, no shouting and all was said in a very small but very angry voice, however there was such force of personality behind it that her words left him shaken. When Miss McCarthy swung round and marched out of the hut to her car Major Ure tried to put it off as a joke, looking round the rest of the men at their meals and shrugging, 'Women.' Nonetheless, he found out in a few short hours that his sentiment was not shared when a phone call came from Surgeon General Thompson who informed him of several things. Firstly, he was calling Ure because he had himself received a phone call from General Sir Douglas Haig, Commander-in-Chief of the BEF, who was incensed. He thought it an absolute disgrace that nurses were being fed and housed for their leisure in a marquee in the depth of winter whilst men, eschewing their natural courtesy towards the fair sex, were loafing around in well-heated quarters. What sort of rotten shower was Thompson allowing to act in this manner under his command? He had better do something about it and pretty damned quick. If the newspapers got hold of it there would be the devil to pay; besides which, it just was not right that nurses were being treated so; what sort of a man was this Ure anyway? He, Thompson, was grossly embarrassed and personally offended that an officer under his command could even countenance the existing state of affairs; Ure was a disgrace and had utterly failed to consider the comfort and actual necessities of the nursing staff at his command. Thompson was sending a team with building materials and Ure had better give them all the help they needed if he knew what was good for him.

The very next morning three lorries arrived and a pre-fabricated wooden deck was built on the lawn next to the marquee. Six men then erected a large Nissen Hut within four hours. When the skin was done they screwed into place a strange looking wooden lining to the whole building, a process that again only took three hours.

'What's that stuff?' asked May. 'I've never seen that kind of wood before.'

'It's called Haskelite love. They bring it from America. We call it plywood. It's not very good insulation to be honest, but it's better than nothing. These huts used to have no lining, but they were as cold as the North Pole in winter. You keep the stoves going and you'll be fine.'

Indeed, as four men installed windows and doors at each end of the hut, two stoves were put into place and a partition built halfway down the building. When it was done the furniture and equipment was moved from the marquee into the hut and for the first time the nurses of number 53 CCS had a decent warm place to eat and relax; they soon made it very homely and it became a popular place to meet, talk, play games, read and even listen to records.

Life went in a similar fashion for the next couple of months and neither of the girls was much inspired to do anything away from Bailleul. It was a hard and bitter winter and though the local shops tempted them in to buy luxuries occasionally, such as fresh butter, eggs, wonderful cheese or fresh bread, they did not stray far. Nellie longed for the cold to break, so that they could at least go on some country walks. In the spring it would be nice to go and gather armfuls of wild flowers to put in the wards. They knew from previous experience that their future patients would appreciate such a thing. It was not very long after their arrival that they became aware of the tension in the air around them and it centred on the forthcoming German attack. Everyone knew very well that it was coming, for although the enemy concealed his troop movements behind the lines as best he could, the presence of large numbers of reinforcements was very obvious to aerial observers. German prisoners, when interrogated, would speak of the huge numbers of troops arriving victorious from Russia and spoke openly of *'der tag'* being the day when they would attack and sweep the Allies into the sea. The air of apprehension was quite tense; the Allied losses during their attacks of 1917 had been very high and rumour said that in some parts of the Western Front the British and French were outnumbered by more than two to one. When the attack came, many doubted they would be able to stop it. May put it quite well one evening in the anteroom after dinner.

'What a place for two lasses from Whitehaven and Wukiton to be, eh Nellie?'

Nellie had to agree that they had certainly by-passed the fire and wished themselves into the frying pan.

'What'll you do if you get captured?'

'Well I'll try not to get captured in the first place. They've got to get through a lot of our lads before they get to us. Anyway the front's nearly ten miles away. We'd have warning enough.'

'You say that Nell, but that's not actually a great distance. Just suppose, if Jerry did take you prisoner; what would you do?'

'It rather depends on what he'd do, May. I'd just try to stay alive, but the Jerries are men, not monsters. I can't believe they'd harm nurses just for the sake of it.'

'I would not bet on that for one minute,' a voice broke in. 'Remember Edith Cavell? Being a nurse didn't save her.'

Nellie and May looked over at the speaker; she was not a member of their nursing staff. They had noticed her when they came into the canteen as a figure dressed in a nurse's uniform, but one that was khaki with some Belgian army badges on it. She also wore riding breeches and boots, but by 1918 women in trousers of all sorts in the battle areas were a common sight, especially in the motorbike despatch riders.

'Elsie Knocker,' and the newcomer held her hand out for both of them to shake.

'I've heard quite a few stories about what the Germans are capable of with unfortunates who fall into their hands. If I were you I'd do my best to stay well clear of them.'

'They are close though,' said May. 'Ten miles does not seem very far away.'

'That's true, it's not,' replied their new acquaintance. 'However, it is possible to operate nearer than that and still not get caught. You just have to stay on your guard.'

'Nurse Cavell was helping men to escape,' said Nellie. 'They shot her as a spy. We are not spies, so they could not do that to us.'

'I admit that they are less likely to shoot a nurse after the belting their world reputation took after they killed Cavell, but I wouldn't put it past them.'

'You mean all those stories about babies being bayoneted and priests being crucified?' said Nellie. 'I don't believe everything I'm told about stuff like that. There's a lot of stories about that are made up to make the enemy look bad. I'm sure they tell stories about us too.'

'I've no doubt they do,' said Elsie, 'but I work in the Belgian sector just to the north of here and a lot of the Belgian boys saw what happened when the Germans invaded their country. Believe me, some of the stories are true. In 1914 I came across a massacre where the Germans had just retreated from a small town near Ghent. They slaughtered twenty-six Belgian military policemen and mutilated their bodies. I saw this. Try to stay out of their hands. If they break through, then run for it if you have time and don't get caught.'

'Baroness, are you scaring my nurses?' asked Matron Wilson.

'Oh I don't think they scare very easily,' replied Elsie Knocker. 'They seem sensible enough and not soft and daft like some.'

'They would not be here if they were that. Have you had your meal?'

'I have thank you. I am much obliged and thank you for the dressings; we ran out completely yesterday and supplies are hard to get from the Belgies.'

'Oh you're very welcome…'

'But it's time for me to go before Major Ure spots that you've been giving me supplies. He doesn't like me anyway, but yes Miss Wilson, it's time for me to go. It's thirty miles back to Pervyse, but my machine will get me there in under the hour.'

With that, Elsie Knocker left to place two well stuffed panniers onto her motorbike and head back to her own hospital; she knew very well where she could rely on people for medical favours.

'Baroness?' asked May. 'She said she was called Elsie Knocker'.

'And so she is, but since her marriage she's better known as Baroness T'Serclaes.'

May and Nellie looked as if they had been shot.

'I see that you've heard of her. Yes, you just met one of the women of Pervyse and though they are unofficial I think they are superb nurses and I give them help if they ask for it. They need all that they can get.'

Baroness T'Serclaes and her friend Mhairi Chisholm were famous. They had set up an independent dressing station one hundred yards behind the Belgian Front line earlier in the war in an old cellar. They had it reinforced with concrete and paid for a steel door to be fitted by Harrods. There they tended the Belgian wounded in their own private CCS. Knocker did most of the nursing, whilst Chisholm transported the wounded to a base hospital fifteen miles away in their own ambulance, often under fire and in awful conditions.

'Well I never!' exclaimed May. 'She looked so ordinary'.

'What did you expect?' laughed Matron Wilson. 'Most people look ordinary. It's not until you see them doing extraordinary things that you realise how different they are. At any rate she's a good egg and I like her. It's easy to 'lose' supplies around here and it helps their wounded a lot. We are all on the same side, so don't go telling Major Ure.'

As if they would.

Early in March the weather broke and the great freeze which had rendered the roads glazed with ice, now turned to water, rain and mud. At least it was possible for people to move around, and so May and Nellie decided to go to Skindles in Poperinghe for an omelette, bread and coffee for lunch; this was on the recommendation of several people who had told them that 'Pop' was a fairly safe place to visit, that there were shops open and that four restaurants did a good trade, the best of which was Skindles. That seemed an odd name for a Belgian restaurant, but it appeared that it had been opened by a lady called Madame Zoe Beutin who wanted to cater for her new clientele and make them feel at home. On asking an English soldier for a suitably British name for her new establishment he had replied without hesitation,

'Skindles, Zoe. Skindles of Maidenhead. A fine place that is.'

So Skindles it was and it made her fortune; she presided over it and insisted on being called 'Mademoiselle Zoe', which is how thousands of British officers came to know her. May and Nellie were nursing Sisters and as such they counted as 'officers' so would have no difficulty getting into a place where ordinary enlisted other ranks were not allowed. It was less than ten miles away and easy to reach with many lorries and buses and tenders heading both ways so it was easy to catch a lift by 'lorry hopping' which everybody did. Soon they stood in the Grote Markt of a charming little town that looked slightly knocked about by malicious shell fire from the distance, but mostly intact and very very busy. This was the gateway to the Ypres Salient and through it poured men and the materials of war. Their lunch was delicious, hot and very cheap; their presence caused quite a stir for though there were many women in evidence round the streets, they were British nurses and that carried a certain cache with the often handsome young officers sitting round the restaurant tables. Whilst finishing her coffee, it was May who caught sight of a painted wooden sign down the street that said 'Toc H'.

'Nellie; do you remember that padre we met on the bus? He had a house called Toc H. Well there it is.'

Nellie craned her neck to see out and it was decided there and then that they would take up the Reverend Clayton's invitation to tea. Paying their bill they presented themselves at the door of Talbot House and saw to their amusement a sign over it which read "Abandon all rank ye who enter here". Inside there was a reception desk, for it appeared that Toc H acted in some ways as a hotel and had rooms for rent. They asked the civilian gentleman behind the desk if the Padre was available, because he had invited them to tea.

'I'll just get him for you ladies; we don't get too many British ladies through that door, so it's something of an honour. Hold on please.'

As the receptionist disappeared, May giggled and pointed at another sign that read, 'If you are in the habit of spitting on the floor at home, please spit here.' Nellie also giggled, 'I can just see my mam's reaction if anyone did that on her lino. She'd have their guts for garters! Look at that one.'

'The waste paper baskets are purely ornamental – By Order!'

One by the staircase caused confusion.

'Now that I don't understand.'

'Nor me.'

'No Amy Robsart stunts down these stairs,' said a jovial voice as the Reverend Clayton came into the hall. 'Well she was the wife of the Earl of Essex in the time of Queen Elizabeth and she died as she broke her neck falling down the stairs.'

'Oh I see,' said Nellie. 'That's a bit grim.'

'Just my gallows humour, I'm afraid' laughed the padre. 'I have such signs up all over the place. Now I promised you some tea, so come along.'

'Please don't put yourself out Padre; we just called in on the off chance.'

'Not at all; my dear young woman you could not have come at a better moment, for we are about to have a tea party. We have just finished service in the church upstairs and some of us are going to drink tea and talk together. Now come along.'

They followed Clayton down a corridor and stared in astonishment as they entered a pleasant room with armchairs and small tables; a tray with fresh tea, cups and sugar was in the middle. Round the table sat three Privates, a Major, a Captain, two Lieutenants and a real live General.

'Gentlemen, as you know, this is a Christian house and I have brought two angels to tea.'

The men all stood and waited until the girls sat, and the Reverend opened the conversation.

'I expect you are wondering what is going on here, but once inside our doors there is no rank. Here we may talk, be at peace, refresh our minds and think.'

'It's lovely,' said Nellie 'but why are you doing it?' Here she waved her hand around the room, at the men at the armchairs and the pictures on the walls.

'You are a Christian, so you know what happened at Emmaeus.'

'I do. Two of Jesus's followers were on the road to Emmaeus

and saw him risen after his crucifixion. They stopped at an inn and talked with him.'

'Correct. Now this is a house of Emmaeus.'

'I don't understand.'

'They saw Christ. They were enlightened. Emmaeus is a place where they were given new hope. Their eyes were opened and they were inspired to change their lives. This is an inn on a new path.'

'I think I see, but it's a strange place to be doing it isn't it, so near to the battle front?'

'No Sister,' said one of the privates. 'It's exactly the right place to be doing it. Here on the road between life and death.'

'I agree,' said the General. 'Here men go to the front and many meet their death. Many survive and go through Hell on earth. Where else is more appropriate to pause and reflect and perhaps to change what you think and believe?'

'This house is home,' stated a Lieutenant. 'It's a place of quiet, of armchairs, civilisation, even of beauty where men come to talk, remember their own homes and families and to set their minds at rest before they go to the front.'

'Exactly,' said Clayton. 'A reminder of what we are fighting for – a better world.'

'But why drop all your ranks? How can you be a general and be seen in the same way outside the door by these privates? In here they do not call you Sir or salute you, so how can you expect them to do it outside?'

'It's a good question,' replied the General, 'And one which I have an answer to that satisfies me. This place is not quite of this world you see. It is outside the normal time and space, sanctified by the will of this man.' Here he gestured at Clayton, 'It's a sort of peace of God; not from war, but of rank. In here we bare our heads and pray not as officer and private, but just as men praying to our God. In here rank would be unnatural.

Out there the normal rules apply.'

'It lifts the weight from your shoulders and allows you just to be you for a time,' one of the Lieutenants said softly. 'In here I'm not Lieutenant Grant. I'm just John Grant from Beauly and no-one expects me to give orders, take responsibility or carry out tasks. It's a true recreation and allows me time to be me.'

'I understand now. I have seen patients die often and wished they had time before they went to make their peace. What you are doing here is a good thing.'

'Thank you Nellie, though not perhaps as good as what is done by you nurses.'

A general murmur of agreement went up and this began some pleasant hours of talk which obeyed the rules of the house. No-one was allowed to talk of war. Nellie and May told their eager audience of the shows they had seen in London and in turn they heard stories from the others of their civilian jobs, sports, families and hobbies. Everyone from General to Private was perfectly at ease, laughing, joking, reflecting and above all, just listening; this, in a life when there is often so little time to listen. When they left in late afternoon, they felt refreshed and they both vowed to each other that they would return. Reverend Clayton had assured them that they were the personification of British womanhood in this town and that their feminine presence had done more to perk up the mood of his afternoon tea than anything else possibly could have. They were welcome at any time.

Their intention to pay a return visit was not to be fulfilled, however. On 21 March the long awaited German attack materialised in overwhelming force on the junction between the British and French armies some eighty miles south of Bailleul across the old Somme battlefields. Although they were too far away to be involved in the massive waves of casualties from that battle, all leave in the Ypres Salient was cancelled as the men and women in that sector braced themselves to face an attack on their positions, which was expected by the hour.

Chapter 26

Retreat

At 4.40am on Thursday 21 March over 8,000 German guns opened fire on the positions of 5 Army, and General Gough's thirteen divisions were attacked by forty-three German divisions. Further north nineteen German divisions attacked General Byng's 3 Army that had six. A wall of orange flame erupted to the east and a sea of fire descended on the British lines. In men the Germans had an 8:1 superiority; they broke through into open countryside. Disaster and defeat loomed for the Western Allies. After three days of hard fighting 5 Army had not broken but was holding the Germans up wherever they could, often with scratch units, then the German attacks stopped. They had run out of their own supplies and had to wait for their lines to catch up; their men were also dropping with fatigue and the outnumbered British had not given up. In the fortified areas now behind German lines, surrounded units fought often to the last man and inflicted thousands of casualties on the enemy. The Germans had gained a lot of territory but most of it was farmland of little strategic value.

The British were of course rushing reinforcements into battle as fast as they could get them. Thousands of men kept back in the UK were convoyed across the Channel as fast as they could be carried; everyone knew that the Germans were not finished, but the big question was as to where they would strike next. In Bailleul May had no doubts at all.

'It's got to be up here Nellie. We'll be next. Just you wait and see. We'll have more work than we can cope with soon enough.'

'Now how do you work that one out May?'

'Think about it. Their big attack has been down south and all our boys have been rushing down there to stop them. Our eyes are off what's going on here. They'll think we're not looking and they'll try it in our sector.'

'Then they'll have it wrong. Everyone is expecting them to try it somewhere else; we'll not be caught on the hop. Just wait and see.'

'Now you sound like Mr Asquith.'

'That's no bad thing. I wish he were Prime Minister again. I don't trust Lloyd George; there's something slimy about him. Seriously May, I wish you'd stop worrying so. There's nothing we can do about it and whatever happens we'll deal with it when it comes.'

May's warnings turned out not to be pessimism, but prescience. On 7 April the Germans opened a tremendous bombardment on the Allies between Festubert and Armentieres. Casualties by the hundred flooded in and the nurses and medical officers of 53 CCS found themselves almost overwhelmed. The wounded continued to flow in as the enemy advanced five miles and were only stopped by suicidal resistance. The average stay for a patient at the CCS was only a day or so, but of course there were men who had to stay longer. Nellie had, as one of her charges, a fine looking lad who had been blown up in the air and whose back was broken. It was the opinion of Major Ure that he could not live, yet for some reason he refused to die. At first she thought that it was the morphine that made him not realize the seriousness of his condition, since all he complained of was a sore back. Yet with good food and bed rest he appeared to be gaining strength. To the amazement of all, at the end of three days he moved his legs and declared his intention of getting up. Nellie told him sternly that he would do no such thing and sent for Major Ure. She did not like Major Ure, for she sensed that he was no friend to women, regarding them as inferior beings, but she did respect his professional abilities. He told the patient quite frankly that there was nothing he could do for him, as he had no X ray machine and he really needed specialist attention. There was a good chance that the man's spine would heal and he showed no signs of paralysis. He could either stay here or he could be evacuated to a base hospital where they had better facilities. The soldier chose to be evacuated, so Major Ure with professional thoughtfulness arranged for him to be removed strapped to a strong plank before being anaesthetised with chloroform. Instead of being taken by a bumpy ambulance to the railway, he was carried on a rigid stretcher by four orderlies the half mile or so to the terminus and woke up in an ambulance train heading for Calais.

May had a gas patient and there was nothing she could do for him except wipe his forehead and pray for his release. He was a blue colour and spent much of his time gasping and coughing while calling for his mother. A comfortable death with someone there was all she could give him and to her great relief he passed beyond human cares at two o'clock in the morning as she held his hand.

For the general run of wounded the only way the nurses could handle the stark numbers of them was to form a sort of assembly line. As the walking wounded came in May stood by the door with a pair of scissors and called the men in three at a time. There was no time to be delicate though poor May found it difficult to be so clinical. She would cut through the stiff filthy bandages that had been hastily put on at the battlefield and tug them off, usually with a quick pull that made the patient wince or yell. Her eyes would fill with tears and she would sometimes sob, but then the man moved on to the medical officer who would examine the wound. He would be very laconic and spat out his instructions, 'Wet dressing', 'dry dressing', 'boric ointment', 'splint', 'three stitches'. The patient then moved on to tables where other nurses waited and applied the prescribed treatment. There were so many casualties that the nurses were on their feet for eighteen hours at a time until they were dropping with fatigue. In many cases the MO simply looked at the wounded man and pulled his eyelids down. If he was satisfied with what he saw then he simply said 'B' and an orderly would tie a label to the man's lapel; he would not be treated at all, but sent straight to the convoy for the base hospital. If the base hospital was similarly overwhelmed then the MO there would order that a label 'E' be placed on the man's lapel and he would be sent straight to England where he would arrive coated in battlefield mud and wearing his original field dressing. He might end up on a fast train to Carlisle or another hospital city. Much the same happened with moribund cases where the MO thought there was nothing to be done. They would be passed up the line while the CCS concentrated its attention on saving those who they knew could be saved.

Six days after the German attack, Nellie and May were tired out, their heads and feet ached, their eyes were red with exhaustion and they were running on nervous energy alone. Over the previous week they and the other nurses had not eaten a proper meal. Sandwiches and tea were brought to them where they worked and they snatched bites and gulps between patients. Matron Wilson would occasionally order them to go and sleep, but they knew that she was in a similar state to themselves and close to exhaustion. Their rooms were at the ends of the wards and of course they could not ignore the cries of patients who needed help or water. The poor nurses in charge of these wards were also overwhelmed and they were lucky if they got three hours of sleep in twenty-four.

Chapter 26 — Retreat

Just outside Nellie's door was a young man who had been there for three days. His leg had been removed and he had a bullet lodged near his heart, which no medical officer felt competent to remove. He was conscious and had such a sweet poetic kind of face that Nellie's protective instincts had been awoken; for some reason he reminded her of Barwise. She would sit and talk to him for a while when she should have been sleeping and would help him drink his water, fluff up his pillow, and read to him.

On 13 April there were over three hundred wounded men in CCS number 53. A hundred of them were crammed into wards and the rest were being processed for evacuation. At 7.00am a huge number of lorries drove up outside the walls and in the courtyard of the building and a tense Major walked up to Major Ure's operating theatre where he had just finished removing a poor lad's arm, and spoke to him. Ure's face, often immobile, registered dismay and he issued his orders. Matron Wilson rushed up to the ward where Nellie and May were asleep and woke them up.

'Come on my girls. Put all your things into a bag now; you leave in ten minutes.'

'Ten minutes Matron? But why?'

'The Germans have broken through. They'll be here in under the hour now hurry.'

Men flooded into the hospital and loaded the wounded into lorries. Everyone who could walk was hurried into whatever space could be found and as soon as a vehicle was filled it sped off down the road to the West. There was no time to save equipment; all that the CCS staff could take was whatever personal effects they could fit into one bag. Ten minutes is not a long time, but the evacuation was quick. The boy outside Nellie's room lay immobile as she came out heading for the stairs; then she noticed that there was no-one else in the ward so she decided to wait with him. He seemed to be asleep, breathing shallowly, perhaps dreaming of home. A few minutes later Major Ure came up the stairs.

'Sister Little you must come now; we are leaving.'

'But there's a patient here.'

'I know that Sister, but you must come. He can't be moved.'

Nellie thought quickly; what misery to be left alone when everyone else had gone. Someone had to take care of him!

'Well in that case I'm staying. He's a patient and he needs me.'

'Sister, your instinct does you credit, but there's nothing you can do. I order you to come now.'

'You can't order me Major. I'm not an army nurse; I'm Red Cross.'

Breathing heavily the Major almost yelled, 'I tell you, you foolish girl that there is nothing you can do for him.' He paused, breathed hard and seemed to think. Then he went on more gently; 'He's dying Sister. He'll be gone very soon. You staying here will achieve nothing except that you will become a prisoner and he will be dead. The Germans will look after him if he's still alive when they get here.'

'I won't let him die on his own. I can hold his hand so he does not feel alone; that I can do. And if the Germans take me prisoner then I'll deal with it when it happens. They're just men when all is said and done.'

The Major looked at her and decided to waste no more time. He clumped off down the stairs and left her holding the dying man's hand. Three minutes later she looked up and there was a Lieutenant standing in front of her with two Tommies.

'Sister; you have a choice. Either you walk down the stairs onto the lorry that is waiting for you at great risk, or these men will carry you. Which is it to be?'

He was a fresh faced lad and not much older than her. She

estimated his age to be no more than about twenty-four but she looked in his eyes and saw something which she recognised. When her mother was determined on something she had a will of steel and she saw the same look in this officer's face. He meant what he said. Time hung, frozen for an infinite mote of eternity, then a shell exploded nearby. In the distance she could hear rifle fire and machine guns. The enemy was close!

One of the Tommies was an older man, perhaps forty, and his eyes were a world of understanding. He spoke, 'It does you credit Sister, and we all love you girls for it, but he wouldn't want you caught by Jerry.' He gestured at the comatose man in the bed.

'Come along now miss.'

A drop of moisture ran down Nellie's cheek from her left eye as the truth of his words sank in, and she stood; as he put his arm round her shoulder all the exhaustion, the strain and the inhumanity of it caught up with her and she dissolved into tears. She wept uncontrollably as he escorted her down the stairs patting her arm saying, 'There there…' and other consoling noises. Just down the road British troops were building a barricade and placing some Lewis guns; they would resist, but there were not enough of them. Bailleul would be in German hands by nightfall and CCS number 53 with all its equipment would be theirs too.

As soon as she was on the lorry it left at speed; shells were hitting the town and though she did not know it, the nearest German storm troops were less than half a mile away. Had she known, it would have made little difference as she cried herself to sleep in May Hollister's arms, sitting opposite Major Ure and Matron Wilson who also slept, leaning on each other, rank, station and propriety all forgotten in the face of common human need. For the moment number 53 CCS had ceased to exist. When Nellie awoke, the front was far behind them and of course the subject arose of what they should do now. Major Ure was clear that his staff and the QAIMNS should report to number 32 stationary hospital at Boulogne, being one of the biggest military hospitals in France. His opinion though was that Nellie and May should not go there.

'You're not Army you see and the reason you Red Cross nurses were sent to the CCS's in the first place was that there was a shortage of trained staff who could do the job. The base hospitals are full of VADs and Territorial Force nurses so you won't see anyone wearing that on them'. Here he gestured at the Reds Cross adorning their apron fronts. 'I think the best thing we can do is take you with us and you can report at Number 8 base hospital which is actually run by the Red Cross. It's a couple of miles further on, but I expect we can get you there somehow. They'll be glad to see you, I should think.'

Nellie thought he was a strange man; she still did not like him, but just now he sounded almost kind.

The Major was right. Number 8 Base Hospital was probably better known as the Baltic and Corn Exchange Hospital, because it received its finance from that august and wealthy association of merchants in the City of London. It had 250 beds and lots of enthusiastic VAD nurses. It stood on the seafront, a converted hotel, at Paris Plage Le Touquet, and after their Nissen huts it looked like a palace to two travel worn and storm tossed nurses. Two fully trained Red Cross nurses were welcomed with open arms by the Chairman and manager, a Mr Henry Obre, and they were quickly installed in two cubicles in the well-appointed and airy hostel that had been built in the grounds to accommodate the nurses. The Matron, a Miss Westnutt, saw the state they were in and told them that she did not wish to see them for another twelve hours. They must eat, bathe and sleep; they could report to her after prayers in the morning. The sheer luxury of clean white sheets, good food and a comfortable bed did much to compensate for the hurried and uncomfortable journey they had just endured and the twelve hours was generous. Although the hospital had 250 beds it had over 300 patients, and many men were on stretchers in the corridors being tended where they were. At 6.30am Nellie and May joined the rest of the nursing staff about to go on duty for morning prayers, a ritual that happened in every base hospital, then they were put to work on the wards. Life soon became a frenetic round of changing dressings, wound irrigation, cleaning and tending to men hurt in all sorts of ways. After their time at the CCS they did not find it hard. Many of the VADs had been at the hospital for years and were as experienced as they were, if not as qualified. The hospital itself was very well equipped indeed with all the latest medical equipment that could be bought. It also had a very enviable recovery rate for its patients. Some of them were acute cases though and needed a more attentive care than less dangerously hurt men. Nellie found herself detailed to look after several men who were very heavily bandaged and not able to leave their beds. One of these was Lieutenant George Vane and he had, so far, been very unlucky.

During the first weeks of the German attacks in March/April he had led a counter attack with his platoon outside the village of Estaires which lay to the west of Armentieres. He had been shot through by a rifle bullet which had smashed the edges of two of his ribs and rendered him unable to continue in combat. A stretcher-bearer of the Royal Army Medical Corps had helped him back to an aid post that had been set up a few hundred yards behind the lines and had started to dress his wounds. As he did so a shell exploded right by them and killed the stretcher-bearer outright, causing great damage to both George's legs. His right leg stayed intact though lacerated, but his left leg was completely shattered. Evacuated quickly and heavily sedated with morphine, he ended up at number 8 Hospital where the very able surgeon Mr Hodinet saved his life by amputating the now useless leg. A very positive young man with a cheery disposition, George was nonetheless in a very bad way indeed and he expected to die. That did not seem to faze him at all, which Nellie found incomprehensible. She knew very well that her role was to comfort him, to sooth him and to help him, if necessary, to let go; to die. Despite this she could not, in this case, stop herself during one of their conversations from asking him why. Perhaps it was because she thought he was so pretty, so young, such a waste. In many ways he was everything that she was not. She was a working class girl from the back streets of Workington and she was here because she had acquired particular skills. George was middle class, probably upper and his parents were well heeled. He had a posh accent and had been privately educated and represented a way of life that she might have seen as soft and effete; but George was not afraid of death.

'Why are you so calm, George. You think you're going to

die, but you smile and laugh and seem to think it's nothing. Aren't you worried at all?'

'No, Nellie. I'm not afraid one bit. I know that looks a bit strange, but I'm not scared of death. Death is nothing; it's what everybody does in the end so why be scared? If I don't die next week or the week after I could die in seventy years time, but in the end we all go the same way.'

She struggled with this. We all want to be immortal, particularly when we are young, but George's bland insouciance in the face of his own imminent demise left her not knowing what to do or say, particularly when he pitied her.

'Poor Nellie. How many people have you seen die? Fifty? A hundred? More?'

'I've lost count.'

'I imagine that you have. I'll just be one more and you'll hold my hand and say nice things. You'll want me to write to my mother just one more time; as you have whenever I get my letters, but you still don't understand why.'

'So tell me George then, since you know. Why?'

He stopped talking for a minute or so then turned to her.

'Why don't I mind dying?'

'Yes.'

'It's the price to be paid. I knew what I was doing, so I will pay the price if need be.'

'The price for what?'

He looked at her almost askance.

'You can ask me that? You of all people? Why are you here Nellie?'

'To do what I can. To help save lives.'

'You save lives; and that's a delay is it not? No-one can really save lives except God if he exists. I doubt he does. What you do is to delay the end, but as I said, we all go the same way ultimately. To some extent the actual time of our end does not matter. The world goes on in the same old way and the time we make our exit not does not affect it in any way at all. Not a smidgeon of the universe is altered by our living or dying, or when it happens. You surely know that?'

'Well I do, but you make it sound like nothing.'

He grabbed her hand and an almost febrile expression came into his face.

'It's not nothing Nellie. You came here to make a difference. That in itself is an absolute good.'

Nellie did not have his education and did not know what this meant, but grasped part of his meaning.

'You say you're paying a price. But what for George? What are you buying by fighting and dying like this?'

It was then that he grew emphatic.

'I volunteered Nellie. Because of Belgium. You know about that.'

'Yes. The Germans invaded Belgium.'

'Exactly. That's why I joined up, me and millions like me. A large nation attacks a small nation; not only that, but a small nation that they had sworn to respect. A treaty signed and sealed with all solemnity by the great nations of Europe and witnessed by our own. How could we stand by and watch a country we had sworn to protect, attacked and over-run by a bunch of militaristic thugs on our own doorstep?'

'Is that all it is? To stop a bully?'

'No. It's far more than that. The Germans are fighting for their Emperor, for their way of life; for authoritarian rule and militarism where people are regimented, may not think for themselves and obey without question. That's not the world I want to see.'

'You think ours is better? With all the poverty and the hunger and the squalor?'

'Yes I do. Don't you see? That's the point exactly. We are

not perfect by any means; I know that. We have people in our country who are obscenely rich and people who are dirt poor, living in hovels with not enough to eat. But we live in hope. Look what happened this year. Working men will have the vote at the next election and women over the age of thirty. It's about hope Nellie; the hope of a better world; the hope for democracy; the hope that we can really make things better for the generations who follow us. That's what I am fighting for and that's why I'm a Socialist.'

'And you really believe that our whole army feels that way?'

'Not consciously, I know. I doubt you'd get a coal miner from Kent or a cobbler from Northampton to say such things, but inside themselves, where it counts that's what they feel. They fight for a square deal, for fairness, for a chance at democracy, for a world where you can hope for better. That's what's on offer; that's what we buy with our blood.'

'And it's worth dying for? It's worth your life?'

His eyes blazed and his answer came, 'Yes. For that sort of world, yes. For me and all the men who have died. If that's what we leave, just the hope of it, then I am happy that my life has been to some purpose.'

That night George lapsed into a fever and Death came to sit at the foot of his bed. Nellie could not see Death of course, though she knew he was there, but he lingered waiting with his scythe for the moment that George would give up. As for Nellie, all she could see was a patient with a fever who was in crisis. Nurses are warriors, and with their comrades, the doctors, they fight an eternal war against their mortal enemies; pain, suffering, disease and death. This war may never be won, but each engagement in it has its victors and its vanquished. Like the trained nurse she was, Nellie prepared for action, then went into battle with every weapon she had. George's sheets were soaked with sweat; they were changed with help from another nurse and an orderly. He raved and was burning up so she applied cold-water soaked towels to his forehead. She took the bandages off his stump and swabbed the wound with Eusol before reapplying fresh dressings. She spoke to him as she worked, telling him to pull himself together and get better. All night she sat with him and held his hand so that he would know that he had an ally on his side, and as morning came he lapsed into a proper sleep and his temperature came down. The cold-water towels were no longer needed to cool the furnace on his brows and Nellie allowed herself to go to bed as a doctor told her that the patient's fever had gone. So had Death because he had lost and Nellie, in hand-to-hand combat with the enemy, had won.

George did not die. It may be that he did not die until he was a very old man with great grandchildren; as was the way with patients, the medical officers decided that he was fit enough to travel and well on the way to recovery. One morning they placed a label on his lapel that said 'E' and he was gone to Blighty, leaving Nellie even more confused. She was not disappointed by his not having to make a sacrifice that he was plainly quite prepared and happy to make; on the contrary she was glad for him. Her own position was what caused her to be puzzled. Why was she expending so much of herself in giving men a temporary respite from the grave in a world and a war where death seemed to be king and the dominating urge seemed to be not to live, but to die and to kill as many men as possible?

May was not so introspective, but her most meaningful conversation was with Sergeant Ted Livesey from Norwich and he knew that Britain was going to win the war.

'Why my love? I'll tell you why. Because we're better than them. That's why they can't win.'

May half expected one of those jingoistic rants that she

heard so often from men who saw the war almost in terms of an international football match, so she almost wearily asked him why we were better than them. Her job was to listen, not to object; to comfort and soothe, not to excite. Excitement might be dangerous, so the patient must be left to gabble as they wished. To her surprise she did not get a rant, but something quite different.

'It's what they're fighting for, Sister. You think about it. Just what are they fighting for? So that Kaiser Bill can lord it over Europe? Or that their generals get to strut about and conquer places? Nah – we're fighting for something better and it shows too don't it?'

'How does it show, Ted?'

'You figure it out. They hit us hard on 21 March and they knocked us about a bit. Are we beaten? Are we jiggery! No – we came back at them and we fought them. Yes I know they beat the Russians, but that's their problem see? They think they can't lose, but we ain't the Russians; most of them are as poor as church mice. What've they got to fight for? The Russians ran, but who are they? Most of their soldiers are peasants. What I'm saying is they outnumbered us by more than four to one and they still couldn't beat us. Now we're reinforcing and fighting back; they're not used to people who fight back as hard as we do. And that's why they're going to lose. We are freedom and hope. They are slavery and militarism. How can they win?'

This lit a hope in May's mind and from then on she would not be moved in her conviction that Germany would lose the war. Certainty is a wonderful thing and a great comforter but Nellie wondered often if it was misplaced. Whatever the German losses, and they were severe, they kept on attacking. The intervals varied but the hammer blow offensives kept coming and the Allies would rush men in to deal with them; then there would be a breathing space. It might be a few days or it might be three weeks, but sooner or later a new German attack would come somewhere. The casualties were almost without number. In the first attack the allies had sustained 255,000 killed and wounded. That might sound like military disaster, but the Germans had lost 239,000. The allies could replace their losses; the Germans could not. For May and Nellie and for the 6,000 British nurses in France it meant sleepless nights, barges, trains and convoys ferrying shattered and wounded men to where they could be helped and a weariness at the sight of blood, pus and suffering.

The lame, the maimed and the chronically injured men could be coped with by the nurses. They grew inured to the sight of what shellfire could do to the human body. The disfigurements must not be commented on and if a man with a massive hole where his nose should be looked at you, then you must look back without flinching. They were men, not monsters, and must be treated as such, no matter what society might do to them when they returned home to become the neighbourhood freak; the man without a face who should have died, but lived. Even the gas casualties could be dealt with in one way or another. The burns and blisters on the skin could be cleaned or poulticed or bandaged, but what gas did internally was in the lap of the gods. The man would be put to bed and then there would be a wait to see what symptoms emerged. If the exposure was severe then the patient would turn blue and die an agonizing death gasping for air. Nurses could do nothing save hold the patient's hand, sooth their brows with wet flannels, and hope that the end would come quickly. Gas cases were relatively common, and Nellie, like other nurses, found that the human mind can get used to anything. She had never hoped before that someone would die, but found herself wishing it time and again so that some poor boy's suffering would be over.

Some of the young ones had never been close to a girl and

grew attached to their nurses in ways that were sometimes an unpleasant surprise. May received a letter from a grateful mother of one patient about what a lovely girl she was and how happy she would be to have her as a daughter-in-law. She knew nothing about the airy structures of marriage, children and cosy house that this boy had constructed in his own head and blenched at the embarrassment of it. Happily the lad in question had been shipped home to convalesce and Nellie helped her to compose a tactful letter putting the mother straight to the effect that wounded men often grew attached to their nurses, but that May knew nothing of this and in fact had a fiancé at home. This last set the seal on it and May never heard another thing about it. The imaginary fiancé was a very useful man to several girls they knew in similar predicaments, but May was not ready for any such person in real life. She had far too much to do, she said, than be wasting time with any of that nonsense.

It was the shellshock cases that probably caused the most trouble. It could take many forms; some men, at the slightest noise, would exhibit signs of panic and dive under the nearest object for protection; this was relatively mild. Others were brought in shaking uncontrollably, quite unable to function whilst others lost the use of their legs. One of the strangest was of a man called Kendall who was brought in to a ward and tied to his bed so that he could not escape. He and two other men had been posted out as sentries in a sap trench thirty yards towards the enemy lines one night, but an enemy bombardment had commenced shortly after their arrival. It was some thirty-five hours before any relief could get through to the three men out on their own and when they arrived Kendall had shouted at them, 'What do you want?'

'Come to relieve you of course,' said one of the new men.

'I don't need no relief. This is my bloody trench; bugger off or I'll plug you.'

Kendall had slid the bolt of his rifle back and was about to shoot the relief, but his two mates grabbed him and forced him down as he screamed. He had gone stark staring mad and was brought to Base Hospital 8 for bed rest, in the hopes that he would recover. He did not and eventually was shipped away in a strait jacket to an asylum in England. Nonetheless, it was a shellshock victim that finally brought Nellie's mind, confused since evacuating Bailleul, back into focus.

She was on night duty sitting at a desk on a landing between two wards. Every so often she had to get up to attend to a patient who wanted water, or a bedpan, or who was calling out in his sleep. There was nothing unusual in such disturbances. This night, however, was not normal; at the far end of one of the wards was a small kitchen and she became aware of a disturbance going on down there where someone was screaming at the top of his voice. Quickly rising from her seat she hurried down the ward, noticing that several beds were empty on the way. As she turned into the kitchen she saw a man throwing himself about the room, banging his head, already bloody, on cupboards and screaming incoherently.

'Watch out Sister; he's got a knife from the drawer.'

The man, whom Nellie recognised as a mild, quiet person who had never given her a moment's trouble, was raving like a maniac.

'He got a letter Miss, earlier this evening. He's been jilted. It must have sent him over the edge.'

The raving man was not waving the knife about in any meaningful way and three convalescent soldiers who evidently knew how to handle themselves disarmed him and dragged him to a bed where they sat on him while Nellie fetched an MO. He was taken away immediately to a specialist hospital. Nellie was left shaking as might well be expected, but the scene cut through her thoughts like a scalpel and her Emmaeus moment, which had been waiting since her talk at Toc H came to her like a revelation back in her room.

'It's death. That's what it's all about. Death, inhumanity and madness. It's all mad and evil and bad. I don't want it. I want life. I'm patching men up and sending many of them back to kill again. And that's what I must do until this war is finished. But that's not what I want to be doing later. I want something better than this.'

A memory came to her and she felt round in the drawer of her cabinet and brought out her book of common prayer. Faint recollection made her fingers turn the pages to a prayer for a sick child and she read:

'…*Look down from Heaven we humbly beseech thee, with the eyes of mercy upon this child now lying upon the bed of sickness. Visit him O Lord with thy salvation and deliver him in thy good appointed time from his bodily pain and save his soul for thy mercy's sake; that, if it be thy pleasure to prolong his days here on earth, he may live to thee and be an instrument of thy glory, by serving thee faithfully and doing good in his generation.*'

This was her apotheosis and it changed her life onto a track that continued until her last day on earth.

'Doing good in his generation. That's what I want – to tend sick children and to bring children into the world. That's about life, not death. When this thing is over I'm going to work with mothers and children.'

At the end of June 1918 May and Nellie had been in France for six months. They were in a well-staffed hospital just a few minutes away from the ferries that ran back to England and Matron Westnutt believed in keeping the rules. These two nurses were entitled to ten days home leave and no matter their protestations that they wanted to stay, their names were placed on the leave roster beginning on Friday 12 July. On the morning of that day both girls set off across the Channel heading for Workington and Whitehaven from whence they had been absent for a year.

Chapter 27

A Family Gathering

Nancy was going through a miserable time at Gretna at the beginning of July 1918. She found her work humdrum and boring now that she was so used to doing it. Sometimes it did occur to her that stirring one of the most dangerous explosives in the world as if it were porridge might be seen as 'interesting' to most people, but it did not exactly engage her mind. She had thought of leaving, but her sense of duty kept her at Gretna, when many girls gave up and left. The workers were all civilian and not conscripted, kept there only by good pay, but even that could not compensate many for the daily grind of dullness it involved. One of those who had left was Gertie. She saw no reason to stay in a hostel at Gretna when she could live at home in Workington and earn almost as good money. She had managed to get a job at the National Shell Factory down on the Marsh and had left, promising to see Nancy when she came home, and urging her to do the same as she was. Nancy thought it all a bit off, because if everyone did that, then HM Gretna would not be able to function. She stuck to her post, but although some of the other girls in her hostel, like Janet, were nice and friendly, there was nothing quite like a familiar face from home around the place. She felt isolated and in a strange land.

Then there was Mr Burt; he was a sectional engineer whose job it was to maintain the factory roofs and as such he ranged widely over the different buildings. In the course of his constant checking, tightening, replacing of panels and sealing of leaks, he came into conversation with many girls and he was generally popular. He was about forty-two, married, and just a lovely man; he had missed his footing on Thursday 27 June and fallen thirty feet through the roof to his death. It did not happen at Dornock, where Nancy was, but at Eastriggs, but the word soon spread that he was gone. This coupled with the desperate news from France sent a wave of depression and black cloud over the factory. It was almost grim, but was coupled with a determination by the thousands of girls involved to grit their teeth and get on with the job of supplying the explosives and ammunition needed to win the war. On Tuesday 9 July Nancy went to her pigeonhole, situated just inside her hostel door, to find that the postman had been and that there was a letter from her mother. This triggered a warm glow inside her and a feeling of anticipation; Margaret's letters always told what the younger children had been up to, what was going on in Workington, and invariably had some of the most up to date gossip going around town. They always brightened her day, made her think of home to the extent that she was almost there, at least in spirit, and were a pleasure she looked forward to. It was perhaps a little unfortunate that she had formed the habit of saving the reading of them for lunchtime. Somehow it comforted her more if she read them over food and a nice cup of tea. Since she was on morning shift her lunch did not come until 2.30pm when she knocked off and made her way to the canteen. It was only when she was sitting down at one of the long trestle tables with her food in front of her, that she actually opened the envelope and began to read. Almost as soon as she did so she stopped eating, her attention entirely given to what she saw:

'Dear Nancy,
Just a short note. Your Dad and me want you to come home for a week starting this Friday. I know it's short notice but Nellie

is coming home on leave and hopes to be with us on Saturday. Barwise is coming home tomorrow and stays until Thursday of next week. I'm sure I don't have to remind you what next Tuesday is. Your Dad wants the whole family together next week and it's very important to us so please arrange it if you can.

love Mother.'

This was not something that could be done by Nancy's Matron; HM Gretna had so much absenteeism that the factory was kept deliberately over-staffed by ten per cent so that it could cope with any reasonable number of people being away. Requests for leave involved filling in a form that went through administrative channels and was usually granted if sufficient notice was given. This was exceptional in that she could only give two days so she went straight to the Welfare Office in the central area of the factory complex and asked to see Mrs Mabel Cotterell as a matter of urgency. Mrs Cotterell had been appointed Chief Welfare Officer in 1917 and had quickly gained a reputation for being wise and efficient; Gretna girls were very well looked after.

In Mrs Cotterell's office Nancy quickly explained what was happening.

'So you want compassionate leave and you need to go on Friday?'

'Yes Ma'am; that's what my mother has asked for.'

'Your sister and brother are both going to be there you said. May I ask why this should be a subject for compassionate leave? It's usually something reserved for people who are sick or dying; or even for funerals. We need every worker to be doing their utmost right now as I'm sure you know. It's very hard over there.'

'Over there.' That phrase was on everyone's lips and not only because of the popular American song that had swept the nation with the arrival of the first 'Doughboys' or US infantrymen in Liverpool the previous year.

'My sister is home on leave from France. She nurses in a CCS over there, Ma'am. And my brother, Barwise, is home on embarkation leave on Saturday. He's nineteen next Tuesday....'

She did not have to finish her sentence as Mrs Cotterell finished it for her, 'And your parents want you all together one last time in case of what might happen.'

'Yes Ma'am,' said Nancy gratefully. 'That's how it is.'

'Well of course you must go.'

'Mrs Cotterell scribbled a note on a pad, ripped off a sheet of paper and gave it to Nancy.

'Take that over to the administrative offices; by the time you get there I shall have telephoned them and instructed them to give you one week's compassionate leave commencing at end of shift on Friday. A mother's instructions are law in this office.'

This was delivered with a twinkling smile that brought an answering one from Nancy and a heartfelt thank you.

'Oh, one more thing; your forewoman is Maude Bruce is she not? Don't forget to tell her; she will need to put in for a temporary stand in for you.'

Evidently Mrs Cotterell took care of details.

So it was that Nancy found herself home on Friday evening in the back room upstairs of number 55 Devonshire Street, the girls' room. After her bedroom in the hostel bungalow it was crowded, as Nellie also arrived that evening and both young women had to squeeze in with Ettie and Ommie. To her surprise Nancy found that Barwise was already there; he had been lucky with the wartime trains and arrived on the evening of Thursday 11 July. For the first time in a year all the family were under one roof and of course they were more than they had been. The latest arrival did not trouble the occupants of the boys' room; he slept in a cot in Margaret and Tom's room. Barwise and John were men now, but squeezed in with Joe and William, who had to move over to make room for them; a thing slightly resented by the younger ones who lost space, but overruled by having Barwise at home again. Family life mostly took place in the downstairs back room where the scrupulously blackened range with its gleaming brass handles dominated the scene. The windows and the back door were open, for though the fire in the range was necessary for cooking and hot water, it did make the room rather warmer than might have been wished in July. There was much conversation and drinking of tea and tales of what the elder siblings had been up to since they last saw each other. Quite which were the most interesting – Barwise's stories of camp life and training, Nellie's descriptions of France and the things she had seen, or Nancy's escapades at Gretna, was impossible to decide. One thing was for certain; the Little family were very involved in this war. Margaret, surveying her table and looking round at the faces, could not help but feel some pride in her children. They all looked so grown-up and had been to places and done things that she could never have dreamed of in her youth. Imagine Nellie in France of all places, and Nancy making explosives. It was Barwise that made her heart bleed. Nellie and Nancy were doing dangerous things, but Barwise would be going into battle and fighting, possibly hand to hand with the enemy who would try to kill him. She could barely face the thought that this could be the last few days that she had to spend with her son and that she might never see him again. So many poor women in Workington had lost their lads; indeed so many across the whole United Kingdom, yet she prayed that hers would not be one of them.

The prayers were literal ones on Sunday when the family put on their best and trouped up to St John's church to listen to Mr Croft's sermon. He spoke on Christian sacrifice and soldiers of Christ putting on their armour to fight the forces of evil, and he said it without ever once mentioning the Germans, though he occasionally referred to 'your adversary'. It was all a bit vague and not one of his best sermons; it was the sort of exposition that might have sent people to sleep in ordinary times, but Margaret did not want any Christian sacrifice to affect her boy and did not feel in the least comforted by it; rather she wished that he did not have to go. A tank had visited Workington on 31 March to raise money for the war as well as to show the steel workers what their manufacture of armour plate went towards. The squat savagery of the thing had stirred up enormous enthusiasm but made Margaret shudder; the Germans had tanks too and they seemed like something from a nightmare. The thought of her son having to face such a monster spitting bullets filled her with fear. He wore his uniform of course, and she looked at him and the strangest thought came into her head of a young knight in his armour dedicating himself to godly combat before he went to war.

After church Barwise picked up his baby brother, Harry, and swung him into the air before giving him an affectionate cuddle.

'One day you'll be in the Border Regiment too, eh little man. You'll show them where to get off!'

'If you mean the Germans,' said Margaret, 'then I hope you don't expect this war to go on until he's grown up!'

'No Mam. Wait till I get over there. We'll finish the job pretty quick.'

Harry did not like being cuddled, especially by a stranger. Khaki may look well on the battlefield, but as a material it resembles sacking and is very scratchy, especially to baby skin. He registered his protest very loudly, as men of his age do, so began to scream the place down. Barwise very quickly handed him over to his mother who carried him back home on her hip. She spent a lot of time with Harry in that position, as she had with all her babies; if you carried them then they did not squall as much as they might do otherwise. Her left arm had stronger muscles than the right as she had carried all her eight previous children in that position. He was a well looked after baby, which might not be said for all in the neighbourhood. Many were simply dumped into a cot basket and left to cry for hours by busy women who had been taught that it was healthy and good for their lungs and just ignored the crying. Margaret took the view that babies cried for a reason and it was usually because they needed feeding or because they were uncomfortable. She set great store by clean nappies and she had a large drawer of them, used by successive children, stitched with loops and ties, cut down from Tom's old shirts. When soiled they were cleaned and boiled, dried and folded again. In this she differed from many, because it was very common for busy women to simply dry wet nappies and use them again without washing. Margaret thought this stored up trouble because a baby would get a rash, be uncomfortable and cry more. None of Margaret's children had died, though the infant mortality rate in town was quite high. This she put down to cleanliness, learned from her mother, and her keeping them to the breast; at nine months Harry was not weaned yet; Mother at Dearham was quite positive that babies kept on breast milk for their first year of life grew better and were generally healthier than those early weaned. Naturally, this threw a great deal of weight onto Ommie and Ettie, who were expected to help with chores, but that too was good because it prepared them for their own children. In their view the worst of these were the regular trips to what they called, quite naturally and in the local vernacular, 'the shithouse' outside in the yard where the hated job of nappy scraping was carried out before they could be boil washed.

Once home Barwise could hardly wait to get his uniform off and put on his civvies, 'Just to feel normal again'. Once he had them on he did not want to put the uniform back on again until he had to; unfortunately it was not to be. On Monday he decided he wanted to go for a stroll round Workington just to look at the old town; Nancy decided to go with him. They took a turn up to Washington Street and down Pow Street, but when they reached Finkle Street they were approached by a young woman in Suffragette colours who had been following them.

'Why are you not in uniform?'

'I don't think that's any of your business,' replied Barwise.

'A young man like you should be in uniform.'

Nancy was about to explode beside him, but Barwise put a hand on her arm to quieten her.

'I think a young man like me should be able to wear what he likes.'

'I've got two brothers and an uncle in France; you should be ashamed that you're not in your country's uniform.'

'And I thought the war was about liberty and the right to choose,' replied Barwise.

'It is!' she retorted without conscious irony, 'and that's why you should be in khaki, fighting for freedom.'

'Well you have your opinion; thank you for it. Now I'll be about my business and you can be about yours.'

'Coward!'

There was an incoherent noise as Nancy exploded at last; 'Wha dist thew think thew is talkn to me brother like that?' Things might have ended up in the police courts, for her fists were clenched, but Barwise caught hold of her. 'Come on Nancy. We've better things to do.' And despite her protests about giving 'that stupid flapper' a piece of her mind, he held her arm firmly in his and they walked off.

'Why did you stop me? I wanted to slap her face!'

'Exactly. That's why I stopped you. Not worth getting arrested for.'

'But she called you a coward.'
'That's right. She did.'
'But don't you mind?'
'Not at all.'
'But why? It's a hard name.'
'Aye, but she doesn't know me does she?'

As far as he was concerned that was the end of the matter and though Nancy fumed he just smiled and walked on.

'Where are we going?'

'To see Matt and the lads.

Down the Station Road they walked, Nancy now very conscious that Barwise was the only young man with no armband to protect him, signifying that he was a vital war worker. No-one else accosted them though and soon they crossed the bridge by the station and reached the boiler works quickly. Barwise, a wise chap, had timed his arrival to coincide with bait time, so they were all glad to see him and very happy to see Nancy. Not many women made their way into their hut, so they moved over in gentleman like fashion and offered sandwiches, which of course were politely refused. This was wartime, food was short and rationing, only introduced a few months before, made food available to all, but not plentiful. The conversation was predictable as it would be; they asked him what life was like in the Army and he asked them how things were at work. It was a pleasant interlude, but Matt was Barwise's particular marra and so gradually the men drifted out on various missions, leaving them to talk.

'You remembered what I said then?'

'I did Matt, but I have to say that I would have come to see you anyway.'

'I know that lad, but I had a definite reason for seeing you before you left so I just wanted to make sure you did come.'

'Every so often I've thought about why you wanted to see me before I went and the best I can come up with is you want to say tata before I get shot.'

'Barwise! Don't talk like that.'

'Well it's a war Nancy; men get shot, and I'm nowt special. It could happen to me, or worse.'

'I don't like that sort of talk though.'

'Nor do I, but I'm a realist; I know what I'm getting into.'

Matt Roach followed this with great interest.

'She's right though Barwise; it's not a thing to dwell on or it could mess your head up. Anyway, I wanted to see you because of something my brother told me.'

'The one who's in France?'

'That's right. He told me that when you get in the German trenches and you're fighting them, your rifle and bayonet are next to useless.'

'How does he make that out?'

'If you think about it for a minute it makes sense. You're in a hole in the ground and you get into a hand-to-hand fight with a Jerry. What's the problem?'

'None. I'll either stick him or shoot him.'

'But that's the point. What if you can't?'

'How do you mean?'

'How long is a rifle with fixed bayonet? Over five feet?'

'That's about right.'

'So what might happen if you're waving it about in a hole in the ground?'

Barwise thought for a moment then said slowly, 'It might get stuck in the earth?'

'That's it. That's what Arthur said. A lot of men get killed because they can't use their rifle in confined spaces. So they use other things.'

'Like what?'

'Oh daggers, wooden clubs with nails in, hand axes; all unofficial stuff.'

'What does Arthur use?'

'These,' said Matt, reaching into his pocket and pulling out a gleaming object. 'I had these run off for you after you were stupid enough to join up you daft bugger.'

'What is it?' asked Nancy.

'They call them brass knuckles Miss, but these aren't brass; they use steel in our shop. Apparently lots of our lads carry these and they buy them specially. You can wear them into battle Barwise and they don't interfere with you using your rifle. If you get in a tight spot you drop your gun and let Jerry have this to the head, preferably on the bridge of the nose or under the jaw. If you can manage it, if his head is back, straight to the Adam's apple; that'll kill him. Otherwise they don't know what's hit them; out like a light.'

Nancy winced.

Barwise took the knuckles and slipped them on. They were a most elegant piece, looking like a set of thick silver rings on his fingers, the whole welded onto a bar that fitted into the grip of his hand like a glove. Anyone put down with these would stay down.

'I want you to carry those with you Barwise and I hope you'll use them if necessary.'

Barwise looked at the knuckles and at Matt's face. It was a gift of true friendship and a gesture to be treasured. He held his hand out and a firm handshake was exchanged,

'Thanks Marra; I appreciate this a lot.'

Matt's face cracked into a grin, 'Aye, well think of it as me doing my bit. Just come home safe you larl cuddy.'

As Barwise walked home with Nancy, Matt Roach's gift in his pocket he had cause to shake his head and wonder at the power of friendship between human beings.

'That man started off by bullying the Hell out of me and I hated his guts. Now he's a pal and thinks of something like that.'

'That's life for you,' said Nancy. 'But even more, that's Workington. Folk look after each other. He's trying to look after you, even when he can't.'

'Aye well I think he did. I feel properly armed with these. They're a good idea.'

'I hope you never have to use them; I don't even like thinking about it. You're my brother and I don't want to imagine you doing that.'

'Nor do I; let's hope I never have to.'

Tuesday 16 July dawned and Barwise was nineteen; and it was now that he received a gift from his father who asked him to come into the yard for a word when family breakfast was over and before he went off to morning shift. Margaret came too.

'What do you want to talk about, Dad?'

Tom Little felt in his pocket and pulled out a package.

Chapter 27 — A Family Gathering

'Your mother and I want you to have this now.'

Barwise opened the wrapping and there was a silver pocket watch. He could find no words.

'We bought it when you were born. We had a farm and money then and we were keeping it for your twenty-first, when you become a man. It seems to us that if you're old enough to go and fight Germans then you're a man now. So it's best you have it today. Happy birthday, son.'

Barwise did not choke up very often, but he did now, though he attempted to conceal it; he thanked his parents repeatedly. He and his father wrung each other's hands, whilst Margaret hugged him as if she did not want to let go. The thought was unspoken, but they all knew that the reason his parents had given him his manhood gift, so long stored away for the day, was so that he might enjoy it for at least a time. He might never return to be present on his twenty-first.

'A man needs a watch,' said his father, rather more gruffly than he needed to. 'Good time keeping is important for many reasons.'

Barwise agreed with that; punctuality was important, both at work and in the military.

'Anyway, I hope you've got nothing else planned for this afternoon and evening young man, because it's a special day for you and the family. We're having our photograph taken at three o'clock and tonight we're all going to the picture house, except Harry.'

'Why not Harry?'

'Daft question,' retorted his mother. 'Because he'll scream the place down. He's staying with Mrs Beeby, in a basket. I'm going to enjoy your birthday night out too.'

Nellie would not wear her red-cross apron for the photograph.

'Why not?' demanded Margaret. 'It's your uniform and

we're proud of you and what you're doing. We want you to wear it.'

'It's difficult to explain Mam. In that uniform I deal with men at war, horrible things and so much suffering. I don't want to look at the family photo in future years and be thrown back to what I see in France. Now that's it, so don't try to change my mind because I won't.'

She would not be moved on the matter and so when the family left the house and walked up to the Van Dyke photographers she wore her plain uniform from Workington Infirmary. They were posed in front of a painted backdrop of what seemed to be a stepped path leading up between a wood and a gorge, the whole framed by dark curtains. Margaret and Tom sat in the front, little Harry on his mother's knee and around them ranged their children. Tom smelled of mothballs as his best suit was carefully preserved in a wardrobe for occasions such as this. A neaty folded handkerchief sat in his breast pocket to emphasise the dignity of the occasion. Ommie sat on her mother's right hand, looking rather bewildered by the whole process; formal family pictures were not something that happened everyday. She had a slight sniffle and her right hand clutched a handkerchief. She had tied her hair back and set a flower in it, as was the fashion with her group of friends. To her father's left sat Ettie looking very grave in her Sunday dress, her auburn hair tied loosely back with a ribbon, while next to her Joe, in an unaccustomed stiff collar looked straight out at the camera almost as if he were standing to attention. Behind him stood William dressed in similar style, but trying hard not to smile. He looked as confident and easy with the situation as could be wished for, solid in the world and sure of himself. Nellie stood, starch and crisp as a civilian nurse, a sisterly hand on Ettie's shoulder in front of her, a slight smile to her eyes and mouth. John stood at the far right, inscrutable in pinstripe, calm and reserved as ever and next to him was Nancy, not in her munitionette uniform, but opting for a white blouse and plain skirt. As she had explained to her parents, the uniform was very unflattering, not very comfortable and scratchy, so she did not wish to wear it; at any rate it was a factory job, not service like Nellie or Barwise and it was not fitting that she should wear it for a family photograph. In the middle at the back stood Barwise, Border Regimental cap badge polished to splendour for the occasion, lanyard looped over his shoulder and uniform pressed as if to go on parade. The photographer, a Mr Todhunter, had trained in the famous studio of Aaron Vandyke in Liverpool, so he knew his business. He told them not to smile and to stay perfectly still; of course they all knew that if you smiled on a photograph you could end up looking as if you'd escaped from Garlands Hospital. Some of the family could not quite repress the shadow of a smile, but it was at the moment of pressing his trigger that Mr Todhunter caught, quite unintentionally, two things that were not meant to happen. The first was Harry, who reached across and grabbed his father's lapel before his mother or Tom had time to react. The baby stared right into the camera and his left arm thrown out seems almost an unconscious clutch. If anyone had moved the picture would have been spoiled, but for ever afterwards it was he who stole the limelight in the image of the family, except for one other; Barwise.

The photographer caught him at a major turning point of his life, when he was about to go to war and to kill or be killed. If the eyes are the windows of the soul then what may be read into his speaks volumes. Earlier photographs of him show almost a devil may care attitude to the world, but not this one. He stands with head slightly tilted, his face wearing an expression that is wistful, vulnerable and open. It is the face of a boy about to go and do what men were expected to do and there is fear there too, of a very controlled sort. There is also resolve, for this was the fifth year of the war and he can have been under no illusions; it was he who was going to face the German's bullets, but even though he probably did not wish to, he had to. It was, as he well knew, a valedictory photograph; one that would stand on family mantelpieces and serve to remember him by if he fell. So he stared levelly into the camera until the shutter fell, with the face of courage, unsure of what was coming, but determined to stand up to it.

Back home Margaret fed her family on a large tattiepot, a staple of their menu anyway, but this one was a wartime recipe. Potatoes could be in short supply although they were not rationed; she had queued and obtained what she could, but padded it out with vegetables which were also not rationed and could be bought from people who had allotments. She had scrimped, queued and saved for flour and produced a pudding in the shape of a jam roly-poly smothered in sweet white sauce. At a time when the family was often only just satisfied with the food they had, it was sufficient to be thought of as quite a banquet. After dinner there was time to sit for a while before depositing Harry with the lady next door who thought him a little treasure. Then the entire family walked up to the Theatre Royal in Washington Street which doubled as a cinema; the performance started at seven o'clock sharp.

The first item on the agenda was amusing in a mild sort of way, but the Littles were a family that did not drink so although they could see the humour in drunken behaviour, they did not relate well to it. It was a new film, just out, called *Goodnight Nurse*. Fatty Arbuckle played a man outside a drug store who was drunk out of his head. Back at his house his wife and butler saw a report from the 'No Hope Clinic' that said they could cure alcoholics. Arbuckle arrived home soaking wet in the rain with two gypsies and a monkey so his wife had him put into the clinic where he was greeted by a blood spattered Buster Keaton carrying a cleaver. He then saw various surgeries that alcoholics were put through so he decided to escape, aided by a half naked woman who believed she was a mermaid. In the course of events he somehow ate a thermometer and was rushed into surgery. He managed to escape by firstly pretending to drown, then by dressing as a woman; which audiences always find hilarious for some reason. Finally when the men in white coats found that he was gone, they gave chase and he inadvertently got involved in the town's annual fat man race.

It was not bad for half an hour or so, but much better was the next turn who was a local comedian called Tom Little, which immediately made Tom and Margaret sit up. Littles are numbered in Cumberland as fleas on a dog, but someone with your own name always gets more attention than most. He had them in stitches with a string of jokes about the daft jam eaters though it has to be said that it was probably more the way he told them than the actual material. He finished off with a little rhyme that brought the house down:

'There was an old man from Whitehaven
Whose whiskers had never been shaven.
He said 'It is best,
For they make a nice nest,
In which I can keep my pet raven.'

As the applause died away Tom leaned to Margaret,
'I bet he'll be in Whitehaven next week telling the same jokes about us.'

The rest of the evening was passed in similar style with two more films, one by Charlie Chaplin and another by Harold Lloyd, interspersed with another comedian, a singer of patriotic songs in which the audience joined and a teller of

Cumbrian shaggy dog stories. The last told a tale in brief of a farmer up Broughton way who asked a carrier to fetch him back a bag of corn from Workington market, which he said he would. That evening the farmer saw the carrier coming past his gate and called out 'Where's my sack of corn?' Without a word the carrier tied the horse up at the gate and set off back to Workington.

'Where's my corn?'

'Ah hev fergot it. Ah'm off back te git it'

'Aren't you tekkin t'oss?'

'Twasn't t'oss that fergot it,' came the reply.

This brought murmurs of appreciation because it fitted much with the county character, 'Aye that's Cumbrians for you,' was said by more than one.

Barwise's nineteenth birthday was a landmark occasion, passed suitably and appropriately in his hometown, with his family and he appreciated every minute of it as a time to treasure. Other things, bad things may be on the horizon, but this day had been lovely.

The next day he put on his uniform again and went for a walk in the town on his own. He headed straight for Finkle Street and sure enough, she was there; the woman in suffragette colours who seemed to have nothing better to do than accost young men and call them cowards. He walked up and stood in front of her, but said nothing. She looked at him, without comprehending at first, then recognition dawned and she went as bright red as a beetroot.

'You didn't say. How was I to know? You should have said.'

'I shouldn't need to. Think on it.'

Then he turned his back on her and walked away.

Speak your mind, say your piece, and you've said enough; folk know what you think. What more is there to say? That's Cumbrian, and Barwise had said sufficient.

Chapter 27 — A Family Gathering

He called in to see his old workmates again, this time in his uniform and bought a few things in shops that he had used since he was a lad. Down to the Yearl he went and after his evening meal he walked along the Harrington Road to the shore lane, down under the railway and onto the shore. There he sat once again indulging one of his favourite pastimes watching the sun go down. As the last glorious rays of the light over the Solway disappeared in the West he may have been excused for thinking sadly that this might be the last Cumbrian sunset that he ever saw. He stared at it and then the afterglow as the dark descended, for a long time.

Next morning, 18 July, Barwise caught a train from Central Station on his own. He had insisted on it. His father and brother had work to go to and the school holidays had not yet started. That bit had been easy; manly handshakes mask a lot of emotions, even when his father had said, 'I'm proud of you son,' and walked out the door with a set face. Farewells had been said early that morning when the working day started and he was not demonstrative enough to want for lingering and sobbing goodbyes. Nellie and Nancy had been resolutely upbeat, eyes bright but with no tears, but his mother had cried. She was not daft his mam. She had not made him promise to come back, or told him to keep his head down. She had just told him to look after himself then cried all over his shoulder; Ettie had followed suit as had Ommie. Joe and William wanted him to be sure to kill lots of Germans. Since he had to go, he was glad to be gone, because the goodbyes could have been so much harder.

Trains in wartime always run in a haphazard fashion. He did not arrive in Ripon until after four in the afternoon but was in camp well before the six o'clock deadline. Lieutenant Tinian was guard commander and was at the gate as he came in. Barwise was lucky; Tinian accused him of not having his lanyard tied straight and fined him sixpence. Other men returning from leave found that their boots were dirty, or their caps were not on at the right angle and were either fined or given extra duties, or both. Two men came in just minutes after the six o'clock deadline and he had them arrested and they spent the night in the guardroom. Clearly the Lieutenant was out to make a name for himself, and indeed he did, though if he could have heard some of the names he would not have appreciated them. It did not matter; on 20 July the platoon entrained with many others and headed south, crossing the Channel and arriving at the great base camp at Etaples outside Boulogne. There they would be broken up and assigned to fighting platoons of the various battalions of the Border Regiment on the Western Front. There would be some days of 'bull' and drill but the Etaples camp was not as grim as it had once been before the days of the famous mutiny of 1917. The strict inhuman regime had become merely strict. Barwise knew his assignment was to 7 Battalion and to his delight he found that among the men of his group both Percy Natrass and Bill Holliday would be going with him. 7 Battalion had been functioning as a pioneer unit since the beginning of the year and until recently had been involved in strengthening defences in the Somme area around the village of Senlis le Sec. Now, however, they had been moved back to Herissart, a small village fourteen miles from Albert and they were about to revert to their true role as combat troops. Barwise and his marras were joining them at this crucial change of role in which they would once again be one of the saw teeth of the British Army.

Chapter 28

Battle

'Halt! Who goes there?' shouted Barwise, and leveled his rifle at the man in the strange uniform who appeared in front of him.

'Easy buddy, I'm just having a mooch around.'

'What do you mean?' asked Barwise who did not know the expression. 'Put your hands in the air and explain yourself.'

The man put his hands up. 'Gee, I was just having a look round. No harm intended.'

Barwise pulled a whistle from his pocket and blew hard; within seconds the duty Sergeant and two men with fixed bayonets came at the double.

Sergeant Hine from Egremont was Barwise's new platoon NCO and not a man to mess about.

'Who the Hell are you? A Yank by the look of you.'

'Howdy Sergeant. I'm Private Elmer Harding, US Army. I just thought I'd come and see a trench for myself. We just arrived in the neighbourhood and I never saw a real trench before, so I thought I'd come and have a look.'

'Aye, and you could be a spy. You three; keep your bundooks on him and if he makes a wrong move, plug him. Keep your hands up, you.'

The Sergeant frisked the stranger, but found no weapons, only an ID card identifying him as Private E Harding who was indeed from the American Expeditionary Force. The Englishman was unimpressed.

'I saw you lot arrive the other day. You can't march, of that

I'm sure. I hope you fight better. Alright you men, take him to Battalion HQ and they can deal with it.'

He turned to Barwise, 'You did right. Pity there's been no time to ease you in better, but you showed sense. Keep on your guard lad and you'll be relieved in about an hour.'

The new intake for 7 Battalion had been seized on eagerly for all sorts of duties as soon as they arrived, which was why Barwise had found himself on sentry duty almost straight away. The Spanish 'flu' had laid many of the veterans low and numbers of them had been taken away to hospitals to recover, or to die. The medics had no answer to this terrible virus, which was to go on to kill over twenty million people world wide and it threw an enormous load onto those who stayed healthy. Herissart was very much in the battle zone and the civilian population had evacuated to other places. 7 Battalion was billeted in the houses, farms and barns of the village that had been a farming community with some sandstone quarrying. The settlement stood on a flat plateau surrounded by deep valleys that were easily defended if the defenders were determined. Amiens was ten miles away, but to the local Germans it might as well have been on the moon. To capture it, the rail switching point for the whole northern part of the front, they would have to go through the Border Regiment; that wasn't going to happen.

For the moment, all was quiet as it might well be. Men on both sides stayed in their shelters as the end of July melted into torrential rain. If 1917 had taught the warring sides anything it was not to court military disaster by attacking in this weather. The local soil was a thick clinging marl overlaying sandstone and when wet it clarted everything. Perhaps to the soldiers it was a welcome respite. Barwise and his friends were released from the regime of discipline and jobs being done for the sake of it, and bided their time between periods on and off duty. They lived from day to day, played cards, shaved, kept themselves as clean as they could, hunted lice and talked a lot. Soldiers learn to make themselves comfortable anywhere and the thirty eight men crammed into the stone barn had laid out straw and military blankets, set planks and stones up for seats and waited. There were men from all over Cumberland though it is perhaps natural that people from the same area tended to congregate together. In the barn were billeted two four-man teams of Royal Army Medical Corps (RAMC) who were attached to a field hospital. When the battalion was in action the field hospital set up aid posts to deal with casualties and evacuate them to a CCS. The men in the barn were stretcher-bearers and for them the ordinary soldier had a profound respect. One of them was Herbert Hayston and he came from Dearham; hearing familiar accents he had come over and introduced himself soon after Barwise, Percy and Bill had arrived. He was a welcome new acquaintance because ultimately their lives could depend on him and his skills. Herbert was not a big man, but strong; he had to be, as they all knew. Carrying a man on a stretcher across muddy fields, in rain, in ice or snow is hard work. It has to be done by four men because the carry can go on for miles. Ropes round the shoulders to carry a large man could wear weeping sores and galls in the flesh of the bearers that must be ignored because the journey had to be done. Barwise liked him, as did the others, because he was full of silent courage and they knew it. He was most particular that his name was Herbert and quickly stifled any attempts to label him as 'Bert'.

'My mam and dad gave me a name and that's the one I use. I don't want another.'

His determination on the point was respected and so to the group he was always addressed as he was christened. Shortly after meeting, they had asked him why he joined the RAMC and not a fighting unit.

'Because I don't want to kill.'

'Are you a conchy? Did they make you come out here because you didn't want to fight?'

'No. I'm not a conchy. I think this is a just war and I want to play my part in it; I just don't want to kill. I want to save lives, not take them. I couldn't kill anyone.'

'Are you religious then? Is that it?'

'No, I'm not particularly religious; it's just not in me to kill people, or things. That man's some mother's son, someone's husband or brother; just like me.'

Among civilians this might have met with roars of disapproval and brought all sorts of imprecations on Herbert's head, but not among these men. There are different sorts of courage, as they knew, but the courage of a man who goes onto a raging battlefield without a weapon, armed only with a stretcher and medical kit is a special sort and worthy of respect even if it sets them apart from you. There was a very good chance they would need Herbert soon, and so he joined their number as a marra even though he would not be going into action with them but would follow on behind.

On 1 August the weather was still slightly rainy, but the divisional command was puzzled by the complete lack of activity in the German lines. Orders came for a reconnaissance patrol to be sent forward to spy out, if they could, what was going on. Second Lieutenant Stewart was detailed to lead it and picked on Barwise's platoon for the job. It had in it a number of new men who needed to be introduced to the battle field.

The wire was cut at dead of night by a work party and at three o'clock on the morning of 2 August Barwise and his pals entered no-man's land for the first time. It was not a fighting patrol, but a *recce*, so they all carried rifles; advancing by sections in short rushes, they soon reached the German wire. This was not an old battlefield where the wire grew, thick as wool on a sheep's back, so it was not sufficiently dense to withstand their wire cutters and they were soon through and approaching the German trenches. There was of course no talking and dire threats had been made towards any man who made a sound; not a single bullet was in the breech and bayonets were fixed. It was pitch black and difficult to see, but all the new men had practiced this sort of manoeuvre. Barwise's heart was pounding, strangely he found not with fear, but with excitement. Up ahead was the enemy and so far he had not reacted so there was apprehension in his mind too, because he expected an alarm and a blaze of fire any minute that would cut them all down. Lieutenant Stewart made a sign imitative of throwing a cricket ball and without a word a grenade was lobbed into the German trench. As soon as it exploded the platoon flooded into that section, but there was no-one there. The lead men hurried round into the next section, but again it was deserted. It soon transpired that the whole German trench was empty; they had gone. Barwise entered a dugout as the Lieutenant called after him, 'Be careful of booby traps.'

'It's bare Sir; they've taken everything and left nowt except a note.'

'What does it say?'

'Dear Tommy. When you are come we are gone, hoping you have much pleasure in our cottages. Why you send so many iron postcards? Eat some yourself. Make peace next time, have you not enough?'

'Cheeky buggers,' said the Lieutenant, entering the dugout. 'They've withdrawn. We'd best report back I think.'

'Why have they pulled out, Sir?'

'I'm not sure Private, but they've been losing a lot of men. My guess would be that they've pulled back to a better position for defence.'

'But they've been attacking us for months Sir. Why would they do that?'

'Again a guess Private, but it's a good question. If we've got them on the run it could mean they're finished.'

This was the mood that ran through the Battalion and through the British Army and was reinforced by the knowledge that they were expecting to launch an attack on the Germans soon. Having been on the defensive since March, the British had got more men from home and transferred from the Middle East where the Turks were all but beaten. On 12 August Barwise found himself in a place called Mericourt and in support positions behind the front lines. The weather by now was beautiful, one of those crisp clear days of summer where the air feels warm with sun and treats the nostrils as you breathe. A support role does not involve most men in activity, so much of the battalion was at ease with cards and brewing tea. So it was that the attack took them unawares.

Mustard gas is subtle; if you have been exposed to it once, then it is hard to detect. It was the new soldiers, fresh from training who noticed it first, though it was very faint; it was an almost intangible spicy sweet smell that reminded many of them of the garlic the French peasants used to eat.

'Gas! Gas!' yelled Percy Natrass. 'Masks on boys!'

Someone found a gas rattle and sounded it frantically as the men scrabbled round in a welter of fear for their gas masks. Barwise's platoon was safe; they had sufficient warning. Unfortunately the rest of the battalion was not so lucky; around two hundred men did not reach for their masks quickly enough and became casualties. This is not to say that they died because although gas can and does kill, it harms far more than it slays. It was not until several hours later that the red spots appeared on the skin of the victims and pain developed where the blisters formed, inside and outside. If the exposure was slight then you would heal. A longer exposure could mean blindness, pneumonia and a whole range of unpleasant symptoms often ending in death. The fear of the gas was greater than its effect, for it had the power to invoke panic among troops, and then anger.

'They're dirty bastards,' said Bill Holliday. 'Who would use stuff like that?'

'Well we do too,' replied Barwise.

'Right enough, so we do, but they used it first. The only reason we have it is because they started it,' said Percy.

'I don't care about who started it first,' said Bill. 'All I know is that it's a filthy thing and inhuman. It just makes me determined that I'm going to kill as many of them as I can.'

'If they don't get you first.'

'That's as may be, Barwise, but at least that would be in fair fight. I don't mind that so much, but this – this isn't even fighting. It's just…'

'Murder?'

'Yes. Murder. That's what it is.'

'But isn't it all the same?' asked Percy.

'How do you mean?'

'I mean that if you're dead, you're dead. Does it matter how? It might be a bullet, or a grenade or blown to bits by a shell.'

'Aye, but there's quick and there's slow. I'd rather have it quick.'

'Well if it's me you're talking about, I'd rather not die at all if you don't mind,' said Percy. 'I'd rather get home and sup John Peel Ale until I drop. I've had enough of this job.'

He had cause to be discontent in the next few hours when another five hundred men had to attend the regimental aid posts to have blisters and spots salved where the gas had its effect on exposed skin, but at least these stayed available for combat. That was where they were now bound, for orders were received that the battalion was to march to Thiepval on the old Somme battlefield.

On 25 August Barwise found himself reliving his training

as 7 Battalion launched a determined attack on the village of Courcelette. Under a creeping barrage the platoon entered the village and found the Germans in occupation though getting out as fast as they could. It was here that Percy Natrass's luck ran out. As he ran down the village street there was no cover and a German behind a wall shot him dead; he fell without a sound. Barwise and Bill did not know he was dead until later, though they were with him and saw him fall down. Orders were very strict on the battlefield. If your marra was wounded in any way you did not stop; if you did so, it was a court martial offence; the attack had to be pressed home. The stretcher-bearers following behind would see to the fallen. There is no justice in these situations, so it would be nice to record that the German was shot dead by a member of the regiment, but he was not. He ran as quickly as he could and got away.

The battalion went through Courcelette and did not stop, heading along a ridge towards the village of Martinpuich. Here the Germans had decided to make a stand and there were trenches, even though the artillery fire had mauled them about. The fighting was hand-to-hand, but the British had the advantage of numbers here. The Lincolnshire Regiment had moved up on the left and Barwise saw their right flank platoon heading forward being urged on by a familiar figure. It was Lieutenant Tinian. He was not leading his men though, but bringing up their rear; perhaps this was a new strategy. Barwise had no time to think of such things because there was a trench to be cleared and his section had a job on hand. The bombers began to work the zig-zags and with Bill as his bayonet man Barwise began the job of rushing round the corners and found three dead Germans very messed about by the grenade just thrown. Of course in training it was a question of rushing and moving on; it had not happened that a live enemy contested the space, which is what now ocurred. The grenade had exploded and it was safe to continue, but so it was for Germans. Two rounded their corner and came for Barwise and Bill; Barwise shot his and Bill went straight for his with a wild yell and a bayonet and the enemy went down with a scream. Barwise stood there looking at the man he had killed and started shaking. Bill stood on guard as the bomber and his helpers came round the corner.

'Ready?'

'Yes,' said Bill. 'Barwise pull yourself together. Work to do.'

'But he's dead. I shot him.'

'Aye and a bloody good job too or he'd have shot you. Like Percy; his number was up. Make sure it's not you next, so snap to it. This could get a bit hot; put your knuckles on.'

Bill didn't go for brass knuckles; he preferred a small dagger, but the brutal matter of factness of his words pulled Barwise round. He was a soldier and this was what he was here to do. Bill's words to Barwise were proven necessary in the very next bay. Here the zig-zags changed into a more typical German trench pattern of square bays. It's more difficult to throw into the next bay for a bomber; he threw the grenade well enough and it exploded; then there were screams from the Germans. Human beings are ingenious and it did not occur to Barwise or Bill that the cries were fake. They rushed round into the next bay to find three Germans very much alive and waiting. Fortunately, Bill was first and had fast reflexes, throwing himself onto the floor as the shots that would have killed him went overhead. Barwise came round the corner just behind Bill to see two of the Germans coming at him. The first he shot. The second reached him, and he found himself grappling in a struggle for his life, Bill was similarly engaged with the third German. Barwise's opponent had an axe and swung it down at him and a strange effect occurred. As the axe came down towards him, everything seemed to slow down and Barwise became almost a disinterested observer as his body took its own actions. He watched as he swung his rifle butt upwards to deflect the axe successfully; then he registered dismay as his fixed bayonet caught in the wall of the trench and momentum tore it out of his hands. Finally, he felt a surge of invincibility as his right fist, steel knuckles in place, swung round to hit the German on the side of his jaw; he went down as if pole-axed and Barwise was still alive. Leaving his opponent making a snoring noise on the floor he turned to look at where Bill was finishing off the other man with his dagger. As Barwise picked up his rifle. Sergeant Hine arrived with more bayonet men.

'Right boys; if they're going to play silly buggers we'll give them something serious to chew on.'

He ordered up the rifle grenade section to bombard the next Germans diggings for five minutes before continuing the work of clearing the area. They captured the German positions and then to their surprise the enemy mounted a counter attack. It was beaten off easily enough, because each platoon set up Lewis guns, but Bill Holliday voiced the puzzlement every man was feeling.

'What the Hell are they playing at? They're on the retreat; why waste men like this? It's mad, that's what it is.'

'They're buying time, Holliday. We've advanced over a mile since this morning and their guns are not far ahead. They want to get them out.'

'Oh right, Sir. Thank you, Sir.'

Lieutenant Stewart had come up and he had a good grasp of both tactics and strategy. A popular officer, the platoon liked him well for his competence, his attention to their needs and the fact that he led from the front. He was right; the stiffening resistance was desperation and a sign that the German forces were about to retreat. That night the battalion encamped in the captured German positions and stayed there next day as the

East Yorkshire passed through them and attacked to the front. Thus, the Cumbrians had a day to rest and gather themselves before they would continue; there was also time to reflect.

'You saw him, Herbert, after he got hit?'

'I did, Bill. Percy got it straight through the heart and I reckon he knew nothing about it.'

'How do you figure that?'

'Seen it before, Barwise. He fell right down with no attempt to save himself so I think he was dead before he hit the ground. Instantaneous.'

'Well that's some sort of comfort I suppose. I'll miss him though.'

'Aye, we all will. But we have to accept that you lose people in this game. It happens all the time; people you have known for years just go. All that training, the education, the life they've had and it only takes a split second to end it all. Might be you next.'

'I hope not.'

'You always hope it's not going to be you,' said Bill, 'but you know damned fine it might be. If it's got your name on it then you've had it. Eh, but Percy missed some rare sport today.'

'Sport?' said Barwise. 'I can't see it as sport. It's killing people. I do it because I have to, or they'll kill me. But I hate it. I bloody hate it.'

'I don't. I've never felt as alive as I do now. It's kill or be killed and I feel on top of the world.'

Barwise looked at Bill long and hard. 'You do now, but it's you doing the killing. What if it's you that gets killed?'

'Then that's just the way it is and so be it. But let me tell you Barwise, there ain't a Jerry alive is going to take me down.'

'You think you're invincible?'

'Yis. Oh I might get blown up or plugged by a bullet but when it's man-to-man there's no-one going to get the better of me. I'm going to come through this just you wait and see.'

'You're cutting edge,' said Herbert.

'How do you mean?'

'They reckon that in every platoon there's two or three men who do most of the killing of the enemy because they like it. They're the cutting edge. The others hate it and do it only if they have to. They'd rather disable the Germans than kill them.'

'Seems to me if we had more of the first type we might win quicker.'

'You may be right Bill,' mused Herbert, 'But I couldn't be one of them. Did you hear about that bloke over at Hetbuterne a couple of weeks back?'

'No. What did he do?'

'It was a man from Maryport…'

'Poor bugger!'

'No seriously, just listen. He was leading a section on patrol and he saw forty or so Germans taking up post and he attacked them.'

'What? With ten men?'

'Yes. They killed loads of them and chased the rest away. Well the word is that he's done it again, two days ago.'

'What? The same thing? Sounds like a mad bugger to me.'

'Maybe he is, but he's at Serre, only about five miles away, so there's a bit of craic going on about it. He was leading a platoon then because he got promoted and there was a machine gun post ahead of him. He went straight at them with rifle and bayonet and they threw grenades at him but missed. He shot six of them and the rest ran off.'

'They would! I like that. Cutting edge; that's me. Yis, I'll go for that. What was that bloke's name?'

'Ned Smith.'

'Well, I take my hat off to him. Proper West Cumbrian, that lad.'

'Aye well you be careful,' said Barwise. 'He might be a hero, but there's lot of heroes end up dead.'

'I can take care of myself, never you fear.'

Bill Holliday had more 'sport' in the next few days as 7 Battalion leapfrogged through the East Yorks on 29 August and attacked Guedecourt. This was not the Somme of 1916, but of 1918 and in very short order the Cumbrians chased the enemy out of the village, through the other side and five hundred yards further on. The following day, advancing by sections they went another fifteen hundred yards to the outskirts of Le Transloy. This cost them between twenty and thirty wounded, to take territory that two years before the BEF could not take with the loss of thousands. They could not take the village, which was strongly held, but settled down to spend the night in some old German trenches; the new German positions were very close. It was here that one of Barwise's platoon got a dreadful fright.

Battalion orders on the subject of urination were quite specific. Men were not to piss in the trench, because it made the place smell and was unhygienic. Happily there was a German latrine that was pressed into service; Robert Gordon from Whitehaven felt the need to go to it in the cold light just before dawn. He found his way to the pots and stood there as he began to piss. In the greyness another figure came up beside him, undid his trousers and also began to relieve himself. Men tend not to look at each other when urinating, but Robert, being a social being, grunted, 'Good Morning,' in a comradely way at the exact time that the other man said 'Guten Morgen.' Robert and the German instantly looked at each other. 'Mein Gott!' came from one, and 'My God!' from the other before they both turned and ran back the way they had come. The others in the platoon thought Robert rather fortunate, because in the ordinary run of things they did not see Germans very often unless they were fighting them. During the day the enemy kept his head down, as the Cumbrians did, so seeing one was a bit like seeing a deer in your garden at the edge of the fells. His bullets and shells were much in evidence, but not the man himself, who was very shy and cautious.

Barwise was now given further cause to think about what he was doing as a man and as a soldier. The platoon was troubled with at least one sniper and Lieutenant Stewart opted to take an aggressive response to this by deploying some of his own. Barwise, being an excellent shot, was one of those sent forward into no-man's land before dawn to see what they could do. He found himself a position on his side of the wire, by an old tree and lay there facing the enemy, covered in a muddy old sack from head to foot. As the sun came up, he heard the rest of his platoon stand to and begin to go about the normal routines of the morning. It was not long before the German sniper showed his hand and a shot rang out. It had no effect, narrowly missing the helmet that Sergeant Hine had held up on a stick to draw his fire. Barwise had seen the muzzle flash of the enemy rifle and he waited, watching the position like a fox watching a chicken, slowly, millimeter by millimeter moving his own weapon to point that way. Eventually the German moved, not very much, but enough for Barwise to make out his shape and where his head was. Taking careful aim he shot the man right between the eyes.

It was strange that he felt no compunction about doing it. He still did not like killing, but this was at a distance and the enemy was trying to kill his own marras. It seemed that it was like remote control and that not being close enough to see the man's face made a difference. 'Real' killing was what he did not like; the close up and personal combat where the enemy was a fellow human being. Bill Holliday did, and that made him very effective in close quarter action, but Barwise knew that he too was effective, just in a different way.

Another angle to his thinking was that he knew he would never ever be able to talk about this to anyone. There was a strong culture among the men of the Western Front, indeed probably all the theatres of war, that they would never talk about their war experiences, how it was. Yes they would tell stories at home, but never the horror; never the bad bits. It was part of being a man at war that you would protect the women and children at home from the knowledge of what you had been compelled to do. Many, indeed, preferred to forget what they had done; Bill and Barwise were two sides of a coin in this matter, for Bill reveled in what he did but Barwise knew that if he lived to marry, to have children and grandchildren, then he would never breathe a word of what he had seen and done, save in the vaguest of terms.

An hour after he had shot the German sniper, there had been no further incident. Barwise heard Sergeant Hine yell, 'Criffel!' at the top of his voice. It was his recall, so he waited. A few minutes later artillery rounds flew over head and landed on the German positions. He immediately left his place as the bombardment continued and rolled back towards his own lines, wriggling, crawling until almost at his own parapet where he yelled out, 'Helvellyn!' then tumbled down into his own trench. The Battalion was being relieved. They marched back a few miles for a couple of days of rest, but they were a good fighting unit and the respite was never going to be very long. On 2 September they were moved forward again to rejoin the fighting and it was now that an incident occurred that showed how far Bill Holliday had gone in what he was prepared to do.

The Lincolnshire Regiment was being held up by stern resistance at a place called Vallulart Wood, and 7 Battalion was given the order to help them. As they moved into position a heavy rainstorm began, obscuring the view and the instruction was given to fix bayonets. The Cumbrians did not need a barrage;

the Germans were too busy trying to keep dry, so 7 battalion rushed the gap to the enemy position and dived down into their trenches. The Germans were taken completely by surprise, as Barwise and his marras waded into them with clubs, daggers, knuckles and entrenching tools, killing numbers of them immediately. The bombers began their work of progressing along and the man that Barwise was attached to came to a bay, hurled a grenade over and Barwise went round like lightning, yelling like a maniac. There was a German still alive in there, blown against the far wall, but otherwise unharmed. His helmet had been blasted off and Barwise went for him with his bayonet. Penetrating the red mist in his eyes, he saw a boy he thought looked very young with blue eyes and light brown hair and the intrusive little thought came into his head, 'That could be me.' The boy cried out in fear; 'Mutti! Mutti!' and Barwise registered that he was in tears crying though he did not know what the boy had shouted. It was then that he thought of how Margaret would feel if someone killed him and he lowered his bayonet.

'Nay, you're a prisoner. Put your bloody hands up,' and he gestured to the lad to do that.

'Kamerad Kamerad!'

'Handy Hock,' said Barwise, parroting what he had learned from older hands.

The German boy put his hands up.

'I'll not kill thee. Thou'lt live to see thee mam agyan and if thew's lucky, to grow old. Now...'

'No prisoners.'

Barwise had not time to finish his sentence. Lieutenant Tinian was beside him; the Lincolnshires had evidently caught up with the Cumbrian men.

'My prisoner, Sir.'

'No bloody prisoners,' said Tinian and raised his revolver.

The German boy screamed 'Nein!' as Tinian fired, but as he

did so Barwise knocked his arm down and the shot went into the wall of the trench.

'My prisoner, Sir,' he repeated with an insistent tone.

Tinian looked at him and smiled. 'You struck an officer. Little, isn't it? Never liked you. You'll make a good example. I'm going to have you shot.'

'Shoot my marra, you bastard?'

Tinian turned round to find Bill Holliday holding a rifle at him. 'Not if I shoot you first.'

Bill shot him and Tinian fell dead, a look of astonishment on his face.

'I never liked him anyway.' Bill looked at the German. 'You,' pointing at him and putting his finger to his lips. 'Keep your mouth shut right! Shhhh!'

The German goggled in disbelief and then nodded his head violently in agreement.

'You shot an officer, Bill. You can't do that.'

'Either he got shot or you got shot. I made a choice Barwise; you made yours as soon as you knocked his arm down. It's simple though, isn't it? Soldiers' rules; your prisoner so you get to dispose of him. He broke the rules.'

Here he spat down at Tinian with a look of disgust.

'Nasty little tick; full of himself. Too many good men get shot; for a change this one deserved it.'

Then he looked at Barwise and told him flatly; 'He was going to murder you Barwise. He didn't need to shoot you or stab you; the court martial would do it for him. That was his weapon of choice. All I've done is stop a murder so it's you that'll go home to your mam and dad not him. Think on it.'

Barwise nodded. The Western Front was Death's empire, and life was cheap.

'I don't have to. Thanks Marra.'

Then he shouted; 'Clear!' and the bomber and his two bayonetmen came round into the bay. What was done, was done. He took his prisoner back into the next bay and reported that the retreating Germans had killed an officer from the Lincolns. Lieutenant Stewart looked at the prisoner and said,

'Wie alt sind sie?'

The boy replied, 'Ich bin sechszehn Jahre Alt.'

The Lieutenant looked weary.

'He's sixteen years old Sergeant. They're sending their children to fight us. Have him sent back to prisoner holding.'

'Interrogation Sir?'

'No. He's told me enough already.'

To Sergeant Hine's querying look, the Lieutenant continued; 'If they're sending boys Sergeant, it's because they've got no men left. They're finished.'

Most of the Germans in the fortified zone just ran away. The battalion captured thirteen machine guns during this attack. They spent the next day improving the defences round their positions and burying the dead. On 6 September they were marched back out of the line for a rest. Before dismissing his men at the end of the march Lieutenant Stewart paraded his platoon.

Chapter 28 — Battle

'I want you to be very aware of what you have done in the last few days. It's been hard fighting and we've taken losses, but what you have done, from a military point of view, is astonishing. In March of this year we were forced out of a whole string of villages in the Somme area and pushed back in some cases for fifty miles. Some of these villages we occupied after hard and bloody fighting in 1916 and 1917; it was a great loss to our side when the Germans took them. In a few short days you have taken those villages back and forced the enemy to run away. I sincerely believe that the end is in sight, because it is quite clear that they cannot stand up to us for much longer. I just wanted to say well done men. Cumberland should be proud of you and I think they will be. You have done things that your children will tell to their grandchildren and they will say your names with awe and regard you as heroes, to be spoken of with hushed voices, and wonder at what you did. What I personally want to say is that I am proud of you all, and that it is a privilege to lead you in this fight for what I hope will be a better world.'

They cheered him, waving their Brodie helmets in the air; then they were dismissed to bivouac and seek comforts where they could. The whole battalion fitted into a railway tunnel where bunks and electric lighting had been installed. In the tunnel were the regimental first aid post and even a small cinema where the various units that visited the tunnels could watch the latest Charlie Chaplin film. In a nearby barn some large vats had been commandeered from a local brewery and pressed into service as baths. The water was changed every so often, but in practice that meant after a hundred or so men had been and had their turns. Clear and hot to start with, it was lukewarm and scummy with bits floating on the top of dubious origin by the time it was changed. By the end of the bath session the towels were indescribable. Needless to say, the position of first platoon to have a bath was enviable. To men covered in dirt and grime, the singing while getting clean was inevitable:

'Whiter than the whitewash on the wall
Whiter than the whitewash on the wall!
Oh wash me in the water that you wash your dirty daughter in,
So that I can be whiter than the whitewash on the wall.
On the wall, on the wall,
On the wall, on the wall,
Oh wash me in the water that you wash your dirty daughter in,
So that I can be whiter than the whitewash on the wall!'

Nobody knew where the jingle originated, but it was sung in France wherever men had baths. It may have begun in the ranks of the music hall performers who were now soldiers, but even though this single verse was the only one, the singers never seemed to tire of it. Generally speaking, singing was a form of leisure much enjoyed by the men in the ranks. Their superiors might indulge their time off duty by writing poetry, or reading or by getting drunk, but to the ordinary soldier a good sing song, even in the trenches on cold nights, was a great way to pass the time. It was not unknown for the opposing sides to sing songs to each other across no-man's land. Barwise's particular favourite was a rather silly new song that was popular with the younger men:

'K-K-K-Katy, beautiful Katy,
You're the only g-g-g-girl that I adore;
When the m-m-m-moon shines,
Over the cowshed,
I'll be waiting at the k-k-k-kitchen door.
K-K-K-Katy, beautiful Katy,
You're the only g-g-g-girl that I adore;
When the m-m-m-moon shines,

Chapter 28 — Battle

Over the cowshed,
I'll be waiting at the k-k-k-kitchen door.'

The Cumbrians had their own version of this, which was far more popular.

'K-K-K Katy, swallowed a tatie
A tuppenny fish, a packet of chips
The night before.
And in the m- m-m-morning,
When she was yawning,
She nearly swallowed the knob off the k-k-k-kitchen door.'

Men who had been serving longer usually preferred songs that referenced a better time, such as *'The Long Long Trail a-Winding'* or *'Keep the Home Fires Burning.'*

Other refreshments were to be found in the local establishments of French citizens who did not mind being too near the firing zone and had been allowed to set up in an area from whence the general population had been evacuated. There were numerous *'estaminets'* where a man could spend pay when it was issued and the bully beef or Machonochie stew of the Army rations could be varied with a plate of eggs and chips. It was one of these that Barwise entered one day and saw a face he knew. There was an RAF squadron just over the way from his billet and a group of men were sitting at a table dressed in the uniform of that infant service, newly formed this year. Among them was Flight Sergeant Edmondson, who had tried to persuade him to transfer; Barwise gave him a nod. The Sergeant, however, got up and greeted him.

'I remember you. Private Little from Workington.'

'That's right, Sarge.'

'I'll confess its grand to have the Border Regiment just

across the road and hear some friendly voices, but I never reckoned to see a face I knew. How are you keeping?'

'Pretty good thanks, Sarge.'

'You're still alive at any rate. Are you sorry you didn't transfer?'

'No, Sarge. It was the right choice. I'd rather be with my marras.'

'Loyal sort of bloke, aren't you. Any more like you at home?'

'Eight more Sarge, four sisters and four brothers.'

'There's enough of you then!'

'My mam would think so.'

John Edmondson laughed, 'I bet she would with that lot on her hands.'

Whatever impulse made him do it, Barwise could never tell, but he reached into his pocket and drew out his family picture. Edmondson looked at it with interest.

'Who's the nurse?'

'That's Annie Eleanor – Nellie to us. She's out here somewhere.'

'Pretty girl. Look, I said you must pop in and see me when this lot's over. Bring her with you if you like.'

'I might just do that, Sarge.'

Conversation between them was not prolonged; it could not be between a Sergeant and a Private, but some men are born to be friends. Barwise had taken to Edmondson just as the Sergeant had taken to him; they were marras and there was no doubt that if he survived then Barwise would look Edmondson up in Aspatria. Over the next few days, they had several short chats and found congeniality in each other's nature that they both knew was the foundation of a good friendship. Life out of the line is made more pleasant by such kindred spirits.

Inactivity could not be suffered for long though. The Border Regiment was considered a fine fighting group and soon they were engaged in rehearsing tactics for their next attack. This had become standard practice and the men took it in good part, because it made them very familiar with what they were supposed to be doing and extremely efficient at doing it. On 5 October 1918 their practice battle was interrupted by orders sending them back into the line. On 5/6 October they took up position in a sunken lane near Gouzeaucourt. In front of them were very thin German defences, stretched to the limit. If they could break through them, only natural obstacles prevented them from reaching open country. The German armies were retreating; advances were now reckoned in miles, not yards, but this enemy was never easy to beat. 7 Battalion had some hard fighting ahead.

Chapter 29

Explosion

'Herbert. What's it like to be shot?'

'I've never been shot, Barwise, so I can't tell you from personal experience.'

'Well, I realize that, but you've met enough men who have been. They must say something about it.'

'That's true, they do, but it varies from man to man.'

'When I got shot, it didn't hurt.'

Barwise and Bill looked across to Robert Wise from Wigton, one of the older soldiers in the platoon.

'I was here in 1916 on the Somme, day one. They got me in the arm. I didn't think anything about it at first, because all I felt was a sort of pressure in my arm. When I looked down there was blood pouring from it, but I can honestly say that the only thing I felt was surprise. The pain came later.'

'Aye, but that's not the way it is with every bullet. I got mine in the leg back in '15 on the Ancre.' This was Fred Bell from Cockermouth. 'It felt like someone hit me on the leg with a cricket bat, very hard, then everything buzzed for about ten seconds before an achy pain started.'

The men who had been wounded all seemed to have different experiences ranging from those already described, to having the sensation of a red hot poker being applied to the place where the bullet hit, and then being thumped by a sledgehammer. A general conversation ensued and it became apparent that every man, if he was to die, would prefer it to

Chapter 29 — Explosion

be by a bullet, quick and clean. Gas they had a horror of, but generally the thing that scared most was the artillery because it chewed people up. A shrapnel shell, filled with one hundred lead balls, timed to explode downwards could trap a man in a cone of destruction that would leave him nothing but bloody chunks on the floor. It was quick, but many men had seen this happen to people they knew and they probably dreaded it more than anything else, simply because it was their most likely death. Artillery killed three quarters of all men who died in battle. They all knew this, but still they faced it every day and did their duty. To a great extent they were the absolute epitome of Britain, because the UK now was literally gritting its teeth and getting on with the war to a finish. It was a dirty nasty job, but it had to be done. It had taken them a long time to get into their stride, but the naïve citizen army of 1916 was now battle hardened, practiced and professional. Now the Germans had no answers left to oppose them with.

Barwise's war commenced in July and ended in October; though his service was short, it was vicious. After nearly a month out of the line and in training for a great attack, 7 Battalion was back in support positions near Bantouzelle by 8 October. Over the next couple of weeks they joined in the general advance that took place after the British Army broke through the Hindenburg line. At two o'clock in the morning of 20 October the Cumbrians entered the village of Amerval and were taken completely by surprise when the Germans counter-attacked them. They were pushed out of the village, but the Commanding Officer, Colonel WE Thomas knew his men well; they regrouped and prepared to attack the Germans. The enemy had held Amerval for months and had time to prepare strong defences. Barwise looked out towards the enemy and a strange sensation came over him. He could not put his finger on it, but a feeling of great reluctance to go any further came on him. Try as he might, he could not shake it. He had previously dismissed the idea of premonitions as nothing but soldier superstition, but he had never felt like this before. It did not matter though; he would have to go forward in the attack whether he wanted to or not. The feeling was still troubling him when he turned and saw the stretcher-bearers waiting to follow the combat troops into action. Among them was Herbert Hayston.

'Herbert; will you do me a favour?'

'Of course I will; you know that.'

'Take my watch will you? You know where I live.'

'Aye, 55 Devonshire Street.'

'If owt happens to me take it there and tell my mam and dad I did my best.'

Herbert had heard this before. Men often handed messages or objects to stretcher-bearers before action and with more or less the same words.

'I'll do that Barwise but I'll give you your watch back tonight. I think you'll need it.'

'But if owt happens to me…'

'I'll deliver it. Now get along with you. You're about ready to go.'

There were of course no noises or whistles to warn the enemy that they were coming, but all three companies of 7 Battalion rushed forward by section leapfrogging in artillery formation. The Cumbrians swarmed over the Germans as the enemy broke and ran. It seemed to turn into a sort of race with the British advancing and halting occasionally to fire at Germans running as fast as they could. Bill Holliday was in his element, face red, and laughing like a loon and grinning widely.

'By, but I'm loving this,' he shouted at Barwise as they advanced at a trot across an open field. 'Look at the buggers run. Come on Barwise; go faster and let's get at them!'

'You're mad Bill. I'm blown out; they run better than I can.'

Chapter 29 — Explosion

'Well I reckon I can catch a couple and I might save one for thee if you're lucky. Rare sport marra; rare sport. Did you ever see men move so fast?'

It was true; the Germans troops in front of them were pelting along as fast as they could go. That this was unusual behaviour for German troops did not occur to Barwise or to Bill or they might have been more cautious. The Germans were attempting to clear the field for a reason they knew well; a stop line had been planted across it. This was an expensive but very effective way of stopping an enemy advance. A line of small underground chambers was dug and filled with explosives. As your pursuing enemy ran onto it, a touch of a wire to a battery could destroy large numbers of the attackers. The German in charge of detonating the mines was a little premature or he would have caused far more casualties. Only the front-runners had reached the stop line when Feldwebel Hertz set them off.

Bill Holliday was in full tilt after the fleeing enemy, laughing with the joy of victory when he vanished from the face of the earth as the first of a series of 8 huge detonations ripped in a line across the field. Whether the explosion he was above buried him or tore him to atoms would never be known. Barwise was not far behind him and the blast from the explosion blew him into the air and tore his uniform to shreds, his jacket and equipment, identity tags and all being ripped from him as if by an angry giant. Something hit his head and he fell to the ground part buried by the earth and lay like a rag doll, to all intents and purposes dead. 7 Battalion reeled from the shock then pressed home their attack, but the resistance was now furious; these were crack German troops and they were not about to give in. The battle rolled on leaving Barwise's limp form where it had fallen.

It was fifteen minutes later when the stretcher-bearers arrived and Herbert Hayston's team found Barwise's body. It did him no good, because German machine guns are no respecters of people with red-cross armbands. A burst killed Herbert's three mates and a bullet entered his leg passing through his thighbone and effectively removing part of it.

Herbert fought down his body's panic, because he knew that shock killed people and especially if they did not act in time. His wound was bleeding but not profusely so he knew that the bullet had missed the artery. The leg felt like a sledgehammer had hit it, but he retained the presence of mind to tamp a field dressing onto both sides of his wound and tie it tight. Walking was out of the question. Then he turned his attention to Barwise, who he saw was breathing but very shallowly, as if most of the life had been blasted from him. He was about ten feet away but did not look to be wounded except for a gash on the side of his head. The only thing Herbert could do was to wait for help and attract attention for both of them. The life of a man has a finite number of breaths, and his heart a limited number of beats. Barwise hung between life and death, his heart beating slowly and his breath almost stilled whilst the grim reaper hovered his scythe over his head.

Then the Germans played one of their trump cards; a series of soft crumps in the area announced the arrival of several gas shells. They hit the ground and a cloud rolled over Herbert and Barwise. Herbert held his breath and fumbled his mask on as best he could. Then he looked over at Barwise, still breathing shallowly and still unconscious, but now making a snoring noise. His equipment had been blown off him; where was it? Herbert saw it lying five feet the other side of him and without another thought he dragged himself on his elbows across to the bag containing Barwise's respirator. Was it intact? Yes it was. Crying with the pain of it Herbert now dragged himself inch by inch back to Barwise. As quickly as he could, Herbert fumbled the mask over Barwise's head and made sure that it was fitting right. Then he passed out beside him. Other stretcher teams found them a couple of hours later and evacuated them to a CCS. The Medical Officer examined Barwise and pronounced him to be moribund; he received no medical attention as his head wound appeared slight, but he had been gassed. Whether he recovered or not was in the lap of the gods, but the CCS could do nothing for him. He was carted outside on a stretcher, placed into an ambulance tender and sent off to a base hospital with a label 'E- dia gas' tied round his wrist. Barwise was going back to Britain, but as a nameless and diagnosed gas casualty since no-one knew who he was.

Herbert woke up as the MO examined him.

'I don't want to lose my leg.'

The MO looked at him, and at his RAMC badges, nodded, then rapped out 'HMU.'

Herbert was as lucky as a man could be in 1918. The Harvard Medical Unit had arrived in France in June 1915 entirely unexpectedly. Funded by Harvard University they brought top grade equipment and some of the best surgeons in the world to help the British War effort. Based in Etaples they did pioneering surgery on wounds of all kinds and of course that was partly why the university had done it. Here was a steady supply of men with the worst hurts the human body could sustain and these surgeons were here to learn how to mend them. Future generations would, and did, benefit from their work. At the beginning of 1918 they began sending surgical teams into the battle areas, attached to Casualty Clearing Stations, which was Herbert Hayston's great luck. He was carried out of the CCS hut where he had been received and into another which had a mobile operating theatre attached to it. Here a clean and fresh-faced young American nurse cut the uniform off him and bagged up his personal possessions. The lousy rags that remained of what he had been wearing, complete with their inhabitants were taken outside and burned in an incinerator. Then she swabbed him down from a basin containing carbolic soap, washed him clean, and shaved all the hair off his head. His own mother would hardly have known him. One thing she did not do was touch the field dressing he had applied to his wound hours before. Shortly he was taken into the operating theatre fully conscious where the American surgeon, a Mr Aylen, awaited him with his team. His dressing was removed and the surgeon explained what was going to happen to Herbert in a precise New England accent.

'Frankly, young man, your leg is in a very bad way and in an ordinary hospital the only treatment would be to amputate.'

'But I don't want to lose my leg.'

'I think nobody wants to do that. You may not have to. I am going to have a look at this wound, for the purposes of which we shall have to put you under, but there is a strong likelihood that we will be able to help you.'

'I hope you can Sir. I would much rather keep it.'

The American gave a dry smile.

'I rather got that message. Okay let's put it this way, if you wake up with a leg we couldn't help you here, but you'll be on the way to someone who can. If you wake up without a leg then no-one could. Sister Enebuske...'

Herbert barely had time to register that the anaethetist was a woman before a rubber mask came over his face and everything went black.

He woke up hours later on a hospital train; he still had both legs and a cloth bag with his possessions was tied loosely to his arm; when he looked in it he found his wallet, his knife and his watch, as well as Barwise's. What had happened to Barwise, he did not know, but hoped that he was alright. His wound ached, but for the first time since before his last action, he smiled. On his lapel was a label HMU, Etaples. These Americans did not hang about. Until 1917 one of their surgeons had been Dr Fred Albee who had pioneered the use of bone grafts in the repair of injured limbs. He had invented a 'bone mill' that was a powered machine, to which a whole range of instruments could be attached. Albee would 'harvest' a piece of bone from somewhere on the patient's body and treat it as a carpenter treated wood. From the bone, perhaps a rib, he could manufacture bone pegs and screws, plates with holes, and cut ledges on surviving bone for inlays. Such was the speed of the process that Albee could screw or peg a bone plate into place in ten minutes flat. When he went back to the US he left a complete bone mill in Etaples and staff trained to use it. On arrival at the American hospital Herbert was taken straight to surgery and operated on immediately. He woke up with a leg encased in two long wooden splints and a well wrapped starched bandage.

'You're a lucky man,' said his surgeon, a Mr Hamilton. 'I found that just over an inch of your femur had been shattered to bits and had to be removed entirely.'

'How does that make me lucky?' asked Herbert.

'Because I was able to patch it up.' The surgeon was smiling and evidently waiting for more questions.

'How did you patch up a thing like that?'

'Good old Yankee know how, Mr Hayston. I took part of one of your lower ribs out; oh don't worry you won't miss it. It's one of the short ones and they don't do much. I used that to fix you up.'

'You stuck part of my rib into my leg?'

'Yep; something like that. It's a bit more complicated, but basically I made four bone splints and pegged them into place to join the two parts of your femur together. It should mend well I think.'

'So I won't lose my leg?'

'Not unless something goes very wrong, but I don't think that will happen. I'm afraid you are stuck here for six weeks in bed before we can consider letting you up. After that you'll be on a crutch for a while, but eventually you'll be able to walk on it.'

'Will it be back to normal by then?'

'Oh no. I wouldn't go as far as that. The bullet did a lot of damage to tendons and nerves. I imagine that you'll always have a slight limp, but you'll get along well enough I think.'

The surgeon smiled, and Herbert thanked him, shaking his hand. For the rest of October, through November he was in bed being cared for by American nurses and being well fed and looked after.

≈

For the unknown moribund case taken off the battlefield with a head wound and suffering from gas inhalation, the prognosis was not so good. Like the CCSs, the base hospitals looked after those they could help. Those who looked beyond help were sent on. Barwise knew nothing of the ferry crossing

Chapter 29 — Explosion

or of the landing at Folkestone, but his normal good luck held, because he arrived there less than twenty-four hours after being evacuated from the CCS. He still had not received any medical treatment, because he was expected to die and the priority was those who could live. At Victoria Station a fleet of ambulances was waiting and hospitals around the UK were primed to expect a flood of casualties. Barwise, still comatose, was taken across London by the London Voluntary Ambulance Service to Euston Station and loaded onto a hospital train heading north. In a dimly lit carriage with thirty bunks in it, and tended by a single nurse, he lay prone, unknowing, and hovering in the shadow land between life and death.

The Army identity discs were not a very efficient way to ensure that men could have a name attached to them if anything happened to them. In other ways though the Army was very efficient indeed. Telegraph messages travel faster than trains and as Barwise was crossing the Channel a telegram boy cycled down from Finkle Street and knocked on the door of 55 Devonshire Street. Margaret opened the door and saw the boy and her mind went blank. So many women in this town had received telegrams and people of her class associated them with one thing and one thing only. She took the telegram from the boy like an automaton and shut the door without saying thank you. He shrugged and rode off; it was a scene he had witnessed many times before.

Ommie came home from school and found her mother sitting in the back parlour staring into space.

'Mam, what's up with you?'

For answer Margaret handed her the telegram and Ommie read:

'Deeply regret to inform you that your son 50464 Private B Little has been reported missing. Letter follows.'

She immediately burst into tears.

'Be quiet Ommie.'

'But Barwise is missing. He's missing.'

'He's missing. He's not dead.'

'It doesn't say that he's dead, but he might be. Lots of them posted missing turn out to be dead.'

'I'll believe he's dead when they tell me he is. I'd know if he was and I don't feel that way.'

Her composure was set firm like cement and she would not be budged. When Tom came home and read the telegram he went out across the yard and into the privy; when he came back his eyes were red, but no-one asked him if he had been crying. Of course not; men did not do that. There was a tension in the house and in a place usually full of light, life and laughter, there was a gloom and a grim clenched up kind of feeling. The family, all except Margaret, felt that they had been given a warning and braced themselves waiting for the blow to fall. Margaret's attitude was not simple obstinacy in the face of the inevitable.

Her father had told her on several occasions that someone had put a rod of steel up her backbone and it was never more true than now, when her eldest son was missing. In the face of this trial she was stoical and that would only change if the news changed. Her attitude transmitted to her children and after a few hours a strange form of determined normality settled over them. The neighbours knew, of course, and were kindly and considerate to the family that might be stricken. People offered to do small things for them like shopping or helping with washing; anything to help ease the family, particularly Margaret, over a time of trouble, but Margaret, as a matriarch, was strong. If the blow fell, she was ready for it; if it did not, then she would rejoice. All she could do for the moment was wait.

Fortune looked in Barwise's direction as he travelled north on the hospital train wrapped in a blanket. The Territorial Force Nursing Service Sister who was in charge of his carriage was a conscientious lady, who was not content to merely administer water, bedpans and words of comfort. Many of her charges were asleep and she found time to tend to her moribund cases. Rattling through the night, Barwise remained completely oblivious as she took scissors and cut what was left of his uniform trousers from him, removed his boots and socks and sponged him clean from head to foot. Then she dried him and wrapped him up warmly, having done all that she could. Although she was quite prepared to give him food and water, since he was unconscious, there was nothing she could do in that way, save make him comfortable. He had had no food nor drunk anything for days when finally the hospital train pulled into the platform at Citadel Station, Carlisle, the hospital city. Along with several other moribund cases he was taken to Fusehill Military Hospital now a giant factory for processing wounded men, with six hundred and eighty beds. Here at last he was seen by a doctor with time to attend to him.

'Now then, what have we here Sister? This man is unconscious. Do we know anything about him apart from the fact that he's been gassed, according to his label?'

'I'm afraid not Sir. He's not even got identification.'

'He is one of ours isn't he? I mean he's not a German?'

'We don't know that either, Sir.'

'Well I'd better examine him then, but first you'd better put him on an infusion. I'm guessing that the cause of this comatose state is some form of shock and dehydration will certainly not help that.'

'Gum Arabic, Sir?'

'No, I think not; he's not got any large bleeding injuries. Plain saline will do the trick I imagine. And if he's a gas casualty you'd better do what you can with that procedure too. Who knows? It might actually bring him round. I'll examine him properly in an hour or so. He's breathing very shallowly and I think the gas might have got to his lungs. He has the spots and the blisters, so best to treat him as a gas case initially and we can deal with the rest later. He's been classified as a moribund up until now I should think, but he does not look quite at that point yet to me.'

Two nurses got to work on Barwise with a large bowl of hot water and sponges.

'He seems to have been washed before.'

'That doesn't matter. Major Knight told us to go through the procedure for gas, so that's what we must do.'

When they had washed Barwise again, they lifted him into a sitting position and propped him up. Then they brought a spray filled with bicarbonate of soda and directed copious amounts of it into his eyes, up his nostrils and into his ears. Then one of them used a wooden spatula to hold down his tongue as they opened his slackened mouth and they sprayed it into his throat. He choked and gagged, but did not awaken beyond a low moan and a fluttering of eyes that had no awareness in them. Finally, one of them found a vein and inserted a needle, attaching a tube and a bottle of saline which she hung up on a hook behind the bed. Then they laid him down and covered him up again.

'You'd better stay with him in case he wakes up.'

The level of saline in the bottle went down slowly and the amount of fluid in Barwise's body went up. He was also warm, so not long after the drip was inserted his comatose state changed, unnoticed by the nurse, into sleep. After an hour or so someone accidentally dropped a tray in the corridor outside and as the noise reached him Barwise awoke with a sharp intake of breath and his eyes opened as he raised his head.

'Oh, so you're awake now are you. How do you feel?'

Barwise made no answer, but stared at her with wide eyes that did not blink. His breathing now was raspy.

'Can you speak to me? What is your name?'

The stare continued and the nurse recognized that he was in shock as Major Knight had thought.

'Now then, you just lie back and take it easy,' she said in a soothing voice. The doctor will be along soon to see you. Gently her hand soothed his forehead back down and he lay staring at the ceiling. It was not long before the doctor returned to see for himself.

'Right, my lad, let's have a look at you. That's quite a knock you've had. Can you tell me how you got it? Do you know your name?'

Barwise said nothing and continued to stare.

'Quite right. Just what I thought. You've had a bang to the head and it's addled your wits. Quite a lot of bruising round the body too. Bed rest is what you need and that's what you'll get. Right Sister; finish the gas treatment now he's conscious, and then feed him. Probably needs a good meal and it will do him the world of good. Now let's have a listen.'

The stethoscope was applied to Barwise's chest.

'Some arrythmia, and quite a lot of wheezing. This chap has been damaged by gas and it's my guess he'll never entirely get over it. It's not as severe as I've seen, but it's not mild. He's been lucky to come away with his life from the exposure he's had. Bed rest again. He probably feels rather poorly, too.'

Barwise made no resistance as the nurses brought a cupful of olive oil and made him drink it to counter the effects of gas in his oesophagus and stomach. Over the next few days he would have to drink several more to help flush out his intestines. When he had drunk this they brought a plate of milky bread slops and made him eat, though he did not wish to and tried to push them away. For two days he lay inert and staring when he was awake, but on the third day he woke up and blinked normally.

'Where am I?'

The VAD nurse who had been sitting beside him reading replied, 'You're in Fusehill Hospital in Carlisle.'

'Carlisle?' A puzzled look came over his face. I know that place. I think I've been there.

'What's your name?'

For a few moments he wrestled to remember, then he admitted, 'I don't know.'

Then he broke off coughing and wheezing. Major Knight told him not to be worried.

'It often happens that we get men who have forgotten their names and everything else about their lives. Don't worry young man; it will come back, I am sure. It's neurasthenia, and with rest, it can fade away. In the meantime, I want you to have some oxygen therapy to help your lungs; and I want you to get up and walk about when you are able to, so that your limbs do not get lazy.'

Chapter 29 — Explosion

Over a period of days Barwise began to walk about the ward as the welt on his head healed. He breathed in a mixture of air and pure oxygen to increase the amount of oxygen in his blood, which was supposed to speed the healing process. His breathing grew easier though the rasping in his chest continued. Major Knight thought that might never go away.

'At least you're not a Jerry,' said Major King. 'I thought you might be at first; I have treated a few, but couldn't understand a word they said.'

October soon gave way to November and by the end of the first week Barwise's head gash had almost fully healed, he was eating normal food and walking about the hospital in the scratchy and ill fitting convalescent uniform they had given him.

'You're a Cumbrian,' said one of the VAD nurses. 'I can tell by your accent.'

'You have a Scottish accent,' said Barwise.

'Very good, you are remembering a lot of things now.'

'What's your name?'

'Caroline Thomas. What's yours?'

Barwise's face took on a pained look as he struggled in his mind.

'I can't remember.'

'Where are you from?'

'I can't remember that either. Where are you from?'

'I'm from Kirkcaldy in Fife. Never mind, I'm sure it'll come soon.'

It came sooner than Caroline Thomas or Barwise might have guessed and it was due to the ingenuity of Major Knight. Barwise had been moved into a convalescent ward and on the evening of Sunday 10 November the Major came into the ward accompanied by a Captain and a Sergeant from the local garrison. The Sergeant bellowed out 'Stand by your beds!'

The patients who were able scrambled out of their chairs or beds and stood at attention. The Captain marched straight up to where Barwise stood rigidly.

The Sergeant then bellowed right in his face.

'Name, rank and number!'

'50464 Little B, Private, Sergeant!'

A look of disbelief came over Barwise's face as Major Knight grinned broadly.

'Unit?' demanded the Captain.

'7 Battalion The Border Regiment Sir!'

'Excellent. And where are you from?'

Barwise's face was a study in wonder as he intoned hesitatingly, 'Workington Sir.'

'Well Rivers, I had my doubts I confess, but you've made your point very well.'

'We've had a few instances like this up at Craiglockart. It's a kind of automatic response to authority and is always worth trying in this sort of case.'

'It's impressive and if I come across it again then I shall try it myself. And thank you also Sergeant.'

'Sir.'

'Yes, Private Little?' This was accompanied by a small smile, not of triumph but of satisfaction.

'I only live a bit down the road, Sir. Can I go home please?'

The Major appeared to be considering this.

Captain Rivers interjected, 'Is the memory loss the only reason you are keeping him here?'

'Yes,' replied Major Knight. 'His gassing symptoms have eased to the point where they are no danger to him. If he exerts then he'll get out of breath, but for everyday walking he's fine. His other injuries have all healed and he's been walking about normally.'

'Then my advice would be to let him go. Home life can be

an excellent therapy. I take it that his military career is over?'

'Oh, absolutely. No question of that.'

'Then if he can move unaided and with reasonable normality, I should let him go home.'

'I concur. Little; report to me at nine in the morning and I'll issue you with the necessary papers.'

So it was on the morning of Monday 11 November 1918 that Barwise walked out of Fusehill Hospital, somewhat dazed to be out in the morning air, but quite sure that he was fine. His friendly Scottish VAD nurse had volunteered to take him to the station and had lent him ten shillings in case he needed money.

'I'll pay you back, Caroline.'

'I know you will. If you can't find me at the hospital you have my home address.'

She waved him off at the station and Barwise felt warm inside; he had her home address up in Fife. He had nothing to read on the train, but did not wish to. He stared out of the window at a green landscape that became more and more familiar as the miles ticked down towards his destination. The beautiful rolling countryside, the foothills of the Lake District studded with dry-stone walls, metal strip fences and sheep and cows flowed past him like a hand soothing his brow. At Aspatria a memory came into his head of a Sergeant Pilot who was a butcher there; he would certainly pop in one day to say hello. At Dearham Bridge he craned over to look over towards where his grandparents lived, though of course he could not see it, and at Maryport he thought of the story his mother had told him. She had gone to a hiring fair there back in the '90s to become a serving maid and thus she had met his father. Strange things seemed to be happening in the streets of the places he passed through. People were running about waving flags; bunting was being put up, while at Maryport the church bells were ringing as if the bell ringers were bursting their muscles.

Past Flimby and Siddick, where the black spoil heaps ran into the sea, he began to smell the town; that sulphur burned-metal smell combined with the salt of the sea; an atmosphere like nowhere else that he knew of or had been. Soon the train rolled into Workington Low Station and he climbed out onto the platform and stood. He stood for a long time and his brows knit in frustration. As he stood, a man came up to him, a man he knew, and he searched for a name.

'Joe! Joe Johnson.'

'Gee, Barwise, I'm glad to see you. You've been posted missing, so man am I happy to set eyes on you. Do your folks know you're here?'

'No Joe. I lost my memory for a couple of weeks and I've only just got out of hospital.'

'Well it's no darn good you hanging round here chewing the fat with me buddy. You better get your ass up the road.'

'I can't.'

'Why in tarnation not? You scared to go home?'

'No, it's not that.'

'Then what?'

'I've forgotten the way.'

'Forgotten the way home? You got smacked on the head boy?'

'Yes. Something like that, but I don't remember that either.'

'Damn! Them dirty Fritzes sure messed you up.'

'Only for a while; my memory is coming back.'

'Which is more than you are, unless I get you there. Just hold on.'

Within five minutes Joe had permission to take Barwise home and walked him up Station Road. The most extraordinary scenes were going on and crowds were gathering in knots everywhere. As at Maryport the church bells were ringing.

'What's going on Joe. Have we won a battle?'

'Jeesus! Ain't you heard? It came in on the telegraph a while ago Barwise. The war's over. The Germans asked for an armistice. We won Barwise. The good guys won.'

Up Oxford Street Barwise's convalescent uniform won him applause, pats on the back, offers of drinks, smiles and lots of cheers. Some knew him and knew that he had been missing.

'By God, Barwise, your mam's going to be glad to see you.'

His mam! A picture of his parents flooded into his mind, and his family; memory flowed like a river. Joe Johnson turned him into Devonshire Street, then stopped him from walking in.

'Gently, Barwise. It'll be quite a shock.'

Inside the house the same air of determined normality prevailed. Everyone knew that it was a veneer, but were set on maintaining it. Ethel Kirkbride had brought the news that the war was over and a discussion about what had happened was going on around the table. There could be no rejoicing in this house.

There was a knock at the door.

'Well,' said Margaret. 'Who knocks on a door round here?'

'The rent man?' said Ethel.

'He's had this week's already. I'll go and see who it is.'

Getting up, she walked out into the passage and opened the door; then she gasped and stood disbelieving. There was her son; her reserve cracked, and she wept.

'We had a telegram to say you were missing. People thought you were dead, but I didn't believe it.'

She knew she was gabbling and that there were probably more appropriate things she could say, but she could not think straight.

Barwise stepped forward and put his arms round her.

'They nearly got me Mam, but they never managed it.'

'Why did you not let us know you were alright?'

'I lost my identity disc and got a bang on the head, so I

didn't know who I was for a while.'

After holding him for what seemed like an age she stepped back to look at him, then said, 'You'd better come in off the street; people are staring.'

Drying her eyes on her apron she led the way through into the back kitchen.

'Hello Ethel.'

'Hello Barwise; I'm right glad to see you safe.'

'Aye; it's good to be back. Put kettle on and mash tea will you? I'm parched. That's a nice teapot Mam; it's got your name on it.'

Barwise was home.

Chapter 30

Fit for Heroes

In some ways the news of the end of the war in Workington was best exemplified in the way it was received by 7 Battalion in France. They had been participating in the great general advance that took place as the Germans retreated, but had been relieved for a rest. The Cumbrians were in billets in Aulnoye when a dispatch rider arrived at about nine o'clock on the morning of 11 November, with a telegram from Brigade Headquarters:

'Hostilities will cease at 11am today. No more firing after that hour. Message ends.'

Fresh from Regimental Headquarters, Lieutenant Stewart called over to Sergeant Hine, 'Sergeant!'

'Sir!'

'Fall the men out. The war is over. There will be no duties today.'

'Yes Sir!'

When the news was given to them, most men simply looked blank. Many of them went back to their beds and went to sleep. They had survived the Great War for civilization and were weary; any thoughts of rejoicing or thankfulness would come later, but for now they were just glad to be alive and wanted to sleep. In many of their minds emotions were mixed; sadness with fear for the future; anger at the war ending before they had invaded Germany to punish them; and hope that for all that had been done, the world would be a better place. It has also to be borne in mind that they were Cumbrians and it is in the character of such people to have a great reserve. They tend not to commit to, or to demonstrate great emotion, but to deal with things matter of factly as they come. Outwardly, nothing would show, whatever was going on inside. Only in London did pandemonium break loose, but to a country, tired of war and fagged out by sheer effort, the end came with a profound sense of relief.

This is not to say that Workington did not celebrate; somebody at the Lifeboat Station sent up a string of maroons between eleven and twelve o'clock in the morning and the public houses filled up, but apart from Central Square, demonstrations of joy were muted and few at first. The town had lost too many of its lads and many people preferred to stay at home, to reflect, and in many cases to weep with memories.

Released from school, Ommie came back from Guard Street first, then the younger children from St John's, and Barwise was overwhelmed with hugs and kisses, weeping and squeals from Ettie. Tom came home from the steelworks with Jack after lunch, having stayed after the hooter to see to his horse. He opened the front door and came into the passageway calling out to Margaret,

'They've lit a bonfire in Central Square.'

Then he entered the back room and saw Barwise. Cumbrian to his bones, he said nothing but sat down, his eyes full of pride, just looking at his son. Then he spoke.

'I'm proud of you my boy, and I'm glad you made it back.'

'I nearly didn't Dad, but I got here in the end. I've lost my watch, though.'

'Watches may be given again. Sons may not. My son is home safe and thank God for it.'

No more needed to be said and conversation lapsed into generalities. It was not long though before Joe asked, 'Dad can we go and see the bonfire?'

Tom looked at Barwise and said to Joe, 'I don't think your brother will be wanting to go out right now. He's only just got home.'

'I don't see why we should not go and look at it,' said Barwise. Days like this don't happen that often. Let's go and see what's going on in town.'

Central Square was the town venue for outdoor civic events and great occasions were celebrated there such as Coronations, flag days and national holidays, especially New Year. Today the police were being indulgent, because the lighting of a bonfire in the square was unusual, but the young men who did it were burning an effigy of the Kaiser and that was excusable by any standards. That gentleman had now fled to Holland and was out of reach of justice, but it was his war and in image he now faced Workington's wrath. A small band of people were dancing round the fire singing:

'A silly German sausage,
Dreamt Napoleon he'd be,
Then he went and broke his promise,
It was made in Germany.
He shook hands with Britannia
And eternal peace he swore,
Naughty boy, he talked of peace
While he prepared for war…

For Belgium put the Kibosh on the Kaiser;
Europe took the stick and made him sore;
On his throne it hurts to sit,
And when John Bull starts to hit,
He will never sit upon it any more.'

Tom, Margaret and Barwise stood and watched as the children joined in, bawling out the chorus, which everyone knew, and allowing a few adults to fill in the verses. Barwise thought of Percy Natrass and Bill Holliday and paused at the black mass of regret inside his head, not wanting to go any further. He knew you could not dwell on what was done, but he was certain that Bill was dead since he had been ahead of him when the explosion happened. What was done was done.

'Do you not want to join in?' asked Tom.

'No,' said Barwise softly. 'I've seen too much to be doing with that.'

Then he drew out a pack of cigarettes, lit one and offered one to his father.

'You didn't smoke when you left home.'

'I started a couple of weeks back. The doctor told me that it would ease my lungs. I got gassed you see.'

Margaret looked at him and said nothing, but she knew he had changed. 'Was it gas that made you lose your memory?'

'No, Mam; it doesn't do that. I think I lost my memory because I got blown up. I can't remember things exactly, but I partly remember I was on the edge of an explosion.'

'Aye,' she thought. 'And it blasted part of you away, because some of you is missing. But I'll put it back my lad. Workington will heal you; it can do that because it's home.'

It had not taken her long to realize that there was a brittle and hard edge to her son that had never been there before. The cockiness had gone out of him and he did not look like a naïve boy any more, even though he was still just nineteen. He had the beginnings of a hard-bitten look and there was something bitter in him. She nodded at the Kaiser effigy burning in the fire.

'Do you hate the Germans?'

'Body and soul, Mam. I loathe the lot of them. Don't you?'

'No I don't. But I didn't have to go and fight them. That was you my dear, and in you it is understandable. But you sound like your uncle Thomas.'

'I remember that conversation. He was right though, wasn't he?'

'Both right and wrong,' said Margaret. 'You know how I feel. We are all God's children and that includes Germans.'

'Aye well for that you have to believe in God.'

'And you don't?'

'No Mam, I don't. Not after what I've seen. You must believe what you want to, but there'll be no more church for me.'

So the explosion had taken his religion away too. That was perhaps what saddened her most. Would he ever get it back? And what of her other two absent children; would they stay with what she had taught them or would the war have stripped that from them too? Hopefully, she would know soon, for the war was over and they would be home before too long.

Little Joe bounced up to his elders grinning all over his face.

'We won the war! We won the war! We beat the Jerries. Did you kill many of them Barwise?'

Barwise's face froze and his expression was unreadable.

Tom spoke immediately.

'Joe; you must never ask anybody that ever again, and particularly not your brother. In fact, let me make it clear; if I hear that again, the person who asks will be very sorry about it.'

'But why?'

'Because I say so; you'll understand when you're older. Now go along and join the others.'

Barwise's expression relaxed, and he met his father's eye with a nod. An understanding was in place and the family honoured it.

The Armistice celebrations, for the moment, were muted. Soon the church bells ceased as the ringers grew tired. The people waving flags and running about got weary of it and after three hours Workington was reacting much in the same way as her soldiers were doing in the field. Men released from working long wartime hours fell asleep. Mothers who had lost sons wept at their memories, unburied now by the coming of peace. Workington would celebrate the peace; but not quite yet. It all had to sink in first, and then it would be done in proper Cumbrian style.

There were of course more measured celebrations once the news had sunk in. On Tuesday 12 November all the children were marched from their school to St John's Church where the Reverend Croft held a service for children. There were so many people attending that they could not all be contained in the building and overflowed outside into the churchyard. It ended with the mass singing of *Now thank we all our God* and this brought a release of some emotion, as many wept to hear the young voices soaring in such a chorus. More bonfires were lit in various parts of town and in the evening the streets were thronged by thousands of people, just talking, walking, drinking, celebrating and several bands played patriotic airs at large junctions. The whole was tempered by the thought, present on most minds, that many lads would never be coming home and great regret that they were not there to join the celebrations. It was all pleasant and rather muted by the official line that the war was not over even if the fighting was. There would have to be talks, then a treaty would be signed; and then there would be national celebrations. It could be months ahead, but without wishing to be premature a modicum of rejoicing was understandable.

Barwise was home, yet did not need to work; officially he was still on the strength of the Army and signed off for a month for convalescent leave. He knew that he would not have to return to active service as the gassing had rendered him unfit; now it seemed that the Army would have no role for him. At the end of a month he had been instructed to return to Border Regiment HQ at Carlisle Castle for a medical, and then his future would be decided. All he had to do for the next few weeks was to pick up, as far as he could, the threads of his life and recover. The last did not seem to be an easy thing to do, because as the weeks went by he still gasped for breath if he exerted himself, but Major Knight had told him it would probably improve a bit and settle down.

The end of the war at Gretna was accompanied by a lot of parties and a lot of drunkenness and the women police were kept very busy. To Nancy the news came as she was on morning shift, but it made no difference in the routine of her shed. You just cannot walk away half way through the manufacture of gun cotton. At any rate the celebrations were curtailed by the supervisors who informed their workers that they had received no instructions that production was to halt. An armistice was not the end of the war; it was a laying down of arms, so that talks could commence. In the meantime, there was an army to supply and so full scale explosive manufacture continued. Nancy carried on stirring the Devil's Porridge right through November as the British, French and American armies advanced through Belgium, liberating the towns and villages as they went. The German army sullenly retreated before them and gradually broke up as they entered their homeland. Close on their heels came the allies and occupied the Rhineland and three bridgeheads over the Rhine. Finally it dawned that the fighting was actually over and would not be starting again.

On Sunday 1 December a note appeared in Nancy's pigeonhole informing her that her employment would be terminated on Thursday 5 December. The factory would be mothballed with a skeleton staff. It thanked her for her services and instructed her to report to collect her pay at close of shift on Thursday. There she would receive two week's pay and twenty pounds as a bonus. She could go home; and she caught the train that same night. Another one of Margaret's children had come home. Now there was only Nellie, somewhere abroad, nursing in a Base hospital; what was she doing? The answer came a few days after the Armistice in the form of a letter:

'Dear Mother and Father; I hope this finds you well and that all at home are in the pink. I was so glad to get your letter today telling how Barwise has turned up. You can tell him from me that he's a bad penny and that's what they always do. Seriously though you tell him from me that if he ever goes missing again and worries us all like that then I shall box his ears for him as is an older sister's privilege.'

'Well she can try,' said Barwise. 'But older than me or not, big sisters have little terror for me compared to the Jerries.'
'If you think Jerry was worse than Nellie when she's got her dander up,' replied his mother, 'Then you've got another think coming.'
Barwise just smiled faintly. He never would tell her what it had been like to fight for his life against someone trying to kill him, nor anyone else.
'Read on Mam.'

'I expect you're wondering when I shall be home now that it's over but the answer is that I don't know. We still have lots of wounded men coming in because the fighting went on until the last minute. The shooting didn't stop at 11.00 either despite what the papers are saying. Some Yanks carried on letting off shells because they wanted to be able to say that they'd fired the last shot of the war; they had to be ordered individually to stop or face charges. I have to stay here for at least another two weeks because we are absolutely inundated with cases of Spanish flu.

Having said that they are going to reduce the number of base hospitals very quickly because they don't need so many. I'll let you know when I can get away, but I think it's a case of expect me when I land.'

'When the news of the ceasefire came through we'd just had a big convoy of flu cases come in and everyone was very busy making boys comfortable in bed. Matron could not go to a little thanksgiving service outside so she asked me to go and represent the nurses. At 11.00 a padre said a prayer and it made me very emotional; it was the prayer of St Francis and I was crying at the end where are the lines;

"Lord make me an instrument of your peace
Where there is hatred let me sow love
Where there is injury, pardon
Where there is doubt, faith
Where there is despair, hope
Where there is darkness, light
And where there is sadness, joy."

Then we sang "Thanks to God" and when we had reached the end where it says,

"Thanks for heav'nly peace with Thee!
Thanks for hope in the tomorrow,
Thanks through all eternity!"

'I just started crying and crying and I don't know why. I'm afraid I made a fool of myself but when they helped me back inside Matron came to me and told me that was why she sent me, because that's what she would have done. She thought that I might not but I'm not as tough as she thinks I am.'

'There were some extraordinary sights later though; all the

flags disappeared from the hospital windows and flagpoles because people took them off to wave them round in the streets. There are lots of Canadians and Aussies here so as you can imagine things got rather merry because they don't mind showing how they feel. A lot of them drank far too much and even some of the patients were a lot the worse for wear. One of them caught May as she was coming to the door and insisted on whirling her round in a dance in the street though she didn't want to. Little groups of men kept going past, each of them waving their flags and singing their national songs. A group of our men were shoveling some coal for the furnaces out back and I told them the war was over. One of them said; "So that's it then. The b***** war's over". Another lad said " What's to become of us? We have lived this life for so long and now we shall have to start again." They seemed to be quite depressed and to be honest I think that is the case with a lot of our people. It's been so long and they've seen so much that I think there is one common thought; Thank God it's all over. Let's go home. That's how I feel if I am frank and I want to get back to Cumberland as soon as I can. I've seen enough to know that there's no place like it and I don't mind if I never leave it for the rest of my life. But I can't come yet. Now the fighting is over they've stopped censoring the letters so I can tell you that hundreds of our boys are down with flu and it's a very nasty type. We have hardly been able to keep pace with the number of people dying...'

Here Margaret broke off with an intake of breath,

'What my daughter has seen! No-one should have to see that.'

'She's a nurse,' replied Tom. 'It's what she wanted to be and she saw people die at the Infirmary before she went.'

'I know that and I know she could cope because she's strong. Someone has to tend the sick, but I never imagined anything on this scale.'

'Be glad it's our Nellie; she'll be better at it than most I think. Now finish the letter eh?'

Margaret read on: '*You just walk down the ward every fifteen minutes or so and you'd see that another one had gone. They'd carry them out on stretchers, covered in a Union Jack and bring another one in. I've never had so much as a sniffle and think I will come through alright. At number 5 Hospital they are over the moon because they've produced an emergency vaccine and all our staff have had it. Not a single nurse or doctor or soldier working here has succumbed to the flu; I do not think rushing a vaccine into use like that would happen in peacetime but I'm glad it has because May and I seem to be protected.*'

'*Anyway you must expect me at short notice because the situation changes from day to day. I hope that it is soon. Love to all, Nellie.*'

'From the sound of that she's rushed off her feet,' said Tom.

'All the nurses I saw were that way,' replied Barwise. 'There were so many people needing their help they could barely cope with the numbers, but they did.'

'I think women have done some amazing things in this war. It's been a real eye-opener to me and I think to a lot of people. At least the matter of votes is settled now anyway.'

'Not really, Dad. They've given the vote to women of thirty-one years old, so mam can vote next time, but not to all the ones who did the big stuff. Think of all them nurses and ammunition girls like our Nancy. Most of them are probably under thirty-one. What do they get from this? No it's daft; if men over twenty-one have the vote then so should women. That job's not finished yet.'

'Well maybe this election will make a difference. There

hasn't been one since 1910. Lloyd George didn't waste any time announcing it.'

'He wants to bounce himself into power for five years as the man who won the war,' growled Thomas.

'Will it make any difference though?' asked Margaret.

'I think it will,' replied her husband. 'I've shifted my ground a lot this last four years. I've seen three of my children go off to war and I don't like what Lloyd George has been doing since he got in. I'm through with the Liberals.'

'You voting Labour, Dad?'

'I am, Barwise. We need something better than what we've had. You mark my words, next election Workington will be practically solid Labour. Tom Cape worked as a miner for twenty-five years and is General Secretary of the Cumberland Miners; he'll speak for us. The Unionist is posh and the Liberal is a lawyer. We need ordinary people in Parliament.'

'After what I've been through, I can hardly disagree.'

'Let democracy speak then,' said Margaret with a grin. 'I once told your father that if I had the vote I'd use it and I will.'

'I remember that as well,' smiled Tom. 'I wonder what Mister would think of all this?'

'He'd come round to it, I know.'

'You had him round your little finger and I'm sure you could have swung him to it.'

December marched on with decisions being made both inside the family, and outside. Barwise suddenly found that he did not have to do anything further with his military career. A letter arrived for him on 5 December informing him that he had been discharged from the Army. He had been thinking that he had to report at Carlisle by the tenth. The letter thanked him for his service, informed him that he was entitled to the General Service Medal and the Victory Medal, which would be forwarded to him in due course, and enclosed a cheque for the amount of the pay owed to him. Within a few days a further cheque for a hundred pounds also came which was a bonus awarded to all servicemen returning from France; a gratuity from a grateful nation. That was that then. The deaths, the blood, the misery and the triumphs; he felt rather let down. Never mind; if he was now a free agent, then he could do as he wished; go where he wished.

Nancy declared that she wanted to see a bit more in life than Cumberland and began looking for jobs. Waitressing was regarded among her peers as an honorable profession and one to which she wanted to return; she did not however wish to go back to the Central Hotel. Her ambition was to master Silver Service, because then she would be able to apply for jobs in first class hotels and great houses anywhere in the world. Not unnaturally her attention was captured by an advertisement in the *Times and Star* that offered an opportunity for a young woman to work in the Derwentwater Hotel at Portinscale. It would be perfect for her, because she could come home very easily during her time off by train from Keswick or Braithwaite. For the right candidate full training would be given in silver service, and the post would be a live in one. She applied straight away by letter and was summoned for interview. Armed with a good character from the Central Hotel and another from HM Gretna, she was interviewed by the manager and got the job. As she told her mother later, 'He told me that they had lots of girls applying, but he was going by the same rule that he used to employ men. If a man has spent any of the last four years serving his King and Country then that more or less meant that he would get a job if all else were equal. I had spent the last two years making ammunition and none of the other applicants had done war service, so I got the job. I start in January.'

'Ethel and I shall be able to cycle out and see you in the summer then.'

'I'd love that. We could have picnics by the lake like we did last year. Mind you I might not be there very long. I plan to go and see a few places.'

'Would you not want tea with us in the hotel?'

'Oh, it's terribly posh Mam and very expensive. I doubt we could afford it.'

'Maybe one day; when we're rich then…'

On 11 December fate took a turn in the road, literally when Freddie Cairns, one of the best-known men in town, drove into Devonshire Street. His small cart with his old horse came down the road and he called out his familiar cry, 'Gather up your old rags and bones.' Any old junk could be taken out to him and he would exchange it for one of his home-made windmills that were very popular with the children. With him on the wagon was a young man, and when the cart reached number 55 Freddie jumped down to help his passenger to the ground.

'Thanks Freddie. I'm obliged to you.'

'Any time Marra. I'll pop back in an hour and take you home.'

The young man put a heavy wooden crutch under his arm and hobbled to the door, on which he knocked. His eyes were filled with pain and determination and that expression was what Nancy saw when she opened the door. It took the words from her and she could say nothing but look.

'Hello, my name's Herbert Hayston. Barwise Little told me he lived here.'

Stumbling to reply, Nancy managed, after a long pause, to say,

'Aye he does. He's in the back kitchen now.'

'I'm glad to hear that; how glad I cannot tell you. I've got something of his to give back.'

'You'd better come in then.'

She led the way down the passage and into the kitchen.

Chapter 30 — Fit for Heroes

'Herbert! I'm glad to see you marra!'

'Not as glad as I am to see you, pal. Last time I saw you I thought you were a gonner.'

'I damned near was. Jerry nearly did for me and I don't know why I'm still alive.'

'Well it's good you are. Anyway I've brought you your watch.'

'My watch! I never thought I'd see it again.'

'You nearly didn't. Jerry nearly did for me too. I got a packet in my leg.'

Briefly Herbert related what had happened to him since they last met.

'Anyway, they told me it's healing well; they let me up after six weeks and here I am. I got discharged in Southampton and paid off. Gammy leg or not I just wanted to get home. My sister Lizzie and her husband can look after me better than any hospital now. They're down in Bromley Street. Another few weeks and I'm going to burn this crutch!'

'That was pretty quick work.'

'Aye well, there's been trouble Barwise. There's been some small riots in Boulogne and other places. Now the fighting's over blokes just want to get home and don't see why they're being kept over there. They're sending people home and getting them out of the Army as fast as they can. I reckon they're scared of a full-scale mutiny. Anyway here I am.'

'A grand day it is too. We'll have a drink or two on it I think.'

'Hang on,' said Nancy. 'You're missing something aren't you?'

'How do you mean?'

'You said last time you saw Barwise you thought he was a gonner.'

'That's right I did.'

'But you brought his watch back here.'

'Well I promised him that I would.'

'You thought you were delivering a dead man's watch to his parents didn't you?'

'Aye I did, and that's the God's truth, but I'm glad it wasn't like that.'

'So how was he last time you saw him?'

'He was in a bad way on a stretcher next to mine in a CCS.'

'You were wounded at the same time?'

'No he was already wounded when I found him.'

'You found him?'

'Aye. My team and I found him, but my marras were all killed by the same machine gun that got my leg.'

Something in him made her stop questioning and conversation continued easily for the next hour. Eventually Freddie Cairns came back with his horse and Herbert went out to meet him.

'Barwise,' said Nancy. 'I'd just like a word with Mr Hayston if you don't mind waiting here.'

'Oh aye?'

'Just wait here, alright.'

Out of the door, and out of earshot Nancy whispered to Herbert Hayston, 'You helped him didn't you?'

'Just a little bit. I wasn't able to do a lot.'

'Look, I swear to God that I won't tell him. What did you do?'

Herbert looked at Nancy and saw she would not let him avoid the question.

'I just put his gas mask on. That's all I did.'

'You saved his life, didn't you?'

'I can't say that.'

Nancy's eyes shone. 'But I can Mr Hayston. I think my brother would not be alive and here if it was not for you. Am

I wrong?'

Herbert looked at her and said, 'All I did was put his mask on. That's it.'

Nancy had worked in an ammunition factory for two years and did not believe that life or opportunity should be wasted. The experience had given her a directness that she had never possessed formerly.

'But it's not it. Mr Hayston. I'm going to say something I should not because it's a bit forward but I speak my mind. I think you may be a man I should like to walk out with.'

Herbert was taken aback, but looked at her and saw an even featured girl with nice eyes. So this was the 'new woman' that was emerging out of the chaos of war.

'Would you like to come to the pictures with me next week?' he said, seizing the initiative for himself.

'I would 'Erbert.'

The deed was done. Fate smiled for the decades ahead.

On Saturday 14 December 1918 the United Kingdom went to the polls. Margaret's polling station was at St John's Hall and she went up there to cast her vote arm in arm with her husband, conscious that she was doing a great thing.

'Just think; women have been fighting for the vote for years and here I am with it. It's just dropped into my lap and I have done nothing for it.'

'Yes you have, Margaret. You are a wife, a mother, a grafter and a citizen of this country. Of course you're entitled to the vote; you should have had it all along.'

'I know you've always been in favour of it. It was one of the things that I liked about you when we first met. You disagreed with your father about it.'

'Aye well, you have it now so use it, and let's change things for the better.'

'You think we can? Just by doing this?'

'I think so; with the right people in Parliament we can make a better world. I don't give a damn for Lloyd George and his sloganeering, "A home fit for heroes to live in". What does that mean? All I fear is that it'll be back to business as usual and it'll end up as it was before. You didn't see them people last night.'

'At the Drill Hall?'

'Yes. The Victory Ball. All the local nobs and bigwigs rolling up in their carriages. I didn't see any of us there Margaret. None of the working people. They were celebrating their victory, but it's not theirs; it's ours. Who won the war if not the ordinary working people of this country with their blood their sweat and their tears? Workington's had all those and in good measure.'

'You sound like you should be in politics.'

'Not me; I don't know enough. They'd run circles round me, but they won't with Tom Cape. He knows his way around and that's what we need. Men who know their way around.'

'Well let's go and vote for him and do our bit.'

Labour won Workington with a majority of 4,495, which probably caused more rejoicing than the Armistice. The world was changing.

Nellie came home, discharged from service on 17 December; with her she brought French cheeses, sausage and bread for the family to sample. The children would not eat more than a mouthful, pronouncing them to be yucky, but Barwise enjoyed some of it as a reminder of the better times in France, and so did Herbert Hayston, now a regular caller and accepting Nancy's calling him 'Erbert. Margaret looked round her back kitchen table and all her children were there. What extraordinary people they were; she had given birth to a nurse, a soldier and a maker of ammunition. Their generation had been called on to meet the greatest challenge Britain had ever faced. They had come through it with fatigue, with effort and with courage. They had seen things that she had never seen and did not wish to; things that no-one should ever have to see. They had done honour to themselves, to their country; and to their mother. She was proud of them beyond all measure and her heart swelled with her pride. Extraordinary they were and of an extraordinary generation.

Margaret asked Nellie if she was going to go back to the Infirmary and nurse there now the war was over.

'No, Mam. I'm going to try to be a District Nurse.'

'Like Alpha?'

'Yes. Just like Auntie Alpha.

Margaret's younger sister, Alpha Nancy Adams, was the first District Nurse ever appointed in West Cumberland.

'Have you any idea where?'

'I'm hoping Aspatria.'

'Why Aspatria?'

'There was an advertisement in the *Nursing Times* for a District Nurse there.'

'Is it working in a hospital?'

'Yes and no. There is a cottage hospital there run by the Coop, but I'd only be based there. Mostly I'd be going into people's homes.'

'To do what?'

'All sorts of things. Helping with births, changing dressings, helping the old; there's a lot of variety in the job. I'd like that.'

'And you wouldn't be too far away.'

'No, and I'd be near enough pop in on Father and Mother at Dearham.'

'They'd like that I know.'

'When's the interview?'

'This coming Friday, Barwise; why?'

'Can I come with you?'

'Well of course, but not to the interview! Why do you want

to come to Aspatria?'

'I've a mind to see someone there.'

'Oh well come along then. I'd be glad of the company.'

Brother and sister took the train to Aspatria early on the Friday, for Nellie's interview was at eleven o'clock. Since they arrived at the hospital at 10.45am Barwise waited while Nellie went in to face the questions and she came out at 11.30.

'Well?'

'They'll let me know. Now we can do your business. Who is it you want to see?'

As they walked towards King Street, Barwise related briefly how he had met John Edmondson of the Royal Flying Corps at Ripon and fleetingly in France in the RAF, and he wanted to look him up.

'Why particularly him?'

'I don't know Nellie. I really don't; I just see him as a marra. But here's where he said he'd be.'

They entered Edmondson's butchers where John Edmondson, freshly discharged from the Royal Air Force, was helping his brother behind the counter.

'Hello Sarge.'

'Well if it isn't young Barwise Little. Hey, but I'm glad to see you. You made it then.'

'I did Sarge – just.'

'You don't have to call me Sarge now,' said the butcher. 'It's John, and it's time we had that pint and that craic. How are you?.. And – oh, you're the girl in the photograph!'

Nellie was a reserved person and not as direct as Nancy. She'd been looking at the meat on display, which was in far more abundance now that the war was over. Barwise was visiting a friend, but she had not really looked at him; now her eyes met those of John Edmondson and the strangest thing happened. Her insides did a flip, she gave a small gasp, and her face flushed. He on the other hand had his mouth open like a goldfish and could not stop looking at her; Barwise noted with some amusement that he looked rather foolish, but so did Nellie. He introduced his sister.

'Well', he said. 'Where can we get this pint? And perhaps a sherry?'

'Barwise! When did you start drinking and what photograph?'

Nellie was glad to seize on this to cover up her confusion.

'John's seen the family picture, Nell. And believe me, if you can go through the trenches and turn down the rum they give you before an attack, then you're a better man than I am. Mam and Dad can think what they like; alcohol has been a friend to me and I like a drink now and then.'

'I'm glad you said that. I've broken the rules myself since I left home and I like a sweet sherry and so does Nancy.'

'Then sweet sherry it is, and no guilt with it. Mam and Dad have their own lives and they can do what they want; but we've got ours, and we do what we like. Agreed?'

'Agreed!'

Nellie got the job. She would start a period of training at the Cottage Hospital in January 1919. Her accommodation would be a small rented house, fully furnished, owned by the Aspatria Coop. Barwise reflected wryly that he thought she would be right at home there. For the future he was now his own boss.

'What will you do now Barwise?' asked Margaret. 'Back to the boiler works with Matt and the lads?'

'No Mam. I've a mind to go and see Scotland.'

'Scotland? Why?'

'I've never been there. And I'm a hammerer. They always need hammerers where there's steel and boilers need putting together.'

'I used to think that when I was a girl. I'd say to myself

when I looked over the water from Maryport, one day I'll go there. I did. Your father took me there after we married. Have you no other reason?'

'I owe someone who lives up in Fife a bit of cash. I've got some now so I think I'll go and pay it back.'

'To always pay your debts is a good rule; and a good reason. Just don't be a stranger.'

He leaned over and kissed her cheek.

'I won't Mam. This is home; Workington is where I belong. That's always where the heart is.'

He looked at Nancy and Nellie, his elder sisters, sitting at the table.

'Come on you two. Let's go for a walk. Sun goes down in an hour. Let's go down to the harbour.'

The nurse, the munitionette and the soldier went for their walk. They sat on a low wall, all holding hands quietly where Barwise liked to sit near the mouth of the harbour and watched the sun go down; it was a special time and they all knew it. They had been tried in the fires of history and had come out as changed people. Out over the grey cold waters of the Firth, the waves were slightly choppy but reflected the light of the setting sun that also tinged the edge of the clouds. Down at the horizon and further away the clouds were dark as the small golden orb of the winter sun dipped into the sea.

'You came here a lot before you joined up didn't you?' asked Nellie.

'I did and I always will.'

'Why?' asked Nancy, always strong minded and down to earth.

'For the glory of it,' came the answer.

She nodded. It was enough.

The light over the Solway to the West dimmed and faded as the planet turned another face to the kind old sun. The light of the steelworks behind them and to their left roared up into the sky, the other light over the Solway that was the life of Workington and of home.

Epilogue

It is not the intention of the author to continue this family saga any further than the end of the First World War. There are reasons for this but perhaps the most important is that the 1920s in Workington were a time of want and distress. It is almost impossible to place a positive spin on an era which has been remembered by so many families as 'the hungry 20s.' It is not fertile soil for a novelist wishing to avoid grim times.

Nonetheless it would be unfair to end this book without some rounding up of loose ends especially as most of my characters were real people. I have of course taken liberties with their history, and their experiences in this book must in no way be taken as anything more than fiction. They are merely what they might have gone through, and many of their generation did experience these things. Reality sometimes has a harder bite than story.

Thomas and Margaret lived at number 55 Devonshire Street for the rest of their lives. In the streets around them lived their children and eventually their children; they were of that community and it was in their blood. They lie now in Harrington Road cemetery with about 23,000 of their neighbours, all citizens of a remarkable town called Workington.

Nellie became a district nurse, as she said she would, and was based in Aspatria for many years. She married John Edmondson and was a happy person, fulfilled and wise.

Nancy married Herbert Hayston who she always referred to as 'Erbert' and eventually, on the death of her parents, they moved into 55 Devonshire Street where they lived on, with their own family, until the 1970s. Her grand daughter Penny

Durham was much help in the researching for this book.

Barwise is not on Workington's Roll of Honour; the list of men from the town who served in the Great War. It might have been updated after the war at some point, but the original roll was made during the war years and any later edition is not extant so the published roll is not complete. Yet 50464 Little B, Private did serve in 7 Battalion The Border Regiment and he did come home a casualty. He was blown up and wounded after being caught on the edge of a mine explosion, and gassed. His name may be found in the medal records. In the 1920s he married Caroline Thomas, lived in Salterbeck, then Moss Bay, and their granddaughter Judith Harris was of great help in the researching of this book.

When I was young and walked through the streets of Workington, Whitehaven and Maryport, I saw this generation of West Cumbrians, and thought them just old people. They did not talk about what many of them had been through and what many of them had done. I did not know then what I know now. For what they did, and what they went through, I think now that I walked among giants. I am proud to be of them.

John Little. April 2018.

Glossary

B.Regt.	Border Regiment as abbreviated on identity discs.
Bait	Lunch taken to work in a tin or box.
Barwise	Pronounced Barras.
Billy Bumley house	Conical shaped coast-watchers' hut near entrance to Workington harbour.
Boggle	Ghost or phantom.
Bowks	Pukes.
Bundook	Rifle; British Army slang.
CE	Church of England as abbreviated on identity discs.
Days of 'bull'	Days spent doing repetitive boring tasks like shining boots or polishing buttons already shiny.
Craic	Chat or conversation.
Dronnie	Person who moved from Dronfield to Workington with the steelworks in 1882–3.
Gothas	Long range German bombers capable of reaching London.
Gowk	Fool.
Gum Arabic	Used to replace blood in the days before transfusions were perfected.
Jock Tamson	Scots colloquial for God.
Larl cuddy	Small donkey. (Sometimes cow)

Larl radgee	Small idiot or incapable person.
Lonnings	Back alleys or lanes; in towns, between the rows of terraced houses.
Lysol	Also Eusol or Dakin's Solution; antiseptics.
Marras	Friends or mates.
Mutti	German; 'Mum.'
Pediculi capitis	Headlice.
Pobbies	Milk and bread slops; the breakfast of many working class people.
Segs	Iron studs on soles of clogs; also known as corkers or caulkers or korkers.
Sponson	Turret attached to side of early tanks.
Tapper	Someone mentally deficient.
Thew	Thou or you.
Whangs	Bootlaces.

PHRASES

Yis lad. Arl 'ave yan.	Yes lad, I'll have one.
That's 'ot cream.	That's all the cream (milk).
Be canny wid the sugar.	Be careful with the sugar.
Shut thee gob or arl lamp thew yan.	Shut your mouth or I will hit you hard.
Mash tea.	Make tea.
Wha dist thew think thew is talkn to me brother like that?	Who do you think you are talking to my brother like that?

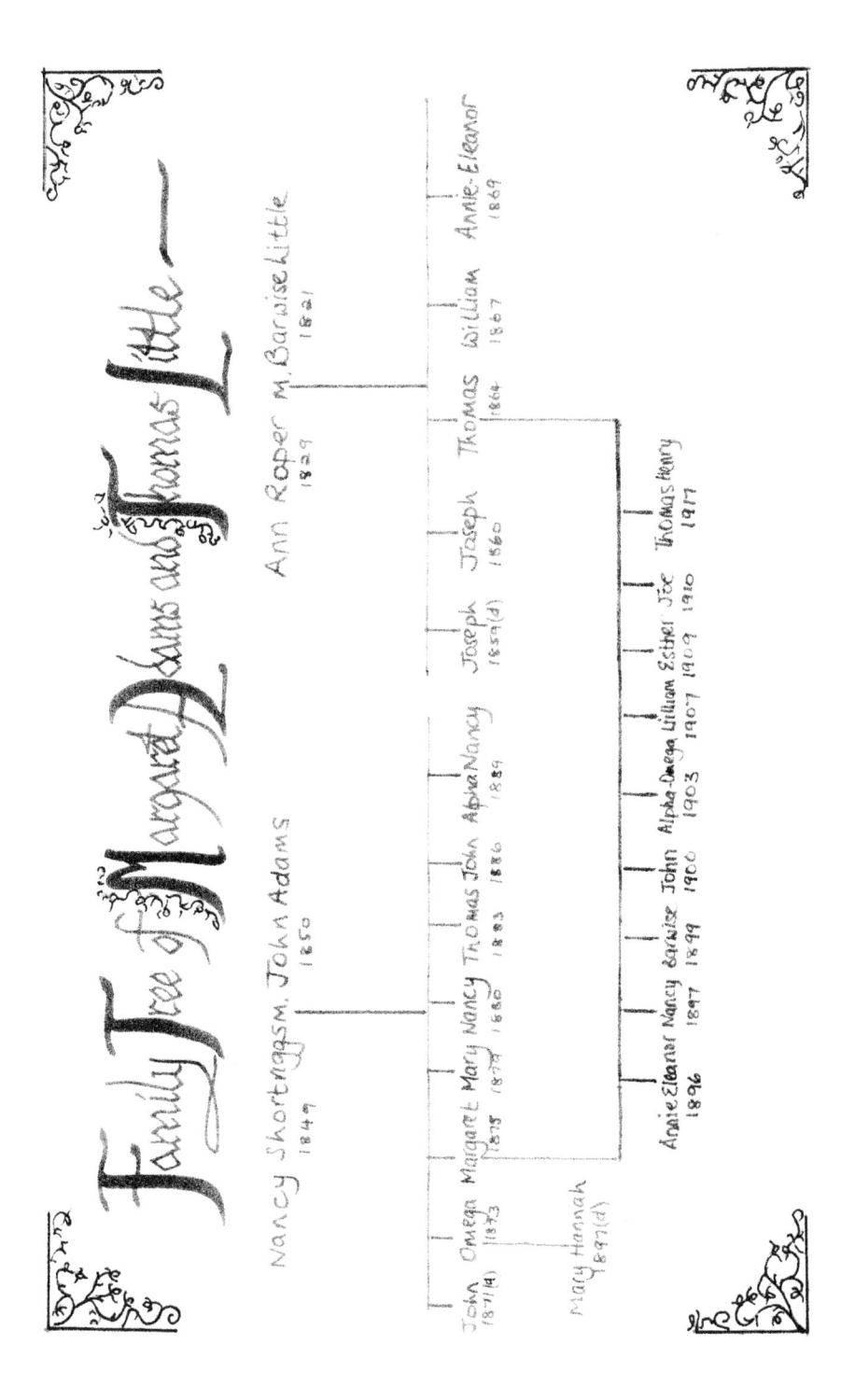

Family Tree of Margaret Barns and Thomas Little

Nancy Shortriggs m. John Adams　　　　　Ann Roper m. Barwise Little
　　　　1849　　　　　　1850　　　　　　　　　　1829　　　　　1821

John	Omega	Margaret	Mary	Nancy	Thomas	John	Alpha Nancy	Joseph	Joseph(d)	Thomas	William	Annie-Eleanor
1871(d)	1873	1875	1877	1880	1883	1886	1889	1860	1859(d)	1864	1867	1869

Mary Hannah
1891(d)

Annie Eleanor	Nancy Barwise	John	Alpha-Omega	Lillian	Esther	Joe	Thomas Henry
1896	1897	1899	1900	1903	1907	1909	1910	1911

Printed in Great Britain
by Amazon